THE EYES OF OTHERS

-- A WATCHTOWER THRILLER --

MIKAEL CARLSON

WARRINGTON
PUBLISHING

DANBURY, CONNECTICUT

The Eyes of Others: A Watchtower Thriller

Warrington Publishing
Danbury, Connecticut
www.mikaelcarlson.com

Printed in the United States of America
Second Edition
ISBN-13: 978-1-944972-81-3 (paperback)
          978-0-9897673-9-2 (ebook)
          978-1-944972-09-7 (hardcover)

Cover designed by JD&J

Novels by Mikael Carlson:

– The Michael Bennit Series –
The iCandidate
The iCongressman
The iSpeaker
The iAmerican

– Tierra Campos Thrillers –
Justifiable Deceit
Devious Measures
Vital Targets
Revealed Secrets
Decisive Endgame

– Watchtower Thrillers –
The Eyes of Others
The Eyes of Innocents
The Eyes of Victims

– The America, Inc. Saga –
The Black Swan Event
Bounded Rationality
Boiling the Ocean

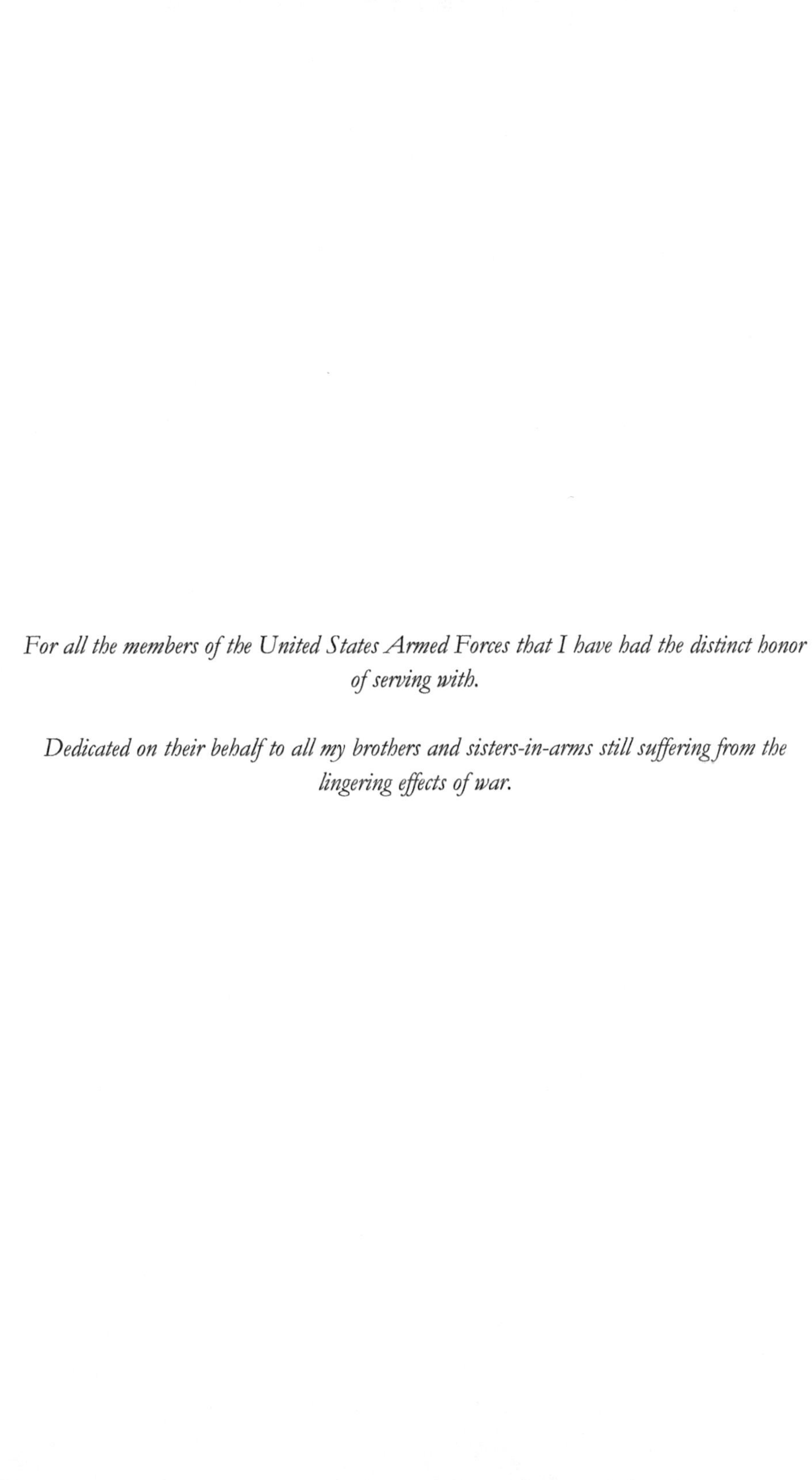

For all the members of the United States Armed Forces that I have had the distinct honor of serving with.

Dedicated on their behalf to all my brothers and sisters-in-arms still suffering from the lingering effects of war.

PROLOGUE
"BOSTON" HOLLINGER

U.S. FORWARD OPERATING BASE
DEIR EZ-ZOR GOVERNORATE, SYRIA

I hate this place. The "graveyard of empires" was hardly a garden spot, but I would take Afghanistan over this hellhole any day. Satan would be eager to return to hell after spending seven months in this Godforsaken place. Syria is always under threat from the government regime, pissed-off rebels, the remnants of ISIS, the Russians, and groups allied with them. It's a mess, and the reason American troops are stuck protecting large oilfields and the potential revenues they could bring in.

None of that matters to me. It's my exhausting, often thankless job that brought me to a desert four hundred fifty miles from Damascus and over five thousand miles from home. As an intelligence analyst, I turn raw data collected from various sources into useful products that help keep the men and women here safe. Commanders here make life and death decisions every week. It's the information that I provide that they base them on.

I pull the small towel out of my cargo pocket as I walk and mop the sweat off the back of my neck as I make my way back to the tent. The temperatures here are already unbearable, and it's only the middle of June. My military deployments have taught me to hate insufferably hot places void of vegetation. The only respite to the misery I manage to enjoy is the time I spend with some of the other soldiers on the base. Some of them have quickly become close friends.

"So, we're haulin' ass across the desert in the MRAP like we stole the thing, and these two Apaches drop down on us from the sun. I swear, man, we never saw 'em," Mexico says, his arms flailing as he acts out every single word in front of the soldiers lounging outside the tent.

"Remind me never to travel anywhere with you in the turret," Colombia says, not bothering to look up as he adjusts the plate in his body armor carrier.

"You can't shoot for shit, anyway," Georgia says, lounging back in her chair as if she's working on her tan.

"I'm an expert marksman, thank you very much."

"Hold on, hold on, I'm not finished," Mexico admonishes. "These pilots must have been bored or something because sneaking up on us wasn't good enough. No, these asshats start practicing their attack runs on us. My driver panics like he's being chased by a hive of hornets or something. He starts dodging and weaving the truck like he's gonna get away from them."

"How long has this story been going on?" I lean over and ask Maryland, who's trying to read a book and pretending not to pay attention to the grunt.

"Twenty minutes or so. Mex is on his third story."

Maryland is the only other guy in this gaggle of unlikely friends who is also in military intelligence. He's the most mission-oriented soldier in my unit. All he wants to do is get the mission done and get home, or so he whines to us almost every day.

"The driver screams at me, 'Find us a place to hide!'" Mexico continues. "So I yell back at him, 'make for the tree line.' Don't you know, he shouted back, 'What tree line?' like we weren't in the middle of the damn desert."

The group roars like it's the funniest thing they've ever heard. Soldiers have a sort of dark humor, and it's something they carry with them when they no longer don the uniform. Mexico has a bright future doing comedy someday, although civilians aren't likely to get most of his jokes.

"He stops us on this little rise, and one of the Apaches comes at us head-on and flies over the MRAP, like ten feet over our turret. I swear, I could smell the pilot's aftershave. The other Apache flares up right next to us. He looks at my driver, and the gun points wherever he looks. My driver looks like he's about to shit his pants, so the guy starts shaking his head, and the cannon moves left and right like he's waving at us."

"Your tall tales are getting taller," Georgia moans from her makeshift lounge chair.

"I'm with her. I can't take it anymore. Which one of you dumbasses gave Mexico caffeine this morning?" I ask the group, knowing the cause of his hyperactivity all too well.

Everyone looks at Louisiana, who's smoking a cigarette as he listens to the story. Maryland points without looking up. Realizing his friends just ratted him out, he puts on a face of mock surprise. The prankster combat engineer of the group, Louisiana would have been my first choice as instigator anyway. What he lacks in stature and athletic ability, he makes up in attitude and intelligence.

"Maryland, why you always blamin' me, bro?" he protests in his Cajun-tinged accent.

"Because you're the one always doing stupid crap," Maryland says, only half-joking.

"Like what? Name one time I've done anythin' stupid." He left that wide open.

"The story about the strip club in Augusta," Maryland deadpans.

"The ATM at the PX in Kuwait," Colombia adds with a grin on his face.

"Something about the flight attendant on the plane to Kuwait," Mexico adds.

"I haven't heard that story yet," Arkansas says, getting nods from his buddies Kansas and Indiana.

The motley group is made up of different military occupational specialties. We have infantrymen, combat engineers, military intelligence, military police, and even a cook who stays quiet for obvious reasons. The food here is also terrible, and he hates us reminding him of that.

After seven months on this deployment, we've become a tight-knit group. It's why we stopped calling each other by our rank and last name, and use our home state or country instead. Most are states and countries like Maryland, Louisiana, Mexico, and Colombia. I got named after a city because Boston sounds slicker than Massachusetts. Together, we're a walking geography lesson.

"How 'bout you, Boston? You wanna add to the list of my transgressions?" Louisiana asks. I don't have to think about it for long.

"Did anyone mention about how you almost burned down the general's house at Lewis-McChord?" I say, smiling. It's funny to me, but not for his commander, who ended up standing in front of a furious colonel for a serious ass-chewing.

"Hold on, wait a sec!" Louisiana shouts before grinning broadly. "I had accomplices for that one."

"Yeah, Sergeant Jack Daniels, Specialist Johnnie Walker, and Private Jim Beam," Colombia announces in his typical cool, James Dean manner.

"The three wise men that manage to turn Louisiana into a complete idiot," Maryland needles.

"Wow. There's a whole lotta sell-outery goin' on here," Louisiana decrees, eliciting snickers from the group.

"What's new in the world, Boston?" Arkansas asks. "We win the war yet?"

"I'm in the SCIF staring at field reports all day. I'd be the last to know."

In intelligence parlance, the "skiff," as it is pronounced, is the Sensitive Compartmented Information Facility where we analyze classified material. It's an enclosed structure with stringent access controls and is restricted solely to personnel who have passed a thorough background check and have been granted clearance to enter. We just think of it as our office.

"Guys, we need to take the fobbits on a field trip one of these days," Indiana says, doing a function check on his M4 carbine.

"Fobbit" is a derogatory word used to shame soldiers afraid to head outside of the base. Just as most hobbits from *Lord of the Rings* never left the Shire, most fobbits never leave the forward operating base. Technically, this isn't a FOB, but the term carried over from the Iraq War.

"Shut up, dude, before you get some unlicensed dental work," Maryland threatens. He likes to talk tough, but the guys know that the dog has no bite.

"Bro, you don't have the strength to open a can of Coke, so what are ya goin' to do?" Louisiana retorts.

For most road warriors trekking to work in the U.S., the biggest concern they have is not to rear-end someone when they cut you off. The only mental energy they expend is listening to the local radio station's traffic report to figure out how to get out of the bumper-to-bumper traffic. A tragedy back home is spilling coffee on your work clothes.

"I'm going to beat you senseless tonight," Maryland says.

"Promise?" he responds, blowing his rival a kiss.

"You guys need therapy. Did anyone—"

A blinding light precedes a deafening blast, and a wall of dust blows over us like a tsunami as I try to keep my balance. Seconds later, the telltale barking of a pair of M240B machine guns rips through the desert air.

"Shit. That was the gate. Let's go!" Kansas says, rallying his fellow infantrymen. They start grabbing their gear when the whistling of falling mortar rounds grows louder.

"Incoming!"

There's no time to react. The round hits the tent, and I feel myself hurtling through the air before crashing on the ground. My ears are ringing… What's going on?

A sharp pain stabs at my head. It feels like it's…split open. I try to move but can't. My body has gone limp.

I see movement above me…everything's hazy. Muffled voices…who is that? Maryland? The infantry guys? Their shouting barely registers…I can't understand.

Hands grab at me…I'm not where I was. There's a piercing pain in my shoulder. I feel like I'm being dragged into… Another bright light destroys my vision and makes me wince. My head is pounding, and it's getting worse. The pain is so bad.

I hear popping sounds. I search the sky above me and see streaks of light…smoke… Another jolt of pain goes through my body as I'm jerked along the ground. I feel dirt kick up into my face as a soldier drops next to me. I try to move my left arm, but nothing happens. I touch my face with my right hand and feel it sticky and wet. Is that blood? My blood?

"Hang in there, pal. We'll get you out of here," a muffled voice reassures me.

There are popping sounds everywhere. They sound like firecrackers. I can't hear or see anything well. My head is swimming. I can't stay awake.

Another small explosion erupts next to me. I can taste the sand kicked up as everything grows dim. I need to get up and try to make my legs move, but nothing happens. Everything sounds more distant now as my world grows darker…and darker.

SIX YEARS LATER

CHAPTER ONE
GINA ATTISON

SENATE SELECT COMMITTEE ON INTELLIGENCE
HART SENATE OFFICE BUILDING, WASHINGTON, D.C.

Senators Colby Washington and Garrett Turner are not stupid men. Despite serving on separate sides of the aisle that delineates the ideological and party divide on Capitol Hill, both understand and play the political game well. They are party loyalists in policy matters and magicians when convincing their constituents of their value.

Unfortunately, like most politicians, they're out of their depth in the act of governing. No elected representative has the breadth of knowledge required to make informed decisions in the complicated mess that our society has become. That's why they hide behind talking points written by their staff and hire people like Gina and Boston to help them navigate the world. That frees the senators up to do what they do best: posture and play politics.

"Admiral Troxell, you're the Director of National Intelligence. You have been brought before this committee because there is credible evidence of a traitor leaking critical information to the Syrians."

"I'm aware of why I was subpoenaed to come here, Senator," the admiral states with a slight edge to his voice.

"Then how can you have the audacity to tell us that you can't confirm the information?"

"It's imprudent to confirm information not proven to be accurate."

"You are saying, then, that there is no leak?"

"We have not confirmed the transfer of any sensitive material to our enemies, no."

Most closed-session hearings of the Senate Select Committee on Intelligence involve sworn testimony and briefings from intelligence agency directors and senior analysts. Most hearing topics include updates on intelligence activities, collection programs, and geographic region or issue analysis. This one is about something far more sensitive.

"Several members of the intelligence community have come forward with viable claims that someone is leaking our secrets," Senator Garrett Turner continues. "They believe that the leak is coming from the Defense Intelligence Agency. Are they liars?"

"I don't know what their motivations are," the director says, recognizing the question from the ranking Republican on the committee more for the accusation it was intended to be.

"But you think that they are wrong?"

"As I have previously testified, I have not been able to confirm the authenticity of their information. If there is a leak in the DIA, it will be found."

Senator Turner leans back in his chair and rubs his chin as his fellow committee members casually watch. "Director, why do I get the feeling that you are not taking this seriously?"

"I assure you, Senator, that is not the case."

Gina eyes Boston standing along the wall on the opposite side of the room. Most information presented here is highly classified and available only to select staff who possess the proper security clearance. Since they both have one, they can trade notes when the time, place, and situation allow for it.

Ahead of this meeting, Boston issued her a warning. He said that this hearing would make things worse before they got better. Whenever politics gets injected, even the best intentions are often laden with conspiratorial fallacies and partisan agendas. It looks like he's right.

"Yes, of course. Then we should assume that you've leveraged outside counterespionage resources to evaluate the claims as Director Karen Weisz generously offered weeks ago."

"No, we have not," Admiral Troxell says with all the confidence he can muster. "All investigations are being conducted internally."

"Internal investigations? You mean by the same agencies who would be publicly embarrassed if a damaging leak were exposed? Does that include the DIA?"

"Yes, Senator."

Gina hears a smattering of groans amongst the committee members. Boston shakes his head slightly. She recognizes the tactic now, and the DNI just fell into the trap.

"Admiral, how does someone in your position as DNI not see the problem with that?"

"We believe in transparency, Senator."

Senator Turner shakes his head. "You lead the agencies that make up the sum of America's intelligence ecosystem. The nature of their business is a lack of transparency. You may be able to stonewall the American public, but not this committee. These failures are having a significant impact on our foreign policy, Director. Don't believe me? Walk over to Lafayette Park when you finish here. I'm sure the president is aware that the American public is losing patience with this administration."

Gina would never admit it, but the senator has a point. The protests in the park are vocal but peaceful for now. The last time the area across Pennsylvania Avenue from the White House looked like this was the fight for racial justice. Now groups are calling for a fundamental change to the country's foreign policy. The protestors want American soldiers out of the Middle East, and their numbers are growing.

"Politics is your job, not mine," Troxell argues.

Senator Turner leans back in his chair. "If you want to keep your position, you should rethink that mentality."

"Senator Turner," Senator Washington says, swiveling in his chair. "I would ask that you refrain from castigating our distinguished guest during this meeting. We all play for the same team."

"Mr. Chairman, former intelligence officials appear on television every night and explain to the American people that someone is leaking information to the Syrians. That information is, in turn, being used to imperil the lives of our servicemen and women stationed there. If the Middle East destabilizes, there will be plenty of blame spread around."

"And I have no doubt that you will find a way to blame the Democrats."

"Who's playing politics now, Mr. Chairman?" Turner sneers.

"Do any of the members have any further questions for the DNI?"

Gina surveys the men and women at the front of the room. There are no questions. Closed-session hearings spare everyone from the political grandstanding in front of the cameras most congressional hearings are known for. The committee members are more interested in seeing how this information can help them and their parties than providing actual oversight of the intelligence community.

"Very well. This meeting is adjourned," Senator Washington says with a rap of the gavel.

"Well, that was fun," Gina says once her boss departs the dais and walks over to her. "When you plucked me out of this room to work on your staff, I thought it was to guide you on policy regarding intelligence matters. I don't like playing politics."

"Creating policy is playing politics, Miss Attison. You've been inside the Beltway long enough to know that."

She knows he's right. Gina is a veteran of the Senate intelligence committee, having come there from the CIA. When the senator became chairman following the last election, he made her a generous offer to join his personal staff to serve as a committee liaison. A Top Secret/Sensitive Compartmented Information clearance is required to be privy to what happens when either Congressional intelligence committee is in session.

Sensitive compartmented information is a classification for knowledge derived from intelligence sources, methods, or analysis. SCI is not a classification itself like Top Secret is. It's why the titles are often used together and generally indicate that the information a holder of that clearance has access to is classified above Top Secret. Gina already had a TS/SCI, and the new position was a bump in both pay and prestige. Only a fool would have turned him down.

"I don't have to like it," Gina argues.

"No, you don't. Garrett Turner bases every decision on the political advantage he gains. The Republicans want to take the Senate back, and they're going to use these leaks to help do that. If the roles were reversed, the Democrats would be doing the same thing."

"Sir, American soldiers are dying over there. Everyone on this committee should be treating them as the priority instead of worrying how it affects their poll numbers."

"I'm a veteran of six tours in the Middle East. I spent most of my military career commanding troops in that Godforsaken part of the world. Nobody understands that better than I do."

Colby Washington was a highly decorated U.S. Army officer before retiring from the service and launching a political career. His overseas tours shaped his political views, especially regarding the use and misuse of American military power. Although a Republican most of his life, he got elected to the Senate as a Democrat because of his opposition to the neoconservative orthodoxy that believes foreign policy challenges are best solved with bombs and bullets. At least, that's the way they used to think.

"I'm sorry, sir. I didn't mean to—"

"Don't worry about it. This hearing should be enough to light a fire under Troxell's ass. The Admiral needs to bring in outside help, and he knows it. Everything in this town is measured in small steps. That's one in the right direction."

The senator walks over to talk to a colleague who is still milling around the room. Gina has seen plenty of men and women like Garrett Turner in her time on Capitol Hill. The people are something to step on when he isn't trying to get their votes. For him, it's all about political bluster leading to the next election. In this town, that's the only priority, no matter how many soldiers die on the battlefield.

CHAPTER TWO
FBI AGENT ZACH FORTE

The door to the pub opens without Zach looking back to see who is entering. He used to be paranoid about having his back to a doorway. Members of the military and law enforcement communities develop a deep obsession with watching what's happening around them. Right now, Zach doesn't care.

"Get me another, Todd."

"Don't you think you've had enough?" the pudgy man asks, not taking his eyes off the television mounted in the corner.

"You're my bartender, not my mother," Zach says, sliding his empty glass down the desolate bar. "Get me another, or I'll find another place to spend my money."

The bartender peels his eyes from the screen and frowns before reluctantly snatching the glass off the bar and adding ice cubes with a generous amount of Jack Daniel's. He acts like it's an inconvenience. It's not like he has anything else to do in an empty Washington dive bar at three in the afternoon.

"Last one. I don't need you staggering out of here to your car and getting pulled over."

"Well, if I do, I'd just show them this," he says, slapping his wallet down on the bar with his gold FBI badge facing up.

"Didn't you learn at Quantico never to harass a bartender about to cut you off?" Matt Remsen asks, pulling up a stool next to him.

"I must have missed that lesson. Get my friend here a scotch and water," Zach instructs the underworked bartender.

"Heavy on the water and hold the scotch."

"Wuss."

The two men came up through the academy and spent their first assignment at the Bureau together. After parting ways for a time, both ended up working for the FBI's Counterintelligence Division in Washington. Matt rose through the ranks faster and then left to run some secret squirrel group based in Virginia. That left Zach to flounder in the ineffective bureaucracy that has mired America's premier law enforcement agency.

"What are you doing here, Matt? Better yet, how did you find me?"

"I came to talk to you. As for your second question, remember that I work for one of the most capable intelligence groups ever assembled."

"You checked the GPS on my phone, didn't you?"

Matt smiles. Tracking anyone in the digital age is easy so long as they use a networked device. A first-grader could have found Zach in this hipster dive bar.

"Yeah."

"What do you want?"

"To offer you a job at Watchtower while you still have that badge. I need someone to run our operations unit. You're my first choice."

Zach shakes his head. "I have a job."

"Not for much longer if Grimman has his way."

Tom Grimman has the unglamorous job of running the Counterespionage Division. They are the guardian of the country's secrets and tasked with monitoring any suspicious behavior of government employees, responding to reported security violations, and developing strategies that subvert enemy intelligence operations. It's a critical job that goes unheralded when done right. When it's done wrong, the whole country hears about it, and suits at the senior levels come for you with pitchforks.

A month ago, they came for Grimman, and he passed the blame on to Zach. As the adage says, shit rolls downhill. Even with an impressive track record of executing counterintelligence operations, he has ended up suspended while they process his one-way ticket out of the Bureau. With nothing constructive to do with his time, he has spent the last couple of weeks at this bar to work on his tolerance.

"I screwed up, and Grimman is protecting his job by making an example out of me. We both know how this movie ends. You should just go."

"Nah. I'm not finished with my drink," Remsen says, taking a sip of his ice water. "You got a bum deal, Zach. Anyone could have made the same mistake. Don't toss away a stellar career over this."

"Anyone could have made it, but they didn't. I did. And then I made matters worse by committing a cardinal sin."

"So, this is how you deal with what? Guilt? You have nothing to be guilty over, and we have work to do," Matt says, nodding at the television on the wall.

Zach looks up to see yet another news report on the happenings from half a world away. Tragic events in Syria have dominated the news cycle for months, beginning when the American death toll began to rise. These segments often segue into reports on the domestic front. Peaceful demonstrations are turning violent with greater frequency.

"It's not my problem."

"Now you're talking crazy. It is when you carry that in your pocket."

Zach follows Matt's eyes to his badge, which is still sitting on the bar. He picks it up and wings it, watching it skip off the dilapidated pool table in the far corner. Matt shakes his head. He'll regret that when it's time to pay the bill.

"That better?"

"Yeah, Zach, it solves everything."

"Good, you can stop nagging me then."

"All right," Matt says, sliding off his barstool. "Know that the offer to join Watchtower stands until you're out of the FBI. At that point, there's nothing more I can do for you."

"Noted."

"There's one more thing. At some point, you're going to end up working security at a mall. When you do, don't whine about it and claim that I didn't try to help. Good luck to you."

The bells on the front door announce Matt's departure. Zach's career at the FBI is about to end prematurely. He can still do the job. He just doesn't know if he wants to anymore.

"Yeah, good luck to me," Zach mumbles, wishing he'd had some a few weeks ago, when he could have used some.

CHAPTER THREE
ERIC "MARYLAND" WILLIAMS

JOINT BASE ANACOSTIA-BOLLING
WASHINGTON, D.C.

Maryland climbs into his gray Chevy Malibu and pulls out of the sea of asphalt that covers the expansive Defense Intelligence Agency parking lot. He points the vehicle for home, less than two miles away. As a federal employee, he qualifies for on-base housing. Besides being safe, it's a nice perk in a city where the cost of living is fifty-three percent above the national average.

Joint Base Anacostia-Bolling is a sprawling military installation situated along the Potomac River south of the National Mall and directly across from Reagan National Airport. Once comprised of two adjoined military bases housing different branches, the combined installation is home to Naval and Air Force units, the White House Communications Agency, and his employer, the Defense Intelligence Agency.

"Seriously?" Maryland asks himself when he pulls off Chappie James Boulevard and into the parking lot of a fast-food restaurant and spots his friend leaning against the back of his car.

He pulls into the spot next to him and kills the engine. The guy is like a bloodhound. Since there is no getting out of this conversation, he might as well get it over with.

"You're nothing if not predictable," Boston says when Maryland joins him between their two vehicles.

"And this must be damn important for you to drag your ass off Capitol Hill to join us in the real world."

"Yeah, it is. Troxell appeared before the intelligence committee today in a closed hearing."

"You get to listen in on all the juicy stuff," Maryland says, grinning. "That must have been ugly."

"It was. Troxell got grilled, but there was also a lot of political posturing within the committee. That's not why I'm here, though. Senator Turner has somebody whispering in his ear that the leak is coming from the DIA. Troxell didn't confirm the rumor, but he didn't dispute it either."

Maryland doesn't react. He's not surprised. Admiral Troxell has always been more of a career bureaucrat than a leader in the intelligence community. He'd throw his mother in front of a bus if it meant saving himself.

"Because we're getting our asses kicked in Syria, and some genius thinks that the DIA makes the perfect scapegoat. Most Americans don't even know who the hell we are, let alone what we do. Trust me, Boston. Nobody here is leaking information to the separatists. In fact, I'm not convinced that there's a leak at all."

Boston exhales. Maryland is one of the senior analysts at the heart of DIA's global mission. His job is to provide analysis of foreign military capabilities to the military. It's not surprising that he's defensive about the possibility of a traitor, especially when the Middle East, particularly Iraq and Syria, is his area of focus.

"You might want to turn on the television and watch something more than Japanese animated porn."

"Not everyone can have a hot fiancée. I watch the news. They're always wrong. The Syrian separatists have had our number, but it doesn't mean someone from the DIA or anywhere else is leaking it to them."

Boston smirks and reaches into his car. He emerges with a manila file folder and hands it to Maryland, who eyes it skeptically before shaking his head.

"Please tell me that you aren't handing me classified information in the middle of a restaurant parking lot."

"It's redacted."

Maryland opens the file, scanning the documents. Most of this hasn't hit the media yet. Every attack by separatists hit a weak spot in the force posture that forced the U.S. military or their allies to pull back. Each time, the Russians were right there to move in within an hour.

"Is this your way of saying that the attacks were all derived from our intelligence?"

"Once is a coincidence. A dozen times is an operation based on intelligence our enemies could never possess without having someone on the inside. Here's the problem: all the recent attacks were based on intel from your section, Maryland."

"Bullshit."

Boston nods at the folder. "It's not, but I'm happy to watch you prove otherwise."

"What does Gina have to say?"

"I haven't talked to her about it yet. It's not something we can discuss over dinner."

Maryland nods. Boston and Gina have a strange relationship. From the outside, they look like the perfect couple. Dig beneath the surface, and a blind man could see issues that neither of them has dealt with. It feels like a relationship of convenience more than a couple in love.

"We have crack counterespionage teams in a dozen different agencies working this. Why are you talking to me?"

"You don't sit in on those meetings, Maryland. The men and women on that committee don't give a damn about the leak. At least most of them don't. It's about politics and power. The strength of the United States and our security interests abroad is a distant second to their reelection chances and campaign coffers. They will politicize this and look for the first scapegoat they can find."

"And you think that's me?"

"Or somebody you work with. I just want to warn you to avoid getting caught in the crossfire, and do a little digging on your own to protect yourself."

"I need to eat," Maryland says, slapping the file against Boston's chest before retreating to the other side of his car.

"What happened to you, man?"

"What do you mean?"

"You were always mission first when we were in the Army. Our brothers and sisters are dying over there. I'm warning you that they may come knocking on your door, and you're dismissing me like it isn't a problem."

"Nobody on my team has done anything wrong," Maryland says, tiring of the conversation.

"In a perfect world, that would be enough. Don't be a spineless candy ass and stick your head in the sand on this one."

"You sound a lot like Louisiana."

"I'm beginning to think he's right about you."

Maryland nods, looking around as the insult sets in. He and Louisiana may be brothers in arms, but they couldn't be more different people. Despite being friends, most things they say about each other isn't flattering.

"I've been in intelligence my entire adult life," Maryland says, resting his arms on the roof of his Chevy. "After everything I've seen, you know what I learned? Don't get involved in other people's wars."

"What happens when the war comes for you? Or me? Or the people we served with and bled with? What do you think is worth fighting for, if not them?"

Maryland doesn't bother responding. He gets into his car and pulls into the drive-thru lane to order his meal, watching Boston grow smaller in his rearview mirror until he turns around the corner of the building. He has made a DIA career out of playing it safe but can't help feeling that Boston is right. If things don't improve in the Middle East and even more casualties start coming home, the next bloodbath may occur when America holds its next election.

CHAPTER FOUR

"BOSTON" HOLLINGER

INTERSTATE 295 NORTHBOUND
WASHINGTON, D.C.

I don't drive angry, but I'm risking a run-in with the military police as I speed down the street leading to the main gate. Once off the base, I press the accelerator down harder, and my forward velocity increases in parallel with my rising anger at Maryland.

We may be friends but have never seen the world the same way. Maryland has always been content to mind his own business and play by the rules. He has this idyllic perception of life that nothing bad can happen to you if you did nothing wrong.

I've seen too much to believe that. Opportunists and manipulators prey on people like Maryland because they never see the terrible things coming their way until it's too late. The disparate viewpoints and approaches to problem-solving have caused us to clash multiple times in the past. Today is no exception.

I point my car in the direction of Interstate 295. The Anacostia Freeway isn't the most direct route to the Capitol but should be the fastest, even at this time. Most of the traffic will be heading in the opposite direction, so it shouldn't be too bad. I press a couple of buttons on the steering wheel, and my call to Gina connects.

"Do I dare ask?"

"Some things never change," I say, turning onto the on-ramp for the interstate.

"What did he say?"

"He's not going to help us. In fact, he acted like he didn't care. He maintained that nobody on his team is the traitor, and so everything will be all right."

"Even after you showed him the file?" she asks, the words dripping with contempt. She has never been a fan of my old Army buddy.

"Especially after I showed it to him. The facts don't fit his reality."

"He grew up near D.C. You would think he'd be savvy about how this city works. I'm going to ask you a question, and don't get pissed at me: do you think the leak could be coming from his team?"

I think about that for a moment. If the FBI interviews him, which they likely will, they won't find his flippant attitude quite so endearing. Despite that, there's no way that a man who doesn't jaywalk would ever cover for espionage or be involved in it himself.

"He would never cover for someone if that's what you're asking. I think he's just afraid to stick his neck out. He doesn't want it to end up under a guillotine."

"That's his choice. Let's hope that we're wrong about all this. You didn't tell him that you talked to me about it, did you?"

"No. I kept you out of it."

"Thank you. Are you heading home since you're practically there?"

"No," I say, checking my mirrors and moving into the left lane. "I have some work to get done. I'll be on the Hill in twenty minutes."

"All right. I'll see you when you get here."

I hang up the phone and shake my head, my thoughts drifting back to my conversation with Maryland. He's an analyst, not a counterintelligence expert. As annoyed as I am that he isn't willing to dig on his end, part of me doesn't blame him.

I catch a reflection in the corner of my eye as a car comes screaming up the Howard Road on-ramp. I don't pay him much mind until he continues straight across the two right lanes instead of merging into traffic. The cars around me slam on their brakes, causing me to react. I'm too late. I feel the speeding car clip my right rear quarter panel at almost seventy miles an hour.

"Whoa, shit!" I exclaim as I fight to regain control. It's a losing battle as my car becomes increasingly unstable. I jerk the wheel left, then right, and then back to the left again. I feel the body rock back and forth on the suspension as I struggle to straighten it out. The tires squeal underneath me. The last jerk of the wheel was too much.

An explosive charge's loud bang announces the airbag deployment when I slam into the barrier dividing the east and westbound lanes. Metal crunches as the car's frame accordion-folds to absorb the energy of the impact. My head isn't so lucky.

It slams into the airbag, causing my vision to burst into stars. A second later, my car bounces off the concrete k-rail and spins back into traffic. Through blurry vision, I watch an oncoming vehicle heading straight for me. I can hear the tires squeal as the brakes lock up. My car comes to a stop underneath me as the driver fights to stop his. My head hangs down as I wait for the impact, but nothing happens. It's over.

I hear the dull voices of people outside. Time seems to wind by at a fraction of its normal speed. My neck aches and lacks any strength, causing my head to roll on my shoulders. Everything is fading as blackness closes in. I close my eyes and feel sleep overtake me.

CHAPTER FIVE

SENATOR GARRETT TURNER

UPPER SENATE PARK
WASHINGTON, D.C.

The early June sunset is still hours away, yet darkening skies are pushing the daylight from the majestic green space that is Upper Senate Park. Located across Delaware Avenue from the Russell Senate Office Building, it's an excellent place for anyone working on Capitol Hill to get away from their desk for a while without straying too far.

Garrett Turner sits on a concrete bench under the line of perfectly spaced trees and stares back at the gathering clouds that have grayed the skies over the Capitol dome. It's the perfect metaphor for his mood as the man who agreed to meet him here strolls down the path in his direction.

"A storm is coming," Garrett says as Colby Washington takes a seat next to him on the bench.

"Are you making an obvious literal observation or a metaphorical one?"

"Both. You're late."

"My world doesn't revolve around you," Colby sneers. "What do you want, Senator?"

"I want to know why you let Troxell off the hook at today's committee hearing."

"Is that what you think I did?"

"No, it's what you did."

"He's the Director of National Intelligence. There was nothing to be gained by putting him through the wringer."

Garrett snickers and shakes his head. "Admiral Troxell oversees seventeen agencies that provide intelligence to this government. There is a leak in one of them that is jeopardizing our national security."

"I'm glad you feel compelled to explain all that to me as if it were my first day here."

"Then act like it isn't. The SSCI holds the executive branch accountable, and right now, the whole thing, from the president on down through the DNI, is being negligent in their jobs."

"Okay, we're done here," Colby says, rising from the bench. "I know it's an election year, and your party is desperate to politicize this, but we—"

"Why are you protecting Troxell?"

Garrett is an unapologetic opportunist, a raging egomaniac, and as ambitious a politician as ever elected to serve in this town. He's the consummate bureaucrat in a building full of them. All those traits have served him well during his meteoric rise. It also means Colby knows that he can't be trusted. If he wanted to meet, it's because he wants something. It might be prudent to find out what.

"I'm not doing any such thing."

"If that had been an open session, would the rest of the country agree with you?" Garrett argues.

Colby retakes his seat. "Not by the time you were done politicizing it, no. Take your hand off my ass and make your move. What do you want, Senator?"

"Do you need flashcards to help you understand?"

"No, what I want is for you to tell me."

"Very well. It's not what I want, for the record. My fellow Republicans demand action. We want you to subpoena the DIA to the Hill to brief us on their investigation. Then we want you to demand that the administration bring in the FBI."

"I know you're not deaf, Garrett. You heard the DNI say that they have an ongoing counterintelligence operation."

"That has yielded no results while someone in their ranks is handing out our secrets like free samples at a Sam's Club."

"Based on what information?" Colby asks. "Do you know something that the rest of us don't? Because you seem certain that this leak is coming from defense intelligence."

"At least I'm arguing that there is one."

"You know, I didn't get elected to the Senate through some affirmative action program. It wasn't an outreach program that brought me here from the squalor of Camden, New Jersey. I earned my military commission, served honorably, and led men in six tours overseas. I serve my constituents and the American people, not you."

Garrett has heard him use a similar line countless times before. His military career helped get him elected, but it doesn't mean he can hide behind it when he runs one of the most influential and secretive congressional committees.

"You serve your party, Senator. Don't pretend that your actions are for anything as noble as the people. I can hear the protest in Lafayette Park from here. Do you think that the president can't hear them from across the street? You're trying to stop the public support for the president from plummeting by pretending this isn't an issue. It's a smart tactic, but it isn't working."

"The president doesn't need my help."

"His whole Middle East policy is about to turn to ashes, giving the Russians carte blanche to do whatever the hell they want there. We're getting our ass kicked by a country that most people can't find on a map. Yeah, he does."

"I'm done with this tango," Colby says, rising again. "If you want to play politics with this, go ahead. We'll see who comes out on top."

Garrett scoffs. "If you don't take firm action to find this traitor and secure this country, it won't be you or your party."

"Garrett, you've always been an arrogant bastard. It's going to be your downfall."

"Wishful thinking on your part, Colby. Enjoy your steak dinner tonight while Americans overseas are dying on your watch."

Colby doesn't bother responding. He walks back up the path toward the Capitol as his archrival sits on the bench. Garrett was hoping to nudge the chairman by talking some sense into him without turning a simple conversation into the Book of Revelation. It didn't work. Now he needs to find something that will give him a push, and has an idea of how to do it that solves a couple of problems.

CHAPTER SIX

GINA ATTISON

NATIONAL MEDICAL CENTER
WASHINGTON, D.C.

Gina bursts through the doors of the emergency room and heads straight to the reception desk. There are calls that nobody wants to get in their lifetime. A doctor telling you that a loved one was in an auto accident is near the top of the list.

"I'm looking for information on Eugene Hollinger," Gina says, her voice firm but panicked.

"I'm sorry, ma'am, I'm in the middle of something—"

"Now!" Gina shouts, slamming her hand on the counter.

Everyone's head in the reception area cranks in her direction, including a guard standing close by who takes a couple of steps closer. The startled nurse notices the determination on Gina's face before turning to him and shaking her head.

"Are you a relative?" she asks, typing his name into her computer.

"I'm his fiancée, Gina Attison."

"He just finished getting an MRI. Let me page the doctor. He can give the prognosis and the details you are looking for. I'll have an orderly show you to the waiting area."

"Thank you," Gina says, her voice softening and eyes expressing gratitude.

The guard walks her over to join a handful of other worried people in a nearby waiting room. She paces incessantly, clutching her hands together to stop them from shaking. After what feels like an eternity, a doctor walks in, causing everyone to perk up.

"Miss Attison? I'm Kathie Osuka. I'm a neurologist assigned to your fiancé, Eugene."

"Call him Boston."

"Boston?"

"It's an old Army nickname. He hates being called Eugene."

"Okay, thank you for letting me know. Your fiancé is going to be okay. He has some scrapes and bruises, but nothing was broken, and there is no apparent internal damage. We're doing some further testing to ensure we didn't miss anything."

A wave of relief washes over Gina. Her nerves subside as if being immersed in a warm bath. She lets out a deep breath.

"Thank God."

"He did hit his head pretty hard, though. He has a concussion, and we're running some tests to see the extent of it."

"That's why you ordered the MRI. What did he hit his head on?"

"We're not sure. Probably the airbag, but the EMTs said that the car hit the barrier at an angle. He might have struck the driver's side window. You said that Boston was an Army nickname. Did he have any previous head trauma while he was in the military?"

"He got a TBI while he was in Syria. He was evacuated to Landstuhl, Germany for evaluation and sent back home."

"IED?"

"No, it was a mortar attack. Boston was badly injured. Most of the soldiers near him when it hit were killed."

"That explains a lot."

The comment unnerves Gina. The relief she felt hearing that he was okay is washed away with the doctor's alarming statement.

"Why? What's wrong with him?"

"I'll know more when I spend time studying the MRI results, but Eugene…Boston…showed some irregularities in his scan."

"What kind of irregularities?"

"I'm not sure. It's something that I've never seen before. I'd like to get Boston's medical records from the military to understand the extent of his previous traumatic brain injury. In the meantime, I'm going to take a closer look at his scan. I may need to consult a colleague of mine, Tara Winters."

"Should I read anything into that?"

"Your fiancé is alive, Miss Attison. I just want to be sure the accident didn't do any additional damage. We'll let you know if we find anything."

"Thank you, Doctor Osuka. Can I see him?"

"Sure. I'll walk you back there. I want to keep your fiancé overnight for observation, but you can visit until he's admitted and moved to a room upstairs."

Gina follows the doctor to a back room in the ER, studying the staff as she walks. The battle-hardened faces come with an emotional detachment from serving in a frontline hospital in one of America's most dangerous cities. Their eyes have witnessed all sorts of unspeakable horrors come through those doors. She is used to working with soldiers called on to take the lives of others. These people are warriors in the cause of saving them. God bless them.

"You know, there are easier ways of getting out of eating Thai food with me," Gina says, earning a grin from Boston as she moves around his bed and gives him a kiss on the forehead. "How's your noggin?"

"Still attached, despite that punk's best attempt to get it knocked off my shoulders. Thankfully, you weren't sitting in the passenger seat. Did you talk to the doc?"

"I did. The doctor said they haven't found your brain, but with the right microscope, there's hope."

"Aren't you the comedian?"

"Boston, I got a call saying you were in a bad accident and I broke a dozen traffic laws rushing to the ER. I didn't find out that you were okay until five minutes ago. I need a little humor right now."

"I'm fine, honey. It's just a bump on the head. They just want to keep me overnight for observation."

"Concussions are serious, Boston."

"Yeah, I have some experience with that."

Gina nods. She feels guilty about not telling Boston about the doctor's inquiry into his previous trauma, but doesn't want to worry him. They may or may not find something, and right now, she's content knowing that her fiancé is in one piece.

A cadre of nurses and orderlies arrives for transport. Gina is asked to leave and decides not to protest, even though it's the last thing she wants to do. There's no reason to add to the ruckus she has already caused in this ER. She kisses Boston and strokes his face.

"I'll be back in the morning. Sleep well, honey."

CHAPTER SEVEN

SPECIAL AGENT ZACH FORTE

J. EDGAR HOOVER F.B.I. BUILDING
WASHINGTON, D.C.

The Federal Bureau of Investigation's headquarters is located in the unsightly J. Edgar Hoover Building on Pennsylvania Avenue, but little real work happens at that location. The pinnacle of hideous late sixties architecture is ill-suited to meet the modern FBI's needs. As a result, most departments are housed in buildings around the district and in Northern Virginia.

Zach is grateful that his counterintelligence job required a lot of fieldwork that allowed him to avoid the office. Unfortunately, there's no avoiding it today.

"Take a seat," Supervisory Special Agent Tom Grimman commands from behind his desk after Zach enters.

"What's this about?"

"Redemption."

Zach shakes his head. "You've done everything you can to destroy my career over the past few weeks. Do you expect me to believe you've suddenly changed your tune?"

A veteran of the FBI, Grimman once distinguished himself following 9/11. He has since morphed into a bureaucratic shell of his former self. Approaching nearly six foot and bald, he looks like an angrier version of Stanley Tucci from the television show *Fortitude*. Whatever this is, it has nothing to do with redemption.

"Is this about the investigation into the Syrian leak?"

"No, I don't want you within a hundred miles of that investigation. This is a special assignment. It's off the books."

"You mean unsanctioned and possibly illegal?"

Grimman sighs and leans back in his chair. "You were a fantastic agent. Top of your class and responsible for helping put away some of the most dangerous threats to our country. You're also irresponsible and unpredictable, and that finally caught up with you during Beaver Cage."

The name of Zach's last operation was more symbolic than the ludicrous moniker suggests. The fact that it went so wrong means it will forever be etched into his memory. Now he wishes it had been named something more provocative, like Dragon's Teeth or Hangman's Noose. Not that a better name would lessen the shame.

"If that is true, why offer me a second chance? Assuming that's what this is."

"Because your brand of irresponsibility and unpredictability is what we need for this operation that I'm planning. The intelligence community is playing their investigations by the book. When the FBI is asked to join – and I expect that to happen at any moment – it's obvious that those methods aren't going to catch this traitor. We need to think outside the box."

"You want me to bend the rules and break laws because pesky things like that are inconvenient."

"That's not the primary reason you're here, but if necessary, yes. We may not agree on much, you and I, but we both want to catch the bastard doing this. I'm giving you the chance to be a big part of that. You can take it, or you can go back to drinking yourself into oblivion. It's your choice."

Grimman waits for a response, but Zach won't give him the satisfaction. His boss had no problem sharing the credit for all of Zach's successes. One operation goes south, and he gets sacrificed as a scapegoat at the altar of political expediency. That's what the bureaucracy has become. Now he's expendable, and his boss is leveraging that.

"Are you going to say anything?" Grimman asks.

"I'll think about it."

"Think fast. We're facing an unprecedented threat to this country. I need to know if you're in before the trumpets sound, not after. We're done here."

Zach leaves Grimman's office and turns the corner to make his way to the elevators. That was far more interesting than he thought it would be. The FBI has landed in hot water over these types of investigations in recent memory. If they were to get caught again, the American public would go crazy.

So why risk moving forward with an unofficial investigation? That's the answer he wants to get. Zach boards the elevator and punches the button for the lobby. If this covert investigation is legitimate and just being kept quiet, he's on board with the idea. He's spent the better part of his adult life protecting America against all enemies, both foreign and domestic. This traitor is an embarrassment to America, and he needs to be neutralized.

CHAPTER EIGHT

"BOSTON" HOLLINGER

NATIONAL MEDICAL CENTER
WASHINGTON, D.C.

I don't know where I am. Everything is blurry and distorted as if I'm staring at the world blanketed in a thick fog. I can feel my body move but can't control it. Is this a dream? If it is, it doesn't feel like one.

Someone is here with me, but I can't make out the face even though the person is only a couple of feet away. I fight to focus my eyes, but nothing happens. The haze refuses to yield no matter how much I will it away. The only sharpness is the raw emotions I feel. Right now, it's fear and anxiousness.

"Call him Boston."

"Boston?"

"It's an old Army nickname. He hates being called Eugene."

"Okay, thank you for letting me know. Your fiancé is going to be okay. He has some scrapes and bruises, but nothing was broken, and there is no significant internal damage."

I feel a wave of relief wash over me. Why am I nervous at all? I hear my name, but I'm right here. What's happening? I hear myself let out a deep breath, but it's not mine.

"Thank God."

"He did hit his head pretty hard, though. He has a nasty concussion, and we're running some tests to see the extent of it."

"That's why you ordered the MRI. What did he hit his head on? The airbag?"

"We're not sure. Probably the airbag, but the EMTs said that the car hit the barrier at an angle. You said it was an Army nickname. Did Boston have any previous head trauma while he was in the military?"

"He got a TBI while he was in Syria. He was evacuated to Landstuhl, Germany for evaluation and sent back home."

"IED?"

"No, it was a mortar attack. Boston was badly injured. Most of the soldiers near him when it hit were killed."

"That explains a lot."

"Why? What's wrong with him?"

A loud noise jolts me awake, and I shoot straight up. The nurse looks at me from the side of the bed as she bends over and picks up the tray she dropped. The look of remorse on her face tells the story.

"I'm so sorry, Boston. It slipped out of my hand. I didn't mean to wake you."

"It's okay."

"Were you dreaming?" she asks, smiling.

I look out the window at the growing daylight. If that was a dream, it was the weirdest one I've ever had.

"Yeah, I think so."

"Anything good?

"No, not really," I say, forcing a smile.

"I'm so sorry for waking you. Would you like to order breakfast? The doctor will be here soon, and it should arrive when she's done with you."

"Uh, yeah, that's fine."

The nurse hands me a menu and leaves the room. I sink back into my pillow, trying to remember what I experienced. Much of it has already faded from memory. I remember hearing my name like I wasn't there. I heard another name: Tara something. It was a season. Damn, why can't I remember?

I give up. Whatever it was, I never want to experience it again. I don't like the feeling that I'm not in control of my body. It doesn't matter if it's real-life or the dream world. I scan the menu, content to satisfy my rumbling stomach if I can't control what's going on inside my head when I'm sleeping.

CHAPTER NINE
ERIC "MARYLAND" WILLIAMS

DEFENSE INTELLIGENCE AGENCY
JOINT BASE ANACOSTIA-BOLLING, WASHINGTON, D.C.

Gina's call last night with news of the accident rattled Maryland. It also changed his frame of mind following his conversation with her fiancé. The two men may not agree on things, but Boston has always been a good friend. Eric knows that he should take the warning he was given more seriously. Too bad it took an auto accident for him to recognize that.

With that in mind, Maryland goes to the desk of a fellow senior analyst on the team and the one man he can trust. Devin Locke is exceptionally qualified for his job, almost to the point of being overqualified. A guy who has worked his way through the ranks, Devin would already be a supervisor if he weren't so damn proficient in his current role. He also owes Maryland some favors, and his phone call this morning cashed one of them in.

"Are you kidding me with this?" Devin asks, leaning back in his cheap office chair after Maryland arrives at his desk.

"Not this time."

"You know, you shouldn't have me looking into this. I could be the mole."

Maryland smirks. "Are you the mole?"

"No."

"If you're not the mole and I'm not the mole, then that's two down."

Devin shakes his head. "Eric, I'm entertaining this because I owe you one."

"You owe me about twelve."

"Fine. Twelve. Regardless, this is a big ask. Every counterintelligence team in the country is looking for the traitor leaking this information. What do you expect me to find that they won't?"

"Nothing. It's what we can do *if* we find something that they won't."

"I didn't think blackmail was your thing."

"Believe me, it's not. The entire intelligence community is on high alert. The directors are already playing politics with this, and fingers are all starting to point at us."

"How do you know that?"

"I know people. Do you want to keep playing games or tell me what you found? I know you started working on it the moment you sat down this morning."

Devin smirks. He did.

"I haven't gotten far, but the first correlation I found happened about seven months ago. The DIA put together a series of products outlining Syrian tactics for the brass at the Pentagon. They were getting predictable, so we thought field commanders could put it to use."

"Did they?"

"Unfortunately. The commander followed the playbook and walked right into an ambush. Eight soldiers were killed."

Maryland shakes his head. He doesn't remember that specific incident. Unfortunately, it was likely buried in the avalanche of tragic reports coming out of that area of the world. It's a sad day when eight patriots' deaths aren't newsworthy, even within the intelligence community.

"Anything else?" he asks.

"Yeah, I've found three more examples where attacks could be linked back to intelligence that we uncovered or products that we produced."

"Nothing from other agencies?"

"Not yet, but I just started. I have to be honest with you, Eric. They may have a reason to point at us."

Maryland lowers his eyes and nods. DIA analysts' products are shared throughout the chain of command, numerous elements within the Department of Defense, and the larger intelligence community. There is no way for them to find out which compartment has the leak, but they can at least start proving it's not them.

"We know what we're looking for. Let's get a list of all the attacks on our troops and infrastructure in Syria during that time. Check them against any intelligence or analysis developed by the DIA. Let's confirm if what you found is a trend or just a couple of examples."

Devin stares at Maryland, checks his computer screen, and returns his gaze to his fellow analyst. This isn't something he's looking forward to.

"That's going to take a while."

"I know. That's why I brought my lunch. I hope you don't have any plans."

CHAPTER TEN

SENATOR GARRETT TURNER

SENATE CAPITOL VISITOR CENTER STUDIO
CAPITOL HILL, WASHINGTON, D.C.

Garrett tries to look interested and engaged, knowing that there are a dozen cameras pointed at him. He agreed to join the Republican Senate leadership for this press conference in the chamber's Capitol Visitor Center studio. No politician misses an opportunity to command more attention and raise their public profile by standing with influential colleagues.

He nods as the leader speaks and surveys the room packed full of journalists. A reporter that Garrett knows once asked him what a room of politicians is really like when cameras aren't rolling. He responded that it smells like careerism and incompetence. Ironically, he uses that same line when describing the congressional press pool.

"We are facing an extraordinary crisis that demands an extraordinary response," the minority leader says, responding to a question. "What's happening in Syria is deadly and is creating a foreign policy nightmare."

"Do you think the rumors of a leak in our intelligence community are true then?" one of the reporters asks.

"It would be easy for everyone to dismiss them as the unsubstantiated product of conspiracy theorists as this administration has done, or even political opportunism to besmirch the president, as his press secretary said yesterday. At what point does a responsible president call for an investigation to determine the truth?"

"Do you think he's hiding something?" another reporter asks.

"You all have colleagues in the White House Press Corps. Maybe if the president ever held a press conference, one of them could ask him. What has it been? A hundred and thirty-two days?"

Presidents have antagonistic relationships with the press. Even Democrats, who much of the mainstream media tend to favor, don't like scrutinizing their decisions. While Republican presidents are often more aloof with the press, the

Democrat currently occupying the White House has brought avoidance to a whole new level.

"Will the Senate Intelligence Committee be calling for an investigation?" a woman in the back asks. It was the opportunity the leader was waiting for.

"Right now, there must be a firm commitment to find and eliminate the threat of anyone leaking our secrets. It is the administration's responsibility to do that. If an investigation is warranted, we will conduct one. Right now, we are focused on keeping Americans sent into harm's way safe. Thank you, everybody."

The press conference adjourns, and the senators move off the raised dais and retreat to the hallway. Garrett thinks the briefing went well, but it will only get a fifteen-second mention on the evening news, at best. There was nothing controversial for social media to pick up on, although publicity wasn't the point. He hopes the press is forced to ask the president a tough question during this term. It would be a first.

Garrett spends some time talking to his colleagues out of the line of view from the Washington press corps. They agree to gather and discuss the response later when the senator feels a tap on his arm. He turns to see his chief of staff offering his phone.

"Grimman."

"Your timing sucks," Garrett says after excusing himself and finding a quiet spot in the hallway.

"Yeah, so I noticed. You guys laid it on thick," the FBI agent says.

"It's the only way you get things done around here. What's your situation?"

"I have a resource on board."

"He'll play ball?"

"He doesn't have a choice in the matter. Let me worry about that. All I need now is your instructions."

Garrett looks back down the hallway to ensure nobody is coming. "I'm working on something. You'll have them soon."

"How soon?"

"When I'm ready to move, you will be the first to know," the senator sneers. "Until then, no contact. Understood?"

"Yeah," Grimman says with a sigh.

"Any update on the start of an official investigation?"

"No, nothing of consequence," Grimman admits. "We're quietly reviewing intelligence reports. They are narrowing it down for when one is sanctioned so that Director Weisz will have a direction to go in."

"I shouldn't be shocked that the administration is dragging their feet on this. I'll be in touch."

Garrett ends the call and tucks the phone into one of his jacket pockets. Karen Weisz didn't become the director of counterintelligence by being reckless. FBI leadership protects their jobs by not doing them, but that doesn't matter. Garrett knows how he can force her hand when the time is right.

CHAPTER ELEVEN
GINA ATTISON

Boston stares at his watch for the tenth time in the past minute and a half, almost willing it to move faster. He hates hospitals, as most veterans do. Despite him being ready to go, it takes a while for his discharge paperwork to make its way through the hospital's bureaucracy.

"Relax, Boston, it couldn't have been that bad."

"Let's hope that you don't have to find out anytime soon."

Gina shakes her head and looks up to see Dr. Osuka walk in with a young woman wearing a matching white lab coat. Her blue-green speckled eyes and olive complexion are characteristic of Persian descent. Gina studies her face and notices a bruise over her eye and slightly swollen cheek that the doctor tried and failed to conceal with makeup.

"What's the word, Doc?"

"Good news. I signed off on your discharge. You're free to go."

"Thank God," Boston says, not taking his eyes off the other doctor.

"That doesn't mean you have a clean bill of health, though. You still have a bad concussion. We're going to want a follow-up scan in a couple of weeks. Can I count on you to keep that appointment?"

Boston looks at Gina. "I doubt I'll have a choice."

"Good. Then before you go, I'd like to introduce you to a colleague I consult with from the VA. Her name is—"

"Tara Winters."

Both women's mouths hang open. He even got the pronunciation correct. She goes by the Persian "tah-rah" instead of the English pronunciation "terra."

"Nice to meet you, Mr. Hollinger," she says, her eyes lighting up and her head dipping demurely as she shakes his hand.

"Please, call me Boston."

"How do you know her name?" Dr. Osuka asks, her head cocked to the side. "Have the two of you met before?"

Gina studies her fiancé. She was wondering the same thing. Dr. Winters's name never came up in their conversations.

"No. I heard you say her name."

"Boston, I've never mentioned her to you before."

"You did in my dream last night."

Gina feels a stabbing pang of jealousy. She already hates this woman. With the olive skin, gorgeous eyes, an athletic figure, and that sultry voice, Tara must have men falling over themselves to spend time with her. Now she may be invading Boston's dreams.

"That must have been quite a dream. What else was in it?"

"I don't remember much of it. You found irregularities in my MRI and needed my medical records or something."

Dr. Osuka glances over at Gina, who shakes her head. "Well, that's intriguing. I'll leave you in the capable hands of Dr. Winters and will see you in a few weeks."

"Thanks, Doctor," Gina says, shaking her hand and then taking a seat next to Boston on the bed.

"I read through your VA and military medical records. You gave the doctors in Germany quite a scare after the mortar attack in Syria."

"It was touch and go for a while there."

"You've been in constant treatment for a traumatic brain injury ever since?" she asks, getting a nod from Boston. "Any negative thoughts, alcohol abuse, depression, sensitivity to sirens or loud noises?"

"I don't have PTSD, Doc." The denial earns him a disapproving look. "Okay, I do, but does any of that explain how I knew your name?"

"No, it doesn't. What symptoms do you have?"

"I'm anxious, jump at loud noises, and I've even mistaken the dresser in my bedroom for a militant once and battered it until my fists bled. I have dreams about my friends in Syria. I see the faces and mortar rounds going off around us. I hear the gunfire. The dream I had last night felt different. It felt real."

Tara's phone vibrates in her pocket. She takes it out and checks it before sliding it back in.

"I'm sorry, but I'm late for an appointment. I would like to meet with you tomorrow morning. I will have the VA send an appointment time and my office location. It will give me a chance to review your MRI some more and a chance for you to get some rest outside this place."

"You don't believe me about the dreams, do you?"

"Trauma can manifest itself in several ways, Boston. I just want to understand how yours is. I'll be in touch," she says, flashing a warm smile before leaving the room.

Gina grabs Boston's hand as they follow her out of the room to his awaiting freedom. He already knows where this insecurity is coming from. He also knows it will take a lot to convince the love of his life to not go with him to the appointment tomorrow.

CHAPTER TWELVE
ERIC "MARYLAND" WILLIAMS

Eric knocks on the door and waits patiently for Boston to answer. Odds are his friend isn't moving too fast these days. After a few more raps don't yield any results, he walks around the house to the back patio. Boston sits in a lounge chair with a book and only looks up when he notices Maryland standing over him.

"You lost or something?"

"I wanted to see if you were still alive," Maryland says, checking the book cover to see what he's reading. "I heard that I might have been in the will."

Boston smirks and slowly sits up, swinging his legs to the ground. Maryland grabs a patio chair and takes a seat of his own.

"How are you feeling?"

"Like I got hit by a truck, which regrettably isn't far from the truth. Everything is sore, and my brain feels like it's sloshing around in my head."

"At least you know that part can't be true."

"I have years' worth of pictures from six different hospitals that prove I have one. I have a meeting with a doctor tomorrow who will want even more proof."

"More poking and prodding?"

Boston reaches over and grabs a beer out of his cooler. He hands it to Maryland, who makes quick work of the cap.

"I hope not. Dr. Winters is a neurologist and PTSD specialist with the VA, so that would be weird."

Maryland grunts. "Ugh. Head doctors are even worse. Is she hot?"

"Gina didn't like her."

"Oh, she must be hot then. Where is the boss?"

"On the Hill, where else?"

One of the reasons the relationship between Boston and Gina works is that they both put in long hours. It's hard to get mad at your future spouse for not being around when you have the same burden. Just as much work goes on during the evening in the nation's capital as during the day. Even with Boston freshly home from the hospital, her being on Capitol Hill isn't a surprise.

"That explains the book and the beer."

"I know you didn't drive over to check up on me when you have a perfectly working cell phone. Are you going to get to the real reason you're here?"

"You need to keep this between us. I had one of my guys do some research," Maryland says, looking around the back yard and keeping his voice low. "Over a dozen attacks on U.S. interests in Syria match up with products generated by the DIA."

"I'm glad you took my advice. The DIA is going to end up under a microscope. Watch your back."

"I may not be the only one. We generated the intel, but in each case, it was widely shared with outside parties."

"Let me guess: CIA and DoD," Boston says, leaning back and earning a nod from Maryland.

"Defense Department for sure, but it was also given to the intelligence committees in both houses of Congress and to the National Security Council."

Boston closes his eyes and rubs his temples. "Politics."

"Yeah. Someone from Langley, the Pentagon, Capitol Hill, or even in the White House could be leaking this intel to the Syrians."

"They aren't. It's leaking to the Russians."

Maryland cocks his head. "What makes you think that?"

"What have I always told you about this game?"

"It's all about power."

That is Boston's worldview, and he shares it every chance he gets. It's his firm belief that every conflict in history and every decision made in politics has to do with power in one way or another. Money may make the world go round, but power is the axis it spins on.

"The U.S. position on Syria doesn't include regime change, even though that's what everyone in this administration wants."

"Yeah, and we're always good for our word. Ask the Sioux and the Cherokee," Maryland mutters.

"The Syrians wouldn't want to test us on that. ISIL is a shell of its former glory and operating in an area the size of a postage stamp. Who does that leave?"

Maryland takes a seat and leans forward, steepling his hands in front of his face. "Russia."

"They've made new deals with the Iranians and already have a naval base on the Med in Syria. They want additional bases in the Middle East to expand their presence and influence in the region. To do that, they need to push us out. Can you think of a better way?"

"Let's assume that's all true. Why are you so bothered by it? And don't say it's because soldiers are dying."

"Because in this political climate, it will work. When someone connects these dots, you'll have two branches of government and the most powerful intelligence agencies in the country all pointing fingers at each other. The public won't know who to believe, so they'll tune in to the media. The talking heads on cable news will spin the stories to earn clicks and support their favorites while demonizing everyone else. In the end, the American people will get fed up and demand we leave the Middle East. When we do, the Russians win."

Maryland takes a long swig from his beer. He can't argue with Boston's logic, as much as he'd like to.

"When did you learn to read the future?"

"You pick up a few things working with Congress."

"Boston, it's not your job to stop it."

"I know. But maybe we should start thinking about finding someone who can."

Maryland doesn't like where this is going. They lost close friends in Syria, and Boston has been obsessed over righting every wrong in the world since that day. It's like he is living for all those who died. The problem is, when you shoulder that much burden, it's only a matter of time before you get crushed. He hopes that's not the path that Boston is on.

CHAPTER THIRTEEN
SPECIAL AGENT ZACH FORTE

The District of Columbia is filled with the same dive bars that dot every big city in America. This one is no different, and Zach knows he should change it up every so often. But he's comfortable in this spot, and Matt Remsen already knows to find him here.

"The Rowdy Squirrel is anything but rowdy, considering that it's ten o'clock," Matt says, climbing onto the barstool next to him while earning a nasty look from the bartender. "Is that soda?"

"Can it be confused for anything else?"

"How much rum is in it?"

"None, unfortunately. What did you find?" Zach asks as Matt points to his soft drink to the bartender's chagrin.

"Grimman wasn't lying. Whatever he wants you to do is off the books."

"How did you find that out?"

"D.C. is a small town, Zach, and everyone who works at Watchtower knows everyone else. Don't worry, the inquiry won't get back to him."

Zach knows that his friend is right: Washington is a large city with a small town's gossip network. People talk, and that can be a good thing or bad. If news of the inquiry ever got back to Grimman, the game would be up. Matt's confidence that it won't is reassuring, but that only goes so far in this business.

"Where is this coming from?"

"That's a good question. We don't know."

"Someone sanctioned it. The FBI is a massive bureaucracy that can't find their way out of a coat closet with two hands and a map, but Grimman is too smart to go off the reservation without a backstop."

"I agree. Someone high up on the food chain is putting him up to it. That's why I want you to take the assignment and let us know what you find."

Zach cranks his head over at Matt. Expecting the reaction, he stares straight ahead at the bottles lining the back of the bar and sips his Coke.

"You can't be serious."

"I help run one of the best intelligence units ever devised. I don't have time for games."

"So you keep saying. Do you know how many laws I will break to do what Grimman is asking?"

"A shit ton, which is why it will double as a Watchtower special assignment."

"That's one way to get me to work for you."

Zach is a loyal agent through and through. While working for the modern FBI infuriates him, he never liked the idea that a covert group exists to work on counterintelligence matters. When he learned that Matt joined it, he felt it was a personal betrayal. That is beginning to change, but the trust hasn't been earned yet.

"I'm not going to use this to force you into Watchtower, as much as I'd like to. We might have a real problem here, Zach. The word came down through official channels this afternoon. The president has directed the FBI to delve into one of the greatest counterespionage efforts in the past fifty years. If Grimman has you doing something that runs counter outside of that effort, we need to know what it is and why."

"Grimman knows we're friends. Why would he assume I don't talk to you?"

"Because he doesn't know what I do. Nobody does except the people who work at Watchtower and you."

Their friendship is a strong one. Matt stood by him through the Beaver Cage fiasco. He's right – Zach would never betray him and hopes that the sentiment works both ways.

"Okay, I'll do it. How do you want me to contact you?"

Matt hands him a slip of paper with a phone number on it. "Call that. It will get routed to me. Do it from an untraceable burner phone. Never call me from your own number. You need to assume that if Grimman put you on something shady, he's taken measures to keep an eye on you."

"I'll let you know when I hear something."

Matt slaps a twenty on the bar that greedy Todd snatches up before he changes his mind. He leaves Zach to nurse a cola that he wishes was something more potent. A safety net has been erected for him now, but that doesn't mean he's enthusiastic about climbing into bed with the devil.

CHAPTER FOURTEEN
EUGENE "BOSTON" HOLLINGER

DR. TARA WINTERS'S RESIDENCE
ADAMS MORGAN, WASHINGTON, D.C.

The voices are muffled. The fog bank envelops me. A figure stands in what looks like an opening…a doorway. My vision is obscured. What is that in my eyes? It streaks my vision in a golden hue.

Something brushes it away. I can see more clearly now. A man in a suit…a bed… As the voices become clearer, I can tell the man is…slurring.

"You are a worthless bitch! You're good for nothing. I don't know why I even bother," he says.

"So why do you, Mark?" I hear myself say. I feel…anger. Burning anger that I can't contain.

"I don't know. It's not for your money. You screwed that up already. And it's not like I enjoy the sex."

"Then get out!" I hear myself scream in a high-pitched wail. "Go screw one of your cheap floozies!"

"Who says I haven't been all along?"

"You're a bastard!" I hear myself yell again. The voice is filled with emotion. It's hurt…and rage.

The man in the suit steps closer. The face is blurry. He comes closer and closer. Then he pulls back his right arm and swings his hand, striking me above the eye. My vision explodes with stars before going all white. The pain…

I wake and immediately touch the top of my eye and cheek, checking for pain or blood. When I find none, I know it was another of those realistic dreams. I sit up and take several deep breaths to get my nerves under control.

"Are you okay? You scared the hell out of me," Gina says, now sitting up and rubbing my back.

"Yeah, just another bad dream."

"It must have been."

I don't tell her what it was about. That will only lead to a couple dozen questions and an hour wasted that I could have spent sleeping. Not that I want to. The realism is startling. Whatever is happening inside my head isn't going away. If anything, it's growing more intense.

* * *

This meeting isn't starting off the way I thought it would. I knew that Dr. Winters maintained her office at her house, but I thought it was something with a separate entrance and maybe even a receptionist posted at a desk. I was wrong.

"Hi, Boston," Tara says after answering the door on the fifth ring in black yoga pants and a sweatshirt. Her long black hair frames both sides of her face, and she makes no attempt to brush it out of the way. The woman in front of me is a far cry from the professional I met yesterday.

"Am I early?"

"Uh, no, I'm sorry. It's been a rough morning. I'm running horribly late and am a bit of a mess. Please make yourself comfortable in the living room. I'll just be about ten minutes."

I pass the time by reading a copy of the *Army Times* that is remarkably current. When Tara returns, she's dressed in a blouse and skirt, with fashionable high heels highlighting a set of legs that would have made Louisiana drool.

"Okay, please, have a seat," she says, gesturing towards the couch while selecting a high-backed chair across from it.

"This is more informal than I thought it would be."

"That's by design. I work with a lot of patients that have PTSD. The familiarity and comfort of a typical living room help put them at ease."

The sound of a door slamming upstairs shakes the house. Tara jumps at the sound and looks at me with embarrassment as I hear someone stomping around upstairs.

"We usually try to avoid loud sounds as well."

"Someone's pissed off."

"As I said, it's been a rough morning."

She picks up her notepad and pen and subconsciously brushes the hair out of her face, revealing the darkening bruise over her eye that she tried to hide with makeup yesterday. It also explains why her hair is down today, and she's struggling not to fuss with it.

"I reviewed all your records last night. You had a significant TBI that was re-aggravated during the accident."

"Hitting a concrete barrier at sixty miles an hour and face planting into an airbag will do that," I say, desperate to move this along. "I want to talk about the dreams I'm having."

"Dreams are typically not a medical condition, Boston."

"I know. I had another one last night. It was different than the last, but the feeling was the same. It was real…like I was there but not able to interpret anything. Everything in the dream was hazy and unclear, and the voices were muffled. The emotion was a different story. It was raw, and I felt fear and pain as if it were happening to me."

"What was the dream about?"

"It's tough to remember. I can only recall pieces."

A well-dressed man comes stomping down the stairs from the second floor and bursts into the living room before she can say anything further. The suit looks too expensive to make him a government employee, so he is private sector all the way: a lobbyist or a lawyer for some big firm, most likely.

"I'm leaving the key on your table out here."

"Fine," Tara responds, the tone of her voice mixing a hint of defiance with a helping of fear.

The man sizes me up like any alpha male would when he thinks someone is moving in on his woman. Whatever went down between these two this morning was as ugly as the bruise over Tara's eye.

"I was wondering if we could—"

"I'm with a patient, Mark."

I lean back on the sofa and look over at the man. Something is familiar with his voice, but I can't place it.

"Yeah, I need to say something. It will only take a moment."

She looks at me with apologetic eyes. "I'm sorry, Boston. Please excuse me for one moment."

Tara gracefully rises from her chair, and her heels click on the hardwood floor as she meets Mark, who is standing at the door in the foyer. They disappear around the corner and try to keep their voices at a whisper, but as the conversation gets heated, their volume goes up.

"It's time for you to go," Tara demands.

"Have it your way," Mark responds, pulling open the front door and slamming it behind him.

The familiarity of the man and his voice eats away at me until the realization hits me like a sledgehammer. I close my eyes and fight to put together the piece of last night's dream.

"Are you okay?" Tara asks, retaking her seat.

"Yeah, I'm fine. Let's get back to it. The dreams. Is there a way to remember what they are when I wake up?"

"There are a few techniques, but they take years to master. What do you remember?"

I close my eyes again, recalling how a woman in my dream used the word "floozies." The man was pompous and sarcastic, and I could feel anger and hurt at his words every time he spoke. Then she called him a bastard.

I remember the slap, but don't remember the face of who hit me. Everything was so blurry and vague in the dream. I try a different approach and superimpose Mark's face on the man's figure from the dream. At once, the haziness subsides. It was him. How is that possible?

"Jesus," I mutter, shaking my head.

"What is it?"

I look up at Tara, not masking the serious look on my face. "What happened to your eye and cheek, Dr. Winters?"

"Oh. Uh, I'm a klutz," she replies, applying a gentle touch to her eye with her fingers. "I walked into something."

I lean forward on the couch. "Would that something be Mark's hand when he slapped you two nights ago?"

Tara's jaw drops, and the blood rushes out of her face as it freezes in shock. I study her reaction. There's no hiding what happened now, and I let out a long exhale.

"How could you know that? I mean, how could you possibly…"

"Has he been cheating on you?"

Tara clenches up. "That's personal."

"He is, isn't he? You confronted him the night before I met you. I saw it in the dream I had last night."

"That's—"

"Impossible? I agree, so please, tell me what I'm about to say never happened. You were having an argument in the house. You said something about screwing floozies, and he said he already was. You called him a bastard, and he slapped you. That's when you decided to break it off and why he left the keys this morning."

Tara is astonished, her hand covering her mouth as she shakes her head, refusing to believe what she's hearing. I sink back into the couch, knowing that her lack of denial means that it went down pretty much as I described it.

"There must be another explanation."

"I hope so. I'm all ears."

"You could be videotaping me."

"I didn't know who you were until we met at the hospital yesterday. This dream I had; it was you and Mark. I watched the whole thing as if I were peering through someone else's eyes."

"Whose eyes?" she asks.

I take a deep breath before responding.

"Yours."

CHAPTER FIFTEEN

SENATOR GARRETT TURNER

OFFICE OF THE SENATE MINORITY LEADER
CAPITOL BUILDING, WASHINGTON, D.C.

Garrett can't help but think he's on the fast track to becoming a major player in the party. He is comfortably ensconced in the Senate minority leader's suite, having already taken the time to appreciate the vaulted ceilings, ornate fireplaces, and nickel-plated brass and crystal chandeliers that adorn the space. It's located across from the Senate Chamber in the Capitol and offers a spectacular sweeping view of the National Mall.

"He's down four points in the last month," the minority leader says from his high-back chair.

"And that's with the media covering up his inept response," the senior senator from Texas says.

"It's too bad he isn't running for reelection this year. It would have been a headache for him," a third senator says.

"Let's keep the focus on winning back the Senate. We need to hold our seats and win three more. Flannigan is losing in Georgia, but we're in decent shape everywhere else. Where do we get four seats?"

"North Carolina, Kansas, and Tennessee are all red states with vulnerable incumbents," the Georgian says.

"Brinkell isn't going to win in North Carolina," Garrett says.

The four men and one woman comfortably seated around the small coffee table all look at him. These are more than Garrett's colleagues. They are the best and brightest members of the party serving in the United States Senate. They are its future, and the responsibility of charting the course to regain the majority falls on their shoulders.

"Why do you say that?" the leader asks. "He has a lead in the polls."

"He's also on the wrong side of a wide enthusiasm gap and is getting outhustled on the campaign trail. Brinkell is low energy, and the guy the Democrats are running is connecting with the people."

"I'm not sure I agree, but let's assume Garrett is right. What else?"

"Maine," the Texan says.

"That's right. We're running that veteran, and she's gaining ground."

"With the right financial push, it could be enough to push her over the top."

"Let's see if an infusion narrows the gap. If it does, we can have some PAC money sent her way."

Money is the lifeblood of politics. Without vast sums of it, there is no campaign structure, offices, ground game to get out the vote, printed materials, rallies, or commercials. It's the reason fundraising is reported so often by the media. A few hundred thousand dollars can be the difference between a win and a loss in a swing state.

"That leaves a fourth seat."

"I'm not sure there is one," one of Garrett's colleagues says, leaning back in his chair.

"There is. Colby Washington's."

"He's not up for reelection this year," the minority leader argues.

"I'm not talking about beating him in an election. I'm talking about him resigning."

"Why would he do that?" the Texan asks.

Garrett smiles at the group. "Missouri has a Republican governor now. Colby resigns, and that hot shit lieutenant governor can be appointed in his place. He does the job until a special election, and with his name recognition, probably wins easily."

"That's all well and good, but it's still contingent on him resigning. Hell will freeze over before he gives up that seat."

Garrett is about to respond when a knock at the door causes the group to turn. He curses the timing.

"Pardon the interruption, Mr. Leader. You need to see this."

"I'm in the middle of something, Patrick. What is it?"

"There has been an attack in Syria. A bombing of a gathering of allies meeting an American envoy. The Pentagon is saying there were no survivors."

The Leader turns to Garrett. "The leak?"

Garrett offers a little shrug. "Probably."

"That's not all, sir," Patrick continues. "Several news outlets are alleging that the American envoy was…"

"Was what?"

"The vice president's son."

CHAPTER SIXTEEN

GINA ATTISON

The Executive Branch takes charge during any crisis. As possible responses are mulled, members of Congress are often consulted. In this case, the CIA, Defense Department, Defense Intelligence Agency, and several other intelligence groups arranged to brief the SSCI on what they have learned about the vice president's son's death.

The committee members are asking prudent questions and have otherwise remained quiet through much of the briefing. The political impact of this is not lost on anyone in the room.

"The convoy left Dayr-al-Zawr at 1400 Zulu time and was traveling to a meeting with Kurdish insurgents when the attack happened," a general from the Pentagon explains.

"Was there air cover and an escort?" one of the committee members asks.

"We had satellite coverage from the National Reconnaissance Office, and the route was monitored by an MQ-4 Global Hawk and an armed MQ-9 Reaper," the representative from the CIA confirms.

"Please continue, General," Senator Washington says from the dais.

"The convoy included an escort of three up-armored Humvees and two MRAPs. The attack began when three IEDs detonated almost simultaneously and took out the escort vehicles. The MRAPs were targeted by RPGs and small arms fire. We are still putting together the details about what happened next."

"Were the attackers noticed by the drones?" another senator asks.

"Not until the ambush was in progress."

"How long was the route monitored before the convoy's departure?"

The CIA official shifts in his seat. "Three days."

Audible grumbling among the senators on the committee erupts as the intelligence and military briefers wait patiently for order to be restored. They knew that would be controversial.

"So, it is safe to assume then that the IEDs were planted along that route at least four days ago," Senator Turner asks.

"No activity was noticed along the route by the drones during the three days prior to the convoy's departure."

"That didn't answer my question, but it doesn't matter. How many people knew about the VP's son's mission? Anyone?"

The intelligence community representatives exchange glances with each other. "We don't have that information, Senator," one of them finally says.

"How many knew the route?"

"We don't have that information either."

Senator Turner leans forward and glares at the man. "The enemy did."

"Thank you for the briefing, gentlemen," the chairman says. "You are all excused."

They waste no time getting out of the room. Most people who find themselves briefing Congress would rather visit a dentist than relive the experience.

"You let them off easy, Mr. Chairman," Garrett Turner says when the doors to the secure hearing room close.

"Excuse me, Senator?"

"Not this time, Mr. Chairman. I've been pleading with you and other members of this committee for weeks to take this seriously. You have all been content to pretend there isn't a major problem."

"You're out of order, Senator Turner."

"I don't care."

"We have been nothing but—"

"The word you are looking for is 'incompetent.' I understand that it's an election year, but you bring new meaning to the word 'inaction.' If Democrats are hoping to bury the problem —"

"I said that you are out of order," Colby says, banging his gavel as he glares at his colleague.

"You are still doing it," Senator Turner says, his arms spread wide. "The vice president of the United States just lost his son to enemy action, and you're conducting the hearing as if it's business as usual."

"I won't repeat myself again, Senator!"

"The death of the VP's son is on you."

"You have some nerve, Senator!"

"I won't stand by and watch you continue to—"

"We need a motion to adjourn," Colby says, speaking over his colleague.

"I move to adjourn," one of the committee members from his party says.

"Seconded."

"All in favor?"

Not a single Republican hand goes up, but Senator Washington doesn't need one to end the session. Democrats have the majority on the committee, and they see that it's about to descend into a political slugfest, even without cameras or witnesses present.

"Hearing adjourned."

Senator Turner doesn't waste any time shooting out of his chair and making a beeline over to the chairman. Boston sees trouble on the horizon and moves swiftly across the hearing room to intercept him. Gina joins the men as they converge while the other committee members vacate the room.

"You had no business adjourning this hearing!" Garrett barks.

"And you had no business making a political mockery of it. Your posturing may make you a hero to the right-wing media, but there is no place for it in this room."

"I ask difficult questions. I know that's a foreign concept to Democrats used to fielding softballs from their propagandist sympathizers in the media."

"You are exploiting the situation for political gain," Colby says, pointing a finger in his colleague's face. "I can't control your behavior outside this room, but in here is a different story."

Garrett smirks and holds his hands up in surrender. "You're right. And while I can't hold you accountable in here, I sure as hell can in front of the American people. You're incompetent. This administration is incompetent. It's time that Americans learn just how weak you are."

"I think you're confused, Senator," Gina says. "This committee provides oversight, nothing more. I shouldn't need to explain that to you. If you're angry with the intelligence community, take it up with them."

"I intend to, Miss Attison. Thank you for telling me how to do my job. Is there anything else you'd like to do for me?" the senator asks, running his eyes over her to punctuate the not-so-subtle message.

The comment was unnecessary. Gina glares at the senator and is about to explode when Boston steps in front of her.

"I think you should choose your words more carefully, Senator Turner."

"Or else what? Is there something you are going to do about it?"

Boston weighs his options. There is nothing he'd like more to do than lay this guy out on the floor. It would also be a death sentence for his career and is likely what Senator Turner wants to see happen.

"You can have policy disagreements and sling mud at each other all you want. The moment you make sexual comments to my fiancée and congressional staffer, you cross a line you had better step back over."

"How's your head, Eugene? You must have hit it hard in that accident to dare talk to me like that."

"At least I have an excuse, Senator."

"Watch yourself. It'd be a mistake to equate your longevity here with job security."

Garrett takes a moment to shoot warning glares at Gina and Senator Washington before stomping off.

"Thanks for the assist," Gina says, touching Boston on the arm. "I was about to lose my shit on him."

"That's the only reason I stepped in. Turner was born an asshole," Boston says.

"I had soldiers like him. The NCOs in my brigade had a unique way of dealing with them."

"How, sir?" Gina asks.

"It usually involved duct tape, rope, a duffel bag, and a high window. Maybe someday we can find out if we can carry Turner up to the top of the Capitol dome."

"It'd give him the media attention he craves, that's for sure," Gina muses.

"Let's get back to work. We still have a long day ahead of us."

CHAPTER SEVENTEEN
ERIC "MARYLAND" WILLIAMS

Service in the military changes someone's perspective on the world in a way only veterans understand. While many of Maryland's co-workers indulge in a trip to the local bar after work or rush home to domestic activities, he is content picking up dinner and crashing on the couch with a beer. It was what he missed most about civilian life during his military deployments to the Middle East.

He pops the cap on a beer and settles deeper into his leather recliner as he flips through the channels. Most of his usual entertainment options include sports. Still, with the massive coverage of the vice president's son's assassination, the allure of getting an update on world events is irresistible.

"The details about the attack in Syria are still sketchy," the reporter says, reporting from the relative safety of Baghdad. "Authorities are still seeking to determine how the ambush was planned and by whom. Until then, the president has ordered all military resources in the region to take extra precautions against an attack, and limit travel outside protective bases. Bob?"

"Thank you for your report, Brian. We have breaking news coming into the news desk," the anchor says, as an appropriate chyron appears on the bottom of the screen. "Newly uncovered information from several unnamed sources places several agencies and government committees in the spotlight and under investigation for leaks that have left the vice president's son among dozens of military servicemembers dead in Syria."

Maryland lowers the bottle from his lips as he sits up in his chair.

"These sources claim a report was authored by the Defense Intelligence Agency that implicates high-level government personnel, including in the White House, of having access to intelligence reports that have been leaked to America's enemies. The document concludes that the leak might not be isolated to one of our intelligence agencies, and could instead be coming from someone in the government's highest offices. That should be terrifying for any American to hear. For more on this…"

Maryland doesn't hear any more of what the anchor has to say. He throws his half-full bottle of beer against the wall, missing his television by inches. He immediately retrieves his cell phone from the end table and finds Boston's number. The call is answered on the first ring.

"I saw it," Boston says before Maryland can lay into him.

"What the hell, man!"

"What the hell, what?"

"Why did you leak it to the press?" Maryland screams into the phone.

"Whoa, why the hell would I leak—"

"Don't lie to me, Boston. Outside of the DIA, you were the only one who knew it even existed."

"Then why not start with your own agency if you're looking for someone to blame?"

"Why would I?" Maryland asks, getting his breathing under control.

"I know you're not a complete moron, but let me spell it out for you anyway. Your report named groups in the White House and Congress, including the committee that I work for. Why the hell would I release that information? To make my life impossible?"

Maryland settles back into his chair. He knows that Boston is right. If the report is taken seriously, both congressional intelligence committees could end up under a microscope. He hadn't thought of that.

"Unless your brain is starved for oxygen, you know that I had nothing to do with that report leaking. So, who could most benefit from the public release of that information? Maybe a career military man turned politician who's been under fire from the beginning?"

"Troxell."

"That's right. The Director of National Intelligence himself, and a man who would no doubt have access to the report you helped write."

"I...I just thought—"

"No, Maryland, you didn't think. We go way back. You know that I'm not out to screw you over for this or anything else. Maybe that's too hard for you to figure out."

Boston hangs up the phone, and Maryland checks the display before holding it against his chest. He shouldn't have jumped to conclusions. He's an intelligence analyst and should know better than that. If Boston is right about Troxell, then Maryland knows he was betrayed by his own superiors.

CHAPTER EIGHTEEN
SPECIAL AGENT ZACH FORTE

IWO JIMA MEMORIAL
WASHINGTON, D.C.

The Marine Corps Memorial is a majestic tribute but is as spooky as hell at night. The ground lighting illuminates the ghostly figures while creating an eerie shadow effect at ground level. Zach is happy to see tourists milling around the statue while he waits for Grimman to arrive.

He admires the monument until he hears his boss arrive behind him. The two men stare for a long moment at the American flag flapping in the light breeze.

"You're late," Zach says.

"We could have met at the office. You do work for me."

"Everyone knows you're pushing me out the door, and I haven't agreed to work for you on this yet."

"You will after you read this," he says, handing Zach a file as they move away from the monument.

The agent studies Grimman's face before looking at the envelope's contents. There is just enough light to see what's in the file. It includes dossiers, a timeline, and relevant personal information on two men and a woman.

"What is this?"

"If I'm right, it's the traitors that are getting dozens of Americans killed in Syria and their intelligence contact."

Alarm klaxons ring inside Zach's head. This is not how things are done. The intelligence being leaked isn't only embarrassing to the United States government. It's severely damaging our national interests. If Grimman is right, his failure to bring this to proper authorities could land him in as much trouble as the spies will be in.

"Eugene Hollinger. He's former military. Purple Heart, Bronze Star…not exactly spy material."

"You know better."

"Okay, so…whoa. He works for the Senate Select Committee on Intelligence?"

"Hollinger has had unfettered access to classified information from every intelligence agency for years now. His fiancée works as the committee liaison on Senator Washington's staff. I'm working on her dossier. She has a high clearance and could be involved as well."

"I thought all the leaks were based on information coming from Defense Intelligence?"

"They are. Keep reading. Hollinger has an Army buddy who works for the DIA. Take a guess at what he does."

"Middle East analysis?"

"Specifically, Syria."

"None of that proves anything."

"That's what I need you for. Counterintelligence groups in a dozen agencies are working night and day but have come up empty. Director Weisz has the FBI zeroed in on the DIA, but what if she's wrong? What if it is someone on Capitol Hill that has access to all these secrets and a means to pass them on?"

"How do you think he's doing that?"

"His doctor. Her name is Tara Winters. Don't let the last name fool you. She's Iranian on her mother's side and has relatives in the elite Republican Guard."

"Why don't you take this directly to Director Weisz?"

"Because she would look at me the way you are now. Look, I have reason to believe Hollinger may be involved in this, but I can't prove it," Grimman clarifies without looking back at me. "I'm so busy doing the director's bidding that I have no time to look into it myself."

"What are you suggesting I do?"

"Watch him and find out if I'm right."

"Are you serious? I'm on suspension, and you want me to spy on an American citizen without cause and without a warrant. It's illegal."

Grimman shakes his head as he fights back his impatience. Zach is missing the bigger picture, and it's pissing him off. How does a guy who made a career out of taking chances suddenly get cold feet?

"If I'm wrong, I'm wrong. No harm, no foul. If I'm right, we catch a traitor responsible for countless deaths and a national security debacle. Besides, do you have any better options? I will make this worth your while."

"What is that supposed to mean?"

"I will provide you a stipend to cover your expenses. When this is over, I'll make sure you get your job back. The choice is yours, Zach, not that it's a hard one."

Every instinct in Zach is screaming for him to walk away from this, only his feet don't move. Matt Remsen is living rent-free inside his head. Grimman is up to something. He needs to find out what his agenda is, and playing along may be the best way to do it.

"All right, I'm in. I'm going to warn you, though. When the time comes, you had better be true to your word."

"Don't worry about that," Grimman says, handing him a burner phone. "Let me know when you start. I had better hear from you soon."

He turns and walks back in the direction of the parking lot. Zach finds a bench with enough light to read through the file a little more. It's quiet and peaceful here.

He stares at the picture of Eugene Hollinger in the dossier. Most targets that are turned by foreign intelligence have some deep dark secret that gets exploited. There isn't anything obvious that he can see. With no evident probable cause, he can only wonder what this guy did to find his way into Grimman's crosshairs. He will need to do a little digging of his own to find out.

CHAPTER NINETEEN

EUGENE "BOSTON" HOLLINGER

VA MENTAL HEALTH CENTER
FRIENDSHIP HEIGHTS, WASHINGTON, D.C.

I hope feeling like a lab rat at a government hospital ends up being useful, because an upset fiancée is the price of admission. After I freaked her out this morning, Tara agreed that the next step to determine a diagnosis was to monitor my sleep activity. I went home, packed an overnight bag, and counted the hours until I could start getting answers.

The decision didn't sit well with Gina. She's not entirely sold on these dreams being a problem, and things are blowing up on Capitol Hill. Her boss is under enormous pressure and needs her more than ever. Unfortunately for him, my health takes precedence over the partisan bickering, so I put in for a few more days of medical leave which got approved.

"Don't mess with them," Tara warns me from the chair in the corner when she catches me touching the contacts taped to my head.

"Sorry," I grumble.

"Why are you so jumpy tonight?"

"I have a lot on my mind. That, and Maryland pissed me off earlier," I say, receiving a confused look in return. "My friend, not the state."

"Oh."

I let my eyes wander around the room. This new VA facility was designed to combat the rising numbers of traumatic brain injuries and mental health issues America's vets from Iraq and Afghanistan face. The clinic may be the vanguard of that fight, but it's lightly staffed at this time of night.

"Tara, can I ask you a question?"

"Sure."

"You have a nice house. How does a doctor working part-time at a veteran's hospital afford a swanky place in Adams Morgan?"

"She doesn't. Her parents do," Tara says, smiling weakly. "It's a long story."

"I thought that maybe it was Mark's place."

"No, he only wishes it was."

"Was that the first time he's ever hit you?" I ask, unsure why I'm asking questions that I have no right getting answers to.

"It was the last time. Mark made a lot of promises that he never delivered on."

"Why did you stay with him?"

"Life's never that simple," she says, refusing to make eye contact and using a tone that reinforces her unwillingness to discuss it any further. "We're ready. Go ahead and lie down."

"How often do you do this?"

"EEGs?"

"No, watch people sleep."

"Not very often, but—"

She stops mid-sentence and blushes after I take off my shirt.

"Sorry. I can't sleep with it on."

"Uh, no problem. Let me know when you're comfortable."

"I'm as good as I'll ever be. Do you think this is going to tell you what's going on with my head?" I ask as she begins hooking up wires to the sensors on my head.

"An electroencephalogram detects brain activity by using electrodes to measure electrical impulses. When you sleep, your conscious mind is off, but that doesn't mean your brain is. In fact, your brain is almost as active in REM sleep as it is when you're awake."

"How do you know if this will capture anything unusual?"

"I don't," she says after attaching the last of the wires onto the electrodes. "But if what you saw was real, this will help us understand what your brain is doing when it happens."

"You mean why I'm seeing someone else's memories?"

"Please don't make me feel crazy for doing this," she says, smiling. Try not to toss and turn too much. You'll yank all the wires off. Sweet dreams."

"God willing," I say, as she turns off the light and I close my eyes.

* * *

"A storm is coming," I hear myself say as someone sits next to me.

I can't tell where I am. I think I see trees, but nothing is distinguishable. The only thing I know for sure is what I'm feeling: seething contempt.

"Are you making an obvious literal observation or a metaphorical one?"

"Both. You're late."

My eyes click open, and I switch on the light perched on the nightstand. In the last two dreams, I felt fear and anger. This time, it was hatred. I try to remember the details when I hear a gentle rap on the door.

"Come in," I say, watching Tara as she walks in holding a printout. "How long was I out for?"

"A couple of hours. Did you have one of those dreams?"

"Yeah. It was a short one, though."

"Where were you?"

"I don't know. I couldn't see much of anything."

"Do you remember what was said?" Tara says, pressing me to remember.

"I don't know. I was talking to someone, but it didn't make any sense, and I forgot most of it the moment I woke up."

"I see."

"What's wrong?" I ask, recognizing the confusion on her face as she scans the printout in her hands.

"You're sure you weren't awake? Maybe thinking about something that happened today?" Tara asks, sitting on the edge of the bed.

"I'm positive. Nothing happened today. What does that thing say?"

"Something that isn't possible. Boston, for fifty-three seconds, you were awake and asleep at the *same* time."

CHAPTER TWENTY
SENATOR GARRETT TURNER

UNDISCLOSED PARKING GARAGE
WASHINGTON, D.C.

Garrett pulls his cherry red Mustang into the garage just after midnight and descends the ramp to the main parking level. The car is a bold statement in a city full of people who like making them. Everybody sees him coming before he arrives. That's useful, except for the times that it isn't. This is one of them.

A message from Grimman appears on his phone, and he scans it quickly. *Met with my resource. We are confirmed for the mission.*

The senator pockets the phone and notices that Abril Lopez is leaning against her car parked along the far wall. Garrett pulls into the adjacent spot and kills the engine. As a United States Senator, he never thought he would be meeting people in a dark, dank parking garage. It's a testament to how he never understood how this world worked in the early days.

"Really? A parking garage?" she asks. "Are you feeling nostalgic for Watergate?"

"No Republican holds an affinity for that era. And don't you dare call me Deep Throat."

Six late-night covert meetings took place under a cloak of darkness at a parking garage beneath the Oakhill Office Building in Rosslyn, Virginia. Reporters Bob Woodward and Carl Bernstein met Deputy Director of the FBI Mark Felt there while investigating the 1972 break-in at Democratic Party headquarters at the Watergate Hotel. Felt was known only to the world as "Deep Throat" for more than thirty years.

"I wouldn't dream of it, Senator. So why all the mysterious cloak and dagger stuff? You've never been this paranoid about sharing information with me before."

"You're a journalist. I'm sure you can connect the dots as to why I'm here."

"Syria."

Abril Lopez doesn't have a rich pedigree. Her inattentive parents and lower-middle-class upbringing meant that education was never prioritized. She managed to attend a community college and did okay, but not well enough to get accepted into a top journalism school. What Abril has are two things that her colleagues in the modern media lack: a strong work ethic and a willingness to hustle. She is going places because her peers are too lazy to outwork her.

"Nothing gets past you, Abril."

"No need to get snarky, Senator. What do you have?"

"This is off the record, in case that wasn't already clear."

"Have we ever been on the record?"

"Now isn't the time to break that streak. The FBI has joined various other counterintelligence groups in investigating the leaks to Syria."

Abril's lips curl in disappointment. "Yeah, we were told that Director Karen Weisz is leading the investigation personally, and that they're targeting the Defense Intelligence Agency as the potential source. That isn't news."

"No, and it also isn't news that the report from the DIA was made public to help deflect the blame and cast suspicion elsewhere."

Abril nods her head. "They wouldn't comment on the authenticity of the report or its origin."

"It's authentic, and it came from the DIA itself."

"How do you know that?"

Garrett cocks his head to the side and makes a face. He can't understand how journalists who fancy themselves the smartest people in a room can ask such stupid questions. Abril at least understands that it was a dumb thing to ask and moves on.

"Okay, the DIA is defending itself? So what? Please tell me that's not why you dragged me here."

"It isn't. The FBI took the report seriously. They have also opened an investigation into members of the Senate Intelligence Committee and the staff that work there."

"Everybody is getting looked at. That's not—"

"One of the staff in question has a clearance above top secret and is engaged to a member of Colby Washington's staff."

"Okay, now you have my interest."

"The investigation started recently. FBI Counterintelligence made the connections. Now they only need the proof."

"I need names, Senator."

"You aren't getting any."

"Then get me the name of a contact in the FBI that can confirm this."

"I'm not doing that, either."

Abril is about to have a meltdown. This story about the potential leak within the intelligence community, government reaction, and the public protests has a spy thriller feel to it that has dominated the front page and been the lead story on news broadcasts for a month. This is the first new wrinkle in a week, and she's frustrated that she can't do anything with it.

"Then this information is good for nothing. I need some corroboration."

"Since when?"

"Senator, I cannot assume the validity of this information. I'm not going to be your personal Zoe Barnes."

"And I'm not going to push you in front of a moving train," he says with a grin.

Zoe Barnes, played by Kate Mara, was a journalist who played big and lost in *House of Cards*. Her meteoric rise was soured by Frank Underwood's increasing reliance on her as his mouthpiece. Eventually, the ethical dilemma proved to be too much, and Zoe tried to break free of his control. She earned her freedom by getting shoved into the path of a Metro train arriving at the station.

"It's not enough."

Garrett frowns. "This is a fast-moving investigation. There is no doubt that there will be movement on it shortly. When it breaks, what I told you will give you the inside line on what's happening. The FBI will deny it, but I can then hand you the corroboration you need. It will be a scoop that no one else can match. It will make your career."

"What do you want in return?"

"What makes you think I want anything?"

"Because you don't give a damn about my career," Abril says, putting her finger in the senator's face. "I'm sure that leaking this information is helping you, but I'm also sure there's more to it."

"Fair enough. I only ask one thing: if this leads back to Colby Washington's office door, don't let anyone bury it."

"What makes you think they will try?"

"Because the liberal media are trying to protect the president. Colby Washington is one of his biggest supporters in the Senate, and everyone will circle the wagons. It's why this drama has been allowed to continue for as long as it has."

Garrett knows how this works. The media plays favorites, and most editors in the country are unabashedly liberal. They kill stories that are damaging to their favorite sons and daughters. It's why NBC rejected stories on Harvey Weinstein when his behavior with Hollywood actresses came into sharper focus. They will not walk out on a limb that could cause a Democrat to fall.

"The media is holding the president accountable," Abril says, offended at the insinuation.

Garrett smirks and gets back into his Mustang. He rolls down the driver's side window after Abril follows him and waits impatiently.

"Ask yourself something. Would the coverage be the same if a Republican were in the Oval? You can wax poetic about all the headlines and stories covering this, but how many of you are really holding the administration responsible? Why did they wait until now to involve the FBI when the leaks started almost a year ago? Think about it. I'll be in touch."

Abril gets a thousand-yard stare to her eyes as she processes that information. Garrett was saving that nugget in case he needed something to get her to play ball. He pulls his car out of the spot and exits the garage, content that she'll do what he needs her to.

CHAPTER TWENTY-ONE
ERIC "MARYLAND" WILLIAMS

JOE BACON ME CRAZY
CONGRESS HEIGHTS, WASHINGTON, D.C.

The Washington, D.C. metro area is filled with quaint little breakfast shops like this one. He met Boston and Gina here because they thought he needed to know what's going on with his friends. After a half-hour of listening to Boston explain the certifiably crazy theory that he ginned up with his doctor, Maryland wishes he had stayed in bed.

"If you really think you are seeing other people's memories, you've been watching too many movies," Maryland says after Gina fails to call him out on his insanity.

"If our positions were reversed, I'd say the same thing. I'm not saying it makes sense. I'm only telling you what I know."

"Gina, please talk some sense into your fiancé."

"It sounds crazy to me, but I'm not a doctor."

Maryland frowns. He's about to continue the argument when a beautiful brunette dressed in jeans and a windbreaker walks through the door. She sees Boston and heads over to them.

"Sorry I'm late, guys. That took longer than I wanted."

"Doctor Tara Winters, this is Maryland, and you've already met my fiancée, Gina," Boston says.

"Hi," she says, shaking their hands.

As the doctor takes off her windbreaker, Gina gives Boston a quick yet unmistakable glare of disapproval. Maryland smirks, knowing his friend was right: she doesn't like his doctor one bit, and now he can see why.

"How did it go?" Boston asks.

"Do you have any idea how cranky doctors are that early in the morning?"

"No less cranky than politicians, I'm sure," Gina quips.

"Gina works on Capitol Hill, too," Boston says.

Tara offers a half-smile to Gina before continuing. "I showed the results of the EEG to a friend. He thought it was broken. He insisted that what we saw isn't medically possible."

"Why not?"

"And please try to explain it without boring us to tears," Gina gripes.

"No guarantees," Tara says, brushing her off. "Okay, there are five stages to the sleep cycle, each progressively deeper than the next until you reach the fifth stage, which is REM sleep. Each of them has telltale signs based on the most prevalent brain waves.

"Brain waves are generated by neurons communicating with each other by electrical changes. They are measured in cycles per second, called hertz. The lower the number of hertz, the slower the brain activity."

"You're killing us here, Tara," Boston says, eager for her to get to the point.

"Stay with me. Traditionally, these fall into five types: delta, theta, alpha, beta, and the newest one, gamma."

"I guess epsilon got screwed," Gina says in a failed attempt at being funny.

"Theta and delta are your deep sleep waves," Tara continues, now completely ignoring her. "Alpha dominates when you first fall asleep, and beta typifies being conscious and awake."

"What about gamma?" Boston asks, still riveted.

"I'm getting there. Now, these aren't separate brain waves but are categorized just for convenience. They help describe the changes we see in the brain during different activities. Our overall brain activity is a mix of all the frequencies simultaneously, some in more significant quantities and strength than others.

"Now, we have markers for all this. For example, in REM sleep, we know what waves the brain produces. One thing it doesn't produce during sleep is gamma waves. They show higher mental activity and consolidation of information seen in advanced levels of mediation."

"Tara, what does any of this have to do with Boston?" Gina asks with an edge to her voice.

"The sleep cycle repeats about four times per night. Boston was in the delta wave portion of your second cycle for seven minutes when he had his dream. That's highly unusual, but then your beta and gamma waves pegged while never leaving delta wave sleep."

"Speak English, Doc," Maryland says, completely lost.

"Delta is deep sleep. When those waves are prevalent, the others can't take charge until the sleeper transitions into REM sleep. In Boston's case, they did, and in a big way."

"So what?" Gina asks, growing increasingly impatient.

"Beta waves are strongest when a subject is conscious and mentally focused. Gamma waves are produced when concentrating. These were produced at the same time he was in his deepest sleep."

"That was the conclusion of this doctor you met?" Gina needles.

"It was the conclusion we both reached. Boston wasn't dreaming last night. His mind was viewing something remotely."

"Viewing what?" Maryland asks, wondering if she will confirm what Boston told them when they first arrived.

Tara leans back and sips her coffee. She sets it down and stares at the cup. When she lifts her head, she exhales.

"There is only one thing that makes all the pieces fit. Boston was right – his dreams aren't really dreams at all. For almost a minute last night, his mind was reliving someone else's memory."

CHAPTER TWENTY-TWO
SPECIAL AGENT ZACH FORTE

JOE BACON ME CRAZY
CONGRESS HEIGHTS, WASHINGTON, D.C.

Zach types the name onto the text editor he opened on his laptop. He repositions the directional mic on his lap and adjusts his earbuds. This is more a breakfast and lunch joint than a coffee shop, but he's alone and won't stick out. His targets at the table didn't notice him walk in five minutes after they did, and were oblivious to him taking a seat a couple of tables away.

"How is that even possible?" Gina asks.

"I have no idea. I need to spend some time trying to work that out with another colleague I know. In fact," she says, looking at her cell phone, "I need to run an errand before I meet him, so I should get going. Boston, I'll call you if I learn anything new. It was nice meeting you, Maryland. Good seeing you as well, Gina."

"You, too," Maryland responds.

Gina doesn't say anything. After a few minutes, she bids her own curt farewell to her fiancé, leaving the two men at the table. There is clearly some strain on their relationship.

"Do you think this doctor knows what she's talking about?" Maryland asks.

"Yeah, I do. These dreams are different, Maryland. I don't know how to explain it any more than that."

Boston and Maryland talk for a few minutes more before paying the check and leaving. Nothing that was said is at all suspicious to Zach. Careful to observe without staring, he watches them load into separate cars and pull out of the parking lot. Once they are clear, he finishes his coffee, packs up his laptop, and retreats to his own vehicle. Zach fishes the cell phone out of his windbreaker and hits redial once he settles into the driver's seat.

"Yeah," Grimman mumbles on the other end of the line.

"I have an update for you."

Zach makes a short report because nothing of consequence happened. He describes who Boston met and what they discussed, omitting any mention of the specifics. It sounded too silly to recount, and could have been a code of some sort that he wants to review first.

"Nothing at all?" Grimman asks when Forte finishes.

"If the doctor is involved in a spy ring, they have no aversion to meeting her in broad daylight in a public place. If these guys are spies, they're shitty ones."

"Not everything is as it seems. Where are they heading now?"

"They just got onto I-695, so they're heading back into the city," Zach says after checking the app on his smartphone.

"Stay on them. The doctor is the key to this whole thing. I'm working on tracking that down now."

"It doesn't sound like they knew each other before Boston's accident," Zach says, hoping to end this insanity.

"Or that's what they want people to think. They could be using it as an excuse to meet now that everyone in Washington is under a microscope. Unless you usually meet your doctor for breakfast."

Zach presses his lips together. Grimman makes a good point, as rare as that is. Still, it's flimsy reasoning. No wonder he kept this assignment off the books.

"Okay, I'll be in touch," Zach says before killing the call.

He consults the tracking application one more time to ensure they haven't deviated from their routes. They haven't, so he heads back towards his apartment for a change of clothes and a couple of hours of shut-eye. He can't run twenty-four-hour operations on his own and will need his rest for tonight.

CHAPTER TWENTY-THREE
GINA ATTISON

Gina drops her pen, leans back, and rubs her tired eyes. The hive of activity in the busy office became as still as a graveyard hours ago. Most of the senator's staff are out eating or back home with their families. She cannot afford to do either right now.

Boston is a forgiving fiancé, mainly because he often works as hard and late as she does. The men and women who make up America's intelligence community didn't take their jobs to work bankers' hours. Twelve- or fourteen-hour days are not uncommon, as are historic stretches when analysts go days with minimal sleep. Boston understands this like few men can, which is why he rarely protests when she calls to explain that she's stuck at the office.

"I didn't mean to scare you," Senator Washington says after the rap on her door jamb causes her to jump. "Burning the midnight oil?"

"Good evening, Senator. Yeah, the assassination changes everything, so I wanted to review what we've been given so far. I didn't realize anyone else was in the office. Can I help you with something?"

"Yes, you can take a break and have a drink with me," he says, unveiling a bottle of scotch and two glasses from behind his back.

"I'm not about to say no to that. Just let me secure these," Gina says, gesturing to the documents on her desk.

She inserts the paperwork in files marked Top Secret and stows them in the safe, ensuring that the tumbler is spun. She pulls out a sheet of paper from a pocket on the side and annotates the log. By the time she is finished, the senator has already poured two generous glasses of amber liquid.

"Cheers. Anything interesting coming out of the intelligence agencies?"

"Not really," Gina says, after taking a sip of her drink. "Just the usual."

"Do you think they are taking this leak seriously?"

"Sir, you know we can't discuss classified material in this office."

The senator grins before setting his snifter on the edge of her desk. "I know. I wasn't referring to the investigation. I was referring to the politicians."

"This is Washington, sir. They will take it seriously so long as it serves their interests."

"All the wrong reasons. Have you ever noticed that the path to Congress is paved with the intentions of people who want to change the system?"

"What do you mean?" Gina asks, taking a sip of her scotch.

"Every single man and woman who works in that infernal building campaigned on the promise to change the way we do business here. Do you think that they were lying?"

"Sir, I'm an intelligence analyst, not a political pundit. My answer doesn't carry much weight."

"Or it carries more."

Gina nods. "Okay, I'll bite. Politicians either had every intention of partaking in the system and lied to get elected, or were naïve outsiders who didn't realize how hard it would be to change it."

"Good observation on both accounts. I fall into the latter group, in case you are wondering. Combat was far easier than this job is."

"Why did you decide to go into politics?" Gina asks as the senator returns his attention to his drink.

"The American people. I pledged to defend the Constitution of the United States against all enemies, foreign and domestic. I wanted to stop the erosion of our rights. It was a fool's errand."

"You sound more like a Republican than a Democrat."

"I've never been an ideologue. It's a sad state in America that people care more about the letter next to a candidate's name than the substance of the policy beliefs behind it. There was once a time when there were liberal Republicans and conservative Democrats. Those days are gone."

"Do you miss the military?" Gina asks, changing the subject. She isn't one to get into a philosophical discussion about liberalism and conservativism.

"Sometimes. I loved Army life but hated the bureaucracy. In that way, the military is like any other government organization. Most of all, I loved the troops. The men and women I commanded on the ground had a knack for cutting through the bullshit. I miss that. It doesn't happen here."

Now, it's Gina's turn to set her drink down and lean forward across her desk. She has the utmost respect for Senator Washington, but he sounds and looks defeated. This isn't the time or place for that. Not now, not here.

"I know you don't need me to tell you this, Senator, but this isn't the military. Politics isn't like war, despite the frequent comparisons to it in the media. Legislative battles are won and lost, but the conflict never ends when governing. There will never be an armistice or ticker-tape parade down the Canyon of Heroes because there will always be other problems to solve or issues to debate."

"Only we don't solve problems in the marble halls of the Capitol. We don't even try. This isn't governing. It isn't about allocating limited resources to meet unlimited demands for them. It's about the accumulation of power, not that it would ever be wielded to change things for the better."

"You're starting to sound like Boston."

"I've always thought highly of your fiancé," the senator says, offering an approving smile. It disappears from his face as quickly as it appeared. "Garrett Turner couldn't care less about someone leaking information to the Syrians. He wants to use the leak as a wedge issue in the election. Every decision we make has a thousand alternatives. It's easy to choose them with the benefit of hindsight and create a wedge issue for voters in the process."

"That's true of all decisions made in a crisis, sir."

The senator leans back and stares at the walls of her office. She went with the spartan design: almost nothing outside of a few pictures and mementos from days long past. Gina has never been one for bragging and has no interest in interior design.

"Would the decisions or required actions be fundamentally different if Senator Turner were the chairman?"

"I don't see how, no."

"That's what scares me. I'm not sure if I'm making the right decisions or the politically expedient ones. That's not who I am, and I don't like what this job is turning me into."

Gina studies the remaining liquid in her tumbler. She likes the senator, but there's nothing she can say to that. She is a staffer, not a cheerleader, and has a job to do here. Her allegiance is to that, not him. It doesn't matter that he's her boss.

"I'm sorry for keeping you here. Why are you here, anyway?" Senator Washington asks, stopping when he reaches the door to her office. "Don't you have a fiancé at home to nurse back to health?"

"Boston's fine."

"No lingering issues from the accident?"

"He should be back to work in a couple of days. He doesn't need me fussing over him. Sir, if I may be so bold, why did you really stop in my office to see me?"

"A fire has been raging between Republicans and Democrats for decades. It doesn't matter who started it or who fans the flames the hardest. It has grown with each election cycle and is now an inferno that may never be extinguished."

"And?"

"The death of the VP's son was a tanker that dumped gasoline on it. We're on the cusp of a firestorm, Gina, and I'm afraid that you're going to be caught right in the middle of it. I just wanted you to know."

The senator nods and disappears from the doorway. Gina hasn't known him for long, but he isn't someone she considers an alarmist. If he felt compelled to take time to give her a warning, things are about to get much nastier.

CHAPTER TWENTY-FOUR

"BOSTON" HOLLINGER

BOSTON'S RESIDENCE
OXON HILL, MARYLAND

The picture emerges of looming dark figures. They are larger than life as light cuts through the haze. A shiver runs down my spine, and a feeling of internal conflict sweeps through me.

"What are you suggesting I do?" I hear myself ask.

"Watch him and find out if I'm right."

"Are you serious? I'm on suspension, and you want me to spy on an American citizen without cause and without a warrant. It's illegal."

The man shakes his head. "If I'm wrong, I'm wrong. No harm, no foul. If I'm right, we catch a traitor responsible for countless deaths and a national security debacle. Besides, do you have any better options? I will make this worth your while."

"What is that supposed to mean?"

"I will provide you a stipend to cover your expenses. When this is over, I'll make sure you get your job back. The choice is yours, Zach, not that it's a hard one."

I can feel the angst of the moment. I want to hand the folder back and walk away, but I don't. I'm conflicted and can feel it eating at me.

"All right, I'm in. I'm going to warn you, though. When the time comes, you had better be true to your word."

"Don't worry about that," the man says, handing me an object. "Let me know when you start. I had better hear from you soon."

He walks away and disappears from my view. I feel myself sit down and stare at the folder but am unable to make anything out. Then it comes into focus. It's a picture. It's my picture.

The sudden shock of seeing my face in a dream jolts me awake. The television is still on, and its light is the only thing cutting through the darkness. I close my eyes and put myself back into the dream.

"I heard a name," I say to myself.

Zach. The name I heard was Zach, and someone wants him to watch me. He will get paid for it. Is he a private investigator?

I shake the thought from my mind. This is no time for analysis or speculation. I focus on the dream as it continues to fade. It was dark. A file was handed over. Large men loomed over us, close to each other, and…there was a flag.

"Iwo Jima," I say to myself.

My eyes open, knowing the lingering elements of the dream are gone. I settle deeper into my chair and stare at the darkness. The shock of what I saw registers for the first time. I am being hunted. But why?

There is no easy answer to that question. I'm an intelligence analyst who works for Congress, not a spy. I don't have dirt on politicians or engage in espionage on either America or her enemies. It makes no sense.

At a loss, I get up and head to the kitchen for a drink. I pour a glass of water from the decanter in the fridge, using the interior light for visibility. Then I close the door, and my night vision is destroyed. I can't see anything but the glowing digital clock on the microwave informing me that it's after midnight. Not seeing anything in the darkness is a metaphor for my problem.

I am too close to this. Gina and Maryland are as well. The only outsider I can trust is Tara, and she's a doctor. She can't understand any of this. That leaves only one person who meets those criteria. I head back to the living room and pick up my cell phone. Maryland isn't going to be happy with this.

The call I place gets forwarded to voicemail. That's not surprising. There is no telling what my old friend is up to these days, but most likely no good.

"Hey, it's me," I say after the tone indicates that it's my time to speak. "I need your help."

CHAPTER TWENTY-FIVE
SPECIAL AGENT ZACH FORTE

DR. TARA WINTERS'S RESIDENCE
ADAMS MORGAN, WASHINGTON, D.C.

Zach sets his binoculars down, feeling like he's living the cliché. Stakeouts are long-honored traditions in law enforcement and a favorite staple for Hollywood depictions of surveillance. Thirty years ago, this was how it was done. Get yourself a pair of binoculars, a vehicle, some snacks, some lousy coffee, and you're set. That is unless the bad guys slip out the back door.

That's the old-school way. Law enforcement agencies across the country have grown up over the years. Although the old methods are still taught and used, they're often replaced by technology. Cameras, tracking locators, and directional microphones increase the likelihood of getting the desired results. Unfortunately for Zach, he's a one-man team forced to do Grimman's bidding the hard way.

"Well, well, well, I guess someone is finally awake," he mumbles when a light clicks on in one of the bedroom windows on the second floor. He stares through his binoculars, frowning that the blinds covering the window are still closed.

He puts the optics down as someone walks up the sidewalk toward him. Unbeknownst to most people, federal law enforcement has fleets of ordinary cars at their disposal to use for any conceivable operation. Only in the movies does the large van packed with cameras, monitors, geeky technicians and sporting a sign reading, "Municipal Electric" sit unmolested on a city street. No longer afforded the luxury of signing out FBI assets, Zach is stuck using his own car. At least his BMW blends in around here.

Zach's cell phone sounds with his familiar *X-Files* themed ringtone as he waves to the guy walking his dog. He waves back, paying the stranger in the car no more attention. Criminals don't wave, or so conventional wisdom would dictate.

"What?"

"Were you asleep?" Grimman asks on the other end of the line, acting like a mother hen.

"No, I'm working," Zach says, remaining purposely vague to drive him nuts.

"Are you drunk?"

"Nope, just high. I smoked a joint out of boredom a couple of hours ago."

"Funny. You were supposed to report in every two hours. Your last call was due almost an hour ago. Do your job," Grimman commands.

"I am. There was nothing significant to report, and lack of sleep makes you cranky."

"I get to determine what's important and what isn't. A concept you'd better grasp quickly."

Zach stares at his phone, struggling against the desire to end the call. He takes a deep breath and places it back against his ear.

"You know what, Grimman, if you want the doctor followed, you can find someone else to do it. Otherwise, I suggest you get off my case."

"Fine. You know what's at stake. Get me some information I can use, and you won't have to keep listening to me."

With that, the call ends. Zach tosses the phone into the passenger seat and rubs his chin. If Remsen hadn't asked him to play his part, he would have told Grimman to go pound sand when he was first handed this unofficial assignment. Instead, he's stuck watching a beautiful doctor whose only crime seems to be that she's Persian.

Zach may be disgraced, but he still is an expert with all the tools of the trade. Despite being initially reluctant to agree to this mission, it's becoming an irresistible puzzle begging to be solved. He's the last dog anyone wants to give a bone, and that's what Grimman has done.

There is only one way to determine if this is a legitimate operation or something else, and it's a considerable risk. Unfortunately, it's also one he's going to have to take.

CHAPTER TWENTY-SIX
SENATOR GARRETT TURNER

THE CAPITALIST PIG CHOPHOUSE
FOGGY BOTTOM, WASHINGTON, D.C.

One of the best things about being a U.S. senator is that they are never kept waiting. Upon his arrival at the restaurant, the hostess immediately seats Senator Turner at an excellent table despite not having a reservation. Like most hot shots inside the Beltway, he doesn't need one.

Moments later, the bespectacled and disheveled head of ZQJ Research enters and makes his way over. Garrett once thought the strange assembly of letters were the initials of the group's founders. He was wrong. It was the odd brainchild of the equally bizarre man he shakes hands with. Z, Q, and J are the three least used letters in the game Scrabble.

"How are you, Cubic?"

"Fine. I wouldn't think you would want to meet me in public," the pollster says, taking a seat at the table.

"Meeting with a pollster during an election year is not uncommon for a politician."

The man nods and tucks his napkin into his collar before scanning the menu and ordering his dinner when the waiter appears. Cubic Zirconia is his actual legal name. Nobody in Washington seems to know his given or family name despite countless attempts to find that information. It's the best-kept secret in a town where nobody can keep one. If there is some hidden meaning behind it, other than him sounding like a stereotypical jeweler, nobody has figured that out either.

"I don't mean to keep you from the trough, Cubic, but I need something from you."

"Does that mean we're skipping the foreplay tonight?"

Garrett grimaces. "I want to know—"

"You want to know what my polls show about how the Republicans are handling the crisis in the intelligence community."

"Yes."

"What makes you think I've been asking the question?"

"Because it's an election year. You have your finger on the pulse of the American people when every other pollster in the country just pretends to."

"All true."

The confirmation of the overly flattering statement was pure arrogance, but with good reason. Cubic Zirconia is the best pollster in the country, bar none. His research is used by the two major political parties, opposite sides of every significant lobbying effort, and countless corporations. It has made him millions, yet he has never been caught compromising his data to appease a client. His lack of public exposure makes him a relative unknown to the nation. He likes it that way.

"So?"

"Let me ask you a question first. Do you think this will be the defining issue in the upcoming election?"

"No, I don't."

"Then why do you care?"

"Because politics isn't always about the hot-button issue. It's about framing the narrative. The Democrats have been doing that for years. Now it's our turn."

Cubic sets his fork down and leans back. "That's interesting coming out of the mouth of a Republican. They're usually the ones screaming about the media setting the narrative."

"Because they do. This time, there is no ignoring what happened to the VP's son."

"And now you're going to politicize it."

"Politics is a dirty business. Americans elect candidates to play in the mud so that they don't have to. We can wax poetic about this being a government of the people, by the people, and for the people, but that noble idea perished long ago. Modern politics is Darwinism – survival of the fittest. Every two years, Americans go to the polls and vote based not on logic or fact, but perception."

"And you want me to confirm that you're painting the right picture."

Garrett leans back in his own seat and nods. Cubic will give him the information he wants, even if he is forced to tap dance to get it. It's how this relationship works.

"If you tell me that more than fifty percent disapprove of the president's handling of this crisis, he looks weak, and so do his surrogates in Congress," Garrett concludes.

"I was wondering what this was really about. It's not about the president. You're looking to flip the Senate."

"That's what wave elections are all about."

"I will never understand why politicians think voters are stupid. The workers who conduct these surveys talk to tens of thousands of people every year. They don't care about foreign policy or how a president handles an intelligence leak. They care about themselves and things like the economy or environment – issues that they perceive affect them personally."

"If that is true, your numbers will reflect it."

Cubic looks down at his plate. He's growing tired of this game and just wants to finish his overpriced dinner.

"Fifty-seven percent are critical about how the president is handling things. The numbers are split down party lines. There is a significant downward movement among those who consider themselves moderate Democrats and Independents. The president's approval rating has dropped five points since our last survey."

Garrett suppresses a smile. The plan is working. The pressure that's being generated has made it to Main Street, and that's a start. Once Abril goes to work, the pressure will become inescapable.

Despite Cubic's philosophical argument to the contrary, modern politics is a popularity contest. In that respect, the presidency carries the same weight as a prom king or queen when it comes to elections. When he begins to fall, his minions in the Senate are sure to follow. To stop the decay in support, they will need to offer the public a sacrifice or two to save their political careers. Garrett is going to hand them the perfect candidate.

CHAPTER TWENTY-SEVEN
ERIC "MARYLAND" WILLIAMS

PADDY'S IRISH PUB
WASHINGTON, D.C.

Paddy's Irish Pub is one of Boston's favorite haunts. Located in a not-so-nice section of southeast Washington, D.C., it's still a local favorite for those who don't like the tourist traps or the trendy bar scene. The place is busy without being overcrowded, which suits Tara, Maryland, and Boston just fine as they wait for the guest of honor.

"How the hell do y'all drive in this damn city?" a voice behind Maryland bellows. "Roads go this way, streets go that way, there are these circles everywhere you have to go around, and in the end, none of them leads to where you want to go."

Every head in the place turns to look at the man with the obnoxious accent pronouncing his disdain for the city's road network. One of Louisiana's trademarks is the grand entrances he makes. Today is no different.

"Good to see your sunny disposition hasn't changed any," Boston says with a smile, sharing a man hug with his longtime Army buddy. Maryland doesn't bother getting out of his chair at the high bar table along the wall they're seated at. A picture of him hugging Louisiana would be considered a keepsake.

"It's been too long, Bos."

"Yeah, it has."

"Where's your delicious fiancée?"

"Working," Boston says, fighting to ignore the sexist comment about the love of his life.

"That's too bad. Well, it's great to see you. Him, not so much," Louisiana says, pointing at the still-seated Maryland.

"Okay, shots fired. Screw you."

"Right back at ya, buddy."

Louisiana extends his hand, Maryland accepts it, and the two share an awkward shake. Their strained relationship from the days in Syria hasn't changed a bit over the years.

"And, oh my good Lord, who might this be?"

"Dr. Tara Winters, it's my honor to introduce the illustrious Vaughn Lormand Cormier Lafourche Rilleux."

Tara looks a little dazed as she tentatively reaches out her hand, which Louisiana takes in his. He holds it longer than appropriate before bending at the waist and kissing it.

"It's an absolute pleasure to meet you, Dr. Winters," he says, dialing up the charm.

"Nice to meet you too…uh, I'm sorry, I only got the Vaughn part of your name."

"That's why we call him Louisiana," Maryland mutters.

"Yeah, I get it now," Tara says with a smile.

"You may call me Louisiana, and you may call me…anytime."

"She's way out of your league, my friend," Maryland warns him.

"There's no such thing, bro. Why didn't you tell me your doc was smokin' hot?"

There's the real Louisiana Boston knows. "It must have slipped my mind."

"You know that I'm sitting right here and can hear you," Tara says, her face red with embarrassment.

"Oh yes, my love, I'm fully aware," Louisiana says, pulling up a chair uncomfortably close to her and taking a seat. "Does it always take this long to get a drink in this town?"

Noticing Louisiana is about to make a scene, a young waiter dressed in a black T-shirt with the bar's name emblazoned on it walks up to us.

"Can I get you all another round?"

"Yes, please," Boston says.

"And you, sir?" he asks Maryland.

"I'm good with the soda for now."

"And what can I get for you, sir?"

"First, I ain't no dang sir. Second," Louisiana says, taking a moment to survey what the others are drinking before pointing to Boston's half-finished beer, "I'll have two of those."

"Sir, I'm afraid it's a house rule that our guests enjoy one drink at a time."

"You 'sir' me again, and you'll find out that my size ten will fit up your ass with the proper amount of force. Now, I just got done with a sixteen-hour drive from the Louisiana bayou to be here. I'm horny, cranky, and not in the mood to have some punk tell me how many beers I can order when he probably doesn't believe in the rule himself. Now, go ahead and tell me how and why you can't fill my order."

The dumbstruck waiter looks at Louisiana for a moment, unsure of what to do. He looks over at Boston, who closes his eyes and shakes his head. If this kid has any brains at all, he'll overlook that rule just this once. Here's the moment of truth.

"I'll get your beers."

"Good man!" Louisiana exclaims as the waiter moves off. "Now, someone wanna fill me in as to why the hell I just drove all the way up here?"

The story takes a while. Boston tells him about the dreams and how they're other people's memories. Tara adds the medical reasoning of how it all works, including her theory about how Boston taps into their memories. Maryland concludes by highlighting the FBI investigation into the leak and how they might be in trouble. Louisiana is on his fourth beer by the time they finish.

"That's a helluva story, Bos. So, let me get this straight. I just traveled halfway across the country to meet you here because you had a dream that wasn't actually a dream about someone targeting you for something that you didn't do and don't know why?"

"Something like that."

"Well, hell, that's just plain stupid, bro."

"I've been telling him that," Maryland quips.

"Well, he ain't gonna listen to you, dude. He's what many people might call 'chicken,'" Louisiana adds, leaning in to Tara.

"I'm not scared of anything."

"Bro, you're scared of a litter of puppies."

"Have they always been like this?" Tara whispers to Boston.

"Since the day they met."

"I still don't understand why you think you have to know them to see their memories, or whatever," Maryland says, not sold on any of this. "I mean, I've never heard anything like that ever before."

"Do you watch science fiction movies?" Tara asks.

"Sometimes. Why?"

"Telepathy is a favorite theme in many of them. Aliens are often portrayed as communicating with each other without words."

"Like in Independence Day?" Louisiana asks.

"Exactly. Everything in the human body is run by electrical impulses. Think of your brain as a computer. It has a hard drive for memory, a processor, and a cooling system. It has input devices and output devices. It also has a way to communicate."

Maryland rolls his eyes. Louisiana is captivated by what Tara is saying, although Boston isn't sure if it's because of her explanation, her attractiveness, or a combination of the two. He won't listen to his previous warning about the doctor being out of his league. Louisiana punches above his weight class when it comes to women, and it works for him.

"It's not implausible that the human brain emits waves like a Wi-Fi signal," Tara continues. "The only thing you need to do is recognize that signal and connect to it. I think Boston has found a way to do that at a near-unconscious level and tap into stored memory like accessing a hard drive."

"All right, so why is he tapping only memories that matter to him? Why not watching someone brushing their teeth or something?" Maryland asks.

"What he sees is generally limited to either a stressful experience or some form of deceit that causes a change in the subject's brain chemistry. I don't know why."

"Okay, so let's assume you really are hacking into other people's heads when you're sleeping, and that it only happens with people you've met. What does this have to do with someone being after you?"

"I don't know. Senators Colby Washington and Garrett Turner are at war with each other," Boston says. "It could have something to do with that or nothing at all."

"Who the hell are they?"

"They sit on the intelligence committee," Maryland grumbles.

"Okay, so we'll just kill these Colby and Garrett fellas, and I'll be home by tomorrow night."

Tara's head shoots around toward Louisiana. Nothing could have prepared her for that statement, including a warning that the man she just met spends his time dabbling in less-than-legal activities. It's not a revelation she'd be overly content with.

"What? Did you say kill them? Like with a gun?" Tara asks.

"Hell no, honey. While that's a traditionally accepted method, I prefer high explosives. It's much more satisfyin' and far less messy."

Tara scans each of the others' faces for signs that he's kidding. Maryland isn't saying anything. Boston joins him in silence. Both convey the answer Tara was looking for…he wasn't joking.

"Is that what you do for a living?" Tara demands. "Blow stuff up like a criminal?"

"Criminal? No, think of me more as a predicament resolution engineer. I help groups solve problems with other groups," Louisiana explains as he slides his arm around Tara's shoulders. "You know, darlin', I'm getting the feelin' you don't much approve of me. You have a problem with killin' traitors to the country?"

She grabs Louisiana's arm and removes it from her shoulders. "Uh, yeah, for starters, I have a big problem with taking another human life."

"Even when it's necessary?" Boston asks, taking up the argument. "There is evil in this world, Tara, whether you want to believe that or not. Even Maryland will agree with that."

"Leave me out of this," Maryland mutters, taking a sip of his soda.

"Who gets to define what is evil and what isn't?"

"Bro, is she for real?" Louisiana asks.

"What do you mean?"

"I mean your moral platitudes."

"Do you even know what a platitude is?" Tara asks, using the most condescending voice she can muster.

There is much more to Louisiana than meets the eye. He may come across as an obnoxious backwater hick, but it's a façade. Underneath lies a conniving, devious, brilliant mind. He's well-read, well-traveled, and street smart. The world underestimates him, and that's his greatest advantage.

Louisiana leans closer to Tara and looks directly into her eyes. "Girl, when was the last time you had a real, earth-shatterin' orgasm?"

"I don't think that's an appropriate question—"

"Have you ever had one?"

Tara's face turns from pink in embarrassment to red with anger. She turns her head to Boston to gauge his reaction before turning her attention back to Louisiana. She leans forward just inches from his face.

"I'm not discussing my sex life with you!" she announces before backing off.

"Okay, that's a no."

"Louisiana," Boston warns.

"I'm just sayin' if she'd had one lately, she'd lighten the hell up."

"I'm leaving."

Tara grabs her purse and storms out of the restaurant without looking back. The men watch her go. Boston gives his friend a pissed off look.

"You still have a way with the ladies, don't you?" Maryland quips, a satisfied smile on his face.

"When was the last time a girl was even that close to you?" Louisiana fires back.

"Was that really necessary?"

"She's wound too tight, Bos. I'm just tryin' to set the mood. She'll be back."

"I need her help, jackass. How do you know that she'll want anything to do with me after that stunt?" Boston asks, hoping he's right.

"Because right now, I promise you, she's thinking about it."

CHAPTER TWENTY-EIGHT
GINA ATTISON

4ᵀᴴ AND A MILE SPORTS BAR
GEORGETOWN, WASHINGTON, D.C.

It's been a long time since Gina walked through these doors. She used to be a regular at 4th and a Mile when she was younger, had more free time, and dated a devout sports disciple. That ended when the relationship soured, and their break-up was inevitable. She had no patience for a man-child who could remember batting averages from 1992 but not their anniversary. This ought to be a fun conversation.

"Jesus," Keith says, peeling his eyes off the screen after she drops into the booth next to him. "Gina? What are you doing here?"

"Seeing you. I'm sorry, guys, can you give us a moment?" she asks his friends at the table.

The men share knowing looks before sliding out of the booth and heading over to the bar. Their thoughts about her motivations for being here couldn't be further off base.

"How did you know I would be here?"

"You're a creature of habit, Keith."

"You say that as if it's a bad thing."

She shrugs. "It's why I broke up with you."

"And now you're here for what? To beg me to come back into your life?"

"No, that ship has sailed."

"Okay. A fling then?"

Gina shakes her head. There is no limit to this man's libido or his arrogance. She decided to break it off with him for both of those reasons long before she got to boring, habitual, and inattentive on the list of his relationship transgressions.

"Not a chance in hell," she says, flashing her diamond ring.

"That's disappointing. Then you're here to plug me for information on the FBI investigation into the intelligence leak."

"That's what I miss about you, Keith. You always get to the right conclusion after all the wrong ones," Gina says.

"You're wasting your time. I don't know anything."

"Oh, I doubt that."

Not everybody who works in the FBI wears windbreakers and chases bad guys like Americans are used to seeing on television. At its heart, the FBI isn't different than any other bureaucracy and requires an army of paper pushers to keep the gears of justice turning.

While not a sexy job, it comes with a benefit – the men and women who perform that function are "in the know," making them the single best sources of information about what is going on there. Keith is one of them.

"I would have a better chance of knowing the location of the Roswell aliens than hearing about what's happening behind those closed doors."

"Which is why you made it a point to find out. I know you, Keith. Don't lie and say you didn't accept that challenge."

Keith smiles and sips his beer. "You're buttering me up."

"And you're a smart guy who's already come to the conclusion that arguing with me is pointless."

"I remember learning that lesson the hard way."

Gina blows him an air kiss, causing him to smirk. "Damn, I miss you. You're still irresistible. Okay, rumor has it that Director Weisz is already under enormous pressure to complete the investigation and catch the leak."

"I could have told you that by watching CNN or FOX News."

"It's far worse than what you've heard on cable news. FBI Counterintelligence has been working on this quietly in the background for over a month. Every lead that they generated has been a dead end. This leak is a ghost, and Weisz is getting desperate."

"Desperate enough to frame someone and lie about it?"

"One would hope not, but the FBI isn't what it used to be." Keith squints and leans forward, suddenly more interested in her for more than her body. "You know something."

"What is Weisz like? Would she sacrifice an innocent American to get the heat off her if she needed to?"

"I don't know her well."

"Answer the question," Gina demands.

"She's a careerist with eyes on being the director of the FBI someday. I suppose that makes her political and capable of anything."

A shiver runs down Gina's spine. Boston was right. She dismissed his most recent memory as something he misinterpreted or didn't see at all. There is no reason to believe Dr. Winters's explanation that this is anything more than just vivid dreams. For the first time, she thinks there may be something behind them.

"Why do you want to know?" Keith asks, grabbing her arm lightly as she reaches for her purse. He withdraws it quickly as not to cross a line. "Come on, Gina. You owe me at least that much."

"I have a bad feeling that a guy I know within the intelligence community is being targeted without cause," she says, not willing to indulge him with the details.

"Okay. If that's true, tell him to watch his back and don't bother playing by the rules. There's one thing I know for sure: if the FBI smells blood in the water on this, they won't be playing by the rules either."

CHAPTER TWENTY-NINE
SPECIAL AGENT ZACH FORTE

DR. TARA WINTERS'S RESIDENCE
ADAMS MORGAN, WASHINGTON, D.C.

Everybody reaches a crossroads at some point in their life. Left or right, the path they choose to take impacts everything that follows. Zach has reached his. Thanks to Grimman, he's being pushed down one he doesn't want to follow.

His superior is taking advantage of him because of the fallout from Operation Beaver Cage. There is no doubt in his mind about that. That one operation has cost him dearly, and not how he envisioned his career would go after he graduated from the academy at Quantico. Life is never fair, and anyone who thinks otherwise deserves what it dishes out.

Zach takes a deep breath and strolls up to the townhouse's front door, thankful that there isn't a video doorbell. He checks the knob. It's locked because nobody in urban America would dare leave it any other way. Zach nonchalantly retreats down the concrete steps to the street and stares back at the sandstone-colored structure, knowing that this place must have cost a fortune.

He continues down the street, careful not to look like a burglar casing places. On a tree-lined street with luxurious homes owned by the wealthy and powerful, taking too much interest will earn unwanted attention. Zach doesn't want to have to pull out his FBI badge and unwittingly start a neighborhood gossip mill.

Careful to maintain the slow gait of a pleasant evening stroll, he walks around the block and down the adjacent street. After a quick look around, he makes his way between a pair of houses and slips into the target's back yard. The dim lighting acts as a security blanket that masks movement and makes the odds of being seen remote.

Zach sneaks up to the back door without disturbing anything or making noise that would alarm a neighbor. He checks the back door in the same manner as the front with the same result before pulling out his rarely utilized lockpick set. Then he notices the deadbolt.

"Shit," he mutters under his breath.

He scans the small back porch and checks under the mat, finding nothing. The top of the door frame and the exterior light also don't house a spare key. Zach moves back down the stairs and feels around the inside of a flower planter. It's only dirt, but he hits the jackpot when he tilts it up and checks underneath.

"Bingo."

Most of the places in this part of the city have alarm systems with central monitoring. If she armed hers, Zach knows he will have to run like hell. He takes a deep breath and holds it, hoping she didn't. He doesn't know the PIN.

He disengages the deadbolt, says a little prayer to himself, and opens the door while listening for the telltale beeping sound. There is none, allowing him to breathe a sigh of relief. The alarm console on the wall has a glowing green light. She never armed it when she left.

"You should be more careful, Miss Winters. There's a lot of crime in this city," he mumbles to himself as his eyes adjust to the darkness.

The ambient light through the back window illuminates a kitchen featuring expensive cabinets, granite countertops, and the modern feel of a recent renovation. Zach pulls out a penlight and shines it around the room. There's a coffeemaker, toaster, blender, bowl of fruit, and no paperwork. Not that he expected there to be any.

The adjoining living room is set up more like a therapist's office than a space for entertaining. It's formal yet comfortable. The woman must be incredibly organized. Everything has its place, and there's no clutter. He can't even find the remote control that operates the seventy-five-inch television hung on the wall.

He checks the workspace in the corner of the room. It takes about five minutes to search the elegant rolltop desk and wood file cabinet next to it. There's nothing on Hollinger anywhere, and this is the most logical place it would be. He flashes the light around the room again, stopping to look at the coffee table and end table. There is nothing but decorative vases on them.

Zach climbs the stairs to the second floor, hoping that she has another office or file cabinet up there. The only rooms on the upper level are the master and spare bedrooms and a pair of bathrooms. Neither of the rooms serves as a backup office. She either keeps her notes on Hollinger electronically or has them with her. Either way, he knows he's screwed.

The sound of someone entering through the front door freezes him in his tracks as the deadbolt slides into place with a telltale click. Zach's heart starts thumping in his chest. He's trapped in here.

There aren't many options for places to hide up here. The master bedroom is out of the question, so he slips into the spare room. The bed doesn't have the clearance to allow him to squeeze under it, so he settles on the closet as his second choice. Footfalls grow louder, announcing someone coming up the stairs. Zach opens the closet door and, mercifully, only finds some long unworn clothes and small boxes. With no time to spare, he climbs in and closes the door.

The hollow core panel door allows enough sound through to hear what's happening. The hallway light switches on, and then he doesn't hear anything. It must be the doctor. Could she know someone is here? Did he make a sound that she heard?

A dozen scenarios run through his head. She cannot be allowed to find him here. Badge or not, entering someone's house without a warrant will mean the end. He didn't bring his weapon. Even under the worst of circumstances, he's not going to shoot the woman without cause. That doesn't mean he didn't come prepared. After spending most of his adult life armed, he wasn't about to enter the house empty-handed.

The bedroom lamp switches on. Zach stops breathing and brings his taser up to chest level as light pours through the space between the bottom of the door and the floor. He focuses on the closet door, expecting it to swing open at any second. There was no conversation announcing the presence of two people. She's the only target. The adrenaline is flowing, being pushed through his veins by the thumping heart in his chest.

A moment later, the light in the room is extinguished. Zach wipes the sweat off his forehead and quietly exhales. The room is still. A series of muffled bangs down the hall gets followed by the sound of running water. He opens the closet door a crack and can hear the shower running.

Zach steps out of the closet and eases himself through the spare room and into the hallway. It's all clear. He pokes his head into the master bedroom and notices the purse and jacket tossed on the bed.

He faces another moment of truth. This is the best chance to escape, but the whole adventure will have been pointless if he finds nothing. He creeps into the bedroom, stepping softly so as not to be betrayed by a squeaky floorboard. The bathroom door is open, and her clothes are strewn across the porcelain tile floor.

Next to her purse on the bed is a manila folder with sheets from a yellow legal pad. On top of the first page is a name: Eugene Hollinger. He finally hit paydirt.

The shower turns off. There is no time to use either the small digital scanner or camera that Zach brought with him. The clock is ticking as he faces yet another crossroads. He makes his decision.

CHAPTER THIRTY

"BOSTON" HOLLINGER

BOSTON'S RESIDENCE
OXON HILL, MARYLAND

There is a finite number of known, indisputable truths in the universe. There is only one applicable to me right now: the harder you fight to stay awake, the faster you find yourself drifting off to sleep. Since the accident and the crazy dream-memories that have occurred, sleep is the last thing I'm looking forward to.

I continue pressing the channel button on the remote in search of anything that will capture my attention enough to help combat my heavy eyelids yearning to shut for the night. It's a losing battle. Alcohol has always made me tired, and tonight's beers at the bar are not helping buck that trend. Even with the stress of the unknown, I know sleep is coming, and it's coming fast.

* * *

I'm nervous, and my heart is beating in my chest like a bass drum. Sweat drips off my brow as I feel the slick clamminess of my hands. Through the blurry haze, I can still tell that it's dark and cramped in here. And silent. I hear footfalls on a floor over my own breathing, and not much else.

I gulp air and hold it in my lungs when a lamp switches on and a sliver of light pours through a crack below me. Where am I? What is this?

I clutch a device in my hands but can't see it through the darkness, much less the haze. I am seized with anxiety and anticipation with no concept of why. The adrenaline rush reaches its peak when the light disappears, and darkness envelops me once again.

An eternity passes until I feel myself open a door. Is this a closet? I don't hear anything other than the sound of running water, and I move slowly into what looks like a hallway. The room at the end is lit, but I can't make out the details aside from a bed and dresser. This could be anyone's bedroom.

I launch myself out of my recliner when I return to reality. The room is shadowy, with the outside streetlight and my LED television providing the only light. Everything is as it should be. Well, not everything.

I close my eyes and run over the content of the dream in my mind several times. When finished, I sit on the couch with my elbows resting on my knees. It's the only logical explanation.

The purse had to be Tara's. That was her apartment in Adams Morgan. It was her in the shower, and someone was with her: a stranger who wasn't invited in. It wasn't a lover or her ex-boyfriend, Mark. It was somebody else looking for information…on me. But why? It's a question that needs an answer, but not the first thing that needs to be addressed.

I reach over to the end table and retrieve my cell, navigate to favorites, and hit send.

"What the hell, bro? Do you know what time it is?" Louisiana barks into the phone.

"Just after three. I'm surprised you're even sleeping."

"Yeah, well, I was. Shouldn't you be gettin' it on with your fiancée if you're lonely?"

"She's still at work," I say, just now realizing that this is probably an all-nighter for her. "Shut up and listen. You need to get over to Tara's. I'll text you the address and will meet you there."

"Bos, I'm okay with that for sure, but will she be?" Louisiana asks.

"Yeah, she will once I explain why we're there."

There is a long pause on the other end of the line. I'm about to argue that we don't have time for a witty comeback when the Cajun finally says something.

"You had one of your crazy visions again, didn't you?"

"Unfortunately."

"And?"

I know this must sound crazy. If the roles were reversed and anybody came to me with this problem, I'd say it was nuts too. But it's happening to me, I know what I saw, and I know a young woman is in danger because of it.

"You have to trust me on this. Tara is in trouble. Just get over there."

CHAPTER THIRTY-ONE
ERIC "MARYLAND" WILLIAMS

The Defense Intelligence Agency is unique because it sits at the crossroads of the Department of Defense and the greater intelligence community. Warfighters and policymakers rely on the DIA for intelligence on the operating environments of foreign militaries. There is some fieldwork to support combat missions, but most analysts like Maryland work at the headquarters facility located along the Potomac River at Joint Base Anacostia-Bolling.

Maryland steps off the elevator when his phone vibrates inside his pocket. He checks the caller ID and grimaces. That didn't take long.

"I just got to work, Boston. Make it quick."

"Louisiana and I are at Tara's. She had a feeling someone was in her house last night and shrugged it off as paranoia until we showed up."

"Anyone would be paranoid that Louisiana showed up on their doorstep, especially her. Why did you rush over?"

"I had a memory. Someone was in Tara's house."

Maryland stops walking. That's an interesting development. Then again, this is Washington, D.C. It's not the safest city in the country by a long shot.

"What was in the dream?" he asks, indulging his friend but still not willing to believe it's a memory.

"Long story short, he was in a closet and searched her room while she was in the shower. He took some notes that she had in her bag."

"Notes?"

"Yeah, the ones from our session and her consultations with other doctors and specialists that she had with her last night. It was also where she outlined her theory behind what's happening in my head. She wrote all of it down, and now it's gone."

"Wait, let me get this straight. You're telling me that someone broke into Tara's house while she was home and stole a pad full of gibberish while the hottest woman ever was naked in the shower? Take the tinfoil hat off, Boston, will ya?"

"I wish I could just pass this all off as me being crazy. It'd be easier to deal with."

Maryland has heard that tone before. He's serious. These dreams are haunting Boston in a way his own post-traumatic stress from their deployment does him.

"Was anyone there when you arrived?"

"No."

"Did you check under the bed?" he asks, not resisting the urge to get a little snarky.

"Well gee, Maryland, I'm sure I didn't think to look there," Boston replies sarcastically. "We searched the whole house. Nobody is here and the notes are definitely gone."

"Why would anybody take them? It's not like you're the mole or these dreams, no matter how bizarre, constitute some clear and present danger to national security."

"That's the million-dollar question, isn't it?"

A pair of analysts walks past Maryland in the otherwise empty corridor. This isn't the ideal place to be having this conversation. Any call held in a hushed voice could be considered suspicious under the best of circumstances. Given the public pressure around the investigation into the leak, these are hardly the best of circumstances.

Maryland is about to say something when another thought pops into his head. What if whoever broke into Tara's house is monitoring his phone? If someone is willing to break into his doctor's house to steal notes, it's not beyond the realm of possibilities that they are being watched. He tries to put the paranoid thought out of his head. Unless it isn't.

"I can't be associated with this anymore," Maryland blurts out.

"You have no choice. You are involved. I need your help, Maryland. Forget your career for a second. Something is wrong with all this. I need your help to figure out what."

"What do you want from me?" Maryland responds, his exasperated tone echoing off the walls of the corridor.

"Just come to Tara's tonight. I'll text you the address. We can talk about the next steps then."

The line disconnects. This is ridiculous, and Maryland wants to scream, but he knows that Boston is right. The leak, the investigation, the politics... Washington is on fire, and Americans are getting uneasy. He wants to believe that whatever is happening to his friend has nothing to do with that.

Unfortunately, his instincts tell him otherwise. After all these years in the intelligence business, he's learned to trust that feeling.

CHAPTER THIRTY-TWO
SENATOR GARRETT TURNER

NEAR CAPITOL HILL
WASHINGTON, D.C.

The senator pulls up behind the unmarked sedan parked on First Street and gets out of his car. This guy has a set of balls on him to demand a meeting before the session is gaveled in. That's not the way this works.

"You have five minutes, Agent Grimman. What is so damned important that it couldn't be handled over the phone?"

"This. Thank me later."

He hands the senator a file that Garrett accepts and scans. "What am I reading?"

"That is the official military personnel record for U.S. Army Sergeant Vaughn Rilleux. This is the FBI file on his activities since," Grimman says while passing over a much thicker folder. "Rilleux was a combat engineer in Syria when Hollinger was there. Now he is allegedly a hired gun for various criminal elements in Louisiana and throughout the South."

"So what?" Garrett asks, wishing his lackey would get to the point without all the drama.

"My source reported that he's in town. Hollinger met with him and the doctor at a bar last night along with an analyst from DIA."

"What was said?"

"I don't know. My source had another assignment. This puts a half-Iranian doctor, a career criminal, a DIA analyst, and a staffer on the SSCI in the same room. That should help with your investigation."

Garrett grins. "Yes, yes, it does. And with his fiancée on Washington's staff, the scandal leads right to his doorstep. Anything else?"

"Are you sure that you really want to hear the details of this?"

"Very much. Out with it."

"That assignment I mentioned meant an unauthorized entry in Tara Winters's residence."

"Did your source find anything?"

Grimman shakes his head. "No, but I didn't expect him to. No spy is that sloppy."

"Is Hollinger experiencing any medical issues after his accident?"

"None that we know of. The neurosurgeon at National Medical Center saw something she didn't like in his MRI, but that's it. He was diagnosed with a head injury, so it's plausible that Winters is working with him for that. It's also damn convenient."

Garrett looks up and down the tree-lined street just outside his gate that leads to his parking lot. He has no fight with Hollinger but the man makes for a useful idiot in taking down the chairman of the SSCI. If he becomes collateral damage, so be it. Men like him are a dime a dozen.

"I suppose you have some sort of plan because, unless they make a mistake, there isn't much I can learn," Grimman concludes. "I don't think you have the time to wait for a slip-up."

"Yeah, I have a plan. It's time to crack some eggs."

"What does that mean?"

"That an omelet is coming. Keep Hollinger and the doctor under surveillance. Stay close to your phone. I may have a task for you later."

Garrett slips his sunglasses back onto his face and climbs into his red convertible, leaving the FBI agent standing next to his own car. He doesn't need to know what comes next. He doesn't rank high enough on the food chain.

One thing about having multiple marriages is that you learn some things. Garrett's first wife was a conniving, self-centered diva who was all show and no substance. His current wife is the opposite. She would do anything for him and their marriage because she loves him unconditionally. Garrett is willing to bet that Gina Attison loves her fiancé and would want to protect him as well.

CHAPTER THIRTY-THREE

GINA ATTISON

RUSSELL SENATE OFFICE BUILDING
WASHINGTON, D.C.

The forecast over the next week calls for "unsettled weather," as the local news's dorky meteorologist characterized it this morning. In typical Washington fashion, even he couldn't make a decisive prediction. Gina can't understand why he just didn't say it would rain periodically.

The walk from the staff parking lot to the Russell Senate Office Building is a long one. She doesn't rank high enough on the organizational chart to merit a spot in the closer underground garage. Parking is at a premium in this part of the city, which is why most staffers take the Metro. She doesn't have that luxury.

Gina peeks up at the sky with concern. The clouds gathering toward the southeast are ominous. It's a metaphor for what is happening in this city and an omen about the storm ahead.

"Hey, Gina. You walk really fast," Justin Triggs says as he bounds up and falls in stride alongside her.

"It could be because it's about to start pouring."

"That's what umbrellas are for. Let's face it. Raindrops falling from the heavens is the easier of the two storms we're dealing with."

Gina avoids making a snarky comment about his pointing out the obvious. The *Herald* reporter has been trying to develop her as a source since her days at the intelligence committee. She thinks he's a nice enough guy, but there is one golden rule on this hill: reporters are to be used but never trusted.

"What can I do for you, Justin?"

"We heard a rumor that the FBI already has a lead on the leak. Have you heard anything?"

"No, and even if I did, you know I won't talk about it."

"I only need one more confirmation to run with the story. C'mon, Gina. Learn to share. Nobody keeps secrets in this town. The only real mystery is who knows them," he pleads, uttering one of the universal truths adopted as canon in the religion of politics. It's not one she believes in. While it's true that everyone has secrets in Washington, most are never exposed.

"Were your other sources on Capitol Hill or in the intelligence community?"

"You know I can't divulge that."

"Who's not sharing now?" Gina asks.

"We both know that Congress is going nuts making political hay over the death of the VP's son. The American people want answers."

Her work is stressful because, despite the intelligence community's consistent warnings of barbarians at the gate, politicians are too often consumed by their own petty infighting to acknowledge the danger. The death of the vice president's son is terrible, but the finger-pointing and blatant partisanship are what make his loss a national tragedy.

"Let no crisis go unexploited," Gina muses. "That's for the DNI to deal with. He runs the entire intelligence network and is a principal advisor to the president and the National Security Council. Why aren't you asking him?"

Admiral Troxell also serves as a whipping boy when things go wrong. He'll be the guy expected to fall on his sword if the president's poll numbers continue to abate over the counterintelligence failure.

"Sure. I'm sure that the DNI will welcome an appointment with a reporter from the *Herald* with open arms."

"Then the admiral and I have something in common."

"Look, Gina," Justin says, grabbing her lightly on the arm as they stop and turn to face each other. "I'm asking you to level with me. Everybody knew that the VP's oldest kid was in the State Department, but nobody knew he was over *there*. He was assassinated in a foreign country because a traitor that counterintelligence can't seem to find within our own government tipped off our enemies.

"The nation is a powder keg right now. That may be the spark that blows this entire administration up. Don't think that they won't find someone to take the fall for it."

"You're cute when you're doing your 'voice of the people' shtick while pointing out the obvious." She leans in close to him. "I can't help you."

Gina finishes the trek to the office unmolested by any other reporters. They are swarming like bees protecting their hive right now, and she is sure that her run-in with Justin wasn't the only instance of a staffer fending off a reporter this morning.

She nods at Colby's receptionist and heads for his office at the rear of the suite. His assistant gestures her toward the senator's door, where he is seated behind his desk in the usual shirt sleeves. She leans in to check if he's on the phone.

"*No, this can't wait any longer… No, we need him taken off the board before this gets any worse…yes…no, do it tonight.*"

Despite the door's thickness, she hears the phone is returned to its cradle, and Gina raps on the door twice.

"Come in."

"Good morning, Senator."

"If I know anything with one hundred percent certainty, it's that this morning can't be characterized as good. I know you have a stack of work on your desk too, Gina. To what do I owe the visit?"

"I got ambushed on the way in by Justin Triggs from the *Herald*. He claims that the FBI has information on the mole and wanted confirmation."

"I assume you didn't say anything to him."

"No, not that I know anything anyway."

He nods for her to close the door, and she obliges. "I haven't been briefed on any possible leads, and to my knowledge, neither has the president."

"Is the press corps making this up?"

"It's Washington, Gina. More likely, someone is leaking misinformation to them. Divulge to the press that there is a lead in the investigation, and the media run with the story. If nothing is announced by the FBI, it looks like they are hiding something or don't have their act together. The public gets even angrier, and the political pressure intensifies. It's not a new tactic."

"Is Garrett Turner behind this?"

The senator smirks. "It's a lengthy list, but he would be at the top of it. I just need you to keep your head down and focus on your job. Just because we are facing turmoil doesn't mean that our enemies aren't making moves against us. Someone could be plotting to use this distraction to their advantage."

"Are we talking about global affairs or politics, sir?" Gina asks.

Colby goes back to reviewing a pile of papers on his desk, signaling an end to the conversation. He is a soldier at heart. She has never seen the man play politics like this. It's disconcerting.

She knows that politics is the great game. It is all about power, and the players work tirelessly to amass more of it. The senator has never been more than a benchwarmer in that match. He believes that he was elected to Congress to serve the people, not himself or his party.

If Colby is caught up in the Kabuki theater of this charade, it must be bad. That conversation was out of character for him. She drops her bag on the desk and crashes into her chair. She takes a long look at the secure safe along the wall, already exhausted from a day that has only just begun.

CHAPTER THIRTY-FOUR

EUGENE "BOSTON" HOLLINGER

DR. TARA WINTERS'S RESIDENCE
ADAMS MORGAN, WASHINGTON, D.C.

It's approaching dinnertime, and I join Tara in the kitchen while she fulfills the promise that she made about cooking a meal for us. Louisiana wanted steaks, but we all agreed on chicken cacciatore after our host insisted that her sauce was to die for.

"Thank you for agreeing to stay here tonight. I mean that. I'm still a little freaked out about the break-in."

"It's no trouble. It's the least we can do considering I dragged you into this," I say, waving a dismissive hand.

"You say that now," Tara says with a smile. "Pray that my mother doesn't call and find out I have three men staying the night here. She still believes that I should be escorted by a family member in public."

I'm about to ask about her Muslim upbringing when Louisiana and Maryland fire the first salvos in their newest battle out in the adjoining living room. Since the moment he arrived, the two of them have been arguing about every conceivable topic. From politics and sports to music and television, all they've managed to agree on is that they have nothing in common.

"I almost wish you hadn't invited him," Tara mumbles as she adds seasoning to the sauce in the pan.

"Maryland or Louisiana?"

"Both. You were right when you said that those two carry on like an old married couple."

"Old habits die hard," I say with a smirk.

"Have they ever gotten along?" she asks, probably curious about why we are all friends in the first place.

"They both have unique perspectives on life. When we were in Syria, the only thing they shared was mutual respect."

"And now?"

"The transition to the civilian world changes every veteran. Maryland stuck with what he's good at and stayed in the intelligence community. Louisiana took a more adventurous approach to life."

"And you? Why Capitol Hill?"

"I just kind of ended up there."

"I see."

"I have a question for you," I say, changing the topic before she starts asking questions that I really don't want to answer. "If these dreams are memories, is there a way to make them sharper? I need to see them better to help me remember and understand them."

"This is medically uncharted territory, Boston. There are common techniques used to recall and sharpen dreams, but they take years to master. Even if you learned them tomorrow, I have no idea if any of them would work for your situation."

"This will be an interesting article for the *New England Journal of Medicine.*"

"I'm not a researcher, Boston," she scolds.

"You know what I mean."

"Of course I do. It was your passive-aggressive way of asking why I'm helping you."

"You're a little creepy sometimes," Boston says, in a complimentary tone.

"Yeah, I've been told that. I just want you to know my motivations are pure. I'm not trying to cash in on an earth-shattering discovery. I'm here to help you through this. That's all."

I'm caught off-guard. It's a solid reason, but it lacks Tara's usual conviction. It sounded more like a convenient excuse, something that's confirmed when she blushes. I'm about to ask if there is another reason when she turns and sticks a wooden spoon in my face.

"Taste."

I slurp down the sauce and smack my lips as I savor the flavor. Tara was one hundred percent right when she insisted that this dish is to die for.

"Amazing."

"Thank you."

"I do have one question for you: why let Louisiana into your house considering…?"

"Considering that he humiliated me last night?" she finishes, returning to her stirring. "I don't know. Maybe it's because someone broke into my home while I was in the shower. The thought scares the hell out of me. If letting someone as obnoxious as him stay here makes me feel the slightest bit more at ease, then I'm all for it. The same goes for you and Maryland. Right now, the more men, the better."

"Spoken like a true woman hiding that fact from her mother. You could have asked Mark to come back."

She stops stirring and stares at the sauce for a moment. When she raises her eyes to meet mine, there is pain in them. I shouldn't have said anything.

"What does it say about our relationship that I'm willing to have three strangers stay here instead of him?"

She doesn't elaborate any further, but she doesn't need to. Mark probably made her feel just as vulnerable as the man who broke into her house did. I put my hand on Tara's shoulder, and she turns back and looks at me. She's a complicated woman—intelligent yet naïve, strong yet vulnerable. We remain still for a moment, almost in a trance, until the sound of Maryland's newest admonishment of Louisiana carries into the kitchen.

"They don't stress you out?" Tara asks with a laugh, breaking our moment or whatever was between us. My guilt sets in immediately.

"I'm used to it," I say, offering an awkward laugh of my own. "They've been stressing me out for years."

"How do you deal with it? Stress in general, I mean."

"Gina and I have demanding jobs. When we are both at the end of the rope, we pack the car and head to a little cabin in the mountains of West Virginia."

"That sounds nice," Tara says without any genuine enthusiasm at all.

"It is, although it's a white-knuckle experience getting to it. The road is a single lane. Parts of it are literally carved into the mountainside and subject to rockslides that can cut you off from the world. Once you get there, the view is breathtaking. The whole area is serene and very peaceful."

"You said the cabin is a secret. How are you able to pull that off?"

"It starts by not blabbing about it to a doctor," I say, getting rewarded with a scolding look. "The cabin belonged to a friend of Gina's who inherited it when her father passed. She didn't want to be responsible for a place in the boonies, so she handed the keys and paperwork over to Gina. There's no official record of the transfer. Gina keeps the deed in an old book. We've never mentioned its existence in public or private…well, until now. Whenever we talk about needing to get away and go, it's done in code."

"Code?"

"When we want to head there for a weekend, we say we need 'Merlot.'"

"Merlot?"

"Yeah. Like the type of wine."

"I know what Merlot is, Boston. What I don't know is why a manly guy like yourself would choose that particular codeword."

I smile at her description of me. "The first time we went there, we learned that the only places around were gas stations with little convenience stores in them. They aren't known for their wine selections, as you can imagine."

"Can they even legally sell them there?"

"I have no idea, but this one did. Beer was out of the question since we wanted to celebrate, and the only thing left was this god-awful bottle of cheap red wine. We both hate Merlot, so we laughed about it all weekend and decided to name the cabin that. So now our trips there are known as Merlot."

"That's a nice story."

"Yeah," I mumble. "I'm surprised I told you that. As I said, nobody knows about it except the two of us … and now you."

"So why did you tell me?" Tara asks, turning to face me.

"I don't know. I guess it's because I find you easy to talk to."

"I'm a doctor, Boston. I need to be easy to talk to."

"That's not what I meant. I guess what I'm trying to say is that I find myself trusting you. That doesn't happen much in my line of work, especially now. If everything you say is true, I have met the person that is targeting me. You have no idea how much that bothers me."

She puts her hand on my arm and gives me a gentle squeeze. She forces a sympathetic smile and looks like she wants to say something but can't find the words.

My cell phone sounds out a familiar ringtone from the pocket of my jeans. I don't need to look at the caller ID to know I need to answer it. There are some calls you just don't ignore. I swear, she has an uncanny sense of intuition. Tara seems to realize that as well as I walk out of the kitchen onto the back porch.

"Hey, honey. What's up?"

CHAPTER THIRTY-FIVE
SPECIAL AGENT ZACH FORTE

The boredom is almost insufferable. Zach has a cell phone with games loaded on it to pass the time, but the tricky part of any stakeout is staying vigilant. Few people can have their face planted into a screen and be aware of their surroundings. He isn't one of them, so his device sits in the center console as he stares out the window.

Minutes feel like hours. Zach varies the time he moves his car to avoid falling into a pattern. The precious minutes spent driving around the block are cherished. The alternative is watching absolutely nothing for no good reason.

His phone vibrates, and the call gets put on speaker. This time, it's not the scheduled check-in with his hyperactive taskmaster of a boss.

"Are you having fun yet?" Matt says.

Zach frowns, not able to even come up with a sarcastic response to the ridiculous question.

"Loads. You should come and join me."

"I'll pass, thanks."

"Anything on that file I gave you?"

"What, are you searching for some kind of absolution for your brief dalliance with breaking and entering?"

"Something like that," Zach mutters.

"I have some people looking into it."

"You have doctors there?"

"No, but the CIA has a cadre of experts they can call on when necessary, and our liaison at Watchtower is well-connected to many of them. Have you heard from Grimman?"

"Far more than I'd like to."

"Has he ordered you to do anything further?"

"You mean did he ask me to violate any more Constitutional rights of sovereign citizens? No, why?"

"Abril Lopez has been asking a lot of questions."

"She's a reporter," Zach says with a shake of his head as he looks down the street at the townhouse. "It comes with the territory."

"Let me clarify: her questions are ones that she shouldn't know to ask. It has the full attention of the Bureau.

"Do you think someone is feeding her information?"

"There's no doubt about it. Justin Triggs is also on the Hill harassing anyone he can find. He's a bloodhound, so I expect him to track a scent when he gets a whiff of it. That's not the case with Lopez. She's a hard-worker and will out-hustle any of her peers for a story, but she's not connected enough to know what she does on her own."

"Matt, please tell me that Watchtower isn't spying on journalists."

"No, we don't do that sort of thing. That doesn't mean we don't do our due diligence and keep tabs on what stories they are chasing."

"I'm sure they would take great comfort in knowing that," Zach mumbles. "Why the call, Matt? What are you trying to tell me?"

"Whoever is leaking information to the media is doing it to ratchet up the pressure in a crisis that doesn't need any more of it. People could start getting jumpy."

"You think that Grimman would be reckless enough to order me to do something else illegal?"

"You weren't chosen for your sunny disposition, Zach."

He exhales on the driver's side window, causing it to temporarily fog up. Zach doesn't like one bit where this is going. Even with Matt covering for him, he is being used. There isn't a respectable human on Earth that cherishes that feeling.

"Matt, this is getting ridiculous."

"I know. Just hang in there a little longer. Let me know if you're ordered to do anything considered out of bounds."

"You mean like breaking into a woman's house who likely has nothing at all to do with a massive intelligence leak that is getting Americans killed half a world away while the real traitor walks free with impunity?"

"Uh, yeah, like that. You know, you're much more articulate when you're sober."

"Gee, thanks."

Zach disconnects the call and goes back to staring out the window. It's another ten minutes before he can take his short sojourn to reposition his car.

He's already exhausted, and it's going to be a long night of watching absolutely nothing happen.

CHAPTER THIRTY-SIX

GINA ATTISON

There is no worse time to live and work in the nation's capital than when the government is in crisis. Everyone's stress level is through the roof. Politicians mobilize their staff to take full advantage of the strife in the never-ending quest for camera time and votes back home. Everyone else is left to suffer the consequences.

Gina doesn't care about any of that. She has a job to do. It's a means to an end, and that end is her sole focus in life: happiness. Everything else takes a back seat. It's a mentality that comes in handy while working here. Washington, D.C. is a city where negativity is a religion, and backstabbing is one of its cherished rituals.

"Excuse me, Miss Attison?" one of the senator's staffers asks, poking her head in her office.

"Yes?"

"There's an FBI agent here to see you."

A surge of electricity courses through her. What the hell could the FBI want?

"Thanks, Olivia. Please send him in."

Gina gets out of her chair and slides on her three-button suit jacket. With heels and dark pants, the outfit is a power suit for women on Capitol Hill. She has a suspicion that it may be needed for this meeting.

"Miss Attison?" the bald man with three-day-old scruff on his face asks from her doorway. "I'm Supervisory Special Agent Tom Grimman, FBI Counterespionage Section of the Counterintelligence Division."

"Nice to meet you, Agent Grimman. Please, have a seat," Gina offers, watching as he obliges following a firm yet brief handshake. "What brings you here?"

"You do."

"I'm afraid I don't—"

"More specifically, I'd like to talk about your fiancé, Eugene Hollinger."

Washington, D.C. is a city built on influence, reputation, and positional power. Americans recognize the political games played among the nation's leadership, but those are only the title fights. The undercards are filled with the staffers who deal with power grabs every day. By interrupting her as he did, Agent Grimman is signaling that he doesn't regard Gina as any type of authority. It's definitely one of those meetings for her.

"I already don't like the direction this conversation is going in, Agent Grimman. If you cut me off again mid-sentence, you'll need a warrant the next time you speak to me."

"If that's what it takes, Miss Attison. I hope it doesn't come to that. How long has your fiancé known Eric Williams?"

"Since they were in the Army. They were in the same unit and were both wounded in a mortar attack in Syria and discharged. Eric held a Top-Secret SCI clearance and landed a position as an analyst with the Defense Intelligence Agency's Middle Eastern Desk. You no doubt already have that information, so why exactly are you asking me?"

"Because we're trying to understand how he also knows Dr. Tara Winters. That information wasn't on his SF-86 when he applied for his clearance."

"To my knowledge, he doesn't know her. We met her after Boston's accident. Any more questions?"

"Lots," Grimman deadpans as he stares intently at her.

"Then ask them or get the hell out of my office."

"Miss Attison, I don't respond to threats. I will not allow your lack of cooperation to prejudice this investigation."

Gina clasps her hands on her desk and leans forward. She was caught off-guard by the FBI agent's arrival and is unnerved by his interrogation, but he's fishing. She understands that this visit is meant to rattle her, and she is determined not to let it work.

"Boston is not the leak. If you think otherwise, you're mistaken. So, I am trying to understand what information you have that could possibly warrant this inquiry. Unless, of course, you count the bigoted insinuation that having a doctor of Persian descent somehow makes her a terrorist and him a traitor."

"We are following leads, Miss Attison. That's all. Are you implying that I shouldn't investigate your fiancé?" Grimman asks, in a voice that dares her to say "yes."

"No, because it's your job. And even if you could stop investigating him, I know you wouldn't. Finding this leak is critical to national security, and that means leaving no stone unturned. I am simply explaining that you're wasting your time, but that's your prerogative."

The comment catches him off-guard. Whatever Grimman's expectations about this conversation were, they were shattered. He shifts in his chair, looking a little less smug than he was when he walked into her office.

"You think that the FBI is targeting Hollinger just to close the case?"

"Look at it from my perspective, Agent Grimman. You show up here asking questions when we both know any evidence you may have about Boston is speculative and lacks credibility. I know this because I live with him. He's not a traitor."

"Yes, but—"

"I also work for a senator who happens to be the chairman of the Senate Select Committee on Intelligence. We both know that there is a political aspect to this."

"Is that what you think this is?" the agent asks, again shifting his weight in her upholstered armchair. "Because I resent the assertion."

"I didn't come to Washington yesterday, Agent Grimman. I know more about the political landscape here than you can hope to learn in three lifetimes. You have a job to do, and that's to find the traitor giving our secrets to our enemies. Understand that I also have a job to do, and that's to ensure you do yours by giving Senator Washington the relevant analysis he needs. That includes a warning that America's premier investigative agency has become political. We both know how that's worked out in the past."

Agent Grimman rubs the stubble on his chin. She's betting that he has put some long hours in on this investigation already. He needs rest and, more importantly, perspective. This is a high-profile investigation that can make or break the rest of his career in the Bureau.

"Your point is well-taken, Miss Attison. Let me ask you one final question: is Dr. Winters attractive?"

"Excuse me?"

He rises from his chair and straightens his jacket. "You heard me."

"How is that relevant to—"

"Your fiancé has been spending a lot of time with her lately. I hadn't realized head injuries require such…personalized care."

"We're done here. Goodbye, Agent Grimman."

He grins and leaves the office, closing the door behind him. Gina leans back in her chair. He scored some points late in the game. What bothers her most is that he's right.

CHAPTER THIRTY-SEVEN
ERIC "MARYLAND" WILLIAMS

DR. TARA WINTERS'S RESIDENCE
ADAMS MORGAN, WASHINGTON, D.C.

"As we have been reporting, the assassination of the son of the vice president may have been planned using information leaked from one of our own intelligence agencies," the female television pundit says by way of introduction. "Joining me to discuss this is Karen Weisz, Executive Assistant Director of the Security Branch of the Federal Bureau of Investigation. Thank you for coming on the program, Director Weisz."

"Thank you for having me."

"She looks like one of her parents was a bird or somethin'," Louisiana observes from the other couch.

"Shut up, will you?" Maryland scolds after missing half of the first question. He's tired of his friend's crap, finding him even more obnoxious than he was in Syria.

"The FBI investigation encompasses all relevant agencies," Weisz explains to the show's host. "It would be premature for me to comment on whether we are focusing on any particular one."

"Director, the assassination of the vice president's son is tragic, but reports are speculating the disclosure leading to his death was not the first instance when classified information was given to our enemies. Some of them have directly resulted in the loss of life."

"Are all cable news chicks this hot now? Because if they are, I need to start watchin' more television."

"We are looking into that as well."

"I find that incredible, Director. Is this administration asleep at the wheel? I mean, if this is true and the leak has been happening for a longer period than Americans realize, I'm wondering if counterintelligence teams are doing their jobs. I'm also wondering if the people elected to hold them accountable are doing theirs."

"Yeah, because if they were, I wouldn't need to be here," Louisiana mutters, testing Maryland's patience.

"We are doing everything in our power to identify if there is, in fact, a breach and find out who is violating the nation's trust by giving those secrets to our enemies."

"Director, the analysis submitted by the Defense Intelligence Agency spells out the nature of the leak very succinctly," the anchor argues, "and their findings have been corroborated. Not only does the leaker need to be found, but someone has to be held accountable. Whether it's the president or members of Congress, our elected officials are equally culpable for not identifying that there was a problem."

Maryland turns the television to a different channel. It's prime time, and he'll take any sitcom over listening to this. Americans are dying because of this leak. All this talking head cares about is assigning blame.

"I was watchin' that, bro," Louisiana cries.

"I don't care."

"What's the bug up your ass?"

Maryland knows that he should never have agreed to come here. Whatever is happening with Boston has nothing to do with him. He's jumping to conclusions based on crazy dreams and taking all of them blindly along for the ride in the process. Boston is a friend, but loyalty has its limits. Louisiana wouldn't understand that. He'd storm the gates of hell with Boston if asked.

"Nothing."

"Yeah, sure. You're embracing life as a low-information voter."

"I work for the DIA, moron. They're investigating the department that I work in. I wrote the analysis she just mentioned. I'm just tired of the media using Americans' deaths for ratings and politicians exploiting it for their own gain. Do you know what's going to get lost in the end? The truth!"

"Okay, relax, bro. Geez."

Louisiana pulls the black duffel bag closer to him and starts removing a myriad of strange-looking homemade devices from it. Maryland knows enough to conclude that most of the stuff in there goes boom. They're not the kinds of things a law-abiding citizen would want to get caught using.

"Is any of that stuff legal?"

"Nope."

"Why did you bring them?"

"Because if we find the mole before the feds do, one of these babies is going to have his name on it," Louisiana deadpans.

"Dinner is almost ready," Tara says after emerging from the kitchen. "I'm just waiting on the garlic bread. I'm sorry that it's taking so long. Boston was supposed to be helping, but he's on the phone with his fiancée."

"Don't worry your pretty self about us," Louisiana consoles with a wink. Tara rolls her eyes and returns to the relative safety of the kitchen.

The two men share a look. They both heard the tone in her voice when she mentioned Gina. It was the vocal expression of seething contempt.

"Why isn't Boston kickin' it with the doc? She's a dime piece, bro."

"You've met Gina, and I know you aren't blind."

"I'm just saying that the doc wants the jambalaya and all our boy is givin' her is the gravy and rice."

"What the hell does that even mean?"

"Well, hell, Maryland, you're the intelligence analyst. Why do you need me to point this out? Tara digs him, the lucky bastard. I'm just wonderin' why he doesn't help himself."

"He's a one-girl guy. Oh, and the girl happens to be a drop-dead gorgeous bigwig staff member for a United States senator who pulls down almost six figures. So, there's that."

"So? Don't tell her."

Maryland shakes his head. He feels terrible for whoever Louisiana settles down with if that day ever happens.

"It's called monogamy, jackass. If you can ever manage to get your mind wrapped around the concept of settling down, you should try it."

"Oh, I understand the concept. Monogamy is like reading the same book over and over. Promiscuity, however, is like readin' the last page of every book in the library."

Maryland is about to chastise Louisiana for his ignorance when Boston emerges from the kitchen and immediately heads over to the expensive wooden blinds that cover the living room window. He peeks between them, scanning the street outside.

"Did we miss somethin'?" Louisiana asks.

"I just got off the phone with Gina. The FBI just paid her a visit at her office on Capitol Hill. He stopped just short of calling me a suspect for being the mole."

"What?"

"That's stupid, bro."

"Yeah, but that's not all. Colby Washington may be somehow involved. She overheard a strange conversation he was having on the phone this morning. She didn't think much of it, but after her conversation with the feds, Gina thinks he may have been talking about us."

Maryland crosses his arms. He can't understand why the FBI would tip their hand if Boston really was a suspect. There is no way he's the mole. If they think that he is, they must be trying a different approach by using Gina to get to him. Since Boston is staring out the window like a paranoid cat, it seems to be working.

"That's pretty flimsy."

"Not when you also consider the memories I'm experiencing. Somebody is after me, guys," Boston says, peeking outside through the blinds. "I think we're being watched."

CHAPTER THIRTY-EIGHT
SENATOR GARRETT TURNER

HIGH STEAKS DRAMA
FOGGY BOTTOM, WASHINGTON, D.C.

Movies love showing a riverside view of Foggy Bottom, with its iconic landmarks like the Watergate, The John F. Kennedy Center for the Performing Arts, and the Memorial Bridge. One of the city's oldest neighborhoods plays host to receptions at the U.S. State Department, watches lobbyists peddle influence, and university students scurry between classes.

Garrett loves this area of the city. While he meets with associates and lobbyists at the Capitalist Pig Chophouse, he prefers to dine with friends at this decades-old bistro. High Steaks Drama is one of the city's best steakhouses, which is why the senator finds himself here so often.

The problem with being a regular anywhere is that you can also be found. For most people, that isn't a problem. For anyone in the public eye, it's a constant nuisance.

"Senator Turner, would you mind if I ask you a couple of questions?" the reporter asks as Garrett puts on his raincoat in the foyer.

"Buzz off, Triggs. I have nothing to say to you or to the *Herald*."

"C'mon, Senator. Don't tell me that you are still bitter about that last article."

"You mean your last hit job?" Garrett asks, sneering.

"It was an accurate piece."

"No, it was an anonymously sourced pile of lies that any decent journalist or media outlet would never have published. Which, of course, is why the *Herald* did."

Justin covers his heart with his hands and dons a dour look. "That hurts."

"Good Night, Justin," the senator says, walking away.

"Are you using the death of the vice president's son to force the resignation of Senator Colby Washington?"

Garrett stops at the reporter's announcement to everyone standing in the foyer. Conversation stops, and the gaggle waiting to be seated stares at the two men. The senator forces a smile, turns, and takes a few determined steps toward Triggs.

"I know that good journalism died with disco, but you're bringing its malpractice to a new level."

"I'm just going off the information I received."

"Yeah, I have an anonymous source that told me all about your affinity for child pornography. See? I can make stuff up, too."

Justin smirks. Senator Turner matched the volume of his original question, and the foyer once again falls silent. He appreciates a man who plays hardball.

"My source is undisclosed but hardly anonymous. Can you answer the question, Senator? Are you using the existence of this traitor for political purposes?"

"I have no interest in forcing anyone's recognition. That said, I think that Senator Washington should resign for the good of the American people and the brave soldiers we put in harm's way over there."

"Yeah. So, you're denying that you are creating an atmosphere that would force the issue?"

The president, DNI Troxell, and both the House and Senate Intelligence Committee leadership have already done that. Our soldiers are being killed, the death of the VP's son is dominating the news, and sensitive information is still being leaked to our enemies."

"What about—"

"No, now it's my turn to ask a question."

Justin rocks back on his heels. "That's not how this works."

"It is now. All these good people heard me answer your questions, so how about you answer one of mine? Why aren't you asking the president why he isn't bringing the full power of the federal government to bear to find the mole?"

"We are asking that."

The senator shakes his head. "No, you're here grilling me on a non-story. The *Herald* hasn't asked one question about it. In your defense, neither has any other media outlet. We're only talking about national security here. It isn't like it's important."

"Can I quote you on that last part, Senator?"

Garrett wants to knock the smug look off his face. The threat of arrest, assault charges, and a public relations fiasco is the only thing keeping this loser out of an ambulance.

"It's funny, Triggs. You're here accusing me of playing politics. Have you ever stopped to think maybe it's you? Oh, wait. What's right. Journalists never choose sides, right?"

The small group around them scoffs and offer sarcastic chuckles. Regardless of political ideology, everyone knows that there is no such thing as an unbiased reporter. Triggs knows it as well.

The senator slaps him on the shoulder and heads out the door. The media has never given him a fair shake. It doesn't matter if the accusations happen to be true in this instance. National security was politicized decades ago. The media helped establish those rules. They are just mad that he is playing the game the way they set it up.

The longer it takes the president and intelligence community to find the mole, the better. Unfortunately, that ineptitude isn't likely to last forever. The good thing is that he doesn't need it to. Abril Lopez just needs to do her job. When the time comes, he has the perfect scapegoat in mind to occupy everyone's attention long enough to matter.

CHAPTER THIRTY-NINE
EUGENE "BOSTON" HOLLINGER

DR. TARA WINTERS'S RESIDENCE
ADAMS MORGAN, WASHINGTON, D.C.

Despite being wired, I can feel my eyelids getting heavy. Tara has only one guest bedroom, so the three guys drew straws to determine the sleeping arrangements. I won, and Maryland ended up with the couch. Louisiana drew the shortest straw and the recliner in the corner, which is probably an upgrade from where he is used to crashing out.

In the low light of the room, I can still make out the closet door. That was what the intruder was hiding in. The thought is still alarming, especially knowing that he may still be around. As the thought fades from my consciousness, I feel myself slipping into sleep.

* * *

I am sitting in a chair at a desk with something hard pressed against my head. Through the haze, I can see the décor of an office. Despite my best efforts, I can't make any of it out. I do feel the discomfort of something hard and plastic pressed against my face.

"Your job is to follow the directions you're given," I hear myself say.

"I understand that, but if he's making a move, why not let him travel down the road a little and see what happens? He has the most to lose if he gets caught."

"Because lives are at stake, that's why. No, this can't wait any longer."

"This is a gutsy play, Colby. You're talking about committing a crime. Are you sure you don't want to think this over?"

My heart thumps, pushing a rush of adrenalin through my blood stream. Stress causes my head to pound. My eyes stare at the desk, closing for a long moment before reopening.

"No, we need him taken off the board before this gets any worse," I say.

"You understand that once we put this in motion, there is no turning back."

A jolt of electricity shoots up my spine.

"Yes."

"Okay, I will get our assets in place and execute the plan tomorrow."

I'm jolted awake. I fumble for the light on the nightstand and go through my memory exercises, trying to recount every aspect of what I saw in the memory as I reach for a pad and pen. My hand struggles to scribble every detail I remember, committing it to paper until I'm content that I have it all.

I bring the phone to life and see that the time on the lock screen reads seven after two. These dreams don't waste any time coming to the surface anymore. They are frequent, becoming more vivid in their feel, and getting worse.

I take a few breaths to purge the lingering raw emotion I experienced before reviewing my notes. The revelation hits me with the force of a brick. I rip the page from the pad and switch the light off. That forces me to climb into my clothes in the darkness before venturing down the hall to Tara's bedroom.

"Tara?" I say, giving her shoulder a firm but gentle shake. I'm surprised at the softness of her skin.

Her eyes open, and she recoils, tugging the blankets up to her chin as she backs up against the headboard.

"It's okay, Tara, it's only me."

"Boston? You scared me! What are you doing in here?"

"I need you to meet me in the living room. Don't turn on any lights," I say.

"Why? What time is it?" she asks, alarm in her voice.

"Just get dressed and meet me downstairs."

I leave her bedroom and descend the stairs carefully, planting my foot firmly on each tread in the darkness. At the bottom, I head for the front window. Louisiana is already there peering through the slats in the blinds.

"You see him?" Louisiana asks me without so much as a glance when I join him.

"No. What am I looking for?"

"The black BMW on the far side of the street about fifty feet up the block. That's our boy. He's got an expensive ride."

I recognize the car from earlier. It's been here all day and moved several times, but that isn't much of a red flag. It's the kind of vehicle that anyone would expect to be parked in this neighborhood.

"How do you know?"

"The interior light switched on and then back off. You don't think any of Tara's neighbors sleep in their cars, do ya?"

"No, probably not. What are you doing up?" I ask Louisiana.

"Couldn't sleep. As you may have noticed, Maryland has some kickin' sleep apnea," he explains, pointing over his shoulder at the lump on the couch whose guttural snoring could wake a hibernating bear. "What's your excuse?"

"I could sleep."

Louisiana looks at me and smirks. "You have one of those crazy dreams?"

"Yup," I say, holding the piece of paper from the notepad with my scribbles on it.

"What's going on?" Maryland inquires, lifting his head off the decorative sofa pillow. It's a lot quieter in this room now without his operatic rendition of a chainsaw.

"We're watchin' our surveillance watch us," Louisiana explains.

"Have you seen any other movement out there?" I ask.

"No, why?"

"We may be in danger."

The warning grabs Maryland's attention and causes him to sit up on the couch. Tara arrives beside us at the window dressed in only an oversized T-shirt draped over her petite frame. It doesn't ride far down her thighs. I told her to wake up and get dressed, and this one article of clothing is all she managed. It makes me wonder what she was wearing before she got out from under the covers.

"In danger from whom?" she asks.

"Oh, my."

"Shut up, Louisiana," she barks, tugging the shirt down. "What are you guys talking about?"

"I had a memory. It wasn't any clearer than the previous ones, but I know what was said."

"What was it?" Maryland asks nervously.

"A guy was on the phone. He was talking about taking someone out."

"Who?" Tara asks.

"Me."

"He said that?" Maryland asks, rising off the couch and joining us near the window.

"No, not exactly. The man mentioned Gina's name. I think it was the conversation she overheard Colby Washington having before she walked into his office. If I'm right, he was talking to the man sitting in that car."

"We're talking about a U.S. senator, Boston," Maryland protests. "They don't have people break into houses or order people killed."

"I can tell you've never been to Louisiana," the Cajun mumbles. "Bet your ass that our politicians have."

"We need to leave here," I say, getting a nod from Louisiana and a confused look from Tara.

"You're leaving? As in walking out my front door at two in the morning?"

"That would sorta defeat the purpose, sweetie," Louisiana reminds her. "We don't want to be followed."

"We can go out the back," Maryland offers half-heartedly.

"We could, but if they have a guy watching the back door, we might as well take Tara's suggestion and go out the front," I counter.

"All right, grab everything you need," Louisiana says, leaving the window and going over to his black duffel bag. "One of you keep watch out the window."

"What are you doing?" Maryland asks out of genuine concern.

"Heading for the back door to find out. Turn the kitchen light on and off if our surveillance reacts. Give me ten minutes. I've got the perfect thing to get us out of Big Brother's crosshairs."

"There's one more thing. You need to stay here, Tara."

She looks at me, her beautiful eyes appearing wounded. She obviously never considered not going with us.

"Why?"

"Because if you come with us, you'll be implicated. The authorities won't see you as a doctor who works for the VA. They'll only see your complexion and heritage."

"What?"

"He's saying that you're half Iranian, love," Louisiana says, still holding the black bag over his shoulder. "That's enough for these people to be suspicious."

"That's insane! My Persian heritage has nothing to do with this. I haven't done anything wrong, and neither have you."

"A point you can make when they bring you in and question you," Maryland says.

"Unless the man outside isn't a fed."

"What?"

"How many agents do you know that drive sixty-thousand-dollar cars?" Louisiana argues. "That could be a hitman here to kill us for all we know."

"Then there's no chance that I'm staying," Tara says, staring at Boston. "Look, I told you that I'm in this to help you. I meant it. If you guys are going, I'm not staying."

As much as I hate to admit it, Louisiana is right. I don't know what their motives are. Neither of the guys says anything. They made their points, and this has become my decision. I can't even explain the stakes to Tara because I can't fully appreciate them myself. "Taking him off the board" could mean anything. I only know that none of those meanings are good.

I nod at Tara, and we all make our way back through the darkness to prepare for our escape.

CHAPTER FORTY
SPECIAL AGENT ZACH FORTE

OUTSIDE DR. TARA WINTERS'S RESIDENCE
ADAMS MORGAN, WASHINGTON, D.C.

The ringing phone jolts Zach in his seat. He scans the area around the car and then stares out the windshield. Everything on the street is perfectly still. With almost no sleep in the past couple of days, he dozed off. He snatches the phone from the passenger seat and answers it before the call gets sent to voicemail.

"Yeah?"

"It took you long enough to answer. You'd better not be sleeping," Grimman warns.

"I wasn't," Zach says, rubbing his eyes with his other hand. "The phone was buried under fast-food wrappers."

"I don't care. Is anything going on there?"

"It's two-thirty in the morning. These guys aren't nocturnal. Nothing is going on here. Do you ever sleep?"

"Nothing more to report?"

"The house has been quiet since Williams showed up. They all crashed out for the night hours ago."

"They're cooking something up."

"Based on what evidence?" Zach asks.

"Two men with SCI clearances, a criminal facilitator, and an Iranian doctor all having a slumber party? Do I need to connect the dots for you? Stay on your toes. Things are progressing as planned on this end."

"Progressing, how?" Zach asks, still determined to understand the endgame.

"That's not your concern."

Zach strokes his chin. There isn't an FBI agent on Earth who likes being kept in the dark. Whether this is an official assignment or not, he should at least be briefed on its objectives. Grimman won't even give him that much.

He read the file he stole before giving it to Remsen. It was medical notes about head trauma following Hollinger's auto accident. There is nothing about this group that smells like treason, despite some of their odd behavior.

Zach is about to press Grimman for more when he sees someone emerge from the front door. It looks like Boston is leading the doctor and Eric Williams straight for the doctor's car.

"Hold on a second. There's some activity here."

"What's going on?"

He studies their body language and watches their heads. They aren't scanning the street or acting nervous like anyone who suspected they're being watched would. Even the doctor is acting normal. Where the hell are they going at this hour?

"They're leaving the house."

"How did you miss that?" Grimman asks.

"I didn't miss anything. They never turned a light on. Three of them are climbing into the doctor's SUV."

"What's the fourth guy doing?"

Zach was so fixated on the car that he never searched for the fourth target. A glint of movement in his windshield corrects that error. Someone is walking in the street straight toward him. They can't have known the house was being watched, much less by him.

"I have to go," Zach says, ending the call with an impatient Grimman and dropping the phone in the passenger seat.

He sinks behind the steering wheel, hoping that the figure is just out for a stroll. He knows better. Hollinger pulls the doctor's SUV out of its spot and flips on the headlights, bathing the street in more unwelcome light. The car inches slowly out of the space along the curb and faces Zach's BMW with the high beams on. There is no hiding how.

The guy he assumes is Louisiana is only fifteen feet away when Zach notices something in his hand. He leans forward toward the windshield, trying to fight the glare from the SUV's bright LEDs.

"Aw, to hell with it," Zach mutters as he feels for the reassuring steel of his weapon and checks for his badge. He reaches for the door handle when the man slaps the top of the cylindrical object and breaks into a sprint. Louisiana covers the distance to Zach's BMW in a flash and slams the coffee can-sized metal device onto the center of the hood.

"Rilleux."

He smiles, the grin apparent even while being backlit from the headlights. Zach fumbles for the door handle when the windshield in front of him explodes in white light as the device erupts on the hood. Flash blindness sets in as Zach's dilated pupils fail to defend his retinas from oversaturation. Sparks fly everywhere from the front of his car. He can feel the intense heat through the windshield as he reflexively tries to shield himself.

"Holy shit!"

Zach struggles to exit the car as the device burns through the hood and begins to melt the engine block. It's the kind of pyrotechnic show you only get with thermite. Zach retreats to the rear of his car and draws his weapon. Louisiana is living up to his reputation. Whether they are spies or not, that was a crime.

The doctor's little red SUV does a U-turn in the street, and Louisiana jumps into the back seat. Zach starts to run towards their SUV some fifty feet ahead as his vision returns to normal. The blistering heat coming from the device forces him to take a circular route around his melting car.

"You're not getting away that easy!" Zach screams as lights switch on in the townhouses that line the street. The thermite is bright enough to turn night into day and cause the paint on nearby cars to bubble. They will eventually succumb to the heat the thermite is throwing off.

The SUV begins to accelerate down the street. Zach isn't going to reach it in time to stop them. In a fit of rage, he settles for the next best thing. He adopts a perfect shooting stance and levels his weapon. The agent lines the sights of his SIG Sauer on the back of the car and squeezes the trigger. He fires one round…then another…and then a third. The rear window of the SUV explodes as Zach adjusts his aim slightly.

CHAPTER FORTY-ONE
"BOSTON" HOLLINGER

DR. TARA WINTERS'S RESIDENCE
ADAMS MORGAN, WASHINGTON, D.C.

The back window shatters, showering glass on Tara and Louisiana. Both duck behind the seat, not that it provides them any protection. Tara screams at the top of her lungs as Louisiana pokes his head between the two front seats.

"Gents, I do believe he's shooting at us," he observes calmly.

"Thank you, Captain Obvious!" Maryland yells in the more expected panicked tone.

I stomp on the accelerator and glance in the rearview mirror.

"Louisiana, I hope you have another idea!" I exclaim as I slam the gas pedal to the floorboards, willing the little SUV to gain some speed.

"Actually, I do."

I look down to see Louisiana holding up a small black device in his hand. He gives me an impish grin and presses a button. The car, already an inferno in the front, bounces in the air as an explosion rocks the rear end. The roar is deafening, and the guy shooting at us only a moment ago is hurled forward and lands face down in the street.

"You're all crazy!" Tara screams from the back.

I watch as the fireball billows into the air and then dissipates quickly. The BMW is now a smoldering wreck. The owners of the cars parked around it will have quite a story to tell their insurance adjusters. Maryland's mouth is hanging open in shock.

"I bet you didn't see that shit in your dreams, did ya, Boston! Spa-doosh!" Louisiana shouts in glee as he slaps my shoulder.

"I only dream about stuff that's already happened, you reckless moron!"

"What the hell was that?" Maryland shouts.

"Plan B."

"Plan B? You call that a plan?"

"Okay, maybe I used a touch too much plastic explosive."

"I told you to disable it, Louisiana, not destroy it," I say, pushing the SUV onto a cross street to get out of sight of our assailant.

"Tomato, to-mah-to."

I make a couple of quick turns. In a part of the city with this much money, police response is measured in seconds, not minutes. The wail of sirens heading in the direction of Tara's house is already growing louder.

I don't know if the guy watching us will stick around to have a discussion with the first responders. Regardless, the neighbors probably saw us pull away. In minutes, the entire city will be looking for Tara's little red SUV. I need to put some significant distance between us and that explosion, and I need to do it fast.

"Your dumb ass is going to land us all in prison!" Maryland shouts, along with a couple other comments I don't hear. He's only moments away from really freaking out about this, so I need something constructive for him to do.

"How's Tara doing back there?" I ask, unable to see her in the rearview mirror. Her screaming and cursing stopped a few moments ago.

"She's curled up in a ball and looks pretty upset," Louisiana reports.

"Then look after her."

"You know I'm not really the touchy-feely support type, right?"

"Just do it."

Louisiana complies, giving me a moment with my distressed friend in the passenger seat.

"Look, Maryland, I—"

"I don't want to talk about it right now," he interrupts. "Let's just not get caught by the police in the next ten minutes and give me a chance to collect my thoughts."

I respect Maryland's decision and pull out my phone to make a call. I know I'm driving and will get chastised by Maryland for it, but it's the least severe of the laws we've broken tonight.

"If they're watching us, there's a pretty good chance they're monitoring that," Maryland warns as I select the number and put the phone up against my ear.

"We have no choice. I'll keep it quick and vague."

"Hello?" Gina asks groggily on the other end of the line.

"Hi, sweetie. I'm sorry to wake you up, but we're in a bit of trouble."

CHAPTER FORTY-TWO
ERIC "MARYLAND" WILLIAMS

IVY CITY NEIGHBORHOOD
WASHINGTON, D.C.

Boston hangs up the phone, having made the most awkward call he's ever dialed. No fiancée would respond well to her betrothed being out on the lam and hunted by a massive police force. Maryland agreed that they were being watched and likely in danger. That feeling was validated when the man shot at them as they fled. Then again, if someone destroyed his car, he would react the same way.

"Are you done with that phone?" Maryland asks when Boston finishes making his arrangements with Gina.

"Yeah, why?"

"They can track it, Boston," Maryland says, holding out his hand.

Boston surrenders it without protest, and he rolls down the passenger window and tosses it out. He fishes through his pocket and does the same with his own.

"Yours too, Louisiana."

"I'll take care of my own, thanks. My love?"

"You've already ruined my life tonight, asshole! You're not getting my phone, too. I'll turn it off."

"The Feds can still access it. Within thirty seconds, they'll have our location. Five minutes later, we'll be in cuffs," Maryland explains. "Hand him your phone, Tara, please."

She crosses her arms and looks out the window as the sleepy city passes us by.

"No."

"Tara, we need—"

"Why would they track it? Was that guy part of the government or not? You said he was there to kill us. The government can't do that. We did nothing wrong!"

The three men share glances with each other. All of that is true. Either this is a rogue operation, or even more terrifying, something else entirely.

"We can figure out the who and why later," Boston says. "We blew up a car."

"The idiot next to me blew it up. I didn't do anything!"

"Regardless, everyone is going to be looking for us. Maryland is right. We need to ditch our phones. *All* of them."

Former National Security Agency contractor Edward Snowden released classified information about government surveillance capabilities publicly that many in the intelligence community knew for years. Among his disclosures was how the NSA uses internal GPS to track the movements of individuals. They gather nearly five billion records a day and store the information in a vast database. What most people don't know is that they can do it in real-time.

Tara hands Louisiana her phone. He turns and tosses their devices out the shattered back window into the middle of New York Avenue.

"Hey Bos, this don't look like D.C. anymore."

"Most of D.C. isn't white marble and ionic columns that you see on the news. This is Ivy City. It's one of the poorer areas of the district."

Ivy City is an industrial neighborhood dominated by warehouses and an Amtrak rail yard. D.C. politicians love to gush about the revitalization of the area that accompanied an influx of nightclubs and young professionals seeking less expensive housing in the district. It's smoke and mirrors. The neighborhood is basically a ghetto that ranks as one of the most dangerous parts of the city.

"My kind of area. It looks like a good place to pick up a new ride."

"He's right," Boston says. "We need to get off New York Avenue. We probably have a BOLO on us by now."

"I'm done with this. Let me out of the car!" Tara demands.

"What?"

"You heard me! I said, let me out."

"Tara, I understand you're upset," Boston says, "but if you think that I'm going to drop you off in this part of town, you're crazy."

Boston's declaration placates Tara long enough for her to notice the run-down warehouses and homes with bars on the windows. This is not an area that a beautiful young woman should be walking around alone in at oh-dark-thirty in the morning.

"I'll get out with her," Maryland says. "I don't want to be a part of this any more than she does."

"We ain't droppin' two women off either."

"Shut it, Louisiana."

"Everybody calm down. Let's take this one step at a time. The first involves getting a new car. Once we're out of immediate danger of ending up in a cell tonight, we can talk this over. If you guys still want out, so be it."

Tara doesn't react in the back seat. Her arms are still welded across her chest, and she's frozen like a statue. Maryland doesn't agree with the plan, but he doesn't argue against it, either. He just shakes his head.

"Make a left at the corner and stop the car, bro. I know where I can get us a new ride," Louisiana says, pointing back to a sign on the brick wall of the warehouse we just passed.

"And just how are you going to do that? Ask someone politely for their keys?" Tara asks, burning anger causing her nostrils to flare.

"Boston, who comes from Louisiana?"

"Gypsies and thieves."

"That's right. Gypsies and thieves," Louisiana repeats.

"Unbelievable," Tara mutters.

Boston brings the SUV to a stop at the curb alongside the faded red brick wall of a warehouse. Louisiana jumps out of the vehicle, shuffles down the dimly lit street, and disappears around the corner. Boston kills the engine and gets out of the car to pace back and forth along the wall. Maryland joins him after ten excruciating minutes crawl by.

"Forget the authorities, Boston. If we stay here much longer, we're going to get ourselves shot. We need to get the hell out of here."

The words are barely out of Maryland's mouth when one of the ugliest cars ever made comes around the corner and stops alongside them. Louisiana puts the vehicle in park and rolls down the window. Boston lets out a little laugh, but Maryland doesn't find it funny at all.

"You stole a nineteen eighties Mercury Sable?"

"I didn't steal it. I reappropriated it," Louisiana says, gesturing at the ridiculous-looking beige car complete with the peeling paint and less than graceful lines.

"You couldn't have picked something from this century?"

"We don't want anythin' with GPS. Besides, it will be weeks before anyone even realizes it's gone, assuming they even care."

"What are we going to do with my car?" Tara asks as she emerges from the back of her SUV.

"You have insurance, right?" Louisiana asks.

"You think this is funny?" Her tone is now something even more dangerous than rage—it's simmering anger just waiting for a release.

"I'm really sorry about this, Tara. If I'd known—"

"Don't! Don't even talk to me right now. You're all certifiably nuts."

"Don't lump me in with them," Maryland mumbles.

"Thanks for the vote of confidence, buddy," Louisiana groans from the driver's seat of the goober mobile.

"We need to find a place to hole up for a while," Boston says, trying to look ahead. "The city is full of cheap motels."

"Hotels will be the first places they check."

"It pains me to ever agree with Maryland, but he's right," Louisiana says. "We need a flophouse off the grid."

"I have a friend," Tara grumbles, looking down as her head shakes in disbelief. "She's out of the country. I've been looking after her place, so the neighbors won't be suspicious. We can go there."

"Where?" I ask.

"S Street, Northwest. Near Logan Circle."

"Great. Right back into the lion's cage."

"We can park behind the house. Besides, they won't be looking for us in this…car. I thought you were—"

"If I'm going to prison, it won't be after living some *Dateline* cliché where a SWAT team busts down the door of a twenty-dollar-a-night motel room."

Sirens blare somewhere off in the distance, causing all of them to stop talking. None except Louisiana have ever been on the wrong side of the law, less a small infraction or two most high school kids find themselves tangled up in. This isn't one of those.

"I hate to be a nudge, but we really should be going."

"Yeah, all right. We just need to make a quick stop. Gina is bringing us some necessities. I arranged to meet her."

"She had better be bringing booze," Louisiana interjects from the front.

Tara nods slowly from the back seat as she stares out the window. If there is a silver lining in any of this, we've had a breakthrough. For the first time since they met, Tara found something she can agree on with Louisiana.

CHAPTER FORTY-THREE
SPECIAL AGENT ZACH FORTE

OUTSIDE DR. TARA WINTERS'S RESIDENCE
ADAMS MORGAN, WASHINGTON, D.C.

Zach is going to have a lot of explaining to do. The police arrive to find him lying dazed in the middle of the residential street. Cautious, they treat him like a victim of whatever transpired. Everything changes when they see his gun.

The restraints get slapped on, and several officers babysit him as fire crews arrive in force. The police secure the scene and begin the process of interviewing neighbors. They find Zach's badge once he is searched, and a severe-looking sergeant steps away to confirm his identity. Still cuffed, he is escorted to a waiting ambulance to get checked out by a pair of EMTs. He's okay but is going to be sore for a while.

"Your story seems to check out, Special Agent Forte," the uniformed Metro Police sergeant tells him. "Your colleagues in the FBI are on the way. They should be here at any moment. Just sit tight until we get this sorted out."

"All right, thanks."

The cuffs are removed as he watches the firefighters continue to douse the parked cars. The flames are out, their light replaced by a myriad of red and blue strobes that bounce of the facades of the swanky townhouses that line the normally quiet Washington street.

Zach will find it problematic to explain why he discharged his weapon three times at the fleeing SUV. The justification would be less of a chore had this been a sanctioned FBI operation. It isn't, and the man who will have to answer for this is approaching him like an angry badger.

"What the hell were you thinking?" Grimman asks, clearly struggling to restrain the volume of his voice despite his anger. "This is a surveillance mission. Look at this mess!"

Grimman makes a sweeping arc with his arm at the chaotic scene around them. Zach doesn't need to see it. He lived it.

"They attacked me, Tom. He set off an incendiary device on my car with me inside it."

"I don't care. You got out. You weren't shot at, yet you opened fire on a fleeing vehicle."

"Would you have rather had me call for support?" Zach asks, offering a smug grin to let his boss know that he knows the answer.

"Under normal circumstances, this would cost you your badge and the train wreck you call a career. Fortunately for you, this incident provided us the answer we were searching for."

"What are you talking about?"

"Hollinger. Innocent people don't blow up cars and run from the law. He's mentally unstable and likely the leak we're looking for. After tonight's escapades, it also confirms that Eric Williams is involved as a coconspirator."

Zach turns away. It's a load of crap. Whether it's true or not, nothing that happened tonight proves anything. There was no good reason for them to destroy his car, but it doesn't mean they're traitors. It's a question he'll be sure to ask when he finds them. Then he's going to hunt for and find the pudgy one who used the thermite to melt his BMW, and he'll cut his balls off.

"Excuse me, gentlemen," the Metro Police sergeant interrupts, giving Grimman the onceover.

"Tom Grimman, Supervisory Special Agent, FBI Counterintelligence Division. Agent Forte reports to me."

Grimman doesn't like dealing with law enforcement or agencies outside of the Bureau. He hates the CIA, despises local police, and doesn't play nice with the rest of the federal alphabet soup agencies. The officer no doubt senses that from the tone of his introduction.

"Your engine block was melted by some sort of homemade thermite grenade. The explosion wasn't caused by the fire reaching the fuel tank, though. An explosive device was attached to the underside of your vehicle."

"What kind of explosive?"

"Still undetermined. We're still collecting evidence for the lab. We will know once they issue a report, but it's likely a plastic explosive. We did find the remnants of a cell phone detonator. We may have questions for you later, but you're free to go, Special Agent Forte."

"Thank you, sergeant," Grimman says with a nod before he walks off. "It's only a matter of time before the director hears about this debacle. That will be a fun conversation. Go home, Zach. Your work for me is complete."

"What?"

"You heard me. You're done. Hollinger and his friends just became the prime suspects as the leak. By dawn, every agency and law enforcement outfit will be combing the city for him. I don't need you anymore and don't want the liability of keeping you around. So, go home."

Zach is about to argue when Grimman's phone rings. He fishes it out of his jacket pocket and walks off without another word to his subordinate.

"Director Weisz, I was just about to call you. We have some developments…"

"When I told you to continue conducting surveillance, it didn't mean that you should open fire in a residential neighborhood," Remsen says, emerging from beside the ambulance.

"I see you're maintaining a nice, low profile. How long have you been here?" Zach asks, surprised to see him.

"Long enough. You fired your weapon?"

"Yeah, I was pissed, so spare me the lecture. They blew up my car. Specifically, the guy they call 'Louisiana' did."

"These guys and their names," Remsen mutters. "Vaughn Rilleux was honorably discharged after serving three tours as an Army combat engineer."

"I know. I read his military personnel file. He's an asshole."

"Yeah, probably. You didn't see the rest of his record. Rilleux is a notorious 'fixer' for criminal enterprises with a penchant for using explosives. He's been implicated in a dozen crimes of varying severity down in New Orleans."

Zach glares at Remsen. "That would have been useful information a half hour ago."

"Grimman knew. Now you do. Do you think that this Louisiana character joined Boston in trafficking information to score a bigger payday?"

"No. It still sounds like a stretch to me. Are you telling me that Watchtower thinks he is?"

"Honestly, the likelihood that he's somehow involved moved up a couple of notches, but we don't know for sure."

"Is there more to this that you're not telling me?"

"Yeah. Did you read the file you took from Dr. Winters before you handed it to us?" Matt asks, causing Zach to perk up.

"I scanned it. It was medical mumbo jumbo."

"It is much more than that, it appears. I'll send you the details. In the meantime, I need you to find Hollinger and his friends before Grimman does. The FBI is getting their marching orders from senators on the Hill, eager for them to name a suspect. We have information that they are enlisting the media to help with that. After tonight, they'll do just that."

"By senators, you mean Garrett Turner?"

"The one and only. Watchtower doesn't know what Turner's motivations are, but they're likely political. To find the real traitor, I need you to find Hollinger before anyone else does. You can use my car."

Remsen hands over a set of keys as Zach shakes his head. "Any more miracles you want me to conjure up?"

"Yeah, restore your car to working condition instead of letting it look like a giant s'more."

"You're hilarious, Matt," Zach says as his friend disappears back around the side of the ambulance.

It's time to get back to work. The only question is where to start.

CHAPTER FORTY-FOUR

GINA ATTISON

MARYLAND AVENUE NE
WASHINGTON, D.C.

Gina closes her eyes briefly before returning them to the road as her phone rings for the tenth time since she left the house. She doesn't need to check the caller ID to know who is blowing her phone up. She also knows that the clock is ticking and she can't ignore it forever.

She steers her Audi onto Maryland Avenue and heads away from the Capitol Building to the northeast. It's less than ten minutes to the meeting place where she agreed to meet Boston. As seething mad as she is, Gina needs to do what she can to help. This is about to turn into a witch hunt, and there is only one group in America capable of keeping the FBI honest.

"Hello?" the groggy voice answers after she selects a number and dials from her cell before pumping the call through her car's handsfree.

"Hello, Justin."

"Jesus, Gina, it's three in the morning," he says, no doubt checking his phone to see who is calling.

"Weren't you the one who once told me that the news never sleeps?"

"Yeah, but that was during the day and after coffee."

"Turn your coffee maker on. You're going to want to hear this. Remember how you are always plugging me for information coming out of the SSCI?"

Justin moans. "I remember how you always turn me down. How do you put it? The thought of betraying my country to enrich the media nauseates me, or something like that?"

Gina checks her rearview mirror. The traffic is light, and anybody tailing her would be easy enough to spot. Just to be sure, she suddenly pulls into a retail store that's closed and makes a U-turn in the parking lot. The move is a simple yet effective countersurveillance technique. The handful of cars behind her drive by. Content that she isn't being followed, Gina pulls back onto the road.

"The thought still nauseates me, but the situation has changed. The FBI is about to name a person of interest in the Syrian leaks."

"You have my attention," the voice perks up. "Who?"

"I'm not going to say. You have sources in the FBI. They can tell you."

Justin sighs, and Gina can almost sense that he is rolling his eyes at her. Journalists used to take pride in uncovering facts and informing the American public. Now they just want to sit at their keyboards, write their articles, and take victory laps about how many clicks and shares they get on social media.

"Okay, so why are you calling?" Justin asks.

"Because it's a frame. Members of the Senate are pressuring the FBI to uncover the leak, and they are offering up a sacrificial lamb."

"How do you know that?"

"Let's just say that I know who they're after. Their accusations lack credibility and hard evidence."

"Okay, assuming you're qualified to make that judgment, is this a political gambit by Garrett Turner to get Senator Washington to resign from the intelligence committee and even the Senate?"

Now it's Gina's turn to be surprised. Maybe Justin isn't as lazy as she thought he was. Not that she shouldn't know better. She just ran into him yesterday digging around Capitol Hill with his shovel.

"Turner is leveraging the lack of committee oversight and failings of the intelligence community to attack the opposition party and the president. That much is true. I believe that the FBI's search for a scapegoat is coming from someone else."

"Who?"

"Colby Washington."

The words have weight. Justin knows that Gina is a high-level member of his staff and would be positioned to know if that were the case.

"That's a hell of an accusation. One that I highly doubt is true."

"It's also front-page material. Go ahead and ask him the question."

"Fine. I will. Are you attributable?"

"That's a stupid question. Call me a 'high-placed staffer on Capitol Hill' only."

"That's not good enough. I use your name, or you hand me additional sources, Gina," Justin demands.

"Your paper has printed countless stories using anonymous sources hundreds of times in the past. Don't hide behind the shield of journalistic integrity when we both know that went extinct years ago."

He sighs. Journalists don't like being reminded of the failings of their colleagues or institutions. He also knows better than to argue with her.

"If I need clarification on anything, can I contact you?"

"Yes. Don't contact my office phone. One more thing: this is time-sensitive. The Bureau will make an announcement the moment the suspect is in custody. By then, it is too late to stop an innocent person from having their life destroyed."

"All right, I'll dig into it. Thanks for the scoop…if it pans out."

Gina disconnects the call and takes a deep breath as she reaches the intersection across from the mall. She just made a rash decision and instead would have liked more time to think this through. Unfortunately, with a manhunt already underway for Boston, time is a luxury he can't afford. Neither can she.

CHAPTER FORTY-FIVE
"BOSTON" HOLLINGER

UNION HEIGHTS SHOPPING PLAZA
WASHINGTON, D.C.

I hold my breath when a pair of headlights pulls into the empty parking lot of the shopping center. It's either Gina or unwanted company. The car stops, the driver apparently uncertain where to go. That's a good sign, but it does little to soothe my paranoia.

"Look alive, guys."

Maryland and Louisiana both stare out the back window as the lights approach. Tara is still fuming and couldn't care less. The vehicle pulls up to our beater car in the dimly lit far corner of the triangular lot. Slamming her vehicle in park and killing the headlights, we watch as Gina climbs out. We do the same, Tara joining us only after we have all exited. I'm greeted with a hug by my none too pleased fiancée.

"Are you okay?" she asks.

"Yeah, I'm fine. I'm glad you're here. Are you sure you weren't followed?"

"Positive. Should I be concerned?"

"If they were watching Tara's, it's not a stretch to believe that they have eyes on our house."

The comment causes her to exhale sharply. "I'm just glad you're okay."

"I'm fine too, thanks for askin'."

"Louisiana… I'm happy you're okay, too. It makes it easier to do this."

Gina walks over and smacks him hard across the face with lightning speed. The sound is loud enough to bounce off the façade of the store. Even if he had known it was coming, there was nothing he could do to stop it.

"Gina…" I say as Maryland chuckles.

"Ow, damn, that hurt!" Louisiana exclaims, rubbing his cheek. "I've been slapped before, but only for stuff that I knew I did. What the hell was that for?"

"For being stupid. This is Washington, D.C., dumbass. It's not some backwater parish in the bayou. You can't blow stuff up here without attracting a lot of attention. Everything is terrorism here, and your recklessness just put a big target on everyone's back!"

"All right, everyone needs to calm down," I say, desperate to defuse the situation. "Come with me, honey."

Gina continues to glare at Louisiana and waits for a witty comeback that doesn't come. She doesn't like it when I tell her what to do, but it's welcome in this instance. One misplaced word from him might result in his tongue getting ripped out. She finally pries her eyes off him and joins me behind her car.

"You never should have called him," Gina says. "He's nothing but trouble."

"What's done is done, honey. You can verbally abuse me over it once we're out of this mess. What do you have for me?"

"A change of clothes, the disposable cell phone, and some cash from our emergency fund. And as much as I'm against it, I brought your weapon."

Boston unzips the backpack and begins to inventory the contents. He pulls the SIG Sauer out of the front pocket and does a press check to see if a round is chambered. Content, he slides the weapon and an extra magazine into the pocket of his light windbreaker.

"I hope you're not planning on using that thing," Gina says. "You don't have a concealed carry permit."

"You can add that to the list of laws we've broken in the last ninety minutes. I don't want to use it either, sweetie, but a guy watching us shot at us as we were pulling away. I'm not taking any chances."

"I hope you know what you're doing."

"So do I. Being the subject of a city-wide manhunt is new to me," I lament. "What is this going to mean for your job?"

"I don't know. The senator has been ringing my cell non-stop. At a minimum, I'm going to have some tough questions to answer. You're not the only one with a security clearance. This had better be worth it."

"I hope so."

"No, Boston, you'd better do more than 'hope so'! You'd better know," she says, poking me in the chest for effect. "You're gambling with our future, so you should know the stakes. We can't survive like this. Fix it, or we're through."

"It's not that easy."

"Then tell me why. Why did you let that maniac blow up a car? Why leave that way? Why were you there at all?"

"I thought that Tara was in danger."

"Well, isn't that special," Gina replies with a sneer.

I don't know what is behind her tone, but I don't have the time to go there right now.

"I saw the conversation you overheard."

"What conversation?"

"The one Colby Washington was having on the phone when you were outside the door. I heard the whole thing."

I explain the details of what I heard and why I know it was him. Gina is a little freaked out when I say that I saw her. After a moment, her temperature comes down a little. For the first time, we have a target to focus on.

"You work with him," I say. "Is he capable of setting me up?"

"He's a soldier—"

"Was a soldier. Now he's a politician."

"One who doesn't strike me as the type to go rogue. Of course, I could say the same thing about Hanssen, Ames, or any of America's most notorious double agents. It's the ones you'd never expect who do the most damage. That's why I tipped off Justin Triggs from the *Herald* on the way here."

"That's gutsy."

"If Colby is behind your surveillance, I want to know. Then I'm going to find out why."

I rub my chin. I have learned the hard way that politicians are slimy creatures by nature. They never give you a straight answer and can almost always be counted on to do only what is in their own best interests. Sometimes that aligns with the will of the American people, but often it does not.

Despite my innate disgust having to work with them at times, they are not all bad people. Their perspectives may be skewed from too many years in Washington, but none of them are the evil, caricatured figures you see on shows like *House of Cards*. That view may change if I'm unjustly labeled a traitor for political purposes.

"I'm going to do the same," I say, slinging the backpack over my shoulder.

"Where are you going?"

"It's better if you don't know."

"Boston—"

"You know I'm right, Gina. I'll keep in touch using them to let you know I'm okay. It's better if you don't know anything more that can compromise you when they start asking questions. I've already put your job in jeopardy. I've already put our relationship in jeopardy. I don't want you to have to lie for me any more than necessary."

"Okay," she says, stealing a glance at Tara, who is waiting with the guys over at our stolen car. "You'd better get going. The police are probably already on their way to our place, and it'd be better if I'm there when they arrive."

I share a quick embrace with her before heading back to the car. It was cold, angry, and almost perfunctory. We pull out of the empty parking lot and head in separate directions. It's a metaphor for our relationship right now. She has every right to be upset and angry, but it feels somehow misplaced. There is no doubt that my mind will spend countless hours trying to figure out why.

CHAPTER FORTY-SIX
ERIC "MARYLAND" WILLIAMS

The four fugitives park the sedan in the short driveway and walk in the back door of Tara's friend's house on S Street near Logan Circle. In the fifteen-minute drive from the mall, they crossed paths with three Metro Police squad cars and held their breath with each one. Fortunately, the dragnet that has been cast is likely searching for Tara's red SUV. None showed any interest in stopping them.

Louisiana starts looking through the kitchen cabinets even before Tara closes the back door. The rest of them leave him to his scavenger hunt and head for the living room. Boston looks around with approval, the backpack Gina gave him still slung over his right shoulder. Maryland stands in the middle of the room and stews with his hands in his pockets.

"This should be a good place to hide for a while," Boston observes.

"This broad had better drink!" Louisiana bellows from the kitchen as the sounds of him rummaging through cabinets echo into the living room.

"It's four in the morning, jerk-off! Shut up!" Maryland shouts. "I'm so tired of him."

"What's your problem?" Boston asks, dropping the backpack on the sofa.

Maryland shakes his head, wondering if the question is a serious one. "My problem? My problem? What the hell are we doing? I mean, we're getting shot at, we've got Crazy Harry over there blowing up cars when he isn't stealing them, and you're blind to it all! Even Miss 'I Abhor Violence' over there is playing along."

"Don't drag me into this conversation," Tara mutters, taking a seat on the couch.

"Crazy Harry?" Louisiana asks, returning from the kitchen with a glass of liquor.

"From *The Muppet Show*. He was always using dynamite," Tara explains.

"I only use C-4, jackass."

"Shut up, Louisiana," Boston scolds.

"I'm just sayin', bro. There ain't no problem that can't be solved with generous amounts of plastic explosive," Louisiana says, saluting with his glass before taking a long sip of whatever he found in the liquor cabinet.

"Yeah, you solved a lot of problems with it tonight, didn't you?"

"You got something to say, Maryland?"

"Yeah, I do. None of what happened tonight was necessary. Someone was watching us. So what? Big whoop. Let them watch. We weren't doing anything wrong."

"No, we weren't, but they weren't just watching, were they? Someone broke into Tara's apartment."

"She wasn't *home*, Boston."

"She *came* home, Maryland. The intruder was in her house while she was there. If he was capable of that, what else do you think he's capable of? And then there's what I saw in the dream—"

"You don't even know what you saw! By your own admission, you can't see much and remember even less."

"I had independent confirmation this time. Gina overheard part of the conversation before I even recalled the memory in the dream. It was Colby Washington. I will bet you any amount of money that the man conducting that surveillance is doing so at his request. I will also bet that he didn't have a warrant or any sort of higher approval, assuming he's in the government at all."

Maryland's face contorts in a twisted expression of disbelief. He shakes his head incredulously, wondering if Boston is even listening to the crazy words coming out of his mouth.

"My, God! You can't be this delusional. This isn't a game, Boston. And it's not some damn movie where you can script the ending. This is our lives you're messing with."

"Me? When do you think I volunteered to be a scapegoat? I didn't, and I'll be damned if I'm going to be the sacrificial lamb slaughtered upon the altar of political expediency. Now, I don't know why they're targeting me, but I will not lie down and play dead just so the FBI and their overlords can throw me in a hole and claim victory for the American people."

"Innocent people don't run, Boston. That's what they'll say when they finally catch up with us. You may be willing to sacrifice everything in the futile hope you'll get your answers first, but I'm done with this."

Maryland stands a little straighter. This is as far as he dares go with them. The world will crash in, and only a fool wouldn't feel compelled to get out of here before it's too late to undo the damage. He turns for the front door when a hand grabs his shoulder and spins him around.

"No, you don't."

The aggressive move catches Maryland off-guard. He thought it was Louisiana and is surprised to see Boston right in front of his face.

"Stop me," he says, shoving Boston hard enough to break his grip.

"Now, boys…" Louisiana chides from the entrance to the kitchen.

Boston grabs his friend again, and they lock arms against each other's shoulders. Tara pulls her feet in as they tussle like a pair of MMA fighters in the octagon. Maryland is bigger and stronger and gets the upper hand quickly. He backs him through the room and slams him against the far wall, knocking a framed painting to the ground. Maryland takes his eyes off Boston, providing him the opening he needs.

A cold and hard object presses against the fleshy part underneath his chin. Maryland doesn't need to ask what it is, nor does he strain to see it. Gina brought Boston his gun.

"Whoa," Louisiana blurts out.

Maryland releases his hold, trying to deescalate things. It doesn't work. The SIG Sauer pressed under his chin doesn't budge.

"Go ahead. Pull the trigger. Show these guys how far you'll take this."

Maryland glances over at Tara, who is watching with her hand covering her gaping mouth. Not surprisingly, Louisiana stands next to her, wearing an amused expression. Neither is coming to Maryland's rescue.

"Is either of you going to say something?"

"I wasn't plannin' on it. But if you two boys are done rough housin'—"

"Shut it!" Boston barks.

"Hey, bro, I ain't washin' his brains off the walls. Shoot him if you want, but I say if he wants to go, let him go. He doesn't have the balls for this."

Boston thinks about it for a moment. Finally, he withdraws the gun and gestures towards the door with it. Maryland doesn't waste time making his way over to it. As much as his mind is screaming to get out of this apartment, he stops and turns to Tara. She's a mess. This has been one hell of a night for her.

"If you want out, now's your chance."

She looks around, uncertain as to what to do. She was adamant in the car that Boston let her go, and must know that this is her last opportunity to get off this train before it plummets off a cliff. She takes a long look at Boston before folding her arms across her chest. Maryland shakes his head.

"Okay, suit yourself. Let me give you a word of advice, Tara. These guys are nothing but trouble. Get out while you still can."

He opens the door and leaves without further incident. He scans the street, knowing that there's a Metro station around this area somewhere. The walk will give him a chance to plan his next move. He needs to find a way out of this mess. More importantly, he needs to stop Boston and Louisiana from getting someone killed. If he doesn't act, that's precisely what's going to happen.

CHAPTER FORTY-SEVEN
"BOSTON" HOLLINGER

S STREET APARTMENT
LOGAN CIRCLE, WASHINGTON, D.C.

I run my hand through my hair and crash onto the overstuffed chair in the corner. Emotions stream through me, none of them good. I don't want to admit it, but I'm losing control, not just of the situation, but myself.

"Well, now I just have to get rid of Boston. Then I can finally get some alone time with you," Louisiana whispers to Tara, hopefully only in an attempt to break the tension.

"No such luck, dude, I'm not going anywhere."

"Too bad."

"What's going to happen now?" Tara whispers, uncertainty apparent in her voice. Maryland must have tempted her with his offer. She declined it for reasons I don't fully understand. She's risking her career and maybe even her life by staying here. For better or worse, she's invested in this now.

"It's been a long night. We should get some rest."

"You don't think Maryland will run to the police?" Tara inquires.

"He knows snitches get stitches," the Cajun muses.

"He'll eventually go to the police if he thinks it'll save his own ass. It's all he cares about. But I know him. Right now, he's having a crisis of conscience about it. I don't think he'll give us up immediately."

At least I hope not. Maryland is a fellow soldier and someone I consider a friend, but we're in uncharted territory. Staying in this apartment is a risk, but leaving opens another: we don't have any other place to go.

"What if he does?" Tara presses, probably harboring the same concern.

"Then I'll find somethin' in my bag of tricks for him," Louisiana grumbles, unzipping his duffel bag and inspecting its contents.

"Haven't you done enough damage tonight with your massive explosion?" Tara asks, dumfounded at his nonchalance.

"Massive explosion? Hell, girl, that was a little one."

"Is he serious?" she asks me before turning back to him. "You think that was little?"

"Oh, hell yeah. That was nothing."

I nod, and Tara contemplates that for a moment. "You're completely off your rocker. I'd hate to see how you get rid of someone you really don't like."

"Aw, hell, sweetheart, that's easy. First, you bury two devices in the road about a car length apart. Then you put a third device between them on a short delay and a fourth off to the side…"

"I don't think she was looking for a real explanation," I say, sinking deeper into the chair. I'm spent, and all I really want to do is close my eyes.

"Then she shouldn't have asked."

"I regret it already," Tara mumbles.

"Anyway, the first two bombs lift the car two or three feet off the ground. The force of the third explosion, since it's delayed, catches the edge of the car and flips it," Louisiana says, using his hand to animate for Tara.

"Three explosions sound a little tame for you," Tara goads.

"Aw, hold on now, honey. That's where the fourth explosion comes in. You see, that one's special. On top of the explosive is barbed wire. Nuts, bolts, screws, or things like that also work."

"Barbed wire?"

"Hell yeah! It's my favorite because it's cheap and you're expected to buy a lot of it for, you know, fencing and stuff. It doesn't raise red flags."

"Okay, why the barbed wire?"

I close my eyes and shake my head. She's going to really regret asking that.

"Because, girl, the explosion tears the barbed wire into thousands of tiny pieces that cut through the car, the passenger compartment, and anyone who happens to be unfortunate enough to be sittin' in it."

"What happens to the occupants?"

"It tears them to pieces," I announce, figuring whatever I say will be less graphic than Louisiana's choice of words.

"That's horrible! How could you do that to someone?"

"You can do anything when you hate them enough."

Louisiana is right. Love and hate may be opposites, but they share one common trait: they both make you do things you probably shouldn't.

"Not me. I could never do that," Tara refutes.

"Never?"

"Never."

"You can't be that naïve, Doc. Are you tellin' me that, push comin' to ever-lovin' shove, you couldn't press the button to rid the world of someone genuinely evil?"

"No…never. An eye for an eye leaves everyone blind."

Louisiana shakes his head with disappointment. "Have you ever been in that position before?"

"No. I haven't. Why does it matter?"

"Because it makes the world a much different place. You lose your idealism and realize that sometimes justice only comes from the barrel of a gun. Trust me, Doc, you may be surprised what you can do."

"I hate to break this lovely chat up," I say, putting an end to this before it gets out of hand, "but we have some bigger problems to work through. Maryland was right about these dreams. I need to cut through the fog and see what I'm looking at. That leads to the second problem. I need to remember the details so I can understand what the hell I'm seeing. And all that has to happen fast because time is running out."

"I don't know what to—"

"What the dream machine over there is asking is if there's some chemical help you can provide," Louisiana clarifies. I give her a nod when she looks over at me.

"I uh…I'm not sure. I know some people who specialize in that. I can give one of them a call. He owes me a favor."

Tara disappears into the kitchen, presumably to use her friend's phone. I massage my temples. The adrenalin has worn off, and the stress is taking its toll. I'm a hunted man. Even if we emerge from this, I know life will never be the same. And then there's Gina and her ultimatum.

"I'm surprised she's still helping after what you pulled tonight."

"I'm not," Louisiana deadpans.

"Why would you say that? I've turned out to be nothing but trouble for her since the moment we met at the hospital."

"Well, that's true," Louisiana muses, "but she didn't leave when we were in the ghetto, or when we met your fiancée at the mall, or even a few minutes ago when Maryland stomped out to find a corner somewhere to sulk in. She's strugglin' with what's happenin', but she's stickin' around. There's only one reason I can think of for that."

"She told me it was because she finds what's happening to me fascinating." The comment causes Louisiana to laugh out loud.

I'm not sure what the hell is so damn funny. Considering Tara's initial reaction to me at our first session, the explanation made sense. Or at least it did at the time. A lot has happened since then, and most people would have bailed a long time ago.

"Yeah, I'm sure she's riskin' incarceration to further her career," Louisiana manages to conclude as his laughter ebbs.

"Okay, genius, since you're so in tune with her, why do you think she's still here with us?" I demand. Louisiana scoots to the edge of the couch and leans forward.

"Simple. The doc likes you, bro. The heart makes people act irrationally. It's the only reason any chick would suffer through this shit."

CHAPTER FORTY-EIGHT

GINA ATTISON

Gina gets nothing but strange looks when she walks into Colby's suite at the Russell Senate Office Building. The usually cordial staff greets her with a degree of animosity that makes the hairs on her neck stand upright. It could be because it's just before six in the morning. It's more likely because they heard about what happened last night, and she's persona non grata. News travels fast on Capitol Hill. Bad news travels at light speed.

"Good morning, Gina. The senator would like to have a word with you. Margo will take your things. Please follow me," the chief of staff announces from the doorway.

She hands the staffer her purse and coat and follows him into the senator's office. Colby has his reading glasses on and is scanning the screen of his laptop when they enter. He pulls them off when she enters. The chief of staff closes the door behind them and stands along the back wall.

"Have a seat, Gina."

Gina selects a chair directly in front of the senator's desk. The fact that they aren't sitting on the sofa is telling. Colby uses the comfortable furniture for informal discussions. This is going to be anything but.

"I've been calling you for hours."

"I got here as soon as I could. I was having a conversation with a pair of detectives from the D.C. police."

"About your fiancé's actions last night?" he asks.

"Yes, sir. The police informed me about the allegations, and I told them what I knew, which isn't much."

"Then you haven't spoken to Boston?"

"No, not since yesterday afternoon. I don't know what's going on," Gina says.

She didn't think she sold it, but the senator seems to be convinced. He nods his head and closes his laptop screen.

"You understand that the allegations against your fiancé put me in a rather precarious position."

"I don't see how, sir," Gina says, forcing him out of his comfort zone by making him explain it.

"As chairman of the SSCI, I brought you here to provide guidance and analysis of intelligence matters. How do you think it looks when your fiancé and his friends are accused of blowing up a vehicle in a Washington neighborhood?"

"*Allegedly* blew up a vehicle. And it wasn't a random one for kicks. If I understand correctly what the police told me, it belonged to an FBI agent watching his house. Funny that they couldn't tell me if there was a warrant for that surveillance. Regardless, none of that has anything to do with me."

"I wish that were true, Gina. You're his fiancée. What he does reflects on you, and you reflect on me. You know how this town works. I can't be associated with his actions in any way. I think it's in both of our interests for you to take some time off. It will be a paid leave of absence until this gets sorted out."

Gina leans back in her chair. The senator's reaction isn't unexpected, but it's no less welcome. It's taken her a lot of long hours to earn this position. She has skillfully navigated him through the shark-infested waters of the intelligence committee in the process. She believes that casting her aside now is…disloyal. Unless there is something more to it.

"Is it in both of our interests, or just yours, Senator?"

"Excuse me?" he asks, his voice filled with a mixture of shock and disgust.

"The soldier who got elected to this seat wasn't concerned about appearances. That colonel would have stormed the gates of hell with the men and women under his command, and would never have abandoned one based on an allegation against one of their spouses. The senator that the soldier became once valued the Constitution, the flag, liberty, and individuals' rights.

"Those days are gone. You don't give a damn about why Boston did what he did. I tell you that a federal agency may have violated his constitutional rights, and you respond by telling me I'm no longer welcome here because it's in 'both of our interests.'"

"His constitutional rights? The authorities are this close to calling it a terrorist attack," the senator informs her, complete with displaying a half-inch gap between his index finger and thumb for effect. "Do you have any idea how many laws were broken last night in that stunt they 'allegedly' pulled? Now he and his coconspirators are fugitives, and I'm not entirely convinced that you're not helping them."

"Coconspirators? Are you so eager to pin this leak on someone that you'll settle for any name they give you?"

He slams his hand down on the desk. Now he's as angry as Gina is. That's another rarity in this office. Or for politicians in general around here unless they are posturing for a camera and their constituents back home.

"I resent the implication that I'm playing politics with this. There's nothing I want more than—"

"Who ordered the surveillance on Boston?"

"What? How would I know?"

"Do you think that he's a traitor leaking information to our enemies?"

Colby steals a glance at his chief of staff posted along the back wall of the office. Gina has her answer. That's precisely what he thinks.

"I don't know whether your fiancé is the mole. I pray to God that he isn't. But there's no denying that he's a fugitive and a person of interest wanted for questioning on charges of espionage. Instead of convincing him to turn himself in and set the record straight, you're justifying his actions and questioning mine. That's what this conversation is about."

Gina leans forward in her chair and glares at the senator. Her time here is up. It's a premature ending, but it's time to move on to the next chapter in her life. It's a hard reality for her to accept, but it does provide her with a refreshing sense of freedom.

"This conversation should be about how you are leading the SSCI to pressure intelligence agencies into finding the man leaking classified information to our enemies. How you're pushing the executive branch to provide our counterintelligence agencies with the financial and manpower resources they need. How you are keeping the American people informed and assuring them that the government with whom they've entrusted such matters is up to the task."

"Gina—"

"That's how leaders operate, Senator. It's something that you understood as a soldier and have abandoned as a politician. By indulging in this distraction, you're enabling a cover-up of the death of the vice president's son and countless Americans."

The senator holds her stare. A long moment passes without any words exchanged.

"Gina, I think you need some perspective."

"And you need to get your priorities straight."

"If that's how you feel, time away won't be sufficient. Your services on my staff are no longer required."

"I don't think you deserve them," Gina says, rising out of her chair to leave. "I thought you might have been different than the rest, but you aren't."

"Good day, Gina," the senator says, prompting his chief of staff to open the door behind her.

Gina retrieves her belongings from the office and takes one last look before switching off the light. The symbolism also applies to her career on Capitol Hill. She hasn't been here long enough to be overly sentimental about the space, but part of her will miss working here.

The chief of staff accompanies her to the door while her peers watch in silence. Gina doesn't bother saying good-bye to any of them. Like with the office, she hasn't formed any bonds that require a tearful departure.

"One thing before you go. Don't even think about going to the media with this."

The chief of staff's demand causes her to stop and face him. "You know, of the many things you and the senator have in common, one is more important right now. I don't work for either of you anymore. Don't presume to tell me what I can and can't do."

She fires off a quick look of disgust and heads down the hall and out the doors of the Russell Senate Office Building for probably the last time. Once on the sidewalk, Gina pulls out her phone and opens Snapchat. It may be passe with kids now, but sending texts to a controlled list of recipients is essential right now. The fact that the "snaps" are assigned a time limit for viewing and have a short retention period for devices and the server is a bonus. It's an excellent means by which to communicate with little concern about a paper trail.

Gina types a message and rereads it: *911 - I've been fired. We need to meet ASAP.* Content, she pockets her phone and heads to her car. Just because she's no longer employed doesn't mean she doesn't have work to do.

CHAPTER FORTY-NINE
SPECIAL AGENT ZACH FORTE

IVY CITY
WASHINGTON, D.C.

Zach checks his watch. It's half past six in the morning. It was already a long night, and the coming day doesn't look like it will be any shorter. He turns his attention back to the D.C. police poring over the little red SUV with the shattered back window in search of evidence. They won't find anything.

They picked a good part of town to dump this car in. A few more hours in this spot, and the locals would have stripped it to the frame. He would have found it himself far earlier had the cell phone he used to monitor the tracker placed on the doctor's car survived the thermite-induced conflagration. It was just dumb luck that a squad car happened past here on a domestic violence call and spotted the SUV.

Remsen's car materializes up the street, and Zach wanders over there. "Any news on our fugitives?"

"No. I have our team at Watchtower combing through everything. They've come up empty. You?"

"They dumped the doctor's car in the perfect spot. There isn't a camera anywhere near here, so that's all I know."

"Did they steal one as a replacement?" Matt asks, all businesslike.

"Probably. Uniforms are canvassing the area residences, but people in this part of town aren't cooperative. A couple of units are checking area Metro stations in case they chose a mass transit option. Either way, they're gone for the time being."

"We'll find them, but I have something new for you to do first."

"I hope it includes a shower and a few hours of sleep," Zach says.

"Yeah, after that. I need you to track down Senator Garrett Turner and have a conversation with him."

Zach's head jerks back to regard his friend.

"What for?"

"We have a contact at the *Herald*. An anonymous tip was phoned in early this morning saying that Senator Washington is setting Hollinger and his friends up as patsies to reduce some of the political heat over the leaks."

"God, I hate politics. How solid is your source there?" Zach asks.

"Very. The call was received by Justin Triggs early this morning from a burner phone. We're trying to track it down but aren't holding our breath that it will lead to anything."

"Why would he try to peg the fiancé of one of his staffers as a traitor and risk the blowback?"

"Bingo. He wouldn't."

"Okay, if the tip was about Washington, then why am I talking to Turner?"

"Abril Lopez. We confirmed that he is feeding her information relevant to the investigation," Remsen says.

"How do you know that?"

"You don't want to know. I have a hunch that Turner is using this situation to his advantage by leaking details to the media. I think he may have arranged the tip, and that's borderline obstruction of justice. The two men hate each other, and Hollinger happens to be the fiancé of one of Colby Washington's prized staff members. It's too convenient."

Zach looks back at the agents searching the car. Law enforcement and politics don't mix. They have a job to do, and all elected representatives and bureaucrats manage to do is get in the way.

"Anything else?" Zach asks, shaking his head.

"Yeah, here's a new phone so that you don't have to keep borrowing other people's. Try not to melt this one. Someone from Watchtower will get you Turner's itinerary. Keep me informed of any developments."

"Will do. What about Hollinger and his friends?"

"Law enforcement is looking for them. They aren't going anywhere today. In the meantime, we will forward any information we get. Just get some rest and be ready to move if we need you to. In the meantime, track down Turner and rattle his cage a little."

Matt leaves Zach to stare at the menacing clouds gathering in the distance as the sun begins to light the horizon. The second wave of the storm is rolling in now, and if the often wrong weather forecasters are to be believed, it will be worse than the last. That's a problem for later as Zach walks back over to the police sergeant in charge of the scene.

"We have uniforms checking the video from the closest Metro station. Nothing yet, but I don't think they're going to find anything," the sergeant says in the raspy voice of a heavy ex-smoker.

"I don't either. Have the uniforms canvassing the area come up with anything?"

"Nothing. No cars seem to be missing from area residences." He uses the term loosely in this neighborhood. "Do you think someone they knew picked him up?"

"Possibly, but I don't think they would take the risk. I'm betting a car from somewhere around here is missing. Keep checking."

"Will do."

There is nothing more for Zach to do here. It's time to go catch a couple of hours of sleep, take a shower, and have coffee. He has a feeling that he'll be needing it.

CHAPTER FIFTY
SENATOR GARRETT TURNER

UPPER SENATE PARK
WASHINGTON, D.C.

Senator Turner is doing his best not to look suspicious. He's been loitering here for over twenty minutes when he spots his target walking down the middle of Delaware Avenue along the west side of the Russell Building. The senator heads in that direction, trying to get the timing right. He comes up alongside Colby just as he passes C Street at the northwest corner of the building.

"It's getting late on an ugly day for a stroll in the park, Senator."

"I told the staff I was on the way to Ebenezer's Coffee Shop across from Union Station, so I'd best return with one of their cups."

"Coffee for dinner. That's dedication. I'll walk with you."

"I'd prefer you didn't. It's going to be a late night tonight. What do you want, Garrett?"

"I heard that you fired Gina Attison this morning. Shrewd political move. Still, her fiancé is a traitor, so it probably won't help you."

Colby doesn't bother looking at him. "*Alleged* traitor, unless you know something that I don't."

"Yes, well, I suppose the legal system will have the final word on that. From what I hear, Hollinger made quite the spectacle in Adams Morgan. The media are already on the scent."

"I know. Abril Lopez called a few hours ago with questions about whether I was fingering Hollinger as a mole for political reasons. I don't suppose you know anything about that?"

"I don't," Garrett says.

Colby smirks. The denial was quick and felt rehearsed. He would bet his pension that not only does Garrett know, but he also orchestrated it.

"What about Justin Triggs?"

"Same answer," Garrett says. This time, he wasn't expecting to hear that name.

"It doesn't matter. Tell me why you are talking to me. Is this gloating or something else?"

"I'm here to do you a favor."

"I doubt that."

Garrett grabs his arm, and the men stop walking to face each other in the middle of the park.

"We may be in different parties and on different planets ideologically, but I respect you. You served our country honorably in two wars that I wanted nothing to do with. We owe you a debt, and I want to repay part of it right now."

The country lost its mind following the terrorist attacks on 9/11. In the aftermath of the mourning for those lost came endless questions about how we could have experienced such a catastrophic intelligence failure. The government was determined to make amends. What resulted was decades of war, countless trillions spent, and tens of thousands of lives lost or changed forever.

Colby Washington can't remember a time when America didn't have thousands of troops in harm's way. It's an indictment of our nation's political leadership and one of the reasons he ran for Congress in the first place. He never wants to see so many sacrificed again without a clearly defined vision of what victory looks like.

"I appreciate your words, Garrett. I also know doublespeak when I hear it. What are you here to say?"

"That the Republican leadership is making a move against you. They know about Hollinger and his relationship with Miss Attison. They are pushing the Democrats to remove you."

"From the SSCI?"

"From the Senate."

"And you're telling me this…why?"

"I want you to resign."

"I bet you do. Good evening, Senator."

Colby turns and heads toward the looming hulk of Union Station. Garrett expected him to walk away and matches his quickening gait.

"You've got to be thinking about retirement anyway. You have already dedicated and sacrificed so much. There are going to be inquiries and investigations. You will spend hundreds of thousands of dollars on lawyers to represent you in countless depositions. In the end, all anyone will remember about you is that you were involved in something shady. When your reelection comes up, you will be primaried by a younger, more vibrant progressive and watch from your sofa on election night as your political career goes up in flames."

"Have you been practicing that speech for long?" he asks.

"It's not one I wanted to have to give. Every six years, we get reelected to serve our constituents, or we don't. Political office is a temp job. The only thing we own here is our reputation. The only thing we truly control is the dignity we enter and leave this office with."

Garrett stops walking. He has said what he came to say. The rest is up to his old adversary.

"I enjoy sparring with you, Colby. You're a worthy opponent. That doesn't mean I want you to get destroyed by the end of the war."

"So, my options are to resign in disgrace or be forever dragged through the mud for something I had no involvement in?" Colby asks, stopping and shaking his head. "You're a lousy negotiator, Garrett. If you want to compel me to take action, there needs to be at least one compelling option. If you and your colleagues want my scalp, come and try to take it. I'll be waiting for you."

Colby spins and continues his journey toward the coffee shop. That went as well as Garrett thought it would. Longshots are a great payday when they come in. Unfortunately, by their nature, they rarely do. If he wants Colby to leave his seat, there are other avenues he can take to make that happen.

CHAPTER FIFTY-ONE
"BOSTON" HOLLINGER

S STREET APARTMENT
LOGAN CIRCLE, WASHINGTON, D.C.

It's dark, and there are no people visible. The scene has its usual fuzziness, only it's worse this time. I'm scanning the area. I'm in a structure…a lit sign…I can't read it. My eyes settle on something. I can only make out…a line of cars.

I'm running…or at least walking fast. I stop and feel myself drop something. I reach down to pick it up with my left hand as my right retrieves something bulky from my pocket.

My eyes move quickly to the object and then away. I can't see what it is. It looks like something is attached. A phone? My arm extends under the rear bumper of a car. It's tough to see the color in this lighting. Is it red? The object is gone when my hand returns from underneath. What did I just do? Is it a tracking device?

I stand and walk back the way I came. I see another car. I can't make it out…

I wake up and find myself staring at the ceiling of a strange room. I immediately try to recount the dream, but it was short, and there isn't much to remember. It was dark and fuzzier than the previous ones. I have a vague idea of what was happening but no context to help me understand it. Frustrated, I drag myself out of bed and head downstairs to the living room.

Louisiana has made himself comfortable in the overstuffed chair as he sips a beer and flips through channels on the television. Tara is on the couch, reading over her notes on me. My first meeting with her feels like months ago.

"Did you have a nice nap, Sleeping Beauty?" Louisiana asks when he notices me come into the room.

"Five hours isn't a nap. It's a coma," Tara says with a big smile on her face.

I check the clock on the wall and notice that it's almost a quarter to eight.

"I needed it."

"Ditto, bro. I only woke up an hour ago."

"And you?" I ask Tara.

"I slept with one eye open in case Pepé Le Pew over there decided to get grabby while I slept."

"Hey, now…" Louisiana objects playfully. "So, what's the plan, Bos? I feel like we're in prison. We're public enemy number one and can't hide here forever."

"He's right, Boston. Did you have any memories during your slumber?" Tara asks eagerly.

"Yeah, and I think it was about Louisiana."

"You saw through the eyes of a devilishly handsome and charming Cajun?"

"Oh, please," Tara says, rewarding his comment with a roll of her eyes and a sarcastic snicker.

"Not exactly. I can't remember much of it, but it looked like someone was bugging a car."

"Bugging it?"

"Or placing a tracker on…actually, it might have been explosives. I don't know."

"Explosives?" Louisiana asks with a raised eyebrow.

"Yeah, it was a device of some sort. The whole thing didn't make sense."

"Are you sure it was a memory?"

"It had the same feel to it," I explain, "but it was fuzzier and darker than usual."

"Was it nighttime?"

"No, I don't think so. It was dark, but not that dark."

"I wonder how recent this memory you accessed is. Let's talk through it, and I'll see if I can help you recover lost details," Tara offers.

I explain the dream as I remember it. I don't know if recounting it will help. Everything was distant, fuzzy, and too random. I think I know what I saw, but I can't even be sure of that. The whole thing might have had nothing to do with the mole and everything to do with us. There's no way to be sure.

"What color was the car?" she asks.

"Red, I think."

"Don't think. See it in your mind and answer. Don't rationalize it. You said there was a hand. Describe it."

"It had a glove on."

"What color?"

"Dark."

"Dark isn't a color, Boston."

"I don't know. Black, brown, gray … I didn't see it clearly enough."

I'm frustrated. The answers just aren't coming. I hop off the sofa and begin pacing around the living room. It doesn't help.

"Forget it, guys, this isn't helping."

"I talked to that friend of mine, Boston. He's willing to help us out with trying to make these memories clearer. We can go there tomorrow if you guys think it's safe to venture out."

"He? Don't tell me you have a boyfriend, sweetie," Louisiana pleads in a near panic.

"He wishes."

"We shouldn't be going out, but I'm not sure we have a choice. One of the first things Maryland gives them will be this address."

"Wait a second, bro. Something just occurred to me. You said you saw a red car in that dream of yours?"

"Yeah. I think so."

Louisiana sits up a little straighter and rubs his chin.

"What are you getting at?" Tara asks.

"Was it the back of the car or the front?"

"Uh, back."

The Cajun nods. "It's exactly how I took out the car that belonged to the guy who was watching us. I placed a small block of plastic explosive with a cell phone detonator right next to the gas tank."

"Then I saw you in this memory?"

"His car wasn't red," Louisiana explains. "And I didn't wear gloves. Tara, you said that these dreams are only based on recent events, right?"

"That's my working theory," she affirms. "Short-term memories have a shelf life. It doesn't appear that Boston is accessing long-term ones, or he would have seen the traumatic death of a parent or someone's bad experience in high school."

"Where are you going with this?"

"Bos, someone you know is out there doing the same thing that I did. They are copying my M.O. Now why would they be doing that unless…"

"Unless someone is trying to set us up."

CHAPTER FIFTY-TWO
SPECIAL AGENT ZACH FORTE

CAPITAL GAS & MINI MART
ANACOSTIA, WASHINGTON, D.C.

The problem with following the itinerary of an elected representative is that they often don't stick to one. The dinner Garrett Turner was hosting downtown was canceled at the last minute, leaving Zach scrambling to catch up to his quarry. He got the runaround from Garrett's chief of staff when he requested a meeting, so he decided to take a more direct approach. He had Watchtower give him Turner's personal cell phone number.

"Garrett Turner."

"Senator Turner, this is Special Agent Zachary Forte with the FBI," he says, using both his title and full given name.

"Good evening, Agent Forte. What can I do for you?"

"I've been looking for you all day. We have some developments in the Hollinger case, and I would like to bring you up to speed."

"I get my updates directly from Agent Grimman or Director Weisz."

Alarm bells go off in Zach's brain. He gets updates from Grimman? Since when? And why would the director of counterintelligence be briefing him? It's interesting information, and Zach decides to use it.

"I'm aware, sir. That's part of why I'm reaching out to you directly. I don't believe they are giving you the full picture."

"That's quite an accusation, Agent Forte."

"Yes, sir, it is. And not one I make lightly."

"All right. Make an appointment with my office for tomorrow morning."

"I'm afraid this can't wait. Can we meet briefly? I can come to you."

"Fine. If it's that much of an emergency, I'm about to leave Ferrandino's Restaurant. Do you know the place?"

"Yeah, it's in Anacostia. I can be there in ten minutes."

"I'm about to head north on Minnesota Avenue. I need fuel and will stop at a service station on the corner of Pennsylvania. Let's meet there."

"The corner of Minnesota and Penn Southeast. See you in ten, Senator."

Zach slams on the accelerator and heads for the river. This feels like a wild goose chase. Garrett Turner is a political scumbag in a city full of them. Any conversation with him will be pointless. Even if he is feeding Abril Lopez information or behind the tip to the *Herald* that has the entirety of the Washington media in a tizzy, he's smart enough not to admit it. Matt is a sensible guy, so there must be a reason for it. Too bad he didn't bother providing an explanation.

Seven minutes later, Zach pulls the car into the service station and parks along the small retaining wall next to the snack shop. He takes his seat belt off and scopes out the inside of the store. Despite being only eight o'clock in the evening alongside a busy thoroughfare, he's the gas station's only potential patron. Garrett Turner is nowhere to be found.

He pours himself a coffee and is paying at the counter when the cherry red Ford Mustang pulls up next to a gas pump under the well-lit overhang. Zach shakes his head. It's exactly the car he would expect a flashy politician to drive.

He walks over as Garrett swipes his credit card in the pump. It takes him a couple of tries to get it right. Apparently, the ability to follow simple instructions on paying for gas is not a prerequisite for being elected to the United States Senate.

"Agent Forte?"

"Good evening, Senator. I apologize for the lateness and the short notice of this."

"It's no problem. What is Director Weisz not telling me? Is Hollinger in custody?"

"No, not yet. Do you know Gina Attison?"

Garrett immediately clams up. "Sure. She used to work for the SSCI and then took a job working for the chairman."

"And she's Eugene Hollinger's fiancée."

"Yes, she is. How is that relevant?"

"Senator, you're not a stupid man. The fiancée of the man being investigated for treason is in a relationship with a woman who is a member of your archrival's senior staff."

"I don't think I like your implication, Agent Forte."

"Today's media firestorm about the manhunt was triggered by an anonymous tip to Justin Triggs at the *Herald*. You wouldn't happen to know who made it?"

"You're testing my patience," the senator warns.

"This will go much faster if you quit jousting and answer my question," Zach replies with equal seriousness.

"No, I wouldn't know."

"Would Colby Washington?"

"Not to my knowledge. Why are we having this exercise when you should be out looking for a traitor like Hollinger?"

"*Alleged* traitor, and he is off the grid. He isn't using his phone or credit cards, nor has he been to an ATM. Every law enforcement officer in the city is looking for the late eighties model Mercury Sable he stole from an auto reclamation shop. He will be found, but I'm more interested in talking to you."

"I'm flattered but can't help you any."

"You say that you don't know who spoke to Triggs, but I think it was you. That qualifies as obstruction of justice and interference in a federal investigation."

Garrett glares at the agent when his phone rings. He stops filling his huge tank to fish the device out of his suit jacket.

"Garrett Turner…I'm sorry, who is this?" he asks, his eyebrows scrunching as he presses his phone harder against his ear. "Hold on one second. Let me take this, Agent Forte. If you don't mind, I'll get back with you in a moment."

Forte smirks and offers a nod. He stops and points to the warning placard sticker on the pump.

"You shouldn't use that thing while fueling up."

Garrett waves a dismissive hand. Zach hates being blown off, but the senator will use any excuse to dodge his questions. He's hiding something, and the investigator in him wants to know what almost as bad as he wants to find Hollinger.

"How did you get this number?" he asks the person on the other end of the line as Zach slowly ambles back toward his car. "Okay, what do you want? No, I'm afraid that isn't going to happen. Hollinger—"

Zach knows that Garrett got interrupted but is too far away to hear the conversation. As he thought, the chat with Turner is pointless. Maybe Garrett tipped off the press, and maybe he didn't. It doesn't change anything. He needs to find Hollinger. This whole sordid affair now revolves around him.

The senator is still on the phone as he hangs the pump handle up and turns to tighten his gas cap. Another phone rings from his car, and he bends down near the fender. Zach stands a little more upright.

The world erupts before his eyes. The force of the blast propels him through the air. His limp body hits something hard before he crashes to the hard ground. The heat is blistering as he buries his head to protect it from the debris peppering him. He doesn't dare move, not that he's sure he can.

Another deafening sound precedes the ground shaking. The air fills with acrid smoke, causing Zach to choke as it fills his lungs. His body is starving for oxygen, and his head is throbbing from the aftereffects of the overpressure wave. Both take their toll as he begins to lose consciousness.

The heat and noise that have enveloped the station subside. Zach inches his arms away from his head and strains to gaze back in the direction of the inferno as he senses the worst is over. His vision is fuzzy, but he recognizes that the fluorescent lights illuminating the pumps have been supplanted with a bright orange glow of flames.

The explosion ruptured the gas pumps that are now feeding enormous sheets of flame. In the middle of the conflagration is what remains of the cherry red Ford Mustang, and presumably its distinguished driver.

CHAPTER FIFTY-THREE
ERIC "MARYLAND" WILLIAMS

It only takes Maryland a few loud bangs on the door for Tara to answer. It's after ten, but he doesn't care if the noise wakes up the neighbors. He assumes that Boston and Louisiana sent her to answer it in case the police are calling. A woman might give them a moment of pause before they barge in. It doesn't have that effect on him.

"It's only Maryland," she announces as Maryland brushes past her into the living room. "And he's alone."

The local news on the television in the living room is covering the same story that prompted him to come here in the first place. An explosion of that size in any city would result in a media obsession and encourage the networks to break into their regularly scheduled programs.

"What the hell did you do?" Maryland shouts as Louisiana enters from the kitchen with Boston in tow.

"What are you even doing here, bro?"

"Getting answers."

"How did you get here?" Boston asks calmly.

"Who gives a damn how I got here?"

"We do. If you want answers to whatever questions you have, you're going to tell us what we need to know first."

"How did you get back here, bro?" Louisiana prods, peeking through the curtains covering the picture window.

"I took an Uber."

"With whose app?"

It's a reasonable question. Maryland's phone got tossed out a window and is likely a pulverized mess in the middle of New York Avenue.

"I had a waitress at a diner do it for me. Now, if you're satisfied, it's my turn. You just committed murder," Maryland says, pointing to the destruction at the gas station playing on the television.

"Check yourself, bro. We didn't murder nobody. Why would I blow up another car?"

"It's what you do!"

"It's what I did at the doc's place because I needed to. I didn't need to do that," Louisiana shouts, also pointing at the television. "I've been here all day. Ask them!"

Maryland glances over at Tara, who nods. He doesn't trust her, but she's more believable and innocent than his two friends are right now.

"And where have you been, bro? Police station? FBI?"

"I've been walking around the city."

"You didn't go home?" Boston asks, more out of surprise than as an actual question.

"Well, that wouldn't be the smartest of ideas, would it?"

"You won't ever accuse me of callin' you smart," Louisiana deadpans.

"Shut up, you psycho," Maryland blurts out.

"Psycho?"

"Yeah, psycho. Are you deaf or plain dumb? Do you know who died in that explosion? Garrett Turner!"

"What? Senator Turner's dead?" The look of incredulous disbelief on Boston's face would be nearly impossible to duplicate by an Oscar-winning actor. He legitimately didn't know.

"How do you know who it was?" Louisiana asks.

"I'm in the DIA, moron. We make it our business to know things before they're splashed all over the news.

"Whoa," Boston says, sitting down on the sofa with his head in his hands.

"The dream?" Louisiana asks, eliciting a nod.

"What dream?"

"What do you care? You bailed on us. You shouldn't even be here."

"Excuse me for thinking there isn't more than one lunatic running around this city with plastic explosives."

Boston absolutely had no knowledge of it, and Maryland doesn't think that Tara would lie about Louisiana's whereabouts. She abhors violence and would never condone a murder.

"Someone out there who knows about what happened last night and is using it to set us up."

"You can't be serious?"

"Boston had another memory, Maryland," Tara offers from across the room. She moved there to steer clear of the carnage in case this turned into something physical. "It was this afternoon and showed someone affixing a device to a red car."

"It made no sense at the time. Now that I have context…everybody on the Hill knows that Garrett drives that red mid-life crisis car. That's what I saw in the memory. I must know whoever killed him."

Maryland has heard enough. Boston's dreams, or memories, have become the bane of his existence. Whether he saw what happened is irrelevant. The bomber might be the other man in the room. The police need to hear this before something else tragic happens. If they won't turn themselves in, that's their decision. His is made, and he turns for the door.

"You're all ridiculous!" Maryland says, heading for the door. "I don't want to hear about your damn dreams again."

"Oh, look, he's leaving again. Shocker."

"Where are you going, Maryland?"

"To do what I should have done the first time I left here. I'm going to the police—"

"You can't do that," Boston states.

"What are you going to do? Shoot me in the back as I leave?"

"Give me the gun, Boston. I'll do it," Louisiana offers eagerly.

"Nobody is shooting anybody. Everyone calm down," Tara interjects, now sincerely worried that this could escalate into something else she doesn't want to be a part of.

"Maryland, why are ya dressed like a ninja?" Louisiana asks, his head cocked to one side.

The three of them give their friend the onceover with their eyes. He has changed, donning black workout clothes that make him look like a thug.

"They were all I could afford with the cash on me, thanks to you clowns."

"Boston, what color were the clothes in the dream?"

"Oh, the hell with this. You want to accuse me of something, go for it. I'm heading over to the FBI. They can ask me themselves."

"You know, screw this, I have a tranquilizer gun somewhere in this bag," Louisiana declares as he starts digging through his black duffel bag of goodies.

"We're not going to drug him," Boston says, stopping Louisiana.

"Damn."

"We're being framed, Maryland. All of us. You're caught up in this, too."

Maryland shakes his head. "Not for long. I am going to clear my name. If you think running will get you anywhere, drive on with your bad selves."

"Whoever did this just killed a United States senator. The son of the vice president is dead. The media are destroying the president over this, and America has lost its patience with the administration. Do you really think anything you say to them is going to make a difference?"

"That's the difference between you and me, Boston. I still believe in the system."

"Don't do this, Maryland."

"It's not your call; it's mine. I am going to tell the feds everything I know, including the location of this place. I suggest you be long gone before I do."

Maryland heads out of the apartment and into the misty night. Boston turns to Tara and sees the concerned look on her face. She has a right to be. They are running out of places to hide.

"Let's grab our stuff," Boston says. "We need to get out of here."

CHAPTER FIFTY-FOUR

GINA ATTISON

BOSTON'S RESIDENCE
OXON HILL, MARYLAND

There is nothing more disconcerting to the average person than a run-in with law enforcement. It's no different for Gina. The most egregious offense she's ever been accused of was going fifty-five in a forty when she first got her driver's license. Now watching black sedans with flashing blue lights pull up in front of her house has relocated her heart into her throat.

Five men in windbreakers with "FBI" emblazoned on them in gold lettering climb the porch and ring the doorbell. They are joined by a man in a suit.

"Remember me, Miss Attison?"

"Yes, unfortunately, I do, Special Agent Grimman."

"Good, I'm happy that there's no need for introductions. We have a warrant to search these premises for information on a fugitive who is about to graduate to the FBI's ten most wanted list," he says, handing her a folded document that she doesn't bother to read. "I think you know him. He bought the ring on your finger."

The remark causes her to twist the diamond engagement ring with her fingers. When Gina realizes that she's doing it, she wrings her hands before gesturing the men inside.

"Let's have a seat, Miss Attison, so we can talk about where your fiancé is."

"I have no idea where he is," she says, as they sit on the sofa and the agents go about their work.

"Have you spoken to him?"

"I believe we've already covered this. Boston called before the incident in Adams Morgan. I haven't talked to him since."

"Still sticking to that story, are you?"

"It's the truth. I don't give a shit whether you choose to believe it."

"Why did you get fired from Senator Washington's staff today?"

"Politics."

"Life is a balance sheet, Miss Attison," Grimman says. "Hollinger landed you in a heap of trouble and has now cost you your job. What else are you prepared to lose for harboring him?"

"I'm not harboring anyone, and the ineptitude of this government cost me my job. And as I explained to you earlier, Boston is not the leak."

That earns her a cynical look. "How would you characterize your fiancé's relationship with Senator Turner?"

Gina stares at him for a moment. She thinks she knows where he's going with this and doesn't like it.

"Frosty."

"I figured as much. Was there enough animosity between them for Eugene to do something drastic?"

"What are you talking about?"

"Senator Turner was killed in that explosion in Anacostia."

"What?"

"He's dead, Miss Attison, and we don't believe it was a tragic accident. He was murdered. That raises the stakes of your involvement.

"I told you, I—"

"Have you been out of your house this evening?"

Gina is on the defensive. One misstep in this line of questioning, and she will find herself in an interrogation room. It doesn't matter if she has nothing to hide.

"I went out for a few grocery items."

"Where?"

"The supermarket. If you want to know which one, I'm sure you can find out on your own."

"What did you pay with?"

"My debit card."

Grimman nods at one of his agents. Gina tracks him with her eyes as he walks outside, presumably to make a phone call. Within fifteen minutes, they will have her financial records and confirmation of the transaction.

"Why did Boston kill Garrett?" Grimman continues.

"What are you talking about? Boston isn't a killer."

"This has not hit the media yet, but Senator Turner's car was destroyed in the exact same manner as the one outside the doctor's house during their…sleepover. The only difference was that they didn't melt the engine block with thermite this time."

The sleepover comment rattles Gina. She is already having trust issues with Boston and the lovely Dr. Winters. Grimman is exploiting that, and she's powerless to stop it.

"Wait, back up," she demands. "Are you telling me that the FBI had him under surveillance?"

"The agent in question is part of my department, yes."

Gina squints at the disclosure. That was an unforced error.

"Isn't that convenient? Under whose authority?" she asks, getting nothing in response. "Maybe I will take a closer look at this warrant after all."

"Read away, but while you do, I'm going to level with you, Miss Attison. If everything you say is true, then I need your help to find Hollinger."

"Even if I could help you, which I can't, why would I do that?"

"You answered the question earlier. Politics. High-profile men are dead, and your fiancé is at the top of the list of suspects. The only way out of this is for us to bring him in. If he's innocent, I promise to ensure that the truth comes out."

Gina forces a smile. Grimman works for the federal government, and his pledge to help is as good as worthless. He's no different than any other bureaucrat. They are all talk and no action. He just wants this off his desk, and if Boston hangs for it, he won't lose sleep over it so long as his boss adds a letter of commendation to his personnel file.

"Look," Grimman continues, "if you cooperate, it means you can get your SCI clearance back and maybe your job on Capitol Hill. Right now, he's a wanted felon and the prime suspect in one of the highest-profile leaks of our nation's secrets since Snowden. Do you really want to be on the wrong side of this?"

"Agent Grimman, you seem like a driven man. People who are so focused on their task don't see the bigger picture around them. I'm sure that Boston does. He won't get a fair shake from you, the FBI, or anyone else in this government considering the media pressure and political climate. I know my fiancé. He's going to stay hidden until the truth comes out. He had nothing to do with this."

"All evidence to the contrary. We will find Hollinger, and if he resists arrest, he might not make it out of that encounter alive. If you love him, you won't let that happen. The only way out of this is to bring him in peacefully."

Gina shakes her head. This is just another tactic to try to secure her cooperation, and it isn't going to work. Boston is going to call eventually, but not on a phone they can monitor. She knows that's what they are looking for. They can rip this house down to the studs and never find it.

An agent shows up and whispers something to Agent Grimman. She's assuming it's the results of the search since the activity has died down. It was a foregone conclusion that it would come up empty.

"You're in the FBI. You don't need my help to find Boston. Since you're done with your search, it's time for you to get the hell out of my house."

"I'm sorry to hear you say that, Miss Attison," he says, rising from the chair. "I'm certain we'll be seeing each other again."

The agents pile out of the house, and Gina closes the front door before turning to lean on it. Her heart is in her chest, and her head is pounding. Boston had better know what he's doing. She knows that her life is about to be put under a microscope. Everything she does from this point forward will have to be done very carefully.

CHAPTER FIFTY-FIVE
EUGENE "BOSTON" HOLLINGER

SOLVASON SLEEP DISORDERS CENTER
CHEVY CHASE, MARYLAND

Given Maryland's tantrum earlier, needing to relocate was a no-brainer. The problem is that there is no straightforward way to do it. Every route we take is covered in cameras and crawling with law enforcement. The car Louisiana stole in Ivy City has likely been identified by now, so we "borrowed" Tara's friend's SUV. They won't be looking for that.

"Your friend has got a sweet ride, Doc. She single?" Louisiana asks from next to me in the back seat of the Infiniti QX80.

"Does he ever stop?" Tara asks from the driver's seat.

"Only when he sleeps," I say, keeping my head ducked down. "Then he just acts like that in his dreams."

Tara is about to say something but clams up in the driver's seat. She grips the wheel tighter and starts to shake.

"What is it?"

"Another cop just passed us. Are we going to make it?" Tara asks, her voice shaky.

"Calm down, love. We'll be fine," Louisiana says.

"Calm down? Seriously? I'm sorry for never having been a fugitive before. How do you know that Maryland is going to the FBI? He didn't go straight there the first time."

"Because you can't trust that punk bitch," Louisiana answers for me. "That weasel would sell out his mama to save his own ass."

"Maryland does things by the book. He stays out of trouble. Now that we have landed him on a wanted poster, he'll be itching to get off it and to return some normalcy to his life."

"How much farther is this place?" Louisiana asks.

We took a circuitous route to get here and have already been on the streets for too long. We won't say it out loud, but Tara has a right to be concerned.

It's late to be out, and one forgotten turn signal or speed limit violation could turn this trip into a disaster. It's why I wanted Tara to drive instead of Louisiana.

"It's up here on the right," Tara replies, pointing to a towering glass building.

"What's that up ahead on the left?"

"The Pavilion," she responds simply. "It's a shopping mall."

"Are you thinking what I'm thinking?" I ask, getting a nod from Louisiana.

"Yeah, jump out with the doc. I'll park it there and meet you back here."

"You know that the office building has plenty of parking."

"That may be true, my love, but this car has a navigation system, which means it has GPS. Once Maryland gives us up, the feds will go to your friend's place and figure out that her car is missin'."

"If they find it at the mall, won't they figure out we came here?"

"Maybe, but it's doubtful," I say. "The mall is a public area with a lot of transportation options, including that Metro station. They won't think we stuck around the area."

"Okay, so why don't we all park the car at the mall and walk back here."

"See, bro? She can't stand to be away from me for even a few minutes."

I shake my head. "The mall has closed-circuit video. If the feds or police check it, they'll be looking for three people, not one. Louisiana knows how to avoid cameras better than any of us."

"True. It's a shame, though. The camera loves me."

Tara pulls the car up to the curb, and she and I climb out. Louisiana takes my place in the driver's seat and takes the car farther up the road before making a left into the mall parking garage. We wait in a shadowy garden on the building's side for what feels like an eternity.

"It wasn't that long of a walk," I say to Louisiana when he finally joins us after almost half an hour. "Ever heard of a thing called exercise?"

"When you're this naturally sexy, workouts are optional," he sputters between breaths.

We walk up to the building's front door and find Tara's friend waiting for us. He's probably been there for the last hour. We're that late.

"Come in, come in," he says, the nervous edge in his voice drawing my immediate suspicion.

"Boston, Louisiana, this is Dr. Steven Kempler. He's one of the center's directors. Steve, this is Boston and Louisiana."

"Unique names," the doctor says with an awkward handshake, prying his eyes off Tara for a fleeting moment to meet ours. "Pleased to meet you. Let's head upstairs."

Steve is as gauche as you get. He's the product of mixing Steve Buscemi with most portrayals of serial killers. He's probably in his early thirties, but the tall, gaunt man with unkempt hair could just as easily be forty.

"You trust this guy?" I whisper to Louisiana as we walk toward the elevators while Tara chats amiably with our host ahead of us.

"Bro, he's got a bigger crush on the doc than I do. Yeah, we can trust him."

"This is where the magic happens," Steve explains as our elevator arrives on the floor where the sleep center is located.

The reception area looks just like the typical doctor's office, complete with the plants, chairs, and obligatory bad art hung on the wall. This place has a decidedly more post-modern feel than most medical facilities. I'm hoping the rooms are cozier.

"The Sölvason Sleep Disorders Center provides comprehensive care for patients with a wide range of disorders, from apnea to night terrors," Steve explains in a well-rehearsed monologue. "Our patients enjoy the advantages of an expertly trained staff, the latest, cutting-edge diagnostic equipment, and personalized attention in a serene and comfortable environment. I have been trying to lure Dr. Winters into working here for years."

"I bet he has," Louisiana grumbles. I had the same thought.

"She explained your case to me, uh…"

"Boston."

"Yes, Boston, of course. I've never heard anything quite like it. It's very fascinating."

"The experience is far less so, I promise you. Tara said that you have something that can help sharpen these memories," I say, trying to move the conversation from a sales pitch to something more constructive.

"I have a compound that helps with lucid dreaming. Your situation is unique. I don't know if it'll work."

"I won't hold you personally responsible if it doesn't, Steven."

"What kind of compound are we talkin' about here?" Louisiana asks, more interested than he should be.

"Galantamine. It's a cholinesterase inhibitor that blocks an enzyme in the brain that breaks down the acetylcholine neurotransmitter."

"Speak English, bro."

"It's a natural supplement that the Chinese have been using as a memory enhancer for centuries. It's FDA-approved and is used as a memory-improvement supplement for Alzheimer's patients. We have begun using it as an oneirogen – a dream-enhancing supplement – with exciting results."

This guy likes his job almost as much as he likes Tara.

"Boston, this chemical compound may serve to lower the threshold to lucid dreaming and thus make it easier and more likely for dreamers to become lucid."

"That's a good thing, right?" I ask.

"It is, but the chemical influences the dreams themselves. It alters them, and we have to assume it may have that effect on memories as well," Tara explains. "Even if the memory itself is not altered, your recollection of it may be. It'd be like watching a movie and remembering a scene wrongly. Only this time, you won't be able to rewatch it."

"The only way to know for sure is to try it."

"You're all balls and no brains, bro," Louisiana adds.

"Excellent. If you're ready to begin, Tara can get you set up in one of our rooms."

"I got a question. If this is a sleep center, why isn't anyone here, you know, sleepin'?"

The comment causes Steven to laugh. "We provide a myriad of services here, and many of them are outpatient. As you might imagine, we are busy on weekends, so we give the staff Wednesday and Thursday nights off. We have the place to ourselves tonight."

"Steve, I actually crashed pretty hard earlier today. I'm not sure I can sleep."

"I can help with that too," he says with a smile. "I'll be back in a jiff. Tara, can you bring him to one of the rooms and set up the EEG?"

"Sure thing."

"I have to make a quick call first. Can I meet you there?"

"Okay. I'll give Steve a hand then and meet you in room eight in ten minutes or so," she says with a smile before walking off after our guide.

"Easy, bro."

"What are you talking about?"

"You've got the jealous boyfriend look on your face."

"You're delusional. I'm engaged."

"I know. Gina's smokin' hot, but there is somethin' about the doc, isn't there?"

"Stop projecting your own fantasies onto me," I say, punching him in the arm before I move to the corner of the patient waiting area. He is right, though. There is something about her.

I pull out the untraceable burner cell and power it up. These are the days when I really miss my smartphone. After the device comes to life, I hit redial and listen as the call gets sent straight to voicemail. I figured Gina would have her phone on and have it next to her while she waited for me to reach out, but I guess not. Where could she be?

CHAPTER FIFTY-SIX
SPECIAL AGENT ZACH FORTE

NATIONAL MEDICAL CENTER
WASHINGTON, D.C.

Zach hates emergency rooms. Despite only being battered and sore, there is nothing physically wrong with him. That's not going to stop the army of doctors and nurses who parade into this small room from keeping him here for far longer than needed.

The other victims weren't so lucky. The clerk working in the store got a face full of glass and was rushed into surgery. A couple of motorists driving by got into fender benders and were taken here as a precaution. Fortunately, I'm told that none of their injuries are life-threatening. The only fatality was Senator Garrett Turner, at least what's left of him.

"Knock, knock. How are you doing, buddy?" Remsen asks as he enters my room.

"It feels like I got hit by a truck."

"You did get blown twenty feet into a retaining wall. What did the doc say?"

"Concussion…blah, blah, blah…contusions, smoke inhalation, blah, blah, blah…I'll live. What's the word?"

"Well, politicians are going crazy, and the media are swarming like locusts. Fleets of satellite vans are parked down the street from the gas station and are covering the explosion like it's the Super Bowl. One more story to add to the voracious machine that is the modern news cycle."

"Typical. And Hollinger?"

Matt shakes his head. "Nothing yet."

"Have they determined the cause of the explosion?"

"Not officially, but it doesn't take a genius to figure it out. Watchtower had the NSA trace the number that called Garrett before the blast. It was a prepaid mobile phone," Matt explains in a hushed tone.

"That's not helpful."

"Only it is. That phone only called one other number in addition to the Turner call. Do you want to venture a guess who it was?"

"Matt, I was nearly incinerated. I'm not in the mood for games. Whose?"

"Gina Attison's."

Zach leans his head up from his pillow and winces at the pain. This case is only getting stranger. Either the fiancée is involved, or she can confirm that Boston is. They need to find out.

"See if you can get me discharged."

"Are you kidding? I started that process before I even came in to see you," Remsen says with a smile.

"About time you got here," Zach says, eyeing Grimman as he walks into the small room.

"Are you okay?" Grimman asks.

"I'm fine. Never better," Zach says, sinking back into the pillow.

"Director Remsen? What brings you here?"

"Zach and I go back to our days at Quantico. When I heard about what happened, I decided to stop in and see him."

"You're not here in an official capacity, are you?"

"No."

Grimman nods and turns to Zach. "Why were you talking to Senator Turner?"

"We were exchanging recipes for this great sangria I found when—"

"Don't play with me, Agent Forte."

"I was checking in on Gina Attison at Boston's house in Oxon Hill. I wanted a coffee and pulled into the station at the same time Turner did. I recognized him and said hi. That's it."

"That's all, huh?"

"Pretty much. The senator dismissed me when he got a call on his cell. He didn't have time for the little people. The gas station had cameras. You can check the video if it survived."

Grimman squints his eyes. He clearly doesn't buy the story but can't refute it either.

"Garrett Turner was an egocentric ass, but he didn't deserve to be incinerated in a massive fireball. Hollinger and his friends are going down for this."

Zach sighs. He's had his reservations all along about Hollinger's role in this mess. The death of a senator in a massive explosion will guarantee that this manhunt gets undivided attention. With the media stoking the fires, everybody is now calling for his head without asking why. Now might be the time to pose that question.

"Unless Hollinger had nothing to do with this."

"Have you been drinking?" Grimman asks.

"Not recently. Unfortunately."

"Forensics issued their initial report a half-hour ago. The explosion was caused by a device under the bumper and triggered by a cell phone. Hollinger and his friends blew up your car in the exact same way. Why would he kill Garrett Turner unless he's the traitor?"

"Because it's too convenient."

"He's the mole, Zach. He's passing information to the Syrians and got the VP's son killed. Now he's on the run and covering his tracks. That much is clear."

"On the run? Yeah, he's running really far. Come on, Tom, something's not right. If you were a mole no longer in a position to pass along information because the entire federal government was looking for you, would you stick around? The longer he stays, the better the chance of getting caught. He could be halfway across the country right now. Why risk a high-profile killing to draw more attention?"

Grimman folds his arms and glares at Zach but doesn't have an answer. With all the pressure being applied, everybody stopped asking questions, including him. They want this issue to go away, and catching Boston is the key.

"What is your theory then?"

"Maybe we have this thing reversed. Maybe Boston suspected Turner of being the mole."

"Yeah, sure, and our mole just blew himself up. Try explaining that to Director Weisz. Mole or not, Hollinger needs to be brought in, Zach. I don't want you within ten miles of him when it happens."

An agent walks in and smiles at Zach. She pulls Grimman away and talks to him in a hushed tone outside the small ER room.

"Sangria?" Matt asks quietly.

"No official capacity?" Zach mocks in return.

The two men share a laugh. "Okay. We're both liars."

"Eric Williams just turned himself in at the Washington Field Office," Grimman announces when he returns. "Maybe he can give us some answers. Get better and then go home and get some rest, Zach. I'll contact you when this is over."

Grimman leaves with the second agent. Matt peeks out the door to ensure he exits the ER. He pulls out his cell and presses a single button.

"Hey Bill, it's me. Get in touch with our contacts in the Washington Field Office. They are about to interrogate Eric Williams, and I want to know everything they say. Roger that. Text me when it's set up."

"That was impressive. What's the plan?"

"It's time to put Watchtower to work. Since Grimman has no more use for you, I have your services at my disposal. Get dressed. The clock is ticking faster, and I need you back on the field. If counterintelligence isn't serious about finding this mole, it falls to us."

"You don't think it's Hollinger either?"

"I don't know. Either he is, or someone desperately wants to make it look that way. If it's the latter, we need to find out who and why."

CHAPTER FIFTY-SEVEN

GINA ATTISON

The ringing doorbell startles Gina. She dozed off on the couch and is jolted at the sound of the chime above her head. She glances at the clock on the wall and rubs her eyes before shuffling over to the door. Two men stand there with their badges out.

"I'm still trying to put this place together following the last ransacking," Gina moans. "If you're here to search it again, you're out of luck."

"We're not here to search anything, Miss Attison. We know it's late, but may we come in?"

"Two in the morning is early, not late. Can this wait a few hours?"

"Unfortunately, no," one of them says, prompting Gina to give him a quick onceover.

"You look like you got your ass kicked."

"I did, in a manner of speaking. I'd rather not have this conversation on your front stoop. Please, may we come in?"

"Sure. It's sweet of you to swing by on your prime suspect's woman," Gina says, stepping aside and watching as the disheveled one trips on the threshold as he enters the living room.

"My name is Special Agent Zach Forte," he says after managing to arrest his fall just in time. "This is Director Matt Remsen."

"You work for Grimman?"

"In a manner of speaking, yes. Director Remsen works for a different division."

"How wonderful for both of you. What do you want?"

"I was the one tasked with surveillance of Boston outside Doctor Tara Winters's townhouse."

Gina's eyes narrow. "I see. Then I guess you took a company car to get here."

The director's lip curls up, but Agent Forte isn't amused at her pointing that out.

"I would normally appreciate your feistiness, but not about that. Your fiancé will answer for that tragedy eventually, but that's not why I'm here."

"Okay, then why are you here?"

"Have you heard about the explosion at the gas station on Pennsylvania Avenue last night?"

"It's all over the news. I didn't think anything could cut in on the twenty-four-hour coverage of the death of the vice president's son. What does that have to do with me?"

The two just stare at her before she does the math. The fresh cuts and bruises lead her to a startling revelation.

"You were there," Gina concludes.

"I was talking to Senator Turner just a few moments before... Well, he received a phone call right before the explosion," Agent Forte relays.

"Good for him."

"The call was from a disposable cell phone," the director interjects, ignoring her obstinance.

"Those things must drive you guys nuts."

"Not in this case, Miss Attison. We obtained the records from the phone carrier and determined that this cell phone had only dialed two numbers in its history. Have you heard of this one?"

Matt tells her the number. When he first mentioned a disposable cell, Gina was afraid it would be one of the two she purchased to communicate with Boston. Fortunately, the number doesn't belong to either of them, not that it realistically could. He would never use that phone to call anyone except her.

"I'm sorry, I don't recognize it."

"We didn't think you would. You will know the second number that was called. It's yours."

"Mine?"

"Yes. Several calls were made to your cell phone from it early yesterday morning. Can you tell me who the caller was?"

"Do you have a warrant?"

"Miss Attison, as you said, it's early. If you want us to get a warrant, you're going to be awake for a whole lot longer."

She purses her lips and walks over to the cell phone sitting on the coffee table. After entering the lock code, she scrolls back through the call history. The list is far shorter than usual now that she's unemployed. She finds the number that the director read off to her and looks at the time. There was only one person who called her at that hour, and it happened multiple times. Gina looks up at the agents.

"Colby Washington."

CHAPTER FIFTY-EIGHT
ERIC "MARYLAND" WILLIAMS

FBI FIELD OFFICE
WASHINGTON, D.C.

Maryland expected this to be much worse. Visions of a dingy jail cell complete with a moldy mattress, steel toilet, and cellmate named Bubba danced through his mind on the way here. At a minimum, he thought he would be shown into a sterile interrogation room with a single light suspended from the ceiling and forced to answer questions while handcuffed to a chair.

He realized he'd watched too many spy movies and television police dramas when he was shown into a small conference room. Maryland may be a wanted man, but not the guy that the professionally dressed agents here really want. That honor is all Boston's.

Several serious-looking men listen to the story, starting with Boston's accident and hospitalization. Maryland is pressed for every detail and relays as many as he can remember.

"That's quite a story," Grimman says from across the small table.

"It's the truth."

He looks at one of the other agents in the room, who gives a slight nod. Agent Grimman is not impressed. His words may be measured, but his body language is screaming that he's measuring Maryland up for a prison jumpsuit.

"You and your friends blew up a car and fled from authorities, yet you want me to believe that you're just a hapless victim in all this?"

"No, no, I didn't know that Louisiana was going to do that. I was already in the doctor's car when it happened."

"And you ran because Boston had a dream."

"It's not just a dream. Boston believes he can see other people's memories. That is why he has been working with Dr. Winters."

"Mr. Williams, I'm sure you can see how we might be skeptical about your story," Grimman says, leaning forward.

"I'm well aware that it sounds completely crazy."

"Do you believe that Hollinger is seeing people's memories?"

"Maryland looks at the table and shakes his head. "I don't know what to believe. I'm only telling you what I know."

"Why didn't you bring this information to us earlier?" another agent asks. It sounds like you had plenty of time to ditch them."

Maryland rubs his chin but remains silent. What is there to say? He was a fugitive and didn't go to the police. That's the definition of aiding and abetting, and he could go to prison for it. He's sure that the agents in this room are thinking the same thing.

"I understand loyalty. That's what it was, right? You helped because that's what friends do. Like his fiancée. You said she brought him a bag. What was in it?"

"I don't know."

"Classified materials?"

"He's not a traitor."

"You just said you didn't know what was in the bag," Grimman says with a smirk. "How is he communicating with Miss Attison?"

"By phone."

"There is no activity on his line."

"Prepaid phone."

"Do you know the numbers?" he presses.

"No."

Grimman studies Maryland for a few moments, trying to determine whether he is telling the truth. There's nothing more unnerving than having every move analyzed by a man specially trained to detect dishonesty. The agent rubs his stubble and leans back in his chair.

"Let's go back to the original question. You waited to turn yourself in and tell us your story. Why?"

"I'm here now. What does it matter?"

"It might not. Maybe it does because now you're complicit in a murder."

"What?"

"Hollinger and your friend Rilleux killed Senator Turner."

"First, Louisiana is not a friend. He's an old acquaintance from my days in Syria. Second, there's no way that either of them was involved in that."

"Why not?"

"Boston is being framed. He's been seeing it…"

Maryland stops talking. He knows how insane this sounds.

"In his dreams? Right?" Agent Grimman finishes, not amused. He draws out the response like a parent who just heard a teenager's lame excuse as to why half the bottle of vodka in the liquor cabinet is missing.

"I don't give a damn if you believe me. I'm not sure that I believe it myself. I'm telling you what I know. Do what you will with the information."

"Hollinger thinks that he is being framed. Who would do that? More importantly, why?"

"I don't know."

Agent Grimman continues to watch him, obviously searching for holes in his story. He turns and looks at the other two agents in the room, checking to see if they have any questions or something to add.

"Okay, Mister Williams, you're free to go."

"That's it?" Maryland asks in utter bewilderment.

"For now, yes. Don't leave town. Local police will want to have a long chat with you about what happened in Adams Morgan once the dust settles in the search for your friend. You are also staring at federal charges of obstruction and aiding and abetting a fugitive. If you know a good lawyer, you may want to give him a call when you get home."

CHAPTER FIFTY-NINE
"BOSTON" HOLLINGER

SOLVASON SLEEP DISORDERS CENTER
CHEVY CHASE, MARYLAND

"Hold on one second. Let me take this, Agent Forte. If you don't mind, I'll get back with you in a moment."

The man smirks and offers a nod. He stops and points to something off to my side. My eyes track his finger to…a gas pump.

"You shouldn't use that thing while fueling up."

A wave of anger washes over me, and I brush him off with my hand.

"How did you get this number?" I ask.

"There are no secrets in this city, Garrett. You know that better than anyone."

"Okay, what do you want?"

"I want you to put the country first for once in your life. You need to stop exerting political pressure on our counterintelligence agencies and let them do their jobs."

"No, I'm afraid that isn't going to happen. Hollinger— "

"Hollinger is only being set up to take the fall. We both know the truth."

The handle clicks, and I return it to the pump before tightening the gas cap.

"So, what are you going to do about it?"

"We're supposed to be fighting for the American people. There was a time when they came first, but you would rather play politics. Fine. I'm going to destroy you, Garrett, and it's going to happen far sooner than you think."

There's a ringing sound. Where is that coming from? I lean over toward the rear of the car. It sounds like it's in the trunk—then everything goes completely black. No fuzzy white haze. Just black.

My eyes open to complete darkness. A moment later, the soft light from the lamp in the corner of the room pierces the darkness. What the hell? I blink twice, confirming I'm still at the sleep center.

The door opens, and Tara comes in wearing a pair of shorts and a fitted T-shirt. Her hair is in a ponytail and, without even trying, she still manages to be sexy. I can't help but be distracted.

"Tara? What are you—"

"Shh! I was monitoring your brain waves from the other room when you experienced the memory. Don't ask any questions. Focus on the dream. Tell me what you saw," she commands as she sits on the edge of the bed next to me.

The drugs must have helped just as Steven thought they would. The fogginess of the dream was gone. I could see everything that was going on. Now, it's about remembering it long enough to describe what I saw.

"It was so vivid. I was at a gas station."

"What were you doing?"

"I was putting gas in a car. A red one," I explain, sorting through the stream of details. It's easier to hang onto the memory this time.

"And?"

"I was talking to someone."

"Focus on the face. Who was it?"

"I think it was the guy from outside your apartment."

"What did you say to him?"

"I'm not sure. It was the end of the conversation. No, wait! I got a call on my cell, and it interrupted us."

Tara slides closer to me on the edge of the bed, leaning closer and causing her shirt to hang far too low on her chest. I force my eyes to stay locked on hers.

"Close your eyes and remember. You got a call. What did the man you were talking to do?" she asks.

"He walked away."

"Okay, you're on the phone now. What did you say to the caller?"

"I'm surprised to hear from you," I recall.

"Who was on the other line?"

"It was muffled…I'm not sure," I say, opening my eyes and getting frustrated that the memory is already fading despite the drugs.

"Close your eyes and focus, Boston. Put yourself back there in your mind. What else was said?" she probes.

"My name was mentioned."

"How was your name mentioned?"

"I'm being set up to take the fall."

"You said it or the voice on the other end?" she continues to press.

"The other guy."

"What did you say?"

I think back to the last part of the conversation. It's fading so quickly. What I remember is clear, but pieces of the dream are starting to slip away.

"He's going to destroy me."

"You or the person at the car?"

"The guy at the car."

"Listen to the guy on the phone. Focus on the tenor, the cadence, the pitch. You know the voice. You know who it is. Now tell me, who is it?"

"It's Colby Washington," I mutter, shocked at the realization. "There was something else at the end of the memory. I heard something. A ringing, I think."

"And then?"

I tense up. I know who I was. It all makes sense now, especially when I think back to the other dream. It was the same red car. I should have recognized the swagger in the voice. And because I was watching the news, I know exactly why everything went all black. It was the last memory he would ever have.

"My God."

"Boston, what is it?" Tara asks, putting her hand on mine.

Steven rushes into the room, holding a printout. Louisiana follows him in, wondering what all the excitement is over. He grins when he notices the two of us on the bed. Fortunately, he keeps his mouth shut for once.

"This is astounding, Tara. Simply astounding! I have never seen readouts like this in my life. These two lines can't be this high at the same time. It's impossible."

"Thank you, Steven. We can review it later. Can you give us a moment?"

"Oh…of course. I'm going to collect more data," Steven says, retreating out the door.

"It musta been a good one, eh Bos?"

"I was Garrett Turner. I just saw the last moments of his life."

"Boston, he's dead. You couldn't have—"

"I know what I saw, Tara. It was him. There's no doubt about it."

"Then I was wrong about how you're experiencing these memories," she concludes, shaking her head. "I was wrong all along."

I think about that for a moment. Tara's original theory was that I somehow tap into the subconscious of someone I know while I'm sleeping. My brain uses that signal to experience their memories. That idea is out the window unless I'm also a medium now. Turner is dead, and I can't tap into the memory of someone who isn't alive.

"You've been right more than you've been wrong. Maybe it's more complicated than you thought. Maybe I somehow downloaded the memory before the senator died."

"Downloaded?" she asks in a curious tone.

It's as plausible a theory as any right now. Right now, I don't care how it works. There is a much larger issue to deal with.

"Tara, it doesn't matter," I say, grabbing her hands. "I think Colby Washington is setting us up for Turner's murder."

CHAPTER SIXTY

GINA ATTISON

This is what a goldfish feels like. It's a recurring thought for Gina as she enters the mammoth station. She is being watched, and it's unnerving. Most law-abiding citizens will never understand the experience of having a pair of FBI agents for shadows. It's one she could have lived without. She doesn't like feeling like a common criminal.

Union Station is a major transit hub for Amtrak that doubles as a tourist area. In addition to the commuters who rely on it, the station sees millions of visitors a year who wander over from the museums and landmarks surrounding the National Mall. As with all busy and well-known places, the popularity bred the need for restaurants, cafés, and even a shopping mall.

Gina knows that coming here is a gamble that's certain to raise a few eyebrows at the FBI. They probably expect her to be meeting Boston. The station is busy enough to cause people to occasionally bump into each other. She finds the crowd annoying, but it's far worse for the men trying to keep her in their line of sight.

After stopping for a coffee, Gina reaches the end of the street-level shops. She needs to do what she came here for before this excursion stops looking at least somewhat normal. Gina ducks into a Victoria's Secret, almost daring the agents to follow her. As she checks the lingerie along the wall, she notices them waiting outside the store. You can always count on men to act the part. They don't want to be perceived as perverts, regardless of what their mission is.

She selects a couple of random nighties and heads for the dressing room, closing the door behind her and hanging the items on a hook. Gina sits on the bench and powers up the device, hoping that Boston has done the same. They may have these to communicate but neglected to set a schedule for when to call.

"Jesus, I've been worried sick about you. Are you okay? Where have you been?" Boston says when the call connects.

"I'm sorry. Things have been hectic. The FBI came over to redecorate the house last night."

"It's that bad?"

"Bad enough that they paid me a second visit at two a.m. I also have a government-funded, around the clock security detail," Gina explains. "At least I don't need to worry about getting mugged."

"Did you ditch them to make this call?"

"I'm at Vicky's trying on nighties."

"There's something to look forward to when this is over."

Gina manages a slight smile. "Yeah, well, you'll never see them on me unless you get out of this mess. Tell me that you're getting somewhere."

"I know who's having us watched. Now I need to know why."

Her heart skips a beat. "Who?"

"Your old boss."

"Senator Washington? There's no way. Look, if this is about the conversation I overheard—"

"I saw it in a dream, Gina. I heard both sides of the conversation."

"He said that he had someone watching you?"

"Not explicitly…it's hard to explain."

Gina's face contorts into a look of confusion as she holds the phone to her ear and there's silence coming from the other end. The senator's conversation was suspicious, but that doesn't mean he's involved. She wants to trust Boston's instincts, but that's not what this is. He's asking her to trust his dreams.

"I saw a memory of someone placing explosives on a car. Then I saw one of Garrett Turner's memories. I put the two together."

"Garrett Turner is dead, Boston," Gina says, unsure of how much he knows and doesn't know at this point.

"I know. I relived the last moments of his life. He was on the phone with Colby when the bomb went off. That bastard arranged the whole thing and is trying to pin the blame on me."

"How did you see one of his memories if he's dead?"

"I don't know. Tara is trying to figure that out. It looks like she was wrong about how this works."

"Shocker," Gina mutters.

"How I'm able to do it isn't important right now. I know what I saw."

"Okay. What are you going to do?" she whispers as she hears someone enter the dressing room area.

Her heart starts thumping in her chest when she hears movement in the dressing room. She doesn't think the FBI agents would be reckless enough to follow her in here, but she's been out of sight for a while. Her fear dissipates when the clatter of hangers is followed by footsteps leaving the dressing room area.

"I'm going to confront him," Boston says.

"That's an epically bad idea."

"Yeah, that's what I've been told," he mumbles. Gina assumes that Louisiana had the same response. Maybe Tara did, too. She hates the idea of agreeing with either of them.

"Take what you know to the FBI. It's time."

"So they can arrest me the moment I walk through the door? I don't think so. You wanted me to end this. This is how I'm going to do it."

"Boston, you need to listen to reason. There's no telling what Colby is capable of. If he killed Senator Turner—"

"I'll be well-protected."

"I don't like this one bit. Do you think that Colby is going to confess?"

"One way or another, yes. Gina, my mind is made up. I have to do this."

"Boston, you promised you would come back to me when this was over. I'm going to hold you to that. For the record, prison doesn't count."

"I know."

Gina hears voices getting louder. It sounds like they're between a customer and an employee, meaning it's only a matter of time before she has company in the adjoining dressing room.

"I have to get going before the feds get suspicious. Good luck."

"Thanks. Take care of yourself, and don't worry about me. I'm not the one who's going to need the luck."

Gina ends the call and powers down the phone. She departs the dressing room with one of the items and pays for it at the counter. It's best to emerge with something after all the time that was spent in the dressing room. She spots her tails and heads out of Union Station, knowing that Boston will need all the luck he can get.

CHAPTER SIXTY-ONE
SPECIAL AGENT ZACH FORTE

Pentagon City is a dining and shopping destination across the highway from the Pentagon and a stone's throw from Arlington National Cemetery. The neighborhood has some of the best shops and restaurants inside the Beltway, and its Metro station is one of the busiest in the system as it services the commuters who live here.

Zach steps out of the shower, towels off, and dresses in some old tactical clothing Matt loaned him. This two-bedroom apartment is far nicer than any place he has lived in his life. If his friend is using this stop to help sell him on the merits of joining Watchtower, it may be working.

Remsen is winding up a call by the time Zach emerges from the bathroom. He hands him a beer.

"Feel better?"

"Much. Thanks."

"My team reported in. Eric Williams was interrogated by Grimman at the field office."

"Where did they lock him up?"

Matt grins and takes a swig from his bottle. "They didn't. They finished and let him walk right out the front door."

"They must want to use him as bait. Did he talk?"

"Apparently, he wouldn't shut up. Grimman had three agents taking notes just so he could ask appropriate follow-up questions. The whole thing is on video. Watchtower is pulling it off the server."

"Anything interesting?"

"He told Grimman about the dreams while trying to explain why Tara Winters is involved. He didn't buy it."

Zach drops onto the sofa. It feels good to be sitting on something that isn't the seat of a car. He rubs his neck. It's been a long couple of days, and he knows that the pace won't stop until Hollinger is in custody and the mole is found. Unlike just about everyone, he believes those two things are mutually exclusive.

"You can't blame him. Grimman doesn't believe anything that doesn't conform to his world view. It sounds crazy to me, too, but it doesn't matter what we think. Hollinger believes it. It also explains why Dr. Winters is still involved."

"All right," Matt says. "Let's play the game. If you thought you were experiencing other people's memories in your dreams, and that could lead you to someone setting you up as a traitor, what would you do next?"

"Avoid Elm Street."

Remsen doesn't miss the *Nightmare on Elm Street* reference, but he would rather not think about Freddy Krueger visiting anyone in their dreams. One of the lectures the two men received at Quantico during their FBI training was the psychological profile of a copycat murderer who replicated those movies' deaths.

"I'm serious."

"So am I. Hollinger will buy as much time as he can. For curiosity's sake, what did Williams say about it?"

"He thinks Hollinger is batshit crazy but swears that he's not the mole. He turned himself in to answer questions about torching your ride and clear his name."

Zach grumbles. That is still a sore spot with him and likely will be for a while.

"Grimman will keep him under constant surveillance to see if Hollinger reaches out to him," Remsen concludes. "He's not the prize, and the police are going to haul him in eventually. There's one more thing. Watchtower intercepted a field report from the agents trailing Gina Attison. She went shopping at Union Station."

"Shopping?"

"If you can believe it. The lovely Miss Attison even stopped into Victoria's Secret to buy some lingerie during her trip there. Do you think she has a man on the side? Because Hollinger isn't coming home anytime soon."

"Victoria's Secret," Zach mumbles, shaking his head. The last woman he dated should take notes. He takes another long slurp from his bottle and rubs his chin. Then it dawns on him.

"Gina didn't go there to shop. She went there for privacy. I bet that she called Boston from the dressing room."

Remsen thinks about it for a moment. "You've got to hand it to her. She's smart. Nothing has popped up on her cell log. She must be using a burner."

"And maybe Boston isn't the only person she's calling from it. Why would a United States Senator have one?"

"You're talking about Colby Washington?"

"Maybe it's time to go to the source to see why he called Gina that night from a burner phone."

"It could have been a coincidence," Matt offers weakly, getting a disapproving look from Zach. He's a director and has been in the FBI for longer than five minutes. He understands that there rarely are coincidences.

"Let's take a trip and find out."

* * *

The drive from Matt's apartment in Pentagon City to Colby's place in Maryland would only be forty-five minutes under normal conditions. These are not normal conditions. This has to be some of the nastiest weather the district has experienced in a while. The rain is hard, steady, and hasn't let up at all. It also makes driving a nightmare for Remsen, who is behind the wheel and struggling to get them there in this mess.

"What do you have, Bill?" Remsen asks, practically shouting to be heard over the rain beating on the windshield.

"Agents went to the address Eric Williams gave Grimman. It belongs to a woman named Andrea Davis. We ran her name through the system. Immigration officials at CBP reported that she left the country via Dulles International over a week ago."

The two men in the car exchange glances.

"Please don't tell me she went someplace crazy like Turkey," Zach warns.

"Paris, France. The trip was booked with an accompanying ticket for a Michael Ramaglia. We ran a check on him. It came back clean."

"Williams told Grimman that Tara's friend was out of the country, so that makes sense. What else?"

"The car reported stolen from Ivy City? It's parked out behind the place and partially covered with an old blanket. We would never have found it. That part of Williams's story checks out too. We contacted the DMV, and Andrea Davis has an Infiniti SUV registered in her name. We're contacting Infiniti's roadside assistance to do a trace on it."

Boston and company might have used it as transport, assuming the FBI was on to the stolen car from Ivy City. A nice SUV wouldn't stand out as much in certain parts of the city as their beater would. If he was trying to flee the area, it might not be a big deal, but for whatever reason, he's staying put around Washington.

"Stay on it, Bill."

"Will do. Where are you now?"

Matt checks the GPS. There's no point in looking for a road sign in this weather. "We're on Route 301 in Waldorf."

"Waldorf?"

"Yeah, it's a small town in Maryland next to White Plains. We're paying Senator Washington a visit."

"Good luck with that. I'll call back when I have something."

Matt disconnects the call. Zach stares out the window as Matt crashes through more standing water on the road. Luck. They're going to need it with Colby Washington, but they may need more of it to reach his house in one piece.

CHAPTER SIXTY-TWO
EUGENE "BOSTON" HOLLINGER

RESIDENCE OF SENATOR COLBY WASHINGTON
WHITE PLAINS, MARYLAND

We drive slowly past Senator Washington's home to get a lay of the land. It sits in a planned suburban neighborhood, a couple of turns removed from Route 213 in Maryland. It's a typical two-story colonial-style house with an attached garage and no place to hide. The trees are all freshly planted, and the only cover is provided by woods to the rear and left side of the house. Unfortunately, it's too far away to be of any use to me.

Louisiana's truck sticks out like a sore thumb in this neighborhood. We're lucky that it's raining hard enough to keep the people who live in the completed homes here indoors. Only slightly more than a dozen houses in this neighborhood have been finished. The rest are either still in the planning stages or are currently under construction.

"You sure ya don't want me to go in?" Louisiana asks, stopping in front of a half-completed house up the road.

"No. I need to do this myself."

"All right. You're an idiot, but I'm cool with it."

"Just stay close. I'll let you know when I'm done."

"Roger that."

I jump out of the truck and start walking back down the street. It's dark out for midafternoon. It's been pouring steadily, making it feel like it is closer to eight p.m. It serves my purposes. The visibility is terrible.

I reach the overhang of the senator's garage and peek through the window. It's still full of boxes from the move. That explains why his car is parked in the driveway. Now to figure out how to get his attention.

I creep over to the passenger side of his car and start rocking it. The car alarm sounds after a few good jolts and is quickly deactivated from the living room window. Damn. I wait a couple of minutes and try again with the same result. Luring anybody outside in this weather is a long shot. The senator may leave the alarm disabled, but I'm hoping his curiosity wins out.

I rock the vehicle again, hoping the third time's a charm. I scurry back to my spot and peer around the corner of the garage to spy the front porch. The smoke grenade and flashbang procured from Louisiana clink against each other on my belt as I move. That won't do. Right now, the goodies from his duffel bag of doom are more trouble than they're worth.

The front door opens, and the scraping of shoes on the covered porch announces someone's presence. The garage juts out from the house's front wall by fifteen feet, giving me a sharp corner to hide behind. Unless Colby suspects something is amiss, I should be able to get the jump on him.

The alarm deactivates with the typical chirping sound. I strain to listen for any sounds from him over the pouring rain. After not hearing anything for ten seconds, I hazard a peek in time to see him turn back towards the door. I spring into action.

Rain covers the telltale footfalls that warn of impending danger as I sprint up the walk and bound up the steps. The senator is crossing the threshold when I grab him and jam my gun into his back.

"What the—"

"Easy, Senator. Walk inside." I jab him with the muzzle just in case he thinks about not complying.

We enter the house, and I close the door with my free hand. I do a quick survey of the open-plan first floor. He's alone. I give him a shove into the living room and back off to a safe distance, my gun trained at his chest.

"You want to tell me what the hell you're doing here pointing a gun at me, Boston?"

"It can't be that much of a mystery."

The Senator grins. "Do you want a drink?"

"You're pretty calm for a man in your position right now," I say, wondering if he thinks this is a sick joke.

"I was in the military just like you were. We've both been shot at before. How would you expect me to react? Now, there's a fine cognac over on the credenza against the back wall. I'm going to walk over there slowly and pour myself one. Join me."

He turns and points toward the back of the living room.

"No, thanks."

"Are you sure? It's Louis the Thirteenth. One of the best cognacs ever distilled on this planet."

"I said no, and if you make one wrong move, I'll drop you where you stand," I warn, sliding two steps to my left to get a better angle on him.

"You've seen too many Liam Neeson movies. You didn't come here to kill me, Boston," he concludes before moving to the credenza. "Why don't you tell me why you're here?"

"Why are you framing me?"

"Excuse me?" he asks as he pours the cognac into a snifter.

"You had a conversation on the phone in your office. You talked about taking somebody off the board. You were talking about me."

"How could…Gina. She was listening at the door. But how did she hear the other side of the conversation?"

"It's a mystery. Tell me I'm wrong."

"You're not wrong, only misinterpreting what you think was heard," Colby responds, taking a sip from his snifter. "I was on the phone with Justin Triggs."

"You're saying that you told the *Herald's* chief Washington reporter that somebody needs to be taken off the board? I don't think so."

"I've had an arrangement with him for years. Most politicians have at least one reporter in their back pocket. We were launching a smear campaign against Garrett Turner to get him to cool his attacks on us. That was what your fiancée overheard. I'm not setting you up for anything, although I'm sure she thinks so. That's why she called Triggs and tried to turn him on me."

"Liar!" I shout, unable to control my anger after his smug response.

I move swiftly, grabbing Colby by the throat and forcing him into an overstuffed chair. The snifter of cognac he's holding crashes to the floor and shatters. I tighten my grip, causing him to gasp for air. He grabs at my wrist when I jam my weapon into his cheek. His resistance ceases, and I loosen my grip, allowing him to breathe.

"You and this administration need a scapegoat. Turner was making this political, and the tactic was working. The American public has turned against you. That's why you killed him and framed me for it!"

"I did no such thing!"

"You were on the phone with Garrett when he died! You said that you were going to end him and then did. Go ahead, deny it. I dare you!"

Washington's jaw hangs slack. "How could you know that?"

"Deny it."

"I can't," he says. "You're right. I was on the phone with him when he died. It doesn't mean I killed him."

"I saw you plant explosives on his car."

"I don't know what you think you saw or how, but it wasn't me."

"Don't lie to me, Colby!"

"I'm not, damn it! Get a grip, Boston. Am I crying that the son of a bitch is dead? Hell no. But I had nothing to do with his death."

"I don't believe you."

He pushes at me as he tries to get out of the chair. I plant my knee into his groin and shove him back into it. I press my nine-millimeter into his forehead.

"Don't try that again."

"Let me up!"

"Not a chance. Not until you start telling the truth."

"The truth? Service to this country has been my life. It's all I have ever done. It's all I have."

"You sound like a politician. I'm not as gullible as the typical voter. You'll have to do better than that," I warn him.

"Look around this room," Colby instructs me. "Go ahead, look. It will tell you everything you need to know about me."

I take my eyes off him and crane my neck to survey the walls. If his collection of photographs, awards, and military accolades in his Senate office is impressive, what he has in his house blows them away. There are pictures with presidents, heads of state, and political leaders, all hanging next to countless commendations. It is his life, but it doesn't mean—

A blow knocks the weapon from my hand. Colby shoves me far enough back to land a heel kick against my chest before I can react. I regain my balance as he launches himself towards the credenza. I dive across the floor to retrieve my gun, but when I turn, he's staring back at me down the barrel of a .44 Smith & Wesson.

"Drop it, Boston. It's over."

"Not a liar, huh?" I ask, placing my weapon on the floor beside me.

"Does it matter? You didn't come here to hear the truth. You want me to say something that matches your perception of reality."

"Are you going to shoot me now?" I ask, trying to determine his intentions, more than a little pissed at myself for letting him get the advantage on me.

"No, that's not how I do things. I'm going to call the police and let them deal with you. Maybe some time in a cell will help you gain some perspective."

"What perspective?"

"That the man framing you is dead."

"What?"

"Garrett was framing you, Boston. Triggs tracked it down this morning. He has a special relationship with Agent Grimman in counterintelligence. He ordered an FBI colleague to conduct surveillance on you and Tara Winters."

"Why?"

"He was using you as a pawn against me. You work for the SSCI. Your fiancée is on my staff. Do the math. He's counting on the embarrassment and public outcry to force my resignation. That's why he approached me outside Capitol Hill and told me to resign. It's why I called him last night. But since you seem to know so much already, you must have known that."

I'm dumbfounded. It's a crazy thought, but at the same time, it has just the kind of logic that the bureaucrats in this town will believe. Could I be wrong about all this? Will I ever get the chance to find out?

"It can't be true. It makes no sense," I say, slowly moving my hand to my belt.

"It makes perfect sense. Tell me something, Boston. How did you know what was said in my office? Or that I was on the phone with Garrett Turner? You can't have known either…unless you are the traitor after all."

He reaches for the phone, and I make my move. I jerk the pin on the flashbang free and roll to my right as I start counting in my head. One. Colby fires off a shot at where I was standing just a moment ago. Two. I toss the grenade in Colby's direction and roll once more, landing on my stomach, clenching my eyes shut, and covering my ears. Three.

The sound is deafening, and the brilliant flash blinds me, despite my precautions. I'm faring better than he is, so I scamper back across the floor on my knees. I'm just getting to my gun when the next shots ring out.

Colby fires blindly, clearly afraid that I'm coming at him while he's incapacitated. He misses but the shots are close enough to cause me to retreat through the living room to the kitchen.

I pull the pin on the smoke grenade and toss it on the area rug next to the couch. It sparks and starts billowing white smoke throughout the room. I fire twice where I knew Colby was once standing, but the return fire lets me know I missed.

"If you kill me, all you'll be doing is sealing your own fate!" Colby screams from the back of the living room. "You'll be adding murder to the charges against you."

"You shot at me first!"

"You put a gun to my head. You have gone off the deep end, Hollinger. I'm just protecting myself," he shouts over the hissing sound of the smoke grenade, which is only now beginning to subside. "I just dialed 9-1-1. The police are on the way. You're a wanted fugitive who held me at gunpoint in my house, Hollinger. What do you think is going to happen when they get here?"

He's right. I am a fugitive. He may be bluffing about calling the police, but even if he is, someone is bound to respond. I need to get out of here. I silently curse myself for not taking Louisiana's advice. He wanted me to bring two flashbangs and two smoke grenades. I settled for one of each. I should have listened to him.

I peek back around the counter that separates the kitchen from the living room. Sparks from the grenade have ignited the rug and couch, and the flames are starting to grow. I have an opportunity here. He won't be able to stay in there long.

"I'm not going anywhere until I get the answers I came here for. I have friends outside the door, and you need to come through me to get out the back. Give it up, Colby!"

"Not a chance," he says, coughing.

The fire is spreading up the walls to the ceiling. There is little to contain the spread – tongues of flame lick the kitchen and the stairs to the second level. A dense layer of smoke hangs in the air, cutting the visibility to only ten feet. The heat and smoke force me to retreat farther into the kitchen and take up a position near the kitchen island.

"Then you're going to burn to death in there. C'mon, Senator, it's over!"

Nothing is happening. Colby only has two escape options. If he tries the front door, I should see it open and can hit him from a distance. It'd be suicide to try coming through me to the back. I tighten the grip on my weapon as a figure emerges in the entryway, a cloth tied around the bottom of his face and a gun aimed right at me. I didn't expect the aggressive move. I dive behind the island just in time to dodge the hail of gunfire.

CHAPTER SIXTY-THREE
SPECIAL AGENT ZACH FORTE

RESIDENCE OF SENATOR COLBY WASHINGTON
WHITE PLAINS, MARYLAND

This is the one time that Matt wishes he hadn't volunteered to drive. The rain is beating on the roof in a steady staccato, forcing the two men to shout at each other across the center console. His phone rings, and he presses a button on the steering wheel to answer it.

"I have you on speaker, Bill. What do you have?"

"A 9-1-1 call was just made from Senator Colby Washington's residence," the agent informs them.

"For what?"

"Nobody responded to the dispatcher, but she reported hearing gunfire. Local police are responding."

"Gunfire?" Matt asks in surprise.

"Floor it," Zach says as he pulls out his weapon and checks to ensure a round is chambered.

Even driving the speed limit in this weather is a white-knuckled experience. Visibility is only a few feet past the hood. The fact that this Suburban has the agility of an armored personnel carrier isn't helping matters any as Remsen struggles to keep it on the road.

"We would get there faster in a boat," Matt says, fighting to keep control after hitting a puddle the size of Lake Erie.

"We'll be there in about a minute," Zach announces as he removes his seat best and wrestles himself into some body armor. "What's the ETA of the local police?"

"Wait one," Bill says on the other end of the line.

Remsen makes a quick left onto a four-lane road and then a right onto Colby's street. It wasn't hard to pick out which place is his. Smoke is billowing from almost every window in the house.

"About five minutes."

"Tell them not to shoot us," Matt says, slamming the vehicle in park.

The two men jump out as gunfire pierces the sound of the roaring inferno engulfing the house. Matt struggles into his own body armor and draws his weapon as Zach kicks in the front door. His heart pounding, he barges into the smoke-filled house.

"FBI!" he screams, sure nobody can hear him over the roar of the flames.

A figure with his face covered wheels around and fires at him. The bullet strikes the wall high and to his right, but it was too close for comfort. Zach tucks his shoulder and rolls away from what is sure to be another shot coming in his direction.

He pops to his feet and assumes a firing stance as the subject fires again in his direction. Zach doesn't bother lining up his sights.

"FBI! Drop your weapon!" he shouts again. The figure either doesn't hear or doesn't care, as he moves to his left when Zach trains his weapon on him..

Remsen moves into the doorway and fires his weapon three times at the man. At least one bullet finds its mark, causing him to collapse to the ground. Flames are everywhere, and the layer of smoke grows denser by the second. He can barely see Matt, only feet away as he begins to choke. Zach gets low to the ground and crawls over to the man clutching his chest. He pulls the rag off his face.

"Oh, shit!" Remsen exclaims from behind him.

"Get him out of here, Matt!"

Zach stares at the senator. The wound is in the center of his chest. There is no surviving that. Matt picks him up over his shoulder and stumbles his way back through the living room.

"Hollinger! This is the FBI!" Zach shouts in the direction of the kitchen. "Drop your weapon and come out where we can see you."

Nothing happens.

Zach crawls back through the kitchen, not seeing anything until he reaches the open back door. He takes a few gulps of air on the back patio before rising to his feet. He raises his weapon level with his eyes and scans the area through the pouring rain. It's clear. He sweeps his eyes over the back yard and catches a fleeting glimpse of a figure before he disappears into the woods behind the house. Gotcha.

Zach keys his tactical radio on his vest, fighting the urge to cough. "Matt, he's on foot and heading into the woods!"

He sprints through the back yard in pursuit, fighting to keep his balance as his boots slip on the wet grass. Briars and shrubs pull at his pants as he enters the thicket beyond the tree line. The underbrush thins out as Zach moves deeper into the woods. Now he contends with battling pine boughs and downed limbs as his boots slide on the muddy ground beneath him.

Hollinger isn't faring much better. He drops to the ground and struggles to get his feet back underneath him. Zach decides on his course of action. Mole or not, he attacked a United States senator. This needs to end right now.

"Freeze, Hollinger!" He doesn't comply.

Zach rushes forward, his heart pounding in his chest, and stops. He takes up a Weaver stance, pauses his breath, and squeezes off a round. It slams into a tree a few feet from its target as Hollinger disappears again.

He pulls the radio off his vest and presses the transmit button. "Suspect heading back toward the road just west of the turnoff."

"Roger," Remsen acknowledges.

After another two hundred feet, Zach has lost sight of his quarry. He slows to a walk, listening in vain for any telltale sign of movement. A figure appears twenty feet in front of him as a branch cracks under his feet. Zach drops to the ground and fires from the prone position. Nothing.

He rises and begins pressing forward. The woods between the house and the road are not that vast. Zach picks up the pace as the slope rises to meet the roadbed raised eight feet above grade to prevent flooding. Another dense growth of briars and shrubs marks the tree line. Zach barrels full steam ahead to hurdle it.

His foot catches a briar, and he plummets to the ground, dropping his radio and weapon to free his hands to break the fall. The hard landing shoots pain up his side. He rolls onto his back and then sits up, his eyes searching for his two lifelines. When Zach turns to look behind him, Hollinger is standing there with a gun pointed at his head.

"Don't try it," he warns.

Zach stays seated and slowly raises his hands to shoulder level.

"You don't want to do this."

"You're right, I don't." It wasn't the response that Zach was expecting.

The unmistakable glow of headlights appears on the road coming toward them. That must be Matt in the Suburban. Zach only needs to stall long enough for him to get here without getting shot in the process. He points down the road at the oncoming vehicle.

"Last chance to surrender."

"I don't think so. Not until I clear my name."

"Colby Washington is dead, Boston. This isn't the way to do that."

He looks surprised. Maybe it was the use of his nickname or the news about the senator. Either way, it caught him off-guard.

"It doesn't matter."

Zach notices that the approaching headlights aren't from the Suburban at all. They belong to an old, beat-up pickup that slows to a stop. Another set of headlights farther off in the distance is coming as well. That must be Remsen, but it'll be too late.

"I know about your dreams, Boston. Or memories."

"Tara's notes. You took them."

"Yeah, I did."

Boston nods. "Then you understand how I know someone is setting me up. Someone I *know*."

He climbs up the embankment to the road and stops next to the truck. The muzzle of his weapon never moves off Zach.

"Two senators are dead. If you really want to find out who killed them, coming with me is your best option."

"Someone handed you a file with my name on it at the Iwo Jima Memorial before any of this went down," Boston says, causing Zach's mouth to hang open. "Who's to say that the mole isn't one of the FBI agents giving you orders?"

"I hate to break up this little fireside chat, Bos, but we're about to have company," the driver of the truck says.

Boston climbs in and pulls the door closed. He keeps his weapon aimed out the open window.

"Hollinger!"

"Don't give me a reason to shoot you," he warns as the truck lurches forward before accelerating.

Zach searches the ground and finds his gun lying in the mud a few feet away. He retrieves it and scampers up the embankment just as Matt pulls up in the Suburban. He gives Zach a onceover.

"Jesus. Are you okay?"

"No, I'm pissed off. We need to get his ass. Let's go."

CHAPTER SIXTY-FOUR
"BOSTON" HOLLINGER

BILLINGSLEY FARM ROAD
WHITE PLAINS, MARYLAND

Louisiana slams on the accelerator, feeding more gas to the roaring engine. This vehicle isn't built for speed, that's for sure. I roll up the window and close my eyes for a moment as I fight to catch my breath.

"I'm guessin' things didn't go as planned."

"What gave it away?" I ask between coughs. "I'm glad I let you tag along on this road trip."

"You should've let me go in with ya," Louisiana admonishes. "What happened with Senator Sketchy?"

"I don't think he had anything to do with any of this."

"Bos, Bos, Bos, you change your mind an awful lot these days. You said you saw him in the memories."

"Yeah, well, I was wrong. Now I'm not sure what I saw."

"He'll be thrilled to hear it," Louisiana says, checking the driver's side mirror.

"Not really. He's dead."

"Dead?"

"That's what my FBI friend said."

"You've grown that close, have ya? Did you—"

"No, I didn't kill him."

Louisiana makes a sharp right turn way too fast for the weather. The back end fishtails out, and he turns into the skid. I hang on for dear life. This beats being in FBI custody, but there was a reason we never let this maniac drive in Syria.

"Do you know where you're going?"

"Does it look like I'm from around here, bro?"

"You're right, we need a plan and fast. The police are going to be all over us in no time."

"The police?"

"Colby called them before we started shooting at each other. Then the FBI interrupted."

"What? How did he…you know what? We need to work on your home invasion skills," he says, shaking his head.

"Another time. That vehicle is gaining on us."

"Your friend from the woods?"

"No doubt."

"Grab the bag in the back seat," he instructs me.

I unfasten my seat belt and retrieve Louisiana's medium-sized duffel bag of destruction. It's filled with homemade and military issue grenades, plastic explosives, detonators, and, not surprisingly, the tranquilizer gun he threatened to shoot Maryland with back at Tara's friend's apartment.

"Jesus, dude," I say, sifting through it.

"I know. It's great, right?"

"Yeah, what do you want?"

"Let's start with the flashbangs."

I pull two grenades out of the bag and push the whole thing down to the floorboards at my feet. I admire the cylinders.

"Where did you get these?"

"Walmart. Straight, or right?" he asks when we come up to a traffic light.

"Go right."

For the second time, he almost loses control as the tires hydroplane on standing water. I check the mirror, hoping the massive Chevy Suburban chasing us doesn't fare as well. It does.

"You know we're going in a circle, right?" Louisiana asks.

"Are you always this calm when the police are chasing you? When do we toss these?"

"It's all about the right timing. Roll down your window."

I look in the mirror. The headlights and flashing blue strobe on the FBI vehicle come up behind us fast when Louisiana lets up on the gas. We roll our windows down and fight the rain pouring into the cab of his truck. I sure hope he knows what we're doing.

"Now?"

"Not yet."

I feel the truck slow even more. I hope that Louisiana isn't planning some insane *Top Gun* move where he hits the brakes, and they drive right by. They're only about fifty yards behind us now.

"Now?"

"Relax, will ya? When I say the word, toss that thing as hard as you can straight in the air." He checks the mirror. "Now!"

I pull the pin and heave the grenade skyward. I count in my head just as I did at Colby's. One…I hope to God this works. Two…three.

I watch in the side mirror as the two grenades detonate within a half-second of each other. We're far enough away to avoid the effects, but the same can't be said for the guys in the Suburban. The flashbangs went off right in front of their windshield.

The SUV loses control and rides up an embankment on the right side of the road. It's about to flip when the driver points it back toward the asphalt. I think he'll make it back to the pavement when his vehicle slams into one of the trees lining the road.

"Nice job, now what?"

"The police are going to be crawling all over this neighborhood in a matter of minutes. At least the torrential downpour will keep the helicopters out of the air. We need to get out of this area and get rid of my truck."

"These are planned neighborhoods on the left and right, Louisiana. One wrong turn, and we could end up not getting out. Most of them only have two entrances and exits."

These types of neighborhoods are meticulously laid out from inception and are constructed in large, undeveloped areas. Unlike most towns where residential areas evolve randomly, planned layouts maximize every square foot of real estate. They can be labyrinths, and we'll be pinned in if we choose the wrong one.

"Uh-oh."

The red and blue flashing lights coming at us from a half-mile up the road mark the local police's arrival at the chase. Without missing a beat or bothering to give me a heads-up, Louisiana makes a hard left and stops.

"What are you doing?"

"Help me," he orders, climbing out of the truck.

Louisiana lowers the tailgate and climbs into the bed of the pickup. It's filled with everything from garden tools to chains and rope. The sirens are growing closer, increasing my own anxiety as he searches for something.

"We don't have time for this."

"Keep your pants on. Here it is," he says, hopping over the side with a black…something. "Help me."

We unfasten the carrier and remove a police-grade spike strip. I grab the end and stretch it across the road right behind the pickup. This guy has everything.

"Nice!" I exclaim when we get back into the truck.

"That'll slow 'em down."

We drive off and are almost out of sight when the police turn into the street after us. They don't make it far. Tires explode on the four cars that hit the spike strip, ending the pursuit before it even starts. We aren't out of danger, but I breathe for the first time since we got out of the truck. I hope to God there is another way out of this neighborhood. A minute later, we hit another main road, and he makes a right.

The air is filled with the unmistakable blare of sirens that sound like they're everywhere. My nerves are shot, and I'm on edge. The adrenaline flowing through me is making it hard to focus on anything. I need to concentrate. The people who get caught are the ones who fail to stay three steps ahead.

"That spike strip won't keep them off us for long. Any idea where we can find new wheels?"

"Yeah, a few. Where do you want to go after that?"

I take a moment to think about it. "Back to the sleep center. I need to talk to Tara."

"Bro, I'm not against seeing my girl, but we'll have to go back through the heart of D.C. Do you think that's smart?"

"No, probably not, but the clock is ticking. We can't run forever, and I can't afford to be wrong about these memories. I need to understand what I'm seeing. Tara's the only one that can help with that now."

I only hope she'll be willing to help. She was upset about how the memories work and angry when I told her about confronting Colby Washington. I decided to do it despite her objections. I'm not sure how well I will be received when I walk back in there.

"You're sure? I mean, the FBI might be on to that by now."

"It's the risk we have to take. These dreams are the key to this story having a happy ending."

"All right, bro, if that's what you want, then back into the belly of the beast we go."

CHAPTER SIXTY-FIVE
ERIC "MARYLAND" WILLIAMS

Maryland is so exhausted that he can't sleep. It's counterintuitive, but his nerves are shot, his anxiety is through the roof, and his mind is racing. It doesn't matter how mentally wrought he is. Sleep won't come. He hasn't been home a half hour when there's a loud series of raps on the door.

He answers and isn't shocked to see two FBI agents standing there. Their appearance, however, is a surprise. Both men are disheveled and smell like they smoked five packs of cigarettes. One has a bandage on his head. The other has pants caked with mud and looks like he's been through hell.

They don't bother greeting Maryland. They brush past him as they walk in.

"Sure, just let yourself in. Search the place if you want. Boston isn't here."

"We know he isn't."

"What happened to you guys?" Maryland asks, no longer able to resist posing the question.

"We ran a Spartan Race."

"Okay, fine. I cooperated with the FBI. Agent Grimman said that I was free to go."

"You were free to go. You're here, aren't you?"

Maryland scoffs and walks over to the table next to his recliner. He seizes his beer and takes a long swig of it.

"Okay, so who are you, and why are you here?"

"I'm Director Remsen. This is Special Agent Forte. We went to pay a visit to Senator Colby Washington this afternoon. It turns out he was involved in quite the firefight when we got there."

Maryland lowers his head. "Was it Boston?"

"Why do you think it was him?" the director asks.

"You wouldn't be here otherwise. How is the senator?"

"Dead," Agent Forte says. "To answer your next question, it wasn't Hollinger that killed him. Senator Washington shot at us when we entered the premises. We were forced to returned fire."

"And Boston?"

"He fled the house through the woods. Hollinger got the jump on me when I caught up to him. Instead of putting a bullet in me, he took off with Louisiana in his truck. We gave chase. That ended with them tossing flashbangs at us and Matt's SUV wrapped around a tree."

Maryland smirks. That sounds about right. The footrace through the woods explains the muddy pants, but not the smoke. The accident explains the bandages. Agent Forte's story is light on the details, but he's not in a talkative mood.

"Ah, I see you met Louisiana."

"That's my second encounter with him. It was my car that he nuked outside Dr. Winters's house."

"That makes you the asshole that shot at us. It sounds like you got what you deserved."

"Yeah, hours of debriefings about why we shot a senator and treatment for our injuries in the pursuit. It's been an enjoyable day, for sure," Agent Forte says, seething with anger.

"What does any of this have to do with me?"

"Nothing," the director says.

"Good. Then get out."

"Not yet. We need your help, Eric. I don't think Hollinger is the traitor, but he isn't making it easy for us to make that argument. After tonight, he's a marked target. You served with him. You know him. What do you think he'll do now?"

"I have no idea. I'm not involved."

Maryland takes another sip from his beer. He's beginning to think Boston is a cat burning through his nine lives. From their near-death encounter with a Syrian mortar round to his Houdini act a few hours ago, that luck will run out eventually. Maryland is happy he got away from him when he did.

"We know that Hollinger sees memories in his dreams. Is that why he went to see Colby Washington?"

"How would…ah, you were the intruder Boston saw at Tara's. You were the one who made off with her notes."

"He experienced that memory?" Director Remsen asks.

"So he says."

The two men exchange a knowing look. They knew about Boston's dreams. Neither realized that Agent Forte was the subject of one.

"Yes, I stole her notes. Answer the question. Why did Hollinger go assault Senator Washington?"

"I don't know. Somebody is setting Boston up. The only thing I know to be true in this whole shitty situation is that he isn't a traitor."

"How do you know that?" the director asks.

"Aside from knowing him for years? He was visiting me at JBAB right before his accident. He knew that the mole was transferring DIA intelligence products and wanted to know who else had access to them. I wrote a report about it and submitted it up the chain."

"The report that got leaked to the media by Admiral Troxell."

"That's right. Boston wouldn't ask me to do that if it was him. I think he suspected someone on the SSCI. Maybe he experienced a memory that pointed him to Colby Washington. It could have been something else. I just don't know."

"What's his next move? Will he skip town?"

"Not a chance. Boston will go back to trying to figure out who is behind all this. He thinks the memories will lead him to whoever is setting him up and maybe even the mole, assuming they are even different people."

"How will he do that?" Director Remsen asks.

"Dr. Winters will help him. She's been working with him to make the dreams sharper."

"Where?"

"I don't know. We went to the apartment near Logan Circle because we had no other options. If they aren't there now, I have no idea where they could be."

"Don't let me find out that you are lying to us, Mr. Williams."

Maryland scoffs. "I'm not hiding anything. But understand something: as much as I disagree with Boston's tactics, part of me is still rooting for him."

"Noted," Agent Forte says as both men head for the door. "One more thing, Maryland. If you think of anything that may help, give me a call. Boston is the brightest blip on everyone's radar now. Two senators are dead, and they'll bring him in by any means necessary."

Agent Forte hands Maryland a business card with his name and number on it.

"And you won't?"

"Hollinger could have killed me in those woods behind Washington's house, but he didn't pull the trigger. It would have made his escape a lot easier. He's not a killer, despite what everyone wants to believe. The only way to get to the bottom of this mess and find the real traitor is for Boston to stay alive."

"You broke into Tara Winters's house and shot at us when we fled. Don't expect me to take anything you say at face value."

"Don't worry, I won't."

The two men leave, and Maryland closes and locks his door, resting his forehead against it. His friend is in serious trouble, and he hasn't done anything to help. As pissed as he is about what they've done, guilt is starting to set in. Unfortunately, it may already be too late.

CHAPTER SIXTY-SIX

"BOSTON" HOLLINGER

SOLVASON SLEEP DISORDERS CENTER
CHEVY CHASE, MARYLAND

It's just before nine p.m. when Louisiana pulls up to the glass building that houses the sleep center. The street is quiet but not completely devoid of activity either. Fortunately, the car Louisiana stole from a rental company after ditching his beloved pickup truck on the way back from Colby's isn't likely to be reported anytime soon.

We had a close call today. We managed to escape being chased by the FBI and used a spike strip to stop a prolonged police chase before it really started. We switched vehicles just as the police dragnet closed in on us. Fifteen more minutes in the truck, and they would have found us. Now, after all that, I'm about to take another risk. The FBI could be waiting for me inside.

"You think she's even here, bro?" Louisiana asks, staring out my window at the building.

"Yeah. Tara has no other place to go. Are you sure you want to risk going to Bolling-Anacostia?"

"Bro, it's time Maryland and I had it out like men. Besides, do you really think the MPs have my picture?"

He has a good point. Gate guards at military installations are concerned with ensuring that visitors aren't carrying explosives that could harm personnel and infrastructure. Although each guard shack is provided names and photos of people they should be on the lookout for, it's doubtful Louisiana is on that list.

"The FBI is probably watching him. I don't think it's worth the risk, but good luck anyway. You have my burner number?"

"Yeah, I got it."

I give him a fist bump and climb out of the car. He has no registration or paperwork for it, so he's toast if he gets snagged trying to enter the base. That's provided he uses the gate at all. With Louisiana, you can't assume anything.

Louisiana drives off towards the shopping mall that we originally stashed Tara's friend's Infiniti SUV in. I turn and walk into the building, passing by the front desk with the inattentive guard, and take the elevator up to the sleep center. When the doors open, I find it empty. A woman's laughter on the other side of the door leading to the sleep rooms is the only indication that anyone is here.

"Tara?" I call out.

The door swings open and she bursts out, covering the distance between us in a flash before throwing her arms around me. I guess she isn't as angry as I thought she would be. I return the hug, feeling a little awkward in doing so after noticing Steven's uncomfortable stance at the door.

"What happened to you?" she finally asks after stepping back and giving me a onceover. I'm still looking a little ragged after my chase through the woods.

"It was a rough day. Colby Washington wasn't involved in any of this, Tara. And neither was Garrett Turner. I don't know what to think anymore."

"What happened?"

We move to the staff lounge, where I proceed to tell the two doctors the whole story about the confrontation with Colby, the resulting firefight in his house, being chased through the woods by the FBI, and how Louisiana and I evaded them. She's not amused, and Steven is in a complete state of shock. Reality just came crashing down on him that I'm a wanted fugitive and that he could be labeled an accessory for helping me.

"I can't believe you! What's going through your head?" Tara finally admonishes once I finish.

"Tara, I'm going to be arrested in the next twenty-four hours. This may be the last chance to find the answers I'm looking for."

"Oh, so you came running back here to me just for that?" she asks, and not in a playful way. It was the wrong thing to say to her.

"No. You're my angel. You need to know that. I've already asked too much of you and dragged you into something I should never have. All I can do now is apologize for that and hope that one day you'll forgive me. But I need to ask for one more favor. Help me see this thing through one more night."

I hope it sounded as sincere as it felt. The last thing I want Tara to feel is like I'm using her. The truth is the exact opposite of that. She's a remarkable woman, sweet and complex, and in different circumstances, someone I would want to get to know a lot better.

Tears well in her eyes before streaming down her cheeks as she stares at the far wall. I think she's going to say no when she turns to Steven, who is sitting there with the look of a jilted ex-boyfriend.

"Steven, would you mind having a guest for one more evening?"

He gives me a hard stare before softening and taking her hand in his. "You know I would do anything for you, Tara."

"Thank you," she says quietly.

"We, uh…we have a laundry machine and dryer here to wash your clothes. They need it."

"Thanks, I appreciate that," I say.

"I'll get him set up in eight," Tara informs him, referring to the room I spent last night in.

"I'll get the galantamine."

"Steven, on that note, I've been shot at, almost burned alive, involved in a car chase…"

"Uh, yeah. I'll get something to help knock you out, too."

I nod, and he disappears down the hall and into a room marked with an "employees only" sign. I follow Tara farther into the bowels of the empty sleep center. She doesn't say a word to me, and the silence is unnerving.

"Did you stay here all day?"

"I didn't have much choice, did I?" she retorts.

"I'm sorry about that. How did—"

"Only the admins were in. Steven told them that I was interested in accepting a position here. Some of them already know me, and most know about Steven's … interest in me. They didn't question it."

We enter the room, and Tara pulls out a set of sweatpants and a T-shirt with the sleep center's name on it from a drawer in a dresser along the wall. From a different drawer, she pulls the sensors and wires out for the EEG. That's not something you find in a typical bedroom.

I strip down to my boxers as Tara powers up the EEG. When finished, she turns around and immediately blushes.

"Sorry, I should have—"

"No, it's okay," she says, averting her head and eyes, but not all the way as I slip the clothes on and sit on the edge of the bed.

"Have you made any progress figuring out how my memory retrieval works considering what we learned last night?"

"No, not really. There isn't enough evidence available," Tara explains in a defeated tone.

"Maybe you'll learn more tonight," I console.

"Maybe."

"Are you mad at me?" I prod.

"No, I'm not mad. I was thrilled when you walked in tonight. I was afraid I'd never see you again when you left, but I'd be lying if I told you I wasn't scared. I just can't bear to think—"

She is interrupted when Steven knocks on the door holding a cup of pills and a small water bottle. This guy is the king of bad timing. Of course, he was probably standing outside the door and planned it that way.

"Thanks, Steven," Tara says as he hands her the pills and water.

"No problem. I'll be in the lounge if you need me."

"That dude's ready to put a ring on your finger," I mumble, sounding far more jealous than I should.

"I know. He's asked me out at least a dozen times."

"How long have you known him?"

"A dozen times *today*, Boston," she clarifies with a slight smile.

"So why are you still helping me? You already got far more than you bargained for."

"My parents are both doctors. Dad is a world-renowned surgeon at G.W. Mom's a clinical psychologist with countless best-selling books. When they had me, I was born with the proverbial silver spoon in my mouth. From the time I could talk, they started grooming me to become them. It was never a question that I would become a doctor, only what discipline I would choose.

"I went to the best schools, had the best tutors, and never had to struggle or want for anything. It was an easy life. Too easy. Unfortunately, nobody ever asked what I wanted. To make a long story short, I rebelled against them and their lofty plans. I chose to work with veterans and help with neurological disorders."

"It's noble work."

"Not according to them. It isn't prestigious enough, so my parents cut me off. They let me stay in the Adams Morgan property because they couldn't bear the whispers among their colleagues about their disgraced only child. It was for their own peace of mind. It had nothing to do with me."

"That couldn't have been easy."

Tears are forming in her eyes again. "It wasn't. The pressure to toe the line in my culture is immense. I began to give in and make changes. You briefly met one of them."

"Mark?"

"I only began dating him because he was successful and from a good family. I knew my parents would approve. I also started looking into positions at Johns Hopkins and other more prestigious medical positions."

"And?"

"Let's just say they both worked out equally well. I've never been passionate about anything…until you came along. For the first time in my life, it felt like what I was doing mattered. That's why I didn't get out of the car in Ivy City or take Maryland up on his offer to leave you. It's why it bothers me so much that my theory was wrong. It's why I'm going to help you finish it now."

I've known Tara for less than a week, and she has shown me more love and support than my fiancée has in the year and a half we've been together. What does that say about our relationship? Gina is beautiful but cold. Tara heats up a room by walking into it. It's no wonder why I'm not taking my fiancée's ultimatum seriously. Part of me doesn't want to.

"Is that the only reason?" I ask, wondering if Louisiana was right in his assessment of her feelings. The comment causes her to look away and blush a little. I guess I got my answer.

"It's the only one that matters," she says, forcing a slight smile at the end.

"Tara, I—"

"Don't. It doesn't need to be said," she says, standing and walking towards the door. "Dream well, Boston."

Tara switches off the light and exits the room. Yeah, dream well. I take the pills, remove my shirt, and climb under the covers. This sleep aid had better be potent because I'm completely wired. The adrenaline rush from this afternoon hasn't dissipated much.

I reach across the bed and retrieve the cell phone from the nightstand. There's one last thing to do before I close my eyes and wish for sleep to come without the need to count sheep. I just hope Gina has her phone turned on.

CHAPTER SIXTY-SEVEN
FBI AGENT ZACH FORTE

Remsen pulls the Crown Victoria sedan up outside the taped-off police line in the typical Washington, D.C. neighborhood. He and Zach hop out of the car and scan the area before flashing their badges to an officer securing the scene. It's just another quiet morning on a sleepy street interrupted by FBI agents and pulsating strobes of D.C. Metro Police vehicles. Half of the neighbors are watching the action from the sidewalk while wondering what's going on.

An agent greets them in the apartment's living room. After a brief introduction, they get down to business. Remsen already got an update from his people at Watchtower, which wasn't much. Without any other leads, they decided to visit the place Boston and his gang were holed up in.

"We've gone through the apartment from top to bottom," the agent informs them. "They didn't leave anything behind."

"They're smarter than that," Zach mumbles, admiring the tastefully decorated living room.

"Is there any indication about where they could have gone?"

"No. The owner's SUV was located in long-term parking at Reagan National. The GPS log indicates that the vehicle was parked for some time in the underground garage at a shopping mall up in Chevy Chase. They could have gone almost anywhere from that location."

"Maybe they know someone up there," Zach says, getting a shrug from Matt.

"We're checking that. I spoke to the homeowner, Andrea Davis. She and her boyfriend are still vacationing in France. She confirmed that Tara Winters had the key and also provided the names of a few friends she might be staying with."

"The doctor came here because she knew that the owner was out of the country. I wouldn't expect to find her dropping in on any of them unless they are traveling."

"We'll check anyway," he says, leaning in. "We heard a rumor that Colby Washington was killed tonight."

Matt shoots a warning with his eyes. "Yeah, he was. Keep that under wraps. The information hasn't been made public yet."

"You know that isn't going to last long, right? Someone is going to get that scoop. The media is all over this story."

"I know, but for obvious reasons, we need it to last as long as it can. The moment this thing goes public, this city will lose its mind."

"Understood," the agent promises before moving off to talk to his other colleagues. "We're wrapping up here. Anything more for me?"

"No, thanks for the update."

The agent moves off, and the two men take a seat in the living room. Matt gingerly touches the bandage on his head while Zach rubs his own shoulders in a desperate attempt to alleviate some stress.

"Thoughts?" Matt asks.

"Yeah, I picked a hell of a day to quit sniffing glue," Zach says, quoting the movie *Airplane!* to the amusement of his friend.

"Besides that."

Zach leans back and reflects on Boston's actions. "Hollinger's response to the surveillance at Dr. Winters's house was unorthodox, and the firefight with Senator Washington can't be explained easily. And then there was the chase through the woods. None of this makes sense unless you factor in these dreams. He is seeing things and trying to interpret them as he goes."

"That makes him a loose cannon."

"But not a traitor. If he is being set up, he'd want to know by whom."

"Colby Washington? Garrett Turner?"

"Or someone else."

Remsen's cell phone rings. He checks the caller ID before placing it on speaker. "What do you have, Bill?"

"We should be thankful that some people still have landlines. There were only three calls from the apartment since the owner left. They all were made to the same individual: a guy named Steven Kempler. He's clean. No criminal history. He's some big shot doctor at the Sölvason Sleep Disorders Center."

Both men sit up and lean forward, a glint in their eyes.

"Let me guess: their office is located up in Chevy Chase," Matt says.

"Yeah. How did you know that?"

Matt ignores the question. "Bill, call the sleep center. Do it from your personal phone and pretend to set up an appointment or something. I want to see if anyone answers."

"It's almost eleven. Won't they be closed?"

"It's a sleep disorders center, so probably not. Let me know what you come up with," Matt says, killing the call as Zach's phone chirps.

"Damn," he grumbles after reading the message. "You've got to be kidding me."

"What is it?"

"I'm being summoned back to the office for a debriefing with Director Weisz about what happened at Senator Washington's house. They're looking for someone to blame, and it looks like I drew the short straw."

"Welcome to the FBI. Ignore it. I'll take care of it. Right now, we have more important things to do."

CHAPTER SIXTY-EIGHT

GINA ATTISON

The cable news alert notifications blow up Gina's phone, and she immediately tunes in to the reports of a fire at Senator Colby Washington's suburban home. The on-scene reporter recites the rumors about a possible intruder, assault, fire, and apparent police chase as the suspect fled the scene. She knows it was Boston. The burner phone is powered on and sitting quietly next to her. Why hasn't he called?

"Authorities have confirmed that the sole victim of the home invasion was Colby Washington, the senior senator from the State of Missouri," the man tells the camera with the flashing lights of fire trucks and the smoldering house in the background. "The senator was found inside and evacuated from the house. Sources have told us that he suffered a gunshot wound to the chest and was rushed to an area hospital. His condition is unknown, as is the cause of the fire. We have learned that it appears to have started in the living room and quickly spread to the rest of the structure. Reporting from White Plains, Maryland, this is Tony Martinez, Eyewitness News."

"Tony, the house belonged to the chairman of the Senate Select Committee on Intelligence. Have authorities commented on this being related to the intelligence leaks that have led to the American deaths in Syria, including the vice president's son?"

"Officials have been tight-lipped about that. It doesn't appear that authorities have anyone in custody and will not divulge whether they have any suspects. The questions about the perpetrator and his motives will have to be answered as this investigation progresses."

Gina's phone vibrates as the news anchor prattles on about the reaction in the senator's home state. Gina snatches it and answers, saying nothing until she reaches the bathroom and turns on the shower. The white noise should disrupt the reception of any directional mic that the feds might be using from the street.

If they planted a modern listening device in the room while searching the house, computer software could filter it out. It's a chance she needs to take.

"Boston?"

"Yeah, it's me. Where are you?"

"The bathroom. The FBI is still parked outside the house. Are you okay?"

"Yeah, I'm fine. Colby Washington is dead."

The news hits her with the force of a hammer.

"They're only reporting the fire and a possible intruder. They haven't said that he's dead. Did you…"

"No, the FBI killed him. At least that's what they told me," he explains. Gina feels herself relax a little.

"They told you that? How—?"

"It's a long story. Colby wasn't setting me up to be the mole," he confesses. "I don't know who's behind it, nor do I know who is leaking our secrets. I'm fresh out of suspects, Gina."

Gina rubs her temples. Maybe these dreams aren't as reliable as he thought they were. It's like he's ruining their lives for nothing.

"What now? You can't run forever. The feds are going to be all over you."

"Hopefully I won't have to. Tara's convinced these memories are triggered by trauma and stress. Hopefully, after what happened today, I will see things very clearly."

She feels a tingly surge of anger at the mention of Tara. "Like she's been right about so many things!"

"Whoa, where did that come from?" Boston asks.

"Seriously? Boston, I've been fired from my job. My security clearance has been suspended. The damn FBI is parked outside our house, and they follow me everywhere! You have to end this."

"I know you're upset. Once I find out who's behind this, everything will be okay."

"Will it? What makes you think that you can figure it all out when half of the federal government can't?"

"Because they stopped looking for the mole when someone pointed their finger in my direction. You have to have some faith in me."

Gina exhales. "All I want to do is put this behind us. We can go to the mountains for some Merlot and disappear for a while.

"And we will," he promises.

Despite the fan in the ceiling whirring away, the bathroom is filling with steam. She can't keep up the charade much longer if the FBI is listening in. As much as she wants more answers from him, the call needs to end.

"Okay, I need to go. Sleep well."

"I'm going to try. Bye."

Gina hangs up and holds the phone against her chest. It's ending tonight. The long story will finally have the ending it deserves, one way or another.

She goes into the bedroom and opens the hollow panel beneath the closet's floorboards. The void is only one plank in width and impossible to detect. That's the only reason that the FBI didn't find it during their search. She replaces the phone and then retrieves another.

Gina knows in her heart that Boston is going to get caught. Once he's in FBI custody, nothing will save him, even if he sees the traitor in a dream. He will answer for Louisiana's recklessness outside Tara's and what he did at Colby's. The authorities will throw the book at him.

It's time to start preparing for bad eventualities. Everything is going to end within the next day, and she needs to be ready. She powers on the second phone and moves back to the bathroom. It's time for a Hail Mary pass to the end zone.

CHAPTER SIXTY-NINE
"BOSTON" HOLLINGER

SOLVASON SLEEP DISORDERS CENTER
CHEVY CHASE, MARYLAND

The image is foggier than usual. The room is small and cramped. A cacophony of steady noise fills the air. I can hear the whir of a fan over my head and the sound of . . . water.

"All I want to do is put this behind us. We can go to the mountains for some Merlot and disappear for a while."

"And we will." I know that voice. It's mine.

The room is getting foggier. It's almost hard to breathe.

"Okay, I need to go. Sleep well."

"I'm going to try. Bye."

I feel the person leave the room and go into another. Everything is clear as I move to a closet and slide over a box. A hand reaches down and opens a hole in the floor, places a device into it, and takes out another. The nails are manicured. A woman's hand . . .

"Da?" a voice says after I move back into the foggy room and dial a number. It's a man's voice . . . with a Russian accent.

"I hope the last information I passed you was acceptable."

"Yes, it will help immensely. Will you ever be in a position to give us more?"

"No. I think you've seen the last of me."

A deep sadness rushes through me. It's not remorse or mourning. It feels shallower than that, like regret.

"That is unfortunate." I can hear the regret in his voice. "What will you do now?"

"I need to leave the country. I must request your help."

"Are you at risk of capture?"

"I don't know. My original plan has been spoiled. Now I'm looking for a way out. I need new travel documents and money."

"I can help with both, but it will take time."

"How much time?"

"A few days. Maybe a week. Can you wait that long?"

"Not here, but I have a place I can go wait far enough away to avoid detection. They have a great Merlot there," my voice says with a laugh.

I shoot straight out of bed and stand in the middle of the floor. I can't catch my breath. I inhale deeper and deeper, and it's still not enough.

"Oh, my God!" I try to blurt out while exhaling.

There's a knock at the door, but I don't answer. I run the dream through my mind. It's unmistakable. Unlike what Colby told me, there's no room for interpretation. I know what I saw and heard. I know who it was, and the thought of it makes me break out into a cold sweat.

"Boston? What is it? What's wrong? He's hyperventilating," Tara shouts to Steven, who has rushed in behind her. The concern is worn all over her face. She edges me back over toward the bed.

"Sit down, Boston. Try to take normal breaths."

"He's awake? How is that possible after the sedative I gave him?" Steven asks, walking over to the EEG. The cords for the sensors were pulled from my head when I jumped out of bed, so the contraption is no longer recording data.

"Boston, it's okay," Tara consoles, rubbing my back while I fight to recover my wind.

"No, it isn't. Nothing's okay," I whisper.

"Tell me what happened."

"I saw it. I saw everything. Unlike the other dreams, I…"

"My God, I've never seen activity like this," Steven says after my voice trails off, staring at the machine.

My heart is racing. I regain my composure and start to control my breathing. Once I do, I quickly begin peeling the connector pads off my head.

"Boston, what are you—"

"How long was I out?" I demand.

"Uh, about two hours, I guess. Why?"

"Are my clothes ready?"

"Yeah, we just pulled them out of the dryer," Steven says, still confused by the urgency.

"Get them."

Steven nods and rushes out of the room without any questions. It sounds like he's eager to please, but more likely just wants me gone.

"Boston, talk to me."

I turn back to see her pleading eyes. What can I tell her? How do I begin to explain what I just saw? How do I convince her when I can't even convince myself to believe it?

"I have to go, Tara," I say, rising from the bed as Steven walks back in with my neatly folded clothes.

"Why? What did you see?"

"Something I never thought I would."

"Here you go."

"Steven, I hate to impose on you further, but I need to borrow your car," I say as I pull off the sweats and put my clothes on in record time. "I'll get it back to you, I promise."

He looks at Tara, searching for any signal to not agree. She's not looking at either of us at the moment, so he receives none. I know I'm hurting her feelings, but this has to come first.

"Okay. It's a light gray Chevy Malibu," he says, pulling his house key off the ring before handing me the one for his car. "It's in the building's parking garage in the basement. Take the elevator down to P1."

"Thanks."

I walk out of the room and down the hall, and Tara follows. I look back and see Steven following as well. She follows my eyes and stops.

"Can you give us a minute?" she asks him.

"Uh…sure," he replies with a forced smile.

"So, that's it? After all this, you're just going to leave and not tell me what's happening?"

"Tara, it's better this way. I can't ask you to go any further with me."

"Why? What did you see?" she pleads once more.

I lower my eyes and stare at the ground. The images and words play in my mind, but part of me still refuses to believe it. It's not something I would ever have considered, and it's tearing me up inside.

"I saw the mole. I know who the traitor is and who is framing me to take the fall."

"Who?" She has a right to know, but I can't bring myself to tell her.

"It's not important."

"Not important? Like hell, it isn't! Tell me, please. You owe me that much!" She stomps over to me and grabs my shirt as I punch the elevator button.

"Tara, trust me, it's better if you don't know."

"So this really is it?" she concludes, the fight dissipating back to hurt again as the tears form in her eyes. I make up my mind. There's really no reason I shouldn't do what I'm about to do now.

I take her face into my hands and kiss her. It's slow, deep, and passionate like most first kisses are. It's something I never thought I would ever do again after getting engaged. Little did I know that I'm engaged to a woman who has been lying to me this whole time.

I hear the ding of the elevator bell, and the doors open behind me. I finally pull my lips away and wipe at the tears with my fingers. As much as part of me wants to stay, I need to go. I need to finish this.

"I have to go. Thank you…for everything."

I step into the elevator and punch the button for P1. I watch her stare back at me, fighting the tears that refuse to be stifled. We hold each other's gaze until the doors finally close.

CHAPTER SEVENTY
ERIC "MARYLAND" WILLIAMS

Television after midnight sucks, but everything is tolerable for someone working on their third six-pack. The pizza that Maryland had delivered earlier is gone except for the box it came in. Maryland is just starting to doze off in his recliner when the piercing sound of the doorbell stirs him awake. He slams his head several times against the headrest. Normalcy will never return until all this is over.

"Who is it?" he asks, not wanting to get out of the chair.

"FBI, Mr. Williams. Open up."

Maryland sighs. Not again. He gets up and opens the door, expecting to see the same disgruntled pair of agents in their rumpled clothes flashing their badges. Instead, Louisiana is standing outside in the rain.

"Very funny. What the hell do you want?"

"It's rainin', dumbass. I want to come in."

"No way. You're a wanted felon. Do you think I'm going to let you set one foot inside this house?"

Maryland starts to close the door when Louisiana kicks it and sends it flying back into his face, knocking him off balance and stumbling back into the living room. The Cajun comes in and closes the front door behind him.

"Get out!"

"Psssh, not a chance. Tell me what you said to the FBI."

"I'm not telling you a damn thing, psycho," Maryland says, rubbing the side of his head.

"Yeah, you really are. You're gonna start from the beginnin' and tell me everythin'. Boston needs your help, and by God, you're gonna give it to him."

"One senator is dead, and he attacked another. That's everything that needs to be said."

"That's where you're wrong. They're both dead."

Maryland shakes off the impact of that comment. "He's a fugitive, and much of that is because of you. You're toxic and poison everything you touch. That's what I told the feds. Now get out!"

Louisiana gets a shove toward the door for good measure. Maryland is about to deliver another when he retaliates with one of his own.

"I'm not leavin' until I get answers from you, bro. So settle down."

"Have it your way."

Maryland pulls out his phone to call the MPs. He isn't sure how Louisiana managed to get on this base in the first place, but he won't want to stick around for their arrival.

Louisiana grabs Maryland's wrist and twists, prying the device from his hand. After a quick check to ensure that no call is connected, he hurls the phone against the far wall. Maryland gnashes his teeth and balls his hands into fists.

He throws a right and connects against Louisiana's jaw. The blow barely fazes him as he responds with a jab of his own. Maryland doesn't see it coming until it's too late. The punch is followed by a hard right that knocks him into the coffee table and then to the floor.

Maryland is pulling himself up on all fours when he gets a hard kick to the ribs. The force knocks the wind from his lungs, causing several hard coughs and gasps for air. He waits for another kick, but it never comes.

"Now, where were we?" Louisiana mocks.

Maryland climbs to his feet and launches himself in a bull rush that there is no hope in dodging. The two men hit the far wall hard and bounce off, grappling until they trip over an ottoman and crash to the ground. Free of each other, they both get back to their feet.

"Okay, bro, now you're pissin' me off."

He fakes a left, but Maryland is ready for the right. He blocks it and strikes him with an open palm to the solar plexus. Louisiana stumbles back as Maryland lands a hard right on his temple, cocking his arm back to hit him again.

Louisiana moves quickly for a guy his size. He closes in and turns his back on Maryland, swinging his elbow and landing into his abdomen before hooking his arm. A split second later, the hip toss sends Maryland flying through the air and crashing on the coffee table. Unlike in the movies, the sturdy piece of furniture groans but doesn't break.

He slides off the edge and collapses to the floor, bringing him eye level with one of the empty beer bottles. He picks it up before using the couch as support to stand and smashes it on Louisiana's head when he moves in for another hit.

The bottle shatters, causing him to wobble. Maryland lunges again. This time, Louisiana was waiting for it, despite seeing stars from the blow to his head. He keeps his balance and twists his body as he secures a headlock. Maryland strikes at his kidneys to try to loosen his grip, but there's no force behind the blows.

He releases the lock and crashes a knee into Maryland's nose, causing blood to gush out and probably breaking it. They grab at each other, each trying to gain the upper hand. After a brief exchange of hits to the head with no power behind them, both miss with simultaneous haymakers in a desperate bid to end things. They crash onto the floor and lie there for a minute. Neither has the fitness level they once did.

They both slide up into a seated position. Maryland leans against the couch as he checks his nose. Louisiana examines his head wound from his spot next to the recliner. He pulls himself up into it and starts laughing, first as a chuckle and then rising into a full belly laugh.

"What's so damn funny?"

"We've been waitin' to do that to each other for years."

As angry as Maryland is, he can't resist a smile. He joins Louisiana in laughing after realizing that the Cajun is right. This day was long overdue and probably inevitable. He only stops when the laughter causes his face to throb.

"You broke my nose."

"Yeah, well, you aren't that pretty anyway. Besides, you busted my head open."

"You weren't using it."

They both start laughing again.

"Boston didn't kill Colby, ya know."

"I know. The FBI told me he fired on them when they charged into his house."

"So why won't you help him?"

"If Boston hadn't gone on the run, those two men might still be alive. The FBI would be searching for the real traitor instead of trying to find him."

Louisiana shakes his head. "Nah. He would be getting railroaded while the FBI claims victory and a traitor still walks free."

"A traitor is still walking free. Nothing you guys have done has changed that. If anything, you've made it worse. This was all for nothing." Maryland moans as he gets up and moves to the kitchen.

He returns with towels and two bags of ice. Both men are sitting quietly and saying nothing when a strange vibrating noise sounds from the corner of the room and gets their attention.

"What the hell is that?" Louisiana asks.

"What's left of my phone, I think."

"Who is it?"

"I have no idea. You broke the screen," Maryland says, picking up and showing him the battered device.

"Is the FBI monitoring your phone?"

"Who knows?"

"Answer it."

"Hello?"

"Maryland, it's me."

"Boston? Where are you calling from?"

"Put it on speaker, bro," Louisiana demands. Maryland obliges by pushing the speaker button several times until he gets it to finally work.

"Louisiana's there?"

"Unfortunately. Where are you?"

"I borrowed Steven's car and just left the sleep center."

"Who's Steven?" Maryland asks, turning to Louisiana.

He shakes his head in disapproval. "Just an enormous tool who's pining for my girl. Where the hell are you goin', Bos? Half the FBI and every cop in the district are out lookin' for you."

"I know who the traitor is."

"What?" the two men say simultaneously.

"Who?" Maryland asks. There is a long pause on his end of the line.

"It's Gina."

Boston goes on to explain the dream he had and how he's sure of it. Louisiana just listens, showing no reaction. Maryland is beyond shocked and not at all sure that Boston is in his right mind. The memories that he sees seem to leave a lot open for interpretation. This must be one of those moments.

"What are you going to do?" Louisiana asks.

"Confront her."

"Not without me you're not," Louisiana demands.

"No, you guys have done enough. I need to do this on my own. I wanted to thank you both for everything and to apologize to you, Maryland. I never should have involved you. This was never your fight. Take care of yourselves."

"Don't do this, Boston," Maryland pleads before seeing through the cracked screen that the call ended.

"He's gone."

"Call him back."

Maryland fights to navigate over to the received calls menu and punches send. It immediately gets sent to voicemail.

"He turned it off."

"Oh, well. What do you have to eat in this place?"

"We have to go after him," Maryland says, a grave tone to his voice.

"Look at you all eager to jump into the fray for once. Boston doesn't want us involved. I'm gonna respect his wishes. I don't get myself messed up in domestic issues."

"Louisiana, he's not going to just confront her. He's going to kill her."

"Am I supposed to be upset about that?"

Maryland shakes his head. He'll never understand how Louisiana can be so nonchalant about this after barging in demanding information that would help Boston. Now he wants a damn sandwich when he's needed most. It's time for a different approach.

"Do you want to see it end like this when you can dream up a much more eloquent way to bump her off?"

"Ya know, that's a good point. Where does he live? I'll drive."

That change of heart was faster and far easier than expected.

"Like hell, you will. We're going to end up with the FBI at some point. I'm not going to add possession of a stolen vehicle to my rap sheet when we do."

Maryland walks over to the small table at the door and grab his keys, jingling them.

"Bro, you drive a Malibu. The car I stole at least has balls."

"We can argue about this, or we can go."

"Fine, I'll drive.

"No way."

"Don't make me kick your ass again. You drive like my grandmother. I wanna get there before the sun comes up."

"Kick *my* ass?" Maryland asks. "That bottle to the head did a number on your memory. We need to do something before we go."

"You need to fix your hair or something? We're wasting time."

Maryland pulls the business card out of his pants pocket and pinches it between his fingers. He's glad he didn't toss it in the trash like he was going to.

"No, we're going to get some help."

CHAPTER SEVENTY-ONE
SPECIAL AGENT ZACH FORTE

Remsen pulls up outside the glass building and slams the beast of a car into park. He surveys the street and then the façade of the sleek building. This isn't a horrible place to hide out, all things considered.

"Are you sure that Bill didn't tip them off?"

"He's CIA, so I doubt it. Let's go find out."

"Do you want to wait for a tactical team?" Zach asks. "Boston's armed."

"Don't get gun shy on me now. We're playing this one on our own. Just be cautious. If Boston is in there, he's not going anywhere."

The agents enter the building and flash their badges to the man behind the desk. Zach instructs the guard to lock the doors and not allow anyone to leave the building, then the men take the elevator up to the sleep center. When the doors open, they draw their weapons and step into the reception area to find a crying woman being consoled by a goofy man in a lab coat.

"Who the hell are you?" the scarecrow-like man barks before recoiling at the sight of their weapons.

"Special Agent Zach Forte, FBI. This is Director Matt Remsen. Are you Steven Kempler?"

"*Doctor* Steven Kempler," he pronounces.

"Good for you. Sit," Zach commands.

"I'll check the back."

Matt heads through the doors leading out of the reception area. His weapon is out and up, eyes searching for any movement that would indicate a threat. Zach knows that his friend can handle himself, so he walks over to the sobbing woman.

"Dr. Winters?"

"Yes," she sobs, with an affirmative nod.

"Where's Hollinger? Is he here?"

"No," she sniffles, "he's gone."

"Where?"

"I don't know. He wouldn't tell me."

"The back is clear," Remsen says, returning from the hall while holstering his weapon. Zach relaxes and follows suit.

"Dr. Winters, Boston is in a lot of trouble. Now's not the time to lie about—"

"I told you, I don't know!"

"She's telling the truth, Agent Forte," Steven says, coming to her defense. "I was here. He didn't say where he was going."

Zach glares at the doctor. "Where is everyone?"

"The staff has tonight off. It's compensation for working weekends."

"What about last night?"

"The same. The center opens for business tomorrow."

Zach nods. It explains why they came here. He sits on the chair next to Tara. Whatever Boston said to her must have been very upsetting. Her eyes are red and puffy like she's been crying for some time. Steven's consolations don't seem to be easing her pain any.

"Can you tell me what happened?"

"He had another memory. He didn't say what it was about."

"Whatever it was, it rattled him. He left in a hurry," Steven adds.

"Dr. Kempler, are these dreams that Boston has really other people's memories?" Matt asks.

"I don't know. It sounds ludicrous, but I can tell you that I've never witnessed anything like it. Mr. Hollinger's brain activity during those periods doesn't match a traditional dream state. After analyzing the data, I believe that Dr. Winters's diagnosis is a sound one. We just can't figure out how it works. I can show you the EEG if you'd like. It's very fascinating."

Remsen offers a shrug. Zach shakes his head, not seeing the point of trying to understand wavy lines on a printout. He needs to find Hollinger, not prove or disprove some crazy diagnosis.

"Do you think he saw something new?" Zach asks after he gets out of the chair and walks over.

"Let's say he did. If you were him, who would you call first?"

"His fiancée. Grimman has agents posted at the house. I'll have Watchtower get orders for them to enter and convince her to bring her phone."

"Agreed. We should also find his friend Louisiana. He'd be on the list, too."

"You got it," Remsen says, pulling out his cell to place a call to wherever he calls home base.

"Is there anything else you can tell me, Tara?" Zach asks, walking back over to the two doctors.

"He kissed me," she whispers, subconsciously touching her lips with her hand.

"He kissed you?"

"He kissed you?" Steven echoes. That was obviously news to him, too. "You didn't tell me that."

Zach rubs his chin. Boston is engaged, and his fiancée is a knockout. Without speaking for Hollinger's integrity, he doesn't seem the type who would step out on his woman, even for a beautiful doctor. Now he knows that something is seriously wrong and sits back down next to Tara.

"I think you need to start again from the beginning, Dr. Winters."

CHAPTER SEVENTY-TWO
"BOSTON" HOLLINGER

There is one universal rule about driving in Washington, D.C.: two dozen routes you can take to get to your destination, and none of them is going to be easy. Even at half-past one in the morning, the most direct route is going to take me forty-five minutes. I could floor it and shave a few minutes off my time, but can't risk getting stopped for speeding by a bored cop looking for something to do.

I make my way through the traffic circle adjacent to American University and hop on to Massachusetts Avenue. I'll take this road past the Naval Observatory and Dupont Circle until I reach Mount Vernon Square. After a turn onto New York Avenue, I'll pick up I-395 and merge into I-695 after the tunnel. It's then left on I-295 for the trip into Maryland and the back roads to my house. The trip will give me plenty of time to think about my options.

I'm struggling to understand what I saw tonight. Could I have misinterpreted what I saw? Could I be mistaken about the whole thing? I mean, Gina is my fiancée. How could she possibly betray our country, and by extension, me?

The intelligence community is small. Most of the staff on the intelligence committees have friends, acquaintances, and contacts in sister organizations. Naturally, we all end up comingling at happy hours across the city. The night I met Gina, a colleague pleaded with me to go to the bar, and it was a last-minute decision to take him up on it. A friend who met us brought a girlfriend who happened to be starting work on Capitol Hill as a staffer on the committee I worked for. There was instant chemistry with the raven-haired beauty named Gina Attison.

The whirlwind romance that followed could rival the best Hollywood love stories. She has been everything a man could want in a woman. There were challenges because we worked together, which was why she took the job with

Senator Washington. Could the whole thing be a cruel fraud, or is there some external factor that I'm missing?

Tara warned me that the drug Steven gave me could interfere with dreams. Could it alter the memories as well? Could this just be a chemical reaction that is leading me to believe that Gina is a traitor? Or was what I saw evidence of the ultimate betrayal?

I have so many questions and so few answers. This exercise isn't helping. I'm trying to talk myself out of having this confrontation. It's me rationalizing away what I saw by pretending it was something my mind conjured up while in a crazy, chemically altered state. The memory was clear. The first part was my conversation with her. There's no reason to believe that the second part wasn't equally valid.

I check the LED clock glowing on the dash. With every second that ticks by, and every foot of asphalt I pass in my borrowed grey Chevy sedan, I get a little closer to a moment I dread. The sooner I get this over with, the better. To that end, I press down harder on the gas pedal.

CHAPTER SEVENTY-THREE

GINA ATTISON

The loud rap at the door announces the company. Gina curses under her breath. It's too soon, but she can't ignore them. They are more likely to break down the door than leave. With two packed bags sitting on the bed, the timing of this is terrible.

"Miss Attison?" a booming voice says from outside the door. "It's the FBI. We know you're home. Open up."

She walks down the hall and through the living room to open the door.

"Good evening, Miss Attison."

"It's one-thirty in the morning, fellas. Does the FBI always make a habit of showing up in the middle of the night?" she asks, trying to sound like anyone would after being woken up. She isn't sure they are buying it.

"May we come in?"

"I'd prefer that you came back in the morning if you need me to answer more questions about Boston."

"I'm afraid I must insist you let us in, ma'am." Gina sighs. This guy isn't going to let her guilt him into coming back tomorrow. This is serious.

"I guess." She runs her hand through her hair as she steps aside and the men enter. "This is getting close to harassment."

"We apologize for that, ma'am, but I'm afraid we have to impose on you once more. We need you to come with us."

"Go with you where?"

"Back to our district office."

"What for?" she asks, being sure to look puzzled.

"Your fiancé has a warrant out for his arrest on espionage charges and is on the run. We believe he may be reaching out to you, and we really need to speak with him."

"What makes you think—"

"We know about the burner phone, Miss Attison," the smaller agent says. "You have been in contact with Mr. Hollinger, which means you have been lying to us. That leaves two paths for you: cooperate, or be charged with obstruction of justice, harboring a federal fugitive, and interfering with a federal investigation."

A shiver runs up her spine. How could these guys know that? She hates being in the dark about what they know. Did they somehow hear the call in the bathroom? Did they get to Maryland or Louisiana?

"Either path means that you're coming with us. We can either walk you out to our car or drag you out to it in cuffs."

"Fine, let's go then," she says in surrender.

"There's one more thing, Miss Attison. We know you have the burner phone on the premises somewhere. You need to retrieve it now, or we will."

They're bluffing. Gina folds her arms across her chest.

"I have no idea what you're talking about."

"We think you do. We know it for a fact," the first agent replies.

"Oh yeah? And how do you think you know that?"

"We're not at liberty to say," the burly man answers.

These guys answer for each other so much, it's like they share a brain. A tennis match involves less head movement than talking to these guys does. Gina finds it infuriating.

"Oh, then it *must* be true. Unless you have a warrant, you aren't searching for anything here, and we can wait. If you want me to go with you, let's go."

"The phone first, Miss Attison."

"Did the steroids you took cause hearing loss? I told you I have no idea what you're talking about."

"The hard way it is," the first agent says, pulling out a set of handcuffs.

Handcuffs limit her options. It would take two dozen agents hours of tearing this house apart with crowbars to find the hiding place, but they will find it with enough effort. If that happens and she's restrained, the game is over.

"Okay, okay. You win. I'll get it for you."

"Where is it?" the second agent asks.

"It's in my purse on the kitchen counter. Do you want to retrieve it, or do you want me to?"

"Go ahead," the first agent says, gesturing with his arm that Gina has permission to enter her own kitchen. She moves to the counter with the two agents following closely, opens her oversized Michael Kors bag, and makes a show of rummaging through it.

"I'd really love to know how you figured out how I had this."

Gina pulls the suppressed SIG Sauer out, spins around, and squeezes the trigger. The men are so close that aiming is optional. The first agent catches the round in the chest. His beefy pal can't react fast enough to do anything about what's going to happen next.

She shifts the weapon to the left and fires again. The gun makes a satisfying chirp as the "silencer" muffles the sound of the shot. In five seconds, both men are hemorrhaging blood onto her kitchen floor. Gina never did like the tile work in here.

The second agent is as good as dead. The first guy is still alert, despite losing blood at an alarming rate. She steps over him and takes a knee, looking him in the eyes. They are wide with fear and disbelief.

Life is not like an action movie. She doesn't have a witty catchphrase or clever quip to punctuate the moment. Gina isn't a killer by nature, despite having done so once when it was called for. She considers herself a fixer of problems. Whether this agent knows it or not, he became one in search of a solution. She stands back up, points her gun at him, and pumps a round into his head.

With the two threats neutralized, she relieves them of their weapons. They might come in handy eventually. Gina also pockets their FBI badges and cell phones. The badges are a lovely keepsake, and their cell phones will alert her to when the men start being missed. The first check-in calls will be coming before too long.

She's on the clock. They are on to her, and a manhunt will be tough to avoid this close to Washington. Gina needs to get out of town and hope that the FBI blames Boston for the murders. He's a suspected spy on the lam and will draw all the attention. She heads to the bedroom to finish packing, no longer content to wait until morning. Twenty minutes from now, she needs to be in her car heading to the safe haven where she can lie low before escaping the country.

CHAPTER SEVENTY-FOUR
ERIC "MARYLAND" WILLIAMS

MARYLAND'S RESIDENCE
JOINT BASE ANACOSTIA-BOLLING

Maryland grimaces as he checks the broken screen on his phone. He'll be surprised if this thing still works. Louisiana is going to owe him a replacement whether he thinks he does or not. After some effort, he gets the phone to dial.

"Forte," the garbled speaker of his phone belches out when the call gets answered.

"Agent Forte, this is Eric Williams."

"Hello, Maryland. I didn't expect to hear from you so soon."

"He calls you Maryland?" Louisiana asks, a little too loudly. Maryland covers his mouth with a finger, willing him to shut his trap just for a few minutes.

"Who's with you?"

"None of your damn business," the big mouth answers. So much for staying quiet.

"You must be Louisiana. You owe me a new BMW. That or I'm going to beat your ass until I feel better about you incinerating mine."

"We have a bigger problem than that," Maryland says, pushing to get to the point. "We got a call from Boston."

There is a noticeable silence on the other end of the line. Maryland and Louisiana stare at each other. Whatever the agent thought Maryland was calling about, it wasn't that.

"When?"

"A couple of minutes ago."

"What did he want?" Agent Forte presses.

"He told us he figured out who the mole is. He's on his way to confront her."

"Her?"

"The mole is his bitch fiancée, Gina Attison," Louisiana says, practically spitting. The qualifiers he always added about her hotness are gone. Now she's at the top of his list of enemies.

Forte must be equally stunned. The silence on the other end drags on until it becomes uncomfortable. Louisiana rolls his hand in encouragement.

"Agent Forte, are you there?"

"Yeah, I'm here. Are you telling me that Hollinger's own fiancée is behind all of this?" he asks, his voice cracking. That, or it was the speaker of this broken phone Maryland is holding.

"That's what Boston told us."

"Where is he now?"

"I don't know exactly. He's heading home to confront her. We need you to stop him."

"Agents are already taking her into custody. We'll try to stop him on the way."

"What do you need us to do?"

"Absolutely nothing. I don't want you within ten miles of his house, understand? You've done enough. We can handle Hollinger."

"Oh, please," Louisiana barks. "You haven't stopped him once yet."

"You're already facing a boatload of charges, Louisiana. You don't want to challenge me on this and add to them. Let the FBI handle it from here."

"I need to tell you, Agent Forte, that Boston may not have been telling us the whole truth."

"I believe he is. We're at the sleep center with Dr. Winters now. He kissed her before he rushed out. Now I know why."

"What?" Louisiana spits. Maryland smiles. Louisiana is visibly jealous.

"Stay put," Agent Forte commands. "We'll be by to talk to you guys later."

The call disconnects. Maryland checks the shattered screen before setting the device in his lap. He bites his lip.

"Now what?"

"Bro, screw the FBI. I don't work for them, and neither do you. I ain't plannin' to sit on the sidelines for this."

"He ordered us to. I'm not about to defy a federal agent."

"You changin' your mind again, bro?" Louisiana asks. "If the FBI has Gina, then we need to stop him before he gets there and finds himself in cuffs."

"Then why did you just let me call them?" Maryland asks.

"Because we could fail. It doesn't mean we don't try."

Maryland stares at the keys in his hand. The FBI is far better equipped to find and stop Boston than they are. The problem is, as painful as it is to ponder, Louisiana is right. They are only interested in apprehending him for treason. If anyone can track Boston down and talk some sense into him, it's the two of them. Maryland has been playing it safe his whole life. Maybe this is the one moment when he needs to throw caution to the wind.

"Screw it. C'mon. Let's roll."

CHAPTER SEVENTY-FIVE
SPECIAL AGENT ZACH FORTE

MASSACHUSETTS AVENUE NW
WASHINGTON D.C.

Their exit from the sleep center was a hasty one. Matt arranged for Watchtower to dispatch some agents to babysit the scarecrow and Tara Winters. She doesn't need bodyguards. She needs a therapist. He's never seen a woman that distraught over love outside of a Hallmark movie.

"I don't care what his current mission is…No, task him to us…Roger, our target should be heading south in a gray Chevy Malibu," Matt says into his cell phone, his finger plugging the opposite ear to blunt the engine noise.

"Shit," Zach says, flooring it when the light up ahead turns yellow. It flips to red a full three seconds before he screams through it.

"Roger, keep me posted." Matt ends the call. "We commandeered an FBI helicopter. Watchtower has him searching the Anacostia River crossings, focusing on the one south of the Navy Yard. The visibility still sucks, though."

"It's better than nothing," Zach grumbles, tightening his grip on the wheel.

"It's forty minutes to Oxon Hill from the sleep center, and he's got at least a fifteen-minute lead on us," Remsen observes as Zach pushes their FBI-issued Crown Victoria as fast as she'll go. "Drive faster."

"Yeah, right," Zach mutters, fighting to keep control of the vehicle. "At least the rain stopped."

Matt's phone chirps in the console again and he sets it to the speaker. He spends more time on that thing than a millennial.

"Remsen."

"Director Remsen, Watchtower Operations," the agent says. "We passed along your request for the agents at Hollinger's house to bring in Gina Attison for questioning to the Counterintelligence Division, and they complied."

"Yeah, and? Is she in custody?"

"We haven't heard back from them," the agent reports.

"What do you mean?"

"We sent the team in to pick her up ten minutes ago. They haven't checked in since."

A pit forms inside Zach's stomach. These are trained agents. They know what the check-in protocols are and wouldn't be irresponsible enough to let their cell phones die. Boston's belief that Gina is the traitor is taking Zach's thoughts to a very dark place.

"Director Remsen? Are you there?"

"Yeah. Keep trying to reach them. Let me know when you do."

Zach's phone rings seconds after Matt ends his call. Grimman's mobile pops up on caller ID.

"Grimman?"

"Zach?" he hears after the muffled sounds of a phone changing hands. "I thought I sent you home?"

"You did."

"Then why am I hearing that the agents tasked to watch Gina Attison were ordered to take her into custody? Nobody in counterintelligence gave that order, so I assume you had Matt Remsen do it. He's the only one with the clout. Go ahead, tell me that you had nothing to do with it."

"Hollinger is going after Gina Attison. He believes she's the mole, and I think he might be right. He's heading to Oxon Hill now."

"How could you possibly know that?"

"It's a long story that I don't have time to tell. You'll get it in the debriefing when this is over."

Zach runs another red light as Grimman thinks this over. The resulting transgression has led to horn blasts from several cars and likely a middle finger or two.

"How sure are you?"

"One hundred percent."

"Zach, listen to me. We can't afford to be wrong about this. Everyone is watching what we do."

Zach shakes his head. Grimman isn't worried about being wrong because the mission might fail. He's concerned about making a decision that could jeopardize his career. If Grimman listens and Zach is wrong, Karen Weisz will sack her subordinate in a nanosecond to deflect the blame. It'd be easy to do since Zach would never be considered a reliable source. Not after Beaver Cage.

"She's the mole, Tom," Zach says, forcing himself to remain calm and speak evenly.

"She's a former staff member of the chairman of the Senate Intelligence Committee. If you swing and miss on this, there will be hell to pay."

"Gina has been implicated, and the agents sent to retrieve her have gone dark. Do you need a map to put the two together? We need to get some people over there."

"I don't have resources to spare. They're all dedicated to bringing Hollinger in."

"They're going to the same place! Use the local police if you need to."

"This is our investigation, Zach. We have to keep this in-house and leave the locals out of this for now."

Zach can't believe what he's hearing. Grimman is more concerned about saving face than apprehending a possible traitor or checking in on his missing agents. It's the only reason not to call for help from local authorities.

"That's a mistake, Tom."

"Hollinger is the primary target, and we will intercept him before he even gets close to home. I can have four units in Oxon Hill in five minutes. We'll set up near the highway exits. If you're sure he's heading home, he'll come right to us," Grimman explains.

It's the most tactically unsound plan that Zach has ever heard.

"What about our missing agents at the house?"

"I will have Ops keep trying to raise them on their cells. I'm sure there's a reason they can't answer. Thank you for the information. Now go home. That's an order."

Zach shakes his head and looks at Remsen. He mouths a word to him. The intent of the message is received loud and clear.

"One more thing, Grimman. Have the agent at Williams's house babysit him until this is over."

"What agent? We pulled everyone off to apprehend Hollinger. He's on a military base, so he isn't going anywhere. I have to go."

He ends the call, and Zach slams his fist onto the steering wheel.

"The idiots in this town can't get out of their own way. Stupid bastards. What do you want to do?"

"Get there as fast as we can, preferably in one piece," Matt says, more concerned with Zach keeping their speeding vehicle from spinning out of control. "Grimman is heading to intercept Boston, and they won't act on Gina until they do. Head straight for his house. We'll check on it ourselves. If he wants to waste his time trying to apprehend Boston on the streets, let him."

This whole operation is going to be a fiasco. The chiefs are so worried about making bad decisions that they refuse to make good ones. That's what politics has done to this country. If Gina is actually the mole, Zach will be damned if he's going to let her get away.

CHAPTER SEVENTY-SIX
EUGENE "BOSTON" HOLLINGER

I check my rearview mirror. The closer I get to home, the more paranoid I become. I see the flashing red and blue strobes behind me in the distance. I can't shake the feeling they're coming for me.

A half-mile and four more checks of the mirror later, I notice the lights from a police cruiser grow larger and brighter. I hold my breath. The car bearing down on me is joined by a second and then a third. My heart tries to pound its way out of my chest. They are coming for me, and I have a decision to make.

I slide into the right lane as I pass beneath the large green sign indicating the turn for I-395. I'm so close to the highway and the anonymity that traveling on an interstate provides. The flashing red and blue strobes bounce off everything around me. It's the moment of truth. If they try to stop me, do I comply and leave my fate to Washington's finest or make a break for it?

My eyes stay glued to the mirror as I make the turn. They're close, and I make my decision. I ready my foot on the gas pedal. If they pursue me, they are going to get the chase of a lifetime. Any moment now…

The first car screams by, continuing east up New York Avenue. The second and third cars follow him. I exhale loudly and breathe for the first time in what feels like minutes. They have somebody in their crosshairs. Fortunately, it isn't me.

My nerves settle down as I get a brief respite from my anxiety. Interstate 395 runs underground through tunnels as it passes through the heart of Washington. A tourist standing next to the reflecting pool and admiring the majesty of the Capitol Building would never know that there's a major thoroughfare running beneath their feet. The tunnels are covered in cameras, so I keep my speed reasonable to avoid attracting unwanted attention. I have the advantage of them not looking for this car.

The road merges into Interstate 695, and I take it east until I cross the Anacostia River. Time is of the essence, and mercifully, traffic is light on the bridge. I give the car more gas, edging up my speed.

I merge onto I-295 for the last major leg of my journey. My mind races ahead. Does Gina know I'm coming? I shake my head. There's no way. Then again, I didn't believe that she could be a traitor, either. It will add some time to the trip, but maybe it's best to take a different exit than usual and approach the house from a different direction. Or is that just a waste of time?

There's no sign of pursuit, so taking precautions might be pointless. I'm too close to home to be this indecisive. I need to fight through my anger and formulate a plan. Do I just question her when I see her? Try to get her explanation of what I saw? Would she even tell me the truth?

No way. If she's been lying this long, I can't believe a word that comes out of her mouth. She needs to be taken down. I can't rely on the FBI or anyone else to do it. This is my responsibility. To do that, I need to get there without her or anyone else knowing I'm coming. Just another ten minutes to go now. I exhale deeply—ten…more…minutes.

CHAPTER SEVENTY-SEVEN
ERIC "MARYLAND" WILLIAMS

Maryland isn't sure what worries him more: the speed he's going, the slick conditions he's driving in, or what they're going to do once they arrive at Boston's. He hopes that Louisiana has a plan, because it takes every ounce of his concentration to weave around cars and not crash into the median. Whatever his pudgy friend is dreaming up had better not involve high explosives. He doesn't need a one-way ticket back to the FBI for more questioning.

"Did you have to wind this thing up before driving it?" Louisiana asks from the passenger seat with no shortage of impatience.

"Bite me. I'm going ninety."

"You need to be going a hundred ninety. How much longer?"

"We're coming up on the Outer Beltway now. Ten minutes tops. We'll be off the highway in three."

"It'd be two minutes if I was driving," Louisiana laments.

"We'd be wrapped around a light pole if you were driving."

Maryland doesn't smile. He's serious in believing they would be.

"How long have you known Gina?" Louisiana asks out of the blue.

"What?"

"Gina…how long have you known her?"

"Since the day after he met her," Maryland says, steering the car around a slow-moving Honda from Utah. "She worked for one of the three-letter agencies but carried herself like a political staff type. She wanted a job on the Senate intelligence committee and got it. Honestly, I never would have guessed she was a traitor."

"You think Boston's right? You think she's the mole?"

"This is a lousy time for twenty questions," Maryland says as he weaves through a small pack of vehicles. Despite the traffic being a far cry from the rush hour crush inside the beltway, he's still coming up on groups of slower drivers who don't understand what the passing lane means.

"Stop your whining. You're not even going that fast. You'll be fine. How would Gina do it? Get hold of classified material, I mean."

"How the hell would I know?" Maryland replies with a sneer.

"You're an intelligence analyst, right?"

"Yeah, I take raw data and turn it into useful information. I didn't read the manual on how to give it to our enemies."

"What good are you then?"

It is a question Maryland has been asking himself. It would be too easy to know if documents went missing. She either passed along pictures of them or just briefed her contacts on what she saw. It could have been a lot.

"The SSCI is the primary legislative oversight for America's intelligence network. It is the perfect position for a spy. She has a TS/SCI clearance and saw everything they provided to Congress."

"Who knows what kind of intel she passed them, bro?"

"Yeah, or for how long. It's worse than that."

"What do you mean?"

"You don't understand how this town works. A bad day for you is getting eaten by mosquitos. This swamp is different. Gina worked for Senator Washington, who was the chairman of that committee. If this gets out, do you have any idea how crazy the media will go? It will send all the rats scurrying around looking for a way off the sinking ship."

"I don't care about that, bro. That's not our problem."

"It's everyone's problem. Whether we want to admit it to ourselves or not, what goes on in this town affects every American. The damage this could cause our country and our intelligence-gathering capabilities is almost immeasurable."

Maryland shudders at the thought. Louisiana may not understand, and he's not alone. Scandals are the easiest way for citizens to lose faith in their government. They create divisions and a loss of trust in leaders by the public that is debilitating and dangerous. A scandal of this magnitude, especially if they got caught covering it up, would shake the republic's very foundation.

"We need to get to Boston," Louisiana mutters, making a show of looking at his watch. Even under the streetlamps, he can't possibly read it. He's always been one for theater. He doesn't need to consult a clock to know they're running out of time.

CHAPTER SEVENTY-EIGHT
SPECIAL AGENT ZACH FORTE

Zach and Matt hurtle down the interstate as they approach the exit to the tunnel that passes under the National Mall. Even with lights blazing, the few cars on the road don't move out of the way fast enough. Several have been greeted with a long blare from the horn. The couple that still took too long were almost run off the road.

Zach's cell phone chimes again. This assignment makes him yearn to be back at the Rowdy Squirrel with a Jack Daniel's in front of him. It's been one of those weeks.

"What?" Zach says, dropping the courtesy.

"Are you on your way to Hollinger's?" Grimman asks.

"You ordered me to head home, remember?"

"I do, but that doesn't mean you listened. In fact, I'm sure you didn't. We acquired an air unit that spotted a gray sedan heading south down I-295 at a high rate of speed."

Remsen slaps the dashboard. That was the helicopter that Watchtower had procured. Somehow, it got reassigned. From the angry look on Matt's face, that doesn't happen very often.

"We're positioned on Livingston, a half a mile south of where it meets Oxon Hill Road. Spotters are posted at the hotel across the street from where Exit 3B comes off the interstate. It looks like our boy is still heading right at us. Where are you?"

Matt turns and cocks his head at him. Zach guesses that it's time to come clean.

"We just got out of the tunnel and will cross the river in a matter of seconds. What's going on at the house?"

"There's still no word from our agents," Grimman says.

Zach's sinking feeling is now a deep concern. Matt has the same look of indigestion that comes with a fear that their agents are down.

"Something's wrong, Grimman. They should have reported back the moment Gina was in custody. You need to get people over there."

"There's no reason to panic yet. It could be anything. We'll check it out after we have Hollinger."

Zach doesn't accept that argument. If Boston is correct and his fiancée is the one who's been leaking information to the enemy, there's every reason to panic. Not that there is a point in trying to convince him.

"Fine. I'll head straight there and see what's up. You don't need me."

"Negative, Zach. Since you decided to disobey orders, I need you to serve as the chase vehicle behind Hollinger if he gets cold feet and decides not to return home. He is the priority."

"Gina Attison is the key to this whole thing! If she escapes—"

"I don't have time to argue with you. You have your orders, and I expect you to actually follow them this time. I'm not showing up to Hollinger's house without support, and the Critical Incident Response Group is still assembling a SWAT team. Until that happens, I need every available agent focused on apprehending Hollinger. That includes you."

Damn these fools and their politics. Under any other circumstances, this would never go down this way. Two agents in peril would result in an overwhelming response from every part of the bureau. What does it say that this isn't?

"Damn it, Grimman, how many times do I have to say it! He's heading there anyway!" Zach shouts into the phone.

"If he sees cars in front of his house, he won't stop in for a chat. If he leaves the city, we might never catch him. This directive comes straight from the top. Do you read me?"

"Roger."

Zach hangs up the call, not liking the result one bit. Matt wastes no time reaching out to the team at Watchtower. The conversation is short. It doesn't sound like there is much they can do.

"Can you mobilize anybody?"

"Not fast enough. We don't have a tactical team and can't stand one up any faster than Grimman can. It's up to us. Head straight to his house."

CHAPTER SEVENTY-NINE
ERIC "MARYLAND" WILLIAMS

RESIDENTIAL AREA
OXON HILL, MARYLAND

Louisiana stares out the passenger window, impatient as hell with his head pressed up against the window as small houses zip by. He's amped up and can't get to Boston's fast enough. They are almost there.

"How do these people stand to live so close to each other?" he asks. Maryland ignores the comment about the cramped suburban D.C. living scene.

"Not everyone lives in a swamp. We're almost there."

"If you had a man's car, we would be already."

"Whatever. Do you have your bag of goodies ready?" Maryland asks, ignoring his comment and prompting him to check his backpack of death in the back seat.

"It's ready if we need it."

"Good. His house—"

A car suddenly pulls out from a side road right into their lane, and Maryland steers hard to the left to avoid it. The car violently responds to the maneuver, shifting him hard in the seat and causing the seat belt to immediately lock into place. The Malibu jumps the curb, taking out fencing and mailboxes as it plows through the small front yards.

"What the—!"

A blinding light pours in from overhead through the windshield. Maryland fights to shield his eyes as his foot searches for the brake. He slams his foot down on the pedal he finds. It's the accelerator.

He jerks the wheel to the right to avoid the light. The maneuver launches the car back onto the asphalt and heading straight for houses on the opposite side. Maryland jerks the wheel back in the other direction, causing the rear end to break loose and send the car into a spin. The rear tire slams into the curb, shifting the vehicle's center of gravity. The sedan flips once, and then twice, before coming to a rest right side up.

Maryland struggles to open his eyes as a half dozen sedans and SUVs screech to a halt and surround them. Men pour out of the vehicles like clowns at a circus. The only difference is, these guys have their weapons drawn and pointed at the car.

"Federal agents! FBI! Don't move!" they shout as they take up position around what's left of the vehicle.

Maryland couldn't move even if he wanted to. He sees blood is gushing from a wound on Louisiana's head. His friend is in worse shape than he is.

The car doors are jerked open. Men yank both of them out and dump them on the ground behind the vehicle. An agent plants a knee in Maryland's back and pushes his head into the grit of the wet asphalt. He grunts at the pressure when his arms are violently yanked behind him, and handcuffs slapped on his wrists.

Unlike Maryland, Louisiana is resisting. It takes three agents to hold him in place while a fourth puts him in bracelets. Once they are secured, another man with a flashlight comes over and shines it into their faces.

"Neither of them is him, sir," one of the agents says.

"What do you mean? This is the right make, model, and color vehicle. Get their identifications."

Someone behind them searches their pockets and confiscates their wallets. The agent checks Louisiana's first, then grimaces when he sees Maryland's name. He shines the light to get a better look at his face.

"Williams? Where the hell is Hollinger?"

CHAPTER EIGHTY

EUGENE "BOSTON" HOLLINGER

OXON HILL ROAD
OXON HILL, MARYLAND

I pull Steven's light gray Malibu off the interstate at Exit 3B and make a left onto Oxon Hill Road before coming up on a red light when I reach Livingston. Two police cars and an ambulance scream through the intersection at high speed. That doesn't look good.

Eager to avoid the authorities, I make the right, turn into a gas station, and backtrack the way I came. My house is a geographic anomaly. My road connects two streets that can be reached from all four directions. I take the scenic backroads that lead to my place from the southwest instead of the east.

It's nearly two in the morning, and the streets are empty in this sleepy suburban neighborhood. After my fourth turn brings me onto my road, I kill the headlights three houses away from mine. The FBI vehicle is parked along the curb opposite Gina's Audi. She's still here.

I pull off to the side of the road, kill the engine on Steven's car, and wait. I don't see any movement in the government vehicle. That's odd.

Careful to remember to disable the interior dome light, I exit the car and sneak up to the dark Crown Vic parked on the curb from behind in a low crouch. As I thought, the vehicle is unoccupied. That's strange because the house is entirely unlit, too. If she's talking to the FBI agents, I wouldn't think it would be in the dark.

The rainstorm has passed, but there's a misty haze in the air that creates halos around the streetlights lining the road. The limited visibility will work to my advantage as I duck into my side yard. I don't own a garage. We park on the street in front of the house and take the long sidewalk to the front door. The back door that leads into the kitchen is never used. I'm counting on that.

I move around the house with caution to the back, taking care not to expose my silhouette to any of the windows. Like most homeowners, we keep a spare key to the door close. Unlike most homeowners, it's not in an obvious spot like under the welcome mat or hidden in a flowerpot. I pry loose a paving stone from the patio and retrieve the key from a clear plastic bag.

I slide the key in the lock and open the back door. The lights lining my street do nothing to provide illumination back here, and the glow of the LEDs from my appliances doesn't generate enough light to pierce the blackness. I step into the kitchen with my gun drawn.

The sticky substance under my feet causes an audible squishing sound when I walk. Curious, I stop before tripping on the two hulking men in suits lying on the floor. It must be the FBI agents. I don't need to check their pulses to know they are gone. I place the back of my hand against the forehead of one of the men. His skin is still warm to the touch, and there is no sign of rigor mortis. They weren't killed long ago.

I gingerly step over them and move through the kitchen and small dining area. After a glance down the hall, I move swiftly into the living area and notice the television is on mute. I sweep my gun back and forth, but the room is empty.

I pause my breathing and listen to the silence of the house. She must have killed the feds and fled. I am allowing myself to relax when a round is chambered in a weapon from behind me. So much for that conclusion. I just made a huge mistake.

"Your room clearing skills suck, Boston. Don't turn around," Gina orders.

I sigh and lower the pistol to my side. There's nothing worse than allowing someone to get the drop on you. That feeling is only magnified when it's your fiancée.

"Did you forget to chamber a round, or was that for my benefit?"

"I reloaded the magazine after killing Tweedle Dee and Tweedle Dum in the kitchen," Gina admits. "Let's live the cliché. Place the gun on the ground and move backward toward me."

It's the same voice she uses when I'm informed that I need to empty the dishwasher. I do as she asks, although in a small act of defiance, I turn to face my fiancée. There's no way I'm going to let her shoot me in the back. The television provides all the light I need to see Gina dressed in black with her hair tied in a ponytail. It's a sexy look for her, and I would say so if I could ignore the fact that she's a traitor. Not that anything about this would cause me to forget. She has a .45-caliber handgun aimed at my chest.

CHAPTER EIGHTY-ONE
SPECIAL AGENT ZACH FORTE

LIVINGSTON ROAD
OXON HILL, MARYLAND

Zach pulls up from the north and surveys the chaotic scene. Black Chevy Suburbans and Ford Crown Vics surround a battered gray car. Agents are swarming everywhere. Local police have roads closed off leading away from the crash site. Zach focuses on the vehicle. Something is very wrong.

"So much for going straight to Boston's," Matt muses from the passenger seat. "We're not getting through this mess."

"We'll see about that."

Both men hop out the moment Zach brings it to a stop and jog the short distance to where agents are standing in their FBI emblazoned windbreakers. He glances up when he hears the circling chopper. He recognizes Maryland and Louisiana, who are pinned on the ground twenty feet from the car while his boss stands over them.

"Grimman! You moron! You got the wrong freaking car!"

"You watch yourself, Forte. I will jam you up for insubordination—"

"Where is Hollinger's car?" Matt interrupts, flashing his credentials and immediately taking command of the situation.

"We're looking for it now, sir," another agent explains.

"Did you head to his place?" he asks Grimman, his eyes boring into him.

"Not yet."

"Have the agents there checked in?"

"No."

"Then what the hell are you waiting for? Get your head out of your ass and get moving!"

"We have to secure the scene and interrogate…"

Zach walks away, letting Matt handle the bureaucratic stuff. He's astonished at the ineptitude. Two agents could be in distress, a possible mole is on the loose, the prime suspect is in the wind, and Grimman is having a meeting. He heads over to where Williams and Rilleux are being restrained.

"Where's Hollinger?"

"I don't know. We were on the way to get him before you assholes intervened!" Maryland chastises.

"I told you to stay put! This is why I didn't want you involved," Zach says, gesturing at the scene around them.

"And let you morons kill him? I don't think so."

"This is Louisiana, I assume?" Zach asks, pointing at the larger man cuffed on the ground.

"This is the guy who's gonna kick your ass the moment you take these cuffs off, buttercup," he mocks.

"Yeah, that's Louisiana…and that's Cajun for he's pleased to meet you."

Zach leans closer to him. "We're going to have a lengthy conversation about my car when this is all over. Stand them up."

Maryland and Louisiana are lifted off the ground by a quartet of agents. They each grunt as they are stood up, the former not challenging Zach's authority. Despite being battered from the accident, the same can't be said for the latter as he tries to shrug off the agents holding him.

"Listen, jackwagon, are you deaf? Boston is about to confront Gina, and you're here screwin' with us."

He's right, insofar as tonight goes. Then Zach remembers how he helped Hollinger get away last time.

"Search the car," he commands, sending two agents over to scour the vehicle.

The staring contest with Louisiana begins. It only takes that long for an agent to bring him a black bag. He sets it down and opens it. Sifting through the contents, he pulls out several blocks of Semtex plastic explosive.

"Let me guess: Play-Doh?" The sardonic statement is enough to humble Louisiana a little.

"Agent Forte, why did the FBI ambush us?"

"The guy at the sleep center told the FBI that Boston was driving a gray Chevy Malibu."

"That figures," Louisiana says with a chuckle.

"Yeah, well, he wasn't driving this one," Maryland adds.

"No shit," Zach retorts.

"You're wasting time," Louisiana says. "If you were headin' to Boston's house, why the hell are you standing here talking to us? Grab your balls and get over there."

Maryland nods his head in agreement. Louisiana may be a bomb-happy thug, but Williams has a good head on his shoulders. It makes no difference that some of his earlier decisions were misguided.

"The clock's ticking, Agent Forte. It's out of our hands now."

"Get our heroes here some medical attention," Zach commands before walking away.

Grimman is on his cell phone, probably talking to Director Weisz. Matt shakes his head. Whatever the conversation is about, it's evident that nobody is in a rush to go anywhere. He nods back at the car, and Zach gets the hint. Someone needs to find out what is going on at Boston's, and that someone is him.

CHAPTER EIGHTY-TWO

GINA ATTISON

BOSTON'S RESIDENCE
OXON HILL, MARYLAND

Gina picks up Boston's weapon and pushes the catch to release the magazine. It slides out of the grip and clunks onto the hardwood floor. Keeping her gun trained on him, she takes a knee. Using the lip on her boot's heel to catch the rear sight, she works the action. The chambered round ejects and chimes as it bounces across the floor. Satisfied that his weapon is unloaded and useless, Gina tosses it on the chair.

"Neat trick," Boston observes dispassionately.

"I'm not without some skills," she says with a smile.

"The walls are closing in on you, Gina. Maryland and Louisiana are on the way. They'll be barging in any minute."

"Oh, Boston, again with the clichés? Maryland would have insisted on waiting for the FBI. Louisiana would have barged in even before you did. Nobody is coming anytime soon."

"I'm willing to let you believe that."

The corner of Gina's mouth curls up. Boston should be glad he doesn't play poker. He can't bluff worth a damn. She reaches into her pocket and pulls out the dead FBI agent's cell phone.

"I'm monitoring the FBI, too. We'll be done before they get here. When they do, I'll be long gone."

"I would have figured that you wouldn't hang around after taking those two agents in the kitchen out."

"They interrupted me when I was packing. I was about to leave when I heard you on the patio. You should have followed some noise discipline, Boston."

"What do you want from me, Gina?" he demands.

"Nothing. I'm just taking a moment to enjoy our final minutes together. Let me guess. You finally saw through my eyes in one of those dreams of yours."

"You called your Russian contact after we got off the phone tonight."

"It figures it would be something like that. Oh well."

Boston shakes his head. Gina knew this day would eventually come. For him, learning of her deception was a revelation he could never have imagined in his wildest dreams. She smiles at the pun.

"Let's move on to our next cliché and ask me why I did it," she says, taunting him.

"I couldn't count on you telling me the truth if I did."

"Oh, don't be like that, honey. I didn't lie about everything. Only about safeguarding America's secrets, loving you…you know, trivial stuff like that. Do you really want to know?"

Gina watches the wave of anger rush over him. He's suppressing the urge to take a chance and lunge at her, but he can't cover even a fraction of the distance in time. He must know that it's suicide to try.

"Yeah, I still want to know."

"Ideals used to mean something in this country, Boston," Gina explains after inhaling deeply. "The founding fathers had a vision for a government of the people, by the people, and for the people. We lost sight of that. Too many have sacrificed for a government and a country that don't give a crap about them."

"The founding fathers? That's your rationale? Bullshit."

"Yeah, it is," she says with a laugh. "Ask yourself who's really getting our soldiers killed in the Middle East. Is it me, or is it the politicians sending them on worthless missions? You don't really think they're over there keeping us safe or defending democracy, do you? It's about politics and economics. They're there to appease big contributors from the defense industry."

"I never realized you were such a pessimist."

"I'm not. I'm a realist. All wars have casualties, but then again, we aren't at war, are we? When you lose faith in the idea of America, nothing else matters anymore except yourself. That's what America is these days. Everyone for themselves."

"Including you?"

"Especially me. Anyone who gets in my way is just collateral damage. That includes you."

CHAPTER EIGHTY-THREE
"BOSTON" HOLLINGER

BOSTON'S RESIDENCE
OXON HILL, MARYLAND

The comment stabs me through the heart. I loved this woman. I was going to spend the rest of my life with her. This is not the Gina I know. She is an entirely different person, and I feel like a fool for having been suckered for so long.

"Collateral damage? Is that all I am to you?"

"Jesus, Boston, why do you always take things so personally? You're an intelligence analyst living with a spy. How bad could you possibly suck at your job to let that happen for years? I was selling secrets long before we even met."

"You bitch," I seethe, taking a step towards her.

Gina moves her finger from the slide to the trigger and tightens her grip on the weapon. I freeze in place. She won't hesitate to shoot me. I comply when she gestures me back with her gun.

"Touchy, touchy. Call me all the names you want. You know I'm right."

"So, what was your plan? Betray everyone and then ride off into the sunset?"

"Not exactly. I always knew that I would eventually get caught. There's nothing more embarrassing than a high-level staffer in the Senate getting arrested for espionage. I assumed that I would know when counterintelligence was closing in before they did. I just had to be ready to bolt at a moment's notice."

I have to hand it to her. She may be a cold-hearted traitor, but she thought it through. The FBI was scouring for the mole in all the wrong places.

"Maryland's report. You had everyone looking at the DIA until I asked him to look into how the intelligence was shared."

"Yeah. I made sure all the information I passed was originated by or handled by the DIA. I wanted investigators looking in the wrong place. I didn't expect him to actually research it. Then that idiot Troxell leaked it."

"Is that why you arranged my accident?"

"Don't be ridiculous. I had nothing to do with that. I sure as hell didn't expect the consequences. I could never have guessed that they would actually be experiencing memories, or whatever. Speaking of that, did you ever find out how it works?"

"Do you think I'm going to tell you?" I snap defiantly.

"Aw, honey, I thought we shared everything," she says, mocking our relationship. "I don't really care how it works. Things would have worked out better for you if what you saw was more irrelevant. I mean, if the memories had been about people taking their kids to the park or a couple strolling on a long walk down to the beach, you wouldn't be looking down the barrel of my gun."

Gina wiggles the barrel of her pistol up and down to prompt me to keep my hands up. Well, that isn't going to work. I hoped that she wasn't paying close enough attention, but I was wrong. I raise my hands back up to chest level. I need a new plan and fast. Time is running out, and it doesn't look like help is coming.

CHAPTER EIGHTY-FOUR
ERIC "MARYLAND" WILLIAMS

LIVINGSTON ROAD
OXON HILL, MARYLAND

Louisiana and Maryland watch as Agent Forte climbs into his vehicle. He fires it up, kills the blue and red strobes, and slams the car in reverse. He yanks the wheel hard and pulls into a driveway before making a left and heading back north up Livingston.

"Do you think he's going to Boston's?"

"That or he's running out for donuts and coffee," Louisiana says.

"He's going the wrong way."

"That sounds about right for the FBI. How close is Boston's from here?"

"Three-quarters of a mile or so that way," Maryland says, pointing in the general direction they were heading before being ambushed by the feds.

"So close."

Maryland watches Louisiana shake his head. He has reached a détente with his longtime adversary. Their fistfight was only an hour ago, but it feels like a week has passed. For better or for worse, their roles in this whole sordid affair are over. Now the final act will be written by Boston, Gina, and the FBI.

"How are you feeling?"

"Like hell, bro. You?"

"Torn."

"Torn? What the hell does that mean?" he asks.

Maryland isn't sure how to explain this. He watches the EMT take his blood pressure in the back of the ambulance. After everything they've been through, there's no doubt that it's high.

"I didn't want Boston to do something stupid. Taking Gina down isn't worth throwing his life away. At least, that's what I thought. We're past that now. Now I'm kind of hoping he kills her before the FBI gets there."

Louisiana chuckles before outright laughing. A second EMT gives him a disapproving look, and one of the FBI agents pokes his head in to see if everything is okay.

"What's so damn funny?" Maryland asks.

"I swear, bro, I'm gonna make a proper villain out of you yet."

"Do they check out?" an FBI agent asks, eliciting a nod from the EMT. "Good, you're coming with me."

The agent helps the two men out of the ambulance, and they walk in the direction of a gaggle of local law enforcement and windbreaker mafia.

"How do you think Tara's holding up?" Maryland asks.

"She's a mess, bro, I promise you. She had a thing for Boston. I guarantee she's freaking out right now."

"I know the—"

"Where's Agent Forte?" the bald agent in charge asks when they reach the group.

"Who?" Maryland asks, playing dumb.

The guy running this shit show isn't amused. "The agent you were talking to a few minutes ago. The one who debriefed…you know who I'm talking about! Where is he?"

"It wasn't my turn to watch him," Maryland says.

He looks at Louisiana, who grins. "Well?"

"No hablo ingles."

"Weaver!" he shouts at one of his underlings. "Have you seen Forte?"

"Negative, boss."

"Get him on the line and find out where he went."

Maryland and Louisiana share a look. The fact that the Bureau can't find one of their own agents is a good sign. Maybe there is hope for Boston after all.

CHAPTER EIGHTY-FIVE

GINA ATTISON

Gina feels the FBI agent's phone vibrate again in her pocket. The calls are more frequent now, like desperate pleas for answers from afar. She is already off-schedule. The longer she plays this game with the man she shared a bed with, the worse the odds get for her. Even knowing that, she can't resist the urge to let this play out. It's utterly satisfying to watch him squirm to hear the secrets she was so good at keeping.

"How did your SCI clearance entitle you to that? I mean, the VP's son's visit to Baghdad was classified at the highest level."

"It's Congress, Boston. People talk too much."

"You mean that your boss did."

"They all do, but he's one of the worst offenders. He leaks more than the Titanic did. I've never met someone so cavalier about safeguarding sensitive information. I just made sure that information made it into the right hands. They took care of the rest."

Gina is gloating, and the more she does, the angrier Boston gets. Not that she cares about his feelings or anyone else's. It's simple math: if he makes a move at her, he dies. If Boston does the rational thing and stays compliant, he dies anyway. The result will be the same. From this distance, Gina knows that she won't miss the shot.

"Why did you kill Senator Turner?" Boston asks.

"To set Louisiana up for it. You see, Maryland was never much of a threat, and you were easy to manipulate. Your crazy Cajun buddy was a different story. He was a wild card. C-4 is easy enough to obtain if you know where to look, and I figured that the FBI would be lazy and finger him for it. It turns out I was right, although I never thought the two of you would be so adept at escaping capture."

"But why *him*?" he presses.

Gina makes a pouty face. "Poor Boston. You're an intelligence analyst incapable of putting all the pieces together. Tsk, tsk. Garrett and Colby hated each other. Once Turner pointed the authorities at you as the mole, he became expendable. His fate was sealed the moment he tried to use our relationship to embarrass the chairman. It was a miscalculation that I made him pay the price for."

"I don't blow cars up, Gina."

"Don't be naïve, Boston. Louisiana may have done the dirty work, but the FBI would think that you were the mastermind. I knew they would mobilize everyone to hunt you down. I pointed you at Colby Washington since you began to suspect him anyway. Then they let another senator die, and you managed to escape again. Go figure."

"Why did you call Justin Triggs before we met at the mall?"

"It was an insurance policy meant to keep the media asking them questions. If they focused on each other, there would be little time to look at anyone else around them. I had no idea that he worked with the senator. Not that it mattered."

Boston sneaks another glance out the window. There is still no hint of movement.

"Our time is running short, love," Gina says, continuing to mock him by using the cutesy pet names they rarely called each other. "It's time for one of us to get on with her life."

"So, where do we go from here?" he asks, staring down the barrel of the gun pointed at his chest.

"I'm going to kill you. Then I'm going to make it look like a suicide. You murdered the agents, had a guilty conscience, and then took your own life."

"It won't work. The FBI knows that you're the mole."

"You're right, Boston. They'll figure it out, eventually. But by that time, I'll be kicking back on a beach somewhere warm. I only need a few days to retrieve my documents and get out of the country."

"They'll never believe it. You won't make it out of the city."

"Right. Well, we're about to find out. You're a fugitive wanted for murder, Boston. With you dead, politicians and bureaucrats will want the case closed. They will use the media to push their narrative. The very men you worked for will be the last to push for justice. It's beautiful, isn't it?"

She raises the gun and points it at his head as her finger moves to the trigger.

CHAPTER EIGHTY-SIX
SPECIAL AGENT ZACH FORTE

Zach frowns as he navigates the car through this suburban hell. Whoever designed these neighborhoods back in the 1960s was on a serious bender.

"Yeah," he says after retrieving the phone and pressing the speaker button.

"Forte, it's Weaver. The boss wants your location."

"In my car," Zach says, making no attempt at disguising his sarcasm.

"Where specifically are—"

"Zach, where the hell do you think you're going?" Grimman barks, having yanked the phone out the other agent's hand.

"Boston's."

"Negative. Stand down. I have a tactical team heading for his location. They'll be there in twenty minutes."

"It may be too late by then."

"Zach, do not go in without them! We're sealing off the area. Hollinger isn't going anywhere," Grimman says, trying to assure him.

"It's not Hollinger I'm worried about."

If Gina is the mole, one of the two of them will die tonight. He needs to stop that from happening. The only way to clear Hollinger is for him to live and for Gina to end up in custody.

"Agent Forte! This is your last chance. Stand down."

Zach ends the call. He's had enough of him. Anything more will only make his insubordination hearing worse. His career in the FBI is over unless Matt comes through on his offer. With that thought, he selects his number.

"Yeah?"

"Matt, are the agents posted outside Boston's house down?"

Zach wants to hope they aren't, but he knows better. They were sent in after Gina a half hour ago and haven't been heard from since. Boston evaded Grimman's ambush and must be there by now. If Gina's there, who knows if he's still alive? Who knows if any of them are?

"Nothing's been confirmed, but more than likely."

"Have there been gunshots reported?"

"No."

Zach bites his lip. Maybe Boston caught up to her and killed her quietly. Maybe she was gone, and he's chasing her. Perhaps the agents are tied up on her living room sofa. There are too many possibilities, and getting to the house is the only way they're going to know. He's sure as hell not waiting fifteen minutes to find out.

"I'm not waiting. I'm going in against orders, Matt."

"I have your back. Watch your six, and don't get yourself killed," Remsen says before ending the call.

Zach takes a deep breath and turns on to Hollinger's street. It's the two-minute warning. He needs a Hail Mary to get everyone out of this mess alive.

CHAPTER EIGHTY-SEVEN
"BOSTON" HOLLINGER

BOSTON'S RESIDENCE
OXON HILL, MARYLAND

If I make it through this, I want to be able to tell the story. More than that, the longer Gina talks, the more time I have. The FBI will be coming eventually. If they don't, then I'm going to have to distract her long enough to make a try for her gun and hope for the best.

"One more thing," I say.

"Seriously? You're full of questions for a dead man."

"I suppose I am," I respond quietly. "Do you really think anyone will believe that I killed those agents and then myself?"

"I don't know and don't care. By the time the FBI even questions it, I'll be long gone. They'll just assume that you killed me or I ran away. There is a natural sympathy for scorned women betrayed by the men they cherish looking to start fresh in a new life somewhere else."

"You're insane."

"One man's insanity is another woman's enlightenment. Now, stop looking so glum and die with a smile on your face. After all, you and your dreams cracked the case of the most elusive mole in modern American history."

I shoot her a glare of pure hatred. She returns it with an evil smile. I can't wait for the chance to wipe it from her face. I peer out the window, desperately searching for signs of a car or some movement on the lawn.

"Still hoping for that last-minute rescue?" she asks, following my eyes.

"It's closer than you think," I say, hoping against hope that it isn't a lie.

"You've seen too many movies, Boston. The ones where the hero wins and the bad guy loses," she concludes.

"People like happy endings."

"Yes, they do. Unfortunately, Boston, this isn't Hollywood."

Gina trains her gun on my forehead. Seven feet away. She isn't close enough for me to stop her.

"I guess a happy ending is out of the question?"

She takes a step closer.

"Not for one of us," she answers with a grin.

I stare down the barrel of her weapon, unflinching. I'm not going to give her the satisfaction of watching me beg for my life. I will never let her know just how scared I am.

"Sleep well, sweetie."

It's a cruel last comment as I watch her index finger begin to move the trigger ever so slightly to the rear. Tires squeal on the asphalt. My window of opportunity is a small one. It's now or never. I begin to lunge for her when she glances at the window.

CHAPTER EIGHTY-EIGHT
SPECIAL AGENT ZACH FORTE

Zach passes a light gray Chevy Malibu parked on the curb, and spots the empty dark Ford Crown Victoria parked across the street from Boston's house as soon as he makes the turn. There's no reason that the agents would be in there with her. Then he notices that Gina's Audi is still parked out front.

"Shit," Zach mumbles, drawing his weapon.

The car slides violently on the wet pavement when he stomps on the brakes. He slams his vehicle into park and jumps out, drawing his weapon and holding it at the low ready. A muzzle flash lights up the room a split-second before a shot rings out in the front room. He's going to need it.

The house is dark except for the light coming from the living room television on the wall. Two more shots follow in quick succession. Zach stays low just in case any of the gunfire gets directed at him as he races across the front yard. He reaches the porch and crouches low on the stoop, fighting to control his breathing. He reaches for the knob and tries to turn it. No dice.

Zach takes a deep breath and backs up on the concrete porch. With his heart pounding and adrenaline coursing through his veins, he rears back and kicks it open. The door flies open, and he charges off-balance through the opening into the darkness of Hollinger's house. His toe catches the threshold, and gravity takes over. Three shots ring out as he careens toward the floor. A searing pain erupts from his left shoulder as snapping sounds fill his ear from the bullets whipping past his head.

His head slams into the wood floor, causing his vision to explode in a kaleidoscope of bright white stars. Another shot rings out as Zach points his weapon at the spot where he saw the muzzle flash. He squeezes the trigger three times from the prone position with his working arm. He doesn't know if he hit anything.

Dazed, Zach is still in the fight but in agony. He fights to keep his weapon trained on where he thinks the gunman might be. Nothing happens.

Darkness begins to close in. Zach is losing blood, and his vision isn't close to normal. He's in no position to give chase. Sirens wail outside as authorities close in. He hears footsteps but is powerless to do anything about them. He can only hope it's the good guys arriving as he succumbs to the drowsiness. Everything goes completely black.

FIVE DAYS LATER

CHAPTER EIGHTY-NINE

ERIC "MARYLAND" WILLIAMS

ARLINGTON NATIONAL CEMETERY
ARLINGTON, VIRGINIA

Seven men stand in a line thirty meters away from the small crowd gathered. They are professionals who, tragically, have performed this solemn ritual hundreds of times. With recent wars in Iraq, Afghanistan, Syria, and against ISIS, so many men and women have given "the last full measure of devotion," as Lincoln once put it.

"Ready! Aim! Fire!"

The report of seven simultaneous shots fired from the honor guard pierces the still morning air. The gunfire causes Tara to jump a little in her chair. For her, the military is a different world. It's a far cry from what she experienced growing up.

"Aim! Fire!"

The firing detail, clad in their navy and royal blue dress uniforms, fire off the second volley as expertly as the first as their shell casings clink on the ground.

"Aim! Fire! Present...arms!"

The men salute with their rifles as a lone bugler standing in the distance sounds *Taps*. Every soldier hates that melody. It's a beautiful tune with tragic connotations. In the military, it signifies the end of a day, or in this case, the end of someone's life. Maryland has heard it too many times.

Boston's parents died when he was a teenager, and his only sibling died of a drug overdose while he was on active duty. With no family present, the funeral gathering comprises only one or two SSCI staffers besides Maryland, Louisiana, and Tara. The narrative has been set, and few will ever know the real truth.

With Gina gone, Boston has been branded a traitor, if not officially. That guaranteed most of his colleagues and politicians on the Hill would not attend the burial. He will be forgotten when the news cycle fixates on the next story. It's a fate he never deserved.

Six soldiers expertly fold a flag at the casket as Tara fights to hold back her tears. The officer in charge kneels in front of her and presents it. Without a next of kin, the flag goes to a close friend of the deceased, and Louisiana insisted that Tara get the honor. Neither man told her that she would receive it ahead of time.

"This flag is presented on behalf of a grateful nation and the United States Army as a token of appreciation for your loved one's honorable and faithful service," the officer whispers. The tears she sought so hard to quell are now streaming down her cheeks.

Maryland, Louisiana, and Tara stay seated as the funeral detail departs. A lone soldier remains behind to stand watch over Boston at the position of attention. Tara rises and walks over to the casket, clutching the flag close to her black dress. She runs her finger along the edge of the lacquered wood, shaking her head in disbelief.

"I feel like I'm the one who's been in a dream. I expect to wake up and see things as they were before."

"Sweetheart, this is as real as it gets," Louisiana says, his words lacking the compassion Maryland knows Tara needs to hear. He was never good about dealing with stuff like this.

"I don't expect you to understand."

"Boston's not the first fallen soldier I've seen buried. He's just the most recent."

"Yeah, well, he's the first one I've had to bury!" she snaps.

Louisiana's face tightens, but he doesn't say anything.

"You loved him, didn't you?" Maryland asks her in a near whisper.

"Does it matter?"

"It matters to us."

"He's dead, Maryland! Murdered in cold blood. He's gone now, so no, it doesn't matter anymore!" Tara screams.

"Ease up, girl. Don't get pissed at us. Focus that rage on the bitch you should be angry at," Louisiana says.

"What good does that do? She's gone forever and gets to live her life. Boston doesn't. Do you think I'll ever be okay with that?"

A long silence grows between them. The two men don't know how to respond. Through some sadistic twist of fate, Tara is now feeling the same emotion they dealt with after the mortar attack in Syria. Good friends died that day while they lived. There was no apparent reason God took some and not others. It's hard to come to terms with that guilt.

"How do you guys do it?"

"Do what?" Maryland asks, kicking at some loose soil.

"Learn to live with the pain."

"I've tried to forget. When we got back from Syria and left the hospital, I got discharged and found a career I enjoy. I spend every day thankful for my life and have tried to get on with living it."

"He also bought a gray loser mobile and became a chickenshit little wimp," Louisiana clarifies with a grin. "Me? I dream up the best way I know to blow things up in a spectacular conflagration of fire and violence. Spa-doosh!"

"And what happens when that isn't good enough?" Tara asks, not reacting to Louisiana's attempt at humor. "Boston never found his answer to the dreams."

"We all leave unfinished business on this Earth. Boston died using that tool to save others. Who knows how much more damage Gina could have done? She could have been responsible for the deaths of hundreds more. That's the only thing that makes his death easier."

"Easier?" Tara snaps, looking as if she wants to choke Louisiana.

"Tara, if you had asked Boston whether finding and stopping the mole was worth dying for, he'd have said it was. He knew it was a possibility when he left you at the sleep center that night. It's also why he didn't want us there."

"And you guys are okay with that?"

"Boston didn't give us a choice, my love."

"You're a piece of work, Louisiana," Tara says in disgust.

"Hey, I'm a glass-half-full kinda guy."

"Well, I'm a full-glass girl, especially if it's a nice wine. I could use a bottle right now. Or three of them."

"Right on! Let's get drunk, naked, and make bad decisions."

Maryland shakes his head. That's basically Louisiana's motto. It's also how he deals with most things in life. For once, Maryland agrees…with some of it.

"I'm all for toasting the fallen until we pass out," he chimes in. "Let's get out of here. I know a place with a selection of Tuscan reds."

Maryland offers his arm, and Tara accepts. They start their walk through the garden of stone back toward the road. After a few steps, he looks around and sees that Louisiana isn't following.

"Are you coming?"

"Yeah. I prefer beer, but I guess I could stomach a glass of Merlot," he states.

Tara freezes in her tracks, her eyes searching back and forth. Her eyes get big before finally settling on his.

"What is it?" Maryland asks, concerned.

"Merlot. The Mountain State Gas Station!"

"What?"

"What's going on?" Louisiana asks, joining them.

"If I told the two of you where I think we might be able to find Gina, what are you willing to do about it?"

"I thought we were talkin' about drinkin'?"

"Yes, we are. Boys, we could all use a glass of Merlot … but we'll have to go to West Virginia to get it. I'll explain in the car."

The three of them move faster now, making the long trek out of the cemetery to their vehicle. Tara has a bounce in her step now. It's a drastic change from just moments ago.

"In a rush to be somewhere?" a man asks Louisiana through the open window of his car.

"Forte? What the hell are you doing here?"

"The same thing you are. Paying respects. Where are you going?"

"None of your damn business," Louisiana retorts as the other two only stare at the FBI agent. "How's the shoulder?"

Zach glances at his sling. "It hurts like hell."

"What do you want, Forte? Because we don't have anything to say to you," Maryland says, crossing his arms across his chest.

"Good. I'll talk. Two years ago, I was assigned a case here in Washington. Someone was leaking highly classified documents to media sources. Even after so much time, the whole Snowden fiasco with WikiLeaks was still on everyone's mind, so there was a lot of attention paid to it. I was told to get to the bottom of the case at any cost.

"After a few months, we got a lead and followed it to a low-ranking analyst in the CIA who had access to some of the deepest secrets that the agency has. I followed him for months, trying to catch him in the act, with no results. The bureaucrats applied a lot of pressure on me, so I dialed it up on him. I confronted him, and he denied everything, of course. He swore that he would never do that. For the next year, I covered him like a blanket. I knew more about his life than I did about my ex-wife. I was there every time he turned around."

"Well, this is a fun trip down memory lane, but is there a point?" Louisiana asks impatiently. "Because I'm really not in the mood to listen to your sob story."

"The police responded to a call from his apartment building one night not long after," Zach continues without acknowledging his insolence. "He had hanged himself. He left a note saying, 'I can't do this anymore. I'm so sorry.' And with that, we got our man. The case was closed. I got a pat on the back and a citation for a job well done. I moved on to the next thing as the bureau's rising counterintelligence superstar."

"Only it wasn't over, was it?" Maryland asks, far more interested in the story than Louisiana is.

"A little over a month ago, we ran a sting operation called Beaver Cage and caught an analyst in the same section as him trying to pass gigabytes worth of classified documents to an agent posing as a publisher from an online blog.

"It turns out that my target didn't kill himself because he couldn't live with being a spy anymore. He did it because he couldn't handle the stress of everyone thinking he was one. My superiors tried to cover it up, and I blew the lid off by filing an anonymous whistleblower complaint to the Inspector General. The same people who congratulated me two years ago threw me to the dogs. I was ostracized and turned to the solace one finds in the bottom of a whisky bottle."

"That's a sad story, but you're wasting our time—"

"I wasn't chasing Boston to apprehend him. I was chasing him to get the truth."

"Boston's dead!" Tara shouts, still clutching the folded flag against her chest. "What did you sacrifice?"

"My career. I resigned from the FBI's counterintelligence unit."

"So, you're not part of this massive cover-up?"

"No. I left because of it."

Maryland shakes his head. Boston almost didn't get buried with military honors. Intelligence agencies are content to label him the mole and announce to the media that the threat has been eliminated. That opinion is being encouraged by members of Congress, no doubt.

"Is the FBI still looking for Gina?"

"I don't know. If they are, it's being done quietly. Finding her isn't a priority. The mole is gone, and that's all they really care about. Justice is another thing entirely, isn't it?"

The three of them look at each other, and Zach smirks. A perpetrator's body language usually gives them away before their words do. It's the same thing here.

"You know where she is, don't you? Good. Someday you'll have to tell me how you figured it out."

"You're not going to stop us?" Maryland asks meekly.

"I told you, I'm not with the Bureau in a counterintelligence capacity anymore. I have no reason or authority to stop you from doing anything. I can be useful to other groups. They are always people looking for a man with my skill set, right, Louisiana?"

All he can do is grin. He knows what Zach is referring to. The former agent turns the key in the ignition and starts his vehicle. He reaches into the pocket of his suit jacket to retrieve a pair of sunglasses, taking a moment to inspect them for smudges before sliding them onto his face.

"Everybody wants this thing buried," he continues. "It's the only reason you all aren't in prison right now. Explanations for the explosions were provided to the Metro PD, and they were told to drop it. Nobody wants your defense lawyers running around town asking questions. A word of warning: there *are* limits to your *get out of jail free* card. Stay off the radar."

Zach puts his loaner car in reverse and turns to look out the rear window. This model doesn't have a rear camera. Louisiana grabs the door of the vehicle, causing him to hit the brake.

"Word of warning to you, Zach: things aren't square between us. Don't think that your letting us find Gina makes things right."

"No, it doesn't. You and I are still going to have a chat someday about what you did to my BMW. Don't think for a second that will be pleasant for you."

The threat issued, Zach backs up out of the space and points his car toward the exit. He offers the three of them a quick salute and heads out of the cemetery.

"Come on," Maryland says. "We have some business to attend to."

CHAPTER NINETY

GINA ATTISON

Gina catches her reflection in the glass of the drink refrigerator. She stares at herself for a long moment. Despite being tucked under a ballcap, wisps of her light-colored hair are peeking out. That's going to take some getting used to. Gina has never thought that being blonde suited her personality, nor having her hair cut this short.

She's thankful that she didn't need to drastically change her appearance. The risk of capture dropped once she made it out of Washington, and nobody knows her here in West Virginia. Regardless, it was prudent to change things up in case authorities decided to start a massive public manhunt. So far, one hasn't materialized.

That development doesn't surprise her. She was on staff for the chairman of Congress's most powerful intelligence oversight committee. They'll remain quiet about the affair to avoid embarrassment now that Garrett Turner and Colby Washington are dead. With nothing to gain, both parties will exert pressure on the FBI to end their investigation. Politicians survive by avoiding scandals.

Gina brings the basket of goodies to the clerk behind the register and pays the bill using cash from Boston's emergency fund. He won't be needing it. She only wishes that she hadn't given him so much in that mall parking lot. Her provisions ran out, and she needs this supplemental food to last another week until it's safer for her to leave the country.

The cabin buried deep in the Appalachian Mountains isn't known to anyone except her and Boston. There's no paper trail for the feds to follow its ownership back to her. It was a secret only they shared. Her biggest fear was that he'd get captured and tell the FBI about this place. Now she can be sure he took that knowledge to the grave. Dead men don't talk.

She swings open the door and leaves the store, carrying three sacks of groceries. After stowing them in the back of the Jeep, she tugs at the zipper on her light jacket to protect against the slight chill in the air leftover from last night's rain. Before climbing in for the trek back to the cabin, she pauses to marvel at the peaceful serenity of this area. It's beautiful here.

A shot rings out from afar, and its report echoes off the mountainsides and down the valley. Gina freezes in place as a flock of ducks flies off and screams their warnings from a nearby pond. Hunters. She exhales. So much for the peaceful serenity.

Gina climbs into the Jeep that she's had quietly parked at a long-term vehicle storage facility for years now. Purchased with cash from a seller on the Internet, its existence was kept a secret, even from her fiancé. Its fading paint, scratches, dents, and overall age don't make it much to look at, but it fits in well in the mountains of West Virginia.

She pulls her keys out and climbs into the driver's seat while thinking about Louisiana. That crazy bastard would have loved to have wired some explosives to the ignition of this car. Gina smirks at the thought as she inserts the key and turns it.

The engine roars to life, and she pulls onto the road heading south. This stretch of highway is a generally flat part of the valley. This region of the Appalachians is characterized by long, even ridges, with long, continuous valleys in between. Her cabin sits on the part of a mountain that directly overlooks an adjoining one, with only a narrow ravine between them.

The combination gas station and convenience store she just left is situated on a two-lane asphalt road more than a dozen miles from the cabin. At least a half dozen shops are closer to her hideout, but she and Boston had frequented them during their trips up here. Despite her change of appearance, Gina doesn't want to tempt fate.

Despite having no indication that anyone is following her, she's on edge. The extra time spent with Boston almost foiled her escape. It was too close, and she knows that the best course was to have shot him immediately and hightailed it out of there. When the FBI barged in, she thought she'd never make it to where the Jeep was stored and slip out of Washington. It was a lesson learned. Deviations from the plan and wasting time are errors not worth repeating. So is failing to be careful.

Gina turns off the main highway onto a smaller road that leads to the cabin. It turns from asphalt to gravel and begins to get steeper as she ascends the mountain. The engine complains, and the tires crunch beneath her as they struggle for traction.

This is the worst part of the trip. Gina has a death grip on the wheel. She is already racked with tension, and the piercing sound of her cell phone causes her to jump. This could only be one person, so she uses the wireless hands-free device affixed to her ear to connect the call.

"Yes?"

"*Privyet*, Gina. *Kak pozhivayesh?*" a man in a thick Russian accent asks on the other side of the line.

"I'm fine, Yevginy. Eager to get out of the States. Has the final payment been made?"

"*Da*. One hundred thousand dollars has been placed in your offshore account in appreciation of your services to the Russian people."

A satisfied smile crosses Gina's lips as she eases back into her seat. With her new passport and identification under an alias and hundreds of thousands in a Grand Cayman account, she should have no problem living out the rest of her life in comfort.

"Excellent. *Spasiba.*"

"*Pozhaluysta.* It is a shame we will no longer be able to do business."

"I'm sorry I can no longer be in your service, but it was inevitable. You're resourceful, though. You'll find another."

"Yes. Americans are selfish and greedy. Recruitment is never a problem," Yevginy says in agreement. "*Do Svidaniya*, Gina."

"*Do Svidaniya*," she says, ending the call on her burner phone and tossing it into the seat next to her. She hopes this will be the last time she ever has to use it.

Gina checks the rearview mirror before returning her attention to the view outside the windshield. Several small rocks are strewn in the road from another all too frequent rockslide on the mountain. It's nothing her Jeep can't easily overcome as she gives the vehicle more gas.

A grin of satisfaction creeps across her lips. She's almost free. In a week, she will leave the country, and her journey as Gina Attison will be officially over. She will win at life because she didn't play the game. Ideology is for fools. For her, it is about money, and more importantly, the lifestyle it can buy. The thought turns her grin into a broad smile.

"You were right, Boston. People do like happy endings."

The Jeep rolls over the debris from another slide. Gina edges it to the left slightly to avoid a basketball-sized boulder that broke free from the mountainside.

A deafening sound rocks the world before a violent shudder erupts beneath her. The vehicle gets lifted off the roadbed as dust and dirt obscure her view out the windows. The force from another blast on the passenger side jars the Jeep hard, then another eruption tears at the floorboards.

Time moves in slow motion. Gina can feel hundreds of cuts tear open her skin like razor blades as she lets go of the wheel and covers her face. The Jeep crashes hard against something as she feels weightless. Her brain can't process what is happening. All that Gina knows is that she's powerless to stop it.

CHAPTER NINETY-ONE
ERIC "MARYLAND" WILLIAMS

APPALACHIAN MOUNTAINS
WEST VIRGINIA

The three of them watch from the opposite mountain as the explosion propels the Jeep over the flimsy guardrail. It begins a slow plummet toward the valley below. The cliff is not a sheer drop. It is more like a steep mountainside with crags and ledges that Gina's car keeps bouncing off every twenty feet. It's a little like watching the Plinko game on *The Price is Right*.

Real-life car crashes aren't like what you see in the movies. The car has not burst into flames on the way down the mountainside as an action film aficionado would predict. Instead, the unimpressive visual effects are only narrated by the sounds of twisting metal hitting rock as the wreck tumbles. It all ends when the shattered SUV comes to rest upside down at the bottom of the ravine more than six hundred feet below.

Tara, Maryland, and Louisiana say nothing. They stare intently at the unrecognizable vehicle as if expecting Gina to crawl out of its twisted remains. It's a ludicrous proposition. If the explosions didn't kill her, the ride down the mountainside certainly did.

Maryland glances over at Louisiana standing off to the left. His hands are in his pockets, and he's wearing a satisfied grin on his face. Mayhem is his middle name, and this is undoubtedly not a new experience for him considering his post-military career choice. This one was personal, though. Gina murdered his friend, and he avenged that death. For Louisiana, it's simple math. Satisfied that there is nothing left to see, he nods at Maryland before heading back toward the road where their car awaits.

Tara is another story entirely. She is looking down at her shaking hand. Principles and ideologies are easy to talk about and far harder to uphold. A person doesn't really know what they are until they are tested. Maryland's, like those of his fellow soldiers, were tested in combat. And Tara's were just now. For all the bluster about believing life was sacred and that there was no way she could ever take the life of another human being, it's her finger that has gone white from pressing the cell phone button that triggered Louisiana's bomb.

Tara notices him staring at her and comes back from whatever dark place she was visiting. She releases the button and tosses the phone at him. Without a word or another glance at the ravine below, she follows Louisiana back down the trail.

Tara had only one request when they put this plan together. She wanted this this responsibility, and now her life will be forever changed because of it. Maryland looks down at the display of the phone. It merely reads, "call ended." Gina's life ended with it. The mole who plagued the country can no longer do any harm.

Maryland removes the battery and smashes the device against a rock before hurling it. It's doubtful anyone other than the three of them will know what happened here. It's a long shot that anyone ever finds Gina's car, and if they do, there's little chance it would ever be traced back to them.

Boston found a cure for his dreams through death. Louisiana got his revenge. Tara got justice for a man she loved and will never get to really know. For Maryland, his life can get back to normal. In this one fleeting moment, everything is right with the world. He stuffs his hands into his pockets and grins. Tara and Louisiana can wait at the car for a while. This is a view worth admiring.

EPILOGUE
SUPERVISORY SPECIAL AGENT ZACH FORTE

NONDESCRIPT OFFICE BUILDING
SOMEWHERE IN VIRGINIA

Zach drags himself out from behind the wheel and studies the ordinary building's façade. The structure is just one of the thousands that house office workers across America. He would never have guessed what secrets it hides inside.

He strolls through the entrance, signs in at the counter after learning that he was precleared, and is given instructions to head up to the fifth floor. After stepping off the elevator, he isn't surprised to see Matt waiting for him in the area that could charitably be called a lobby.

"Did you have any problems finding the place?"

"No," Zach says, scanning the room, unimpressed.

"I know, it's nothing to look at. The CIA is great at hiding in plain sight."

"This is a CIA facility?"

"One of the many. How's your shoulder?"

"Still painful," Zach says, subconsciously adjusting his arm in the sling.

Charging into Hollinger's house was nearly a suicide mission. Gina was waiting for him, and tripping over the threshold again as he barged through the door saved his life. The shot Gina aimed at the center of his chest struck him in the shoulder just above the pectoral muscle. Instead of finishing him off, Gina decided to flee before the rest of the cavalry arrived.

"Don't get shot next time. It could have been worse. Speaking of which, I heard you went to Hollinger's funeral last week. How was it?" Matt asks, making his way over to a door and using a biometric scanner to gain access.

"Sparsely attended."

"Did you make contact with his friends?"

"Yeah, I did. Louisiana still owes me for my car."

Remsen chuckles. "Good luck getting that debt settled."

"They know something about Gina's whereabouts. I'm sure of it."

"Remind me never to question your instincts. They knew, all right. Two days ago, your buddy Louisiana used explosives in the mountains of West Virginia to knock her car off a cliff."

"Seriously? Talk about burying the lead! How could you not tell me that when it happened?"

"I didn't want to spoil the surprise. I sent out a team to confirm it was her. The case is closed on Gina Attison."

Zach nods. It was a long path, and it led him here. Only time will tell whether the journey was worthwhile. As much as he won't shed a tear over the death of that traitor, there is a lot of collateral damage in Gina Attison's wake.

The two men walk down a long corridor and make a turn to the left. The halls are covered in cream-colored paint and absent any décor on the walls. It's the most sterile place he's seen since his first apartment.

"How did you get the CIA to loan you this place?"

"Pooling resources is one of the perks of being in Watchtower. Are you ready to see this?"

"Do I have a choice?"

Matt smirks and opens the door to a spacious room. Two doctors turn to look at the men who interrupted their conference. On a bed in the center of the room is their patient with his head covered in gauze. Amazingly, he can still manage to breathe through it.

"He looks dead."

"It was touch and go for a while there," Matt says, joining Zach in staring at Frankenstein's monster.

"Has he regained consciousness?"

"We're keeping him in a medical coma," the doctor says, rising from his rolling stool. "It's the best thing for his recovery."

"I wonder if Boston would agree with that."

"He had significant trauma," the second doctor explains. "The bullet missed his brain stem by millimeters but did incredible damage. We had to reconstruct his entire facial structure."

Zach studies a pair of LED monitors with the before and soon-to-be after pictures of their newest asset. He can see some similarities, but nobody would ever recognize him, including his own mother.

"Obviously, the change in appearance will work to our advantage," Matt explains.

"What are the chances he kept his…gift," Zach asks.

"We won't know for a while."

"Can you gentlemen excuse us for a moment?" Zach asks the two doctors.

The men look at each other then at Matt. He nods, and they leave the room without a word.

"They are on the CIA payroll. They can be trusted."

"I don't care. Matt, tell me that you realize the risk in this. By faking his death, you took Boston's life away from him. How do you think he will react to that when he wakes up?"

Zach has thought about that a lot since the fateful night at Boston's. It's a morally compromising situation for him. Counterintelligence is inherently an immoral game, but he has always worked hard to keep his honor and integrity intact. The endeavor with Matt may have forced him to cross a line, even if his friend maintains that the rewards are worth the risks.

"I know that Boston won't react well. That's why you're here. As a member of Watchtower, you're going to be his case officer."

"You're kidding me, right? First, that's a CIA position. I'm FBI. Second, I'll be lucky if he doesn't kill me the first chance he gets."

"Positions in Watchtower are somewhat fluid," Matt says, rocking back and forth on his feet. "You'll come to learn that. As for what Boston will do, yeah, it's a risk. Look, he's in for a recovery that will take the better part of a year. Without our intervention, he wouldn't be alive at all. It took the best surgeons in the world to save him, and for as good a hospital as it is, none of them work at GW."

"Yeah, I'm sure that will convince him not to kill me. Or you."

"Then find a way, Zach. Our system of government is on the brink of extinction. We are facing threats that you cannot begin to imagine. Gina Attison was nothing. We need him and his skills now more than ever. I'm counting on him to help us fight them. I'm counting on you to ensure he does."

"No pressure."

Matt smiles and pats him once on his uninjured shoulder. "Welcome to Watchtower. Come on, we need to get over to the office. There is a lot to get you up to speed on over the next few weeks while you heal up."

Zach looks back at Boston one more time. Like it or not, the two of them are now locked in this journey. They are men with irrelevant pasts and uncertain futures. They are reborn, in a sense, and he's not sure that's a good thing. Time will tell.

America will have a new secret weapon to fight its enemies, both foreign and domestic. By merely closing his eyes, Boston can glean information that nobody else could ever learn. With the right training, he could be an irreplaceable intelligence asset. The only thing left to do is convince him to make the sacrifice being asked of him. That may be the most challenging assignment Zach has ever been handed.

ACKNOWLEDGEMENTS

Thank you to all my readers who let Michael Bennit into their hearts to make that series a rousing success. Boston, Tara, Maryland, and Louisiana were a far different cast of characters, so I hope you enjoyed their journey as well. For anyone who did not read the Michael Bennit series, it is my sincere hope that you give them a chance to win you over as well. I also have started the Tierra Campos series and am thrilled with the direction it's going in.

As always, my heartfelt appreciation goes to Michele, whose patience and understanding makes it possible to pursue my dream. Writing is a labor of love, with a heavy emphasis on the labor part. I simply could not do any of this without her. My family has also been incredibly supportive of me. To my mother Nancy, my sister Kristina and brother-in-law Ken, and my nephew Gibson: thank you for always being there and showing your unwavering support.

My military career came to an end during the completion of the first edition of this novel. The time since my retirement has given me ample opportunity to reflect on my service. I met some of the greatest men and women our nation has to offer while serving with distinction in the United States Armed Forces. It was an honor to wear the uniform with you. With heartfelt gratitude for your service, I dedicate this novel on your behalf to those wounded in combat.

The first edition of this story was plagued with problems and formatting errors. I have turned to Book Butchers and Michael Waitz to get them sorted out. Special thanks also go to Dave at JD&J Book Cover Designs for the incredible new cover art.

A NOTE FROM THE AUTHOR

The Eyes of Others was based on a screenplay I wrote in 2009, and the novel's first edition was published in 2015. There were a lot of changes that were made when I adapted the screenplay to print. It was meant to be a standalone story. And then something happened.

Boston has a unique gift, and it's unlike anything else I've seen in political fiction. He's the ultimate truth detector. His death in the first edition seemed like a waste of a character who has really grown on me. I did leave the door cracked open for his return since you never actually see him die. The problem was that there was no compelling way to bring him back.

The second edition is the same story, with a few repurposed characters, different jobs, and a different ending. He's in rough shape but legally dead and now in the hands of the mysterious Watchtower team. It will make for some intense drama and exciting missions in future novels.

Boston's team in Iraq was based loosely on some of the men and women I met while training at Fort Jackson, S.C. There was no shortage of personality in that group, and it was an honor to take some of their antics and character traits and incorporate them into the fictional figures in this novel.

The most memorable is Louisiana, loosely based on Kenneth, a friend of mine who served with the 101st Airborne at Fort Campbell, Kentucky. He was a great NCO and has one of the best senses of humor of anyone I ever met in uniform.

This book takes a negative view of our nation's intelligence and law enforcement agencies, namely the FBI. As with the armed forces, there are both good and bad members of our federal agencies. Many of them are great people just doing whatever they can to keep the American people safe from threats. The dim view I created for Grimman is not at all indicative of how I view the FBI.

The description of brain waves, how dreaming works, and dream recollection techniques were well-researched and fundamentally accurate. To my knowledge, there have never been any instances of someone being able to access another's memories. The mind is still a frontier in that we are only scratching the surface in our understanding of how it works and what we are capable of as human beings.

I endeavored to deliver a plausible scenario where Boston could do this and a reasonable theory as to how. As a nod to the changing understanding our medical professionals are often faced with, it was written that Tara was incorrect in elements of her early theory. Maybe someday we will discover if the paranormal ability Boston had is feasible, but in the meantime, I hope I provided enough to make for an exciting story.

ABOUT THE AUTHOR

Mikael Carlson is the award-winning author of *The iCandidate* and the Michael Bennit Series of political dramas. He is also writing the Tierra Campos series, following the award-winning lead book *Justifiable Deceit*. *The Eyes of Others* is the first novel of his new series of Watchtower thrillers.

A retired veteran of the Rhode Island Army National Guard and United States Army paratrooper, he deployed twice in support of military operations during the Global War on Terror. Mikael has served in the field artillery, infantry, and in support of special operations units during his career on active duty at Fort Bragg and in the Army National Guard.

Academically, Mikael has earned a Master of Arts in American History and graduated with a B.S. in International Business from Marist College in 1996.

He was raised in New Milford, Connecticut, and currently lives in nearby Danbury.